SHE FEARED THE FUTURE
THAT WAS ABOUT TO EMBRACE HER

Crenna looked at the creature that Pawago, the hot-blooded Oneida war chief and her promised husband, had dragged before her. She, as headwoman of the tribe, had to decide the captive's fate.

The creature seemed human—or nearly so. It was a man with a face the color of the moon, and blue eyes like the sky.

Crenna remembered the prophecy of the medicine man— the prophecy that the moon men would come one day and burn the forests of the Oneidas and make the rivers run red with Oneida blood.

And Crenna was afraid of the man who stood before her, looking into her eyes, afraid because she knew she could not bring herself to kill him. . . .

MANITOU'S DAUGHTERS

Great Fiction From SIGNET

BOOK I

MANITOU'S DAUGHTERS

THE INDIAN HERITAGE SERIES

by
Paul Joseph Lederer

A SIGNET BOOK
NEW AMERICAN LIBRARY
TIMES MIRROR

*This book is dedicated to the remarkable
and generous Miss Lillian Gish with
gratitude and admiration—and to the
memory of Dorothy.*

NAL BOOKS ARE AVAILABLE AT QUANTITY DISCOUNTS
WHEN USED TO PROMOTE PRODUCTS OR SERVICES. FOR
INFORMATION PLEASE WRITE TO PREMIUM MARKETING
DIVISION, THE NEW AMERICAN LIBRARY, INC., 1633
BROADWAY, NEW YORK, NEW YORK 10019.

SIGNET TRADEMARK REG. U.S. PAT. OFF. AND FOREIGN COUNTRIES
REGISTERED TRADEMARK—MARCA REGISTRADA
HECHO EN CHICAGO, U.S.A.

SIGNET, SIGNET CLASSICS, MENTOR, PLUME, MERIDIAN AND NAL
BOOKS are published by The New American Library, Inc.,
1633 Broadway, New York, New York 10019

First Printing, September, 1982

1 2 3 4 5 6 7 8 9

PRINTED IN THE UNITED STATES OF AMERICA

IN THE DAYS BEFORE THE West Wind blew away the Stone Giants, the land of the Oneida had been ice and fog, a frozen world where no one could live, inhabited by Great Heads who howled and shrieked through the endless night as they searched for human food. All of that was before Hinu, the Thunder God, had rid the earth of giants and chased his evil brother, Ka-tash-hauht, the North Wind, from the land so that the earth could heed the gentle urging of the Sisters and ripen into sweet abundance.

When the ice had withdrawn, the trees had budded and come to trembling life. The grass had awakened beneath the melting hoarfrost; the birds had returned from the desolate mountains, and Manitou had smiled.

It was a place for the Oneida to dwell, at one with all of the spirits, respecting the wishes of Hinu, the laws of Manitou, the ways of the Sisters, of Goweh, of Tar-huhyiawahku, the Holder of the Heavens.

Once a year Ka-tash-hauht returned, blustering out of the north, darkening the skies, his wrath flashing in the heavens, and the earth turned cold, the trees were stunned to lifelessness, the grass was covered with snow. But in time the warm weather would return; in time the earth would green again and renew itself. That was Manitou's promise to his people, the Oneida.

Now it was spring and the river glittered in the sunlight, the long grass flowed in the wind, and the returning ducks darkened the skies. Ka-tash-hauht was banished. The land was fruitful.

Crenna stood on the high pine ridge overlooking the village. She could see all the way to the great river, to the humped blue mountains beyond. The breeze was soft and fragrant as it reached out and toyed with the buckskin fringes of her dress, as it ran teasing fingers through her long black hair.

Below, within the palisaded village, smoke rose from

near the longhouses as hides were tanned over numbers of small fires. A party of women was working in the large field beyond the south wall, planting corn and beans, pumpkin and sunflowers. Fish was hung up to dry on long racks beyond the meeting lodge. The people were busy, happy, and strong.

He appeared from out of the pine woods on silent feet, moving like the wind through the trees, and before Crenna could turn around, Pawago had her locked in his strong bronzed arms and he lifted her from the ground, whirling her around, kissing her throat and lips.

"No! Enough, Pawago."

He only laughed. He placed her on her feet and stood looking into her black, black eyes, wiping back a strand of hair which had fallen across Crenna's forehead.

"So elegant a woman, so strong and sure in council, yet our headwoman is shy."

"You surprised me," Crenna said, her eyes flickering to the village once more before returning to the face of Pawago.

His nose was prominent, finely molded, flanked by fierce eyes. The coppery flesh of his face was stretched taut over high cheekbones and a slightly sharp chin. He wore his hair roached, as did most of the Oneida men. A two-inch-long, inch-wide bristle of coal-black hair ran from his forehead to the long, flourishing scalp lock which hung from the back of his skull.

On this day Pawago wore heavy stone earrings, and he smelled of laurel—he was fresh from the sweat lodge.

He grinned at Crenna. "Let us take a walk down along the Heron Lake."

"I have business to attend to, Pawago," she said, placing her hands flat against his solid chest. She met his gaze again, and then found she could not hold it. With some anger she looked away. Why was it she could not look into those dark eyes of Pawago for long? He was only a man, after all, and in the council, she spoke with assurance to the greatest of the Iroquois warriors.

It was only because they were to be married, she decided, and with that thought Crenna's heart began racing slightly. She pushed away from Pawago, smiling carelessly.

"Have you spoken to Wakami yet?" Pawago wanted to know.

"She is still holding out," Crenna had to tell him.

Pawago's eyes flared with brief anger. "Surely, Crenna, you have the persuasiveness necessary to gain Wakami's vote."

"She believes we need another Turtle Clan chief," Crenna answered.

"Turtle Clan?" Pawago scoffed. "We need the strongest sachems, no matter the clan. That should be your argument, Crenna."

"And it will be," she promised him. She felt vaguely confused as she always did in the presence of this strong Oneida warrior. It was a feeling which irritated her, but which she had as yet been unable to overcome. She laid her cheek against his chest, listening to the slow, heavy beating of his warrior's heart. Pawago's hand stroked her hair and ran down her spine, and when she looked up, his eyes had softened.

"Let us walk to the lake," he said.

"Then who will speak to Wakami for you?" Crenna asked.

"I would rather have the day to spend with you than become sachem," Pawago said, and she almost believed him. "We are going to the East River," he informed her.

"Why? Who is going?" she asked, drawing back. No one had said anything.

"I, with your brother Manto, sixteen warriors."

"But why?"

"The Munsee have invaded our hunting grounds," he replied with a shrug.

"Yes, I had forgotten." It had seemed unimportant. The Munsee were a weak confederation. The council had believed a warning, the hanging of spirit masks, would send the Munsee fleeing.

"I will miss you," Pawago said, and he smiled. Her hands rested on his strong shoulders and he bent his face to hers, kissing her lips.

"I will miss you, Pawago. Take care."

"I will. Does a man who is about to marry such a creature as Crenna take risks?"

"Have you spoken to my father, Pawago? Does Yushta think this battle is necessary?"

"Battle!" Pawago laughed. "They will flee like rabbits at

3

the first sight of an Oneida warrior. There will be no battle, Crenna. But we cannot let them hunt in our land."

"No." She shook her head in agreement. "Be careful, my warrior. Manitou's blessing upon you."

"Manitou has blessed me," Pawago said. "He has given me you, Crenna."

He kissed her again, and Crenna felt an upsurge of emotion, a tangle of responses, sensual, vaguely intellectual; pleasure, pride, and a faint uncertainty. His lips were eager, his shoulders and chest sun-warm, hard, and pleasurable. But those eyes—she could not meet their gaze. With a smile and a last soft kiss, Crenna turned away and strode down the piny slope toward the village. Pawago, smiling thinly, watched her go, admiring the erect carriage, the fluid grace of hips and long legs.

"I will go to the lake with you, Pawago." The voice, slightly mocking, came from the forest behind the young Oneida warrior. He recognized the voice and turned slowly, his smile vanishing.

Kala came from out of the shadows. Her hair was loose down her back; she had just washed it, obviously. Her smile was taunting and Pawago stared at her.

Kala's hips twitched from side to side with more emphasis than necessary. Her eyes were hooded, sensual. Her lips formed a soft pout. Kala had those full, wide lips which were meant for kissing. They always looked slightly bruised, puffy, and deeply intriguing.

"I am not so busy as my sister," Kala said, and she walked brazenly to him, not halting until her breasts were inches from Pawago's chest, until her scent, clean and ripe, was in his nostrils.

"Go away, Kala," Pawago said.

"Do I frighten you?" she asked.

"Nothing frightens me. I am to marry your sister."

"But Crenna seems not to care, Pawago." Her finger stretched out and traced a weaving pattern across Pawago's chest. He caught her by the wrist and forced her hand away. Her pout deepened.

"It is not right," Pawago said. Still he was excited. She could see the pulsing of his throat, see his eyes dilate, his nostrils flare.

"If I were headwoman, you would not say that, Pawago," Kala whispered.

4

"That had nothing to do with it." He turned away angrily, looking northward across the marshes toward the lands of the hated Algonquin. She was so near to him that he could feel her moist breath on his back. Her hand rested briefly on his shoulder, and her touch sent a mighty surge through Pawago's brain.

"You and I understand each other, Pawago," Kala said quietly. "We are people who want things. And what we want, we get. My sister is headwoman, competent and clever, but she does not understand people the way you and I do."

"I want to hear no more of this, Kala. Crenna and I will be married. You and I are family, or will be."

"And you will share our lodge," she said with a faint laugh.

"You are evil, Kala."

"I am a woman, Pawago—and you know it. We both know who is the evil one among us."

Pawago whirled and his eyes flashed. "Go away, Kala. Do me that favor."

"What if I were headwoman, Pawago?" Kala asked with a bright, deep smile.

"But you are not."

"What if I were the headwoman and Kala could make you sachem? How then would you feel about me? Whom then would you prefer to marry?"

Pawago was silent, looking into those mocking eyes, and Kala burst out laughing.

She walked away, glancing once over her shoulder. Pawago watched her go. It was not the same as watching Crenna walk. Crenna you watched with admiration, with amazement at her grace and bearing. Kala you watched with eyes of a hungry man.

Again she laughed, and then she was gone, disappearing into the pines, and Pawago turned away angrily, fingering his scalp lock for a minute before striding toward the village himself.

Crenna looked into the longhouse, but Wakami was not there. Her sister, the old one, told Crenna that Wakami had gone to the marshes to see about the planting of rice. Crenna thanked the old one and walked slowly across the camp, watching the tangle of children playing in the center of the camp, noticing the bales of reeds which would

5

be used to make mats being stacked near her lodge. A dozen women were entering the palisaded village through the river gate, carrying water in earthen pots. Crenna's youngest sister was among them.

"Have you seen our father?" Crenna asked.

Sachim, whose smile was mild and distant, whose eyes were large in her fine skull, shook her head. "Not since the morning meal, Crenna. Is something wrong?"

"Nothing at all," Crenna said, but there was no use lying to Sachim—she knew everything.

She was frail and tiny, beautiful in a sensitive, fragile way. She had been born small, given no chance to live by the women and Yo, the shaman. But she had lived, and although still a girl, her eyes reflected that ancient wisdom of the spirits, as they always had. Sachim was special, an intimate of the spirits, a distant, loving person whom no one could hate.

She stood watching as her sister strode away, her dark eyes deep and mysterious.

Where was Yushta? The old man never wandered far from the village these days. He was vigorous still, but he was a settled man now. A long time ago, before Crenna had been born, Yushta had won his chieftainship through valor. He was a Solitary Pine Tree, one of four in the Oneida camp, a chief whose position was not hereditary and which could not be taken away, a man of exceptional wisdom. It was said that Crenna had inherited his strength of character, his oratory skills, much as Sachim had inherited their mother's spirituality.

Crenna walked through the longhouses, finding women at their work. They lifted happy faces to her and smiled. In turn she greeted them, pausing to watch their strong brown hands turn rawhide into supple moccasins. If the moccasins were for a child, they carefully cut holes into the soles, knowing that the spirits would not take a child so ill-shod on a long journey through the darkness.

Coming out into the bright sunlight, Crenna saw the warriors forming up, saw Pawago take command of the men. Their faces were painted now—Pawago wore the black and red paint of doom and death.

She watched them for a time, until they hefted their warbags and strode through the gate and disappeared into the marshes. Crenna's heart raced slightly. Always there was someone who did not return. She whispered to Manitou. Do not let it be Pawago or my brother Manto.

Walking past the great gray granite boulder from which the Oneida people had been named, Oneida meaning "people of the stone," Crenna walked the river path toward the hut of the solitary shaman, Yo.

Already she could smell the acrid potion the shaman was brewing on this day. She hurried on, startling a trio of red squirrels from the path. They bounded up a tall, woodpecker-pocked pine, chattering and scolding Crenna as they went. She laughed out loud and walked on.

"Good morning, Crenna."

She halted abruptly. He came from the shadows of the deep pines, a shy and frail man whose eyes glowed with challenge, whose mouth only occasionally softened into a smile.

"Good morning, Ta-Tando," Crenna said, greeting her youngest brother. "Have you seen Yushta?"

"Our father is with the shaman," Ta-Tando said, tilting his head toward the hut in the pines. "I was waiting to see him myself, but now it is too late." He offered Crenna a rare smile, and she returned it warmly. Ta-Tando was close to Crenna, perhaps because his mother had died early. Yet he was a strange, enigmatic boy on the brink of manhood, and he did not share the secrets of his soul even with her.

"What was it you needed?" she asked. Ta-Tando only shrugged, but she saw his eyes lift to the marshes, and she turned, barely able to make out the strong dark forms of the war party as they crossed the land, moving toward the East River.

"You wanted to go with them?" Crenna asked.

"I did not care," Ta-Tando said, lifting his shoulders. His eyes told her that he did care. Slight, unprepossessing, Ta-Tando was jealous of his manhood. Proud, seemingly arrogant, he was a caldron of unhappy emotions inside, Crenna knew. He would have admitted none of that. In his mind's eye he was brave, a born leader, destined for greatness. Just what that destiny was, not even Ta-Tando knew.

"Pawago assures me it is simply a patrol, there will not even be a battle," she said.

"Pawago is a brave man," Ta-Tando said with obvious

7

admiration. "He was willing to let me go with them. It was Manto who would not allow it."

"Your brother loves you; he did not wish to see you hurt."

"Manto is jealous of me!" Ta-Tando exploded. "And how can I be hurt if there will be no battle, Crenna?"

"I meant your brother did not want to take a risk. He knows that Yushta would be crushed if you were hurt." She smiled and rested a hand on Ta-Tando's shoulder.

His anger was gone, but not his resentment. He shook his head heavily. "Manto will not allow me to grow up."

"Manto cannot prevent it, Ta-Tando. And I think you are grown." Again she smiled, and her brother returned it weakly.

When Ta-Tando was gone, Crenna continued along the forest path toward the hut of the shaman, Yo. The smell of his potion grew stronger as she approached the small frame-and-elm-bark structure which was nestled in a teacup valley surrounded by towering spruce.

The sound of a turtle-shell rattle being rhythmically, emphatically shaken was audible now, and Crenna listened to the chanting which accompanied it.

Earth Sisters, now is the time for the planting of corn
Come live in our corn and make it grow ripe
It is the food of our people.

Crenna listened, at the same time watching the women busy in the fields. That evening the planting festival would be held and there would be dancing to amuse the spirits. Yo was propitiating the Sisters so that they would return with goodwill to the Oneida corn.

After a while the chanting ceased and Crenna went to the hut, which was painted with sun and moon symbols. She tapped once and heard Yo's cracked voice summon her.

Crenna's father sat naked in one corner of the hut. Yo, glistening with perspiration and oils, sat in the center of the hut, his narrow rib cage rising and falling with the exertions of his dance.

"Welcome to the headwoman of the Oneida," Yo said.

The shaman's tattooed body was covered with sacred symbols. No one but the shaman could know the meanings of all those marks; but Crenna knew some of them. They were prayers, for the most part, prayers which Yo had cut into his body and which he carried with him night and day so long as he would live. He also had commemorated great events of the years of his life: the forming of the great and powerful Iroquois League of which the Oneida were a central member; the flight of a comet across the skies; the defeat of the hated Algonquin at Fawn Meadows.

"What is it I can do for you, Crenna?" Yo asked.

"I wished to speak to my father, Yo. I did not wish to interrupt."

"The Sisters must be pleased to see our beautiful head-woman in my hut," Yo said. His narrow, scarred face crinkled into a smile.

Yushta had risen and put on his breechclout. He came across the smoke-filled room and hugged his daughter, looking into her eyes with tender regard.

"The shaman who sees all sees truly when he says my daughter is beautiful," Yushta said, and Crenna smiled. These two old foxes always made a fuss over her, especially when they wanted something from the headwoman.

"When you are finished, Father, I would like to speak to you."

"All right." Yushta said his good-byes to Yo and followed Crenna out into the clear light of the spring morning. The air was fresh, filled with pine scent.

Together father and daughter stood overlooking their village and then together they walked through the forest, watching the trees sway in the wind, the doe which bounded away at their approach, the far blue hills to the east. At last they came to the hidden falls.

Here the creek fell in a thin silver sheet over the lip of water-polished gray stone and swirled briefly, before the water spirit, no longer angry because he had fallen, continued on placidly.

Red fern grew abundantly, and vines clinging to the cedar cast mottled shadows. The sunlight sparkled on the water.

Yushta seated himself on the low, smooth stone which overlooked this favorite spot, and he was silent, studying the currents of the stream, watching the fish break water as they snapped at fallen insects.

"What is it, Crenna, that my daughter wishes?" he asked eventually.

"I need your help with a tribal matter, Father."

"Crenna needs my help?" he asked with faint irony.

"It is about Pawago."

"I see." Yushta nodded meditatively and turned his eyes to Crenna. "But what is it I can do which Crenna cannot?"

"Wakami wishes to have a Turtle Clan man made sachem. And so she will not give her consent."

"You do not need her consent, Crenna," Yushta reminded her. "You have the power to do what you will."

"I do not wish to do it that way, Father. It would only cause unhappiness and friction. Wakami would feel ashamed if her wishes were disregarded. In undermining Wakami I would only be undermining my own position. She would oppose me at every turn afterward."

"True. You have the wisdom of your mother," Yushta said. For a moment he was silent, breaking a small twig with his gnarled old fingers. Perhaps he was thinking of Crenna's mother, who had been taken by the spirits. "What can I do?" he asked.

"You can talk to Wakami and convince her that we need strong chiefs, regardless of clan. She will listen to you."

"Why would she?"

"One hears . . ." Crenna smiled. "One hears that Wakami, who has lost her second husband, is looking for a third. A man of position, a great warrior and good hunter."

"Does one?" Yuhsta frowned, but that expression was replaced by a smile. "Now I see why she brings me new moccasins," he said as if the idea was entirely new to him. Wakami had been pursuing Yushta shamelessly for months. "What of Pawago, Crenna? Is he really the best man? Or is it because you and he are to be married?"

"Pawago is a strong warrior. The young men follow him willingly. He is able."

"And impulsive?"

"At times, but so are we all."

"But in a sachem, it is not good." Yushta tossed the broken twig away and shrugged. "I will speak with Wakami," he said.

Crenna kissed her father good-bye and left him to himself. She walked through the forest, followed by a scolding jay which hopped from bough to bough, squawking loudly.

The forest was deep and the day crisp. She seemed to be walking through long corridors. A never-ending series of corridors within a great temple. Manitou seemed near, and his goodwill was something which could be felt against her cheek, which warmed her heart. The temple was silent and comforting, the wind chanted gentle songs in the treetops. The jay squawked again, breaking the spell. Crenna picked up a pine cone and threw it at the jay. It fluttered away, still complaining.

Yo was squatted outside his hut, watching Crenna's approach. He grinned and nodded his head as with some secret understanding.

His grin was toothless, his eyes sparkled as brightly as a child's out of his incredibly wrinkled, parchment-colored face.

His tattooed arms hung limply over bony knees as he crouched there. Crenna saw that he had drawn a design in the earth between his feet, a strange design she had never seen before: a many-rayed sun, a moose's antlers, three stick figures of men who stood on the antlers, supporting the sun.

He offered no explanation of the picture and so she did not ask—these shamans must have their secrets. If they revealed all they knew, how then could the spirits confide in them?

"Did you enlist your father's help, Crenna?"

"Yes."

"He would do anything for you," the shaman said.

"Yes, I know that. And I would do anything for Yushta."

She stood, hands behind her back, her weight on one foot, watching the shaman.

"Then it is all settled?" he asked.

"It will be."

"Then why are you not happy, Crenna?" Yo asked, and as Crenna started to respond with an automatic denial, she realized that Yo had seen her inner face. She was not pleased at all, and yet she could find no reason for this dissatisfaction.

11

"Perhaps it is the dark moon we have been having," she answered, and Yo smiled, rising.

"Perhaps it is only that. Or the strangers who have brought their bad magic with them."

"Strangers?" Crenna was puzzled briefly.

"The visitors to the Mohawk lands, Crenna. All the people have been speculating on the significance of these strangers."

"I have been too busy with my own problems to listen to gossip, Yo."

"Gossip? I am afraid there is more to it than that. May I show you something, Crenna?" the shaman asked, and she agreed. She followed Yo into his hut and watched as he searched for and found an ancient hide with symbols written on it. He brought it to where she had seated herself on the floor and unrolled the skin.

"This, you see was made in the Grandfather Times," Yo told her. "This is not the original hide. It has been copied many times over. The tale is faithfully reproduced, however."

Crenna, with only half her attention, watched as Yo excitedly unrolled the hide and pointed out certain figures with his bony finger.

"In the Grandfather Times, men came out of the Great Sea. Men from the bottom of the sea, or perhaps from the far side of the moon, where the sun never reaches, because their skins were as white as snow. Where they came from is in doubt; what they wished is a mystery.

"They wore sun-mirrors on their breasts and carried glittering weapons in their hands. They had yellow hair and red hair, and hair grew all across their faces, masking their features."

Crenna looked at the ancient skin, seeing the depictions of great canoes rising from the sea, of men glittering like the sun coming ashore, their faces masked by hair. The tale was not new to her, although she had never seen this skin before.

She had always accepted it as simple myth, as the children accept the story of Long Nose, who comes to carry away the bad boys and girls.

"What happened?" she asked politely.

"You see here, Crenna." Yo's finger flowed across the pictographs, and he continued, "The people of the north met these Moon Men and offered them food and drink, and then after a time the people decided they must kill the demons. Then there was a battle and many people were killed. But the demons were driven off. They returned to their canoes and left, sailing toward the edge of the earth. It was that battle which saved the land of the northern people from the demons. Now," Yo said, "they have returned."

"When was this? Who saw them?" Crenna wanted to know.

"The Mohawks, no one else."

"The Mohawks are liars," Crenna said.

"But they have proof. When the Moon Men were killed, they removed their shells. Shells brighter than copper, and of greater strength."

"But they are dead. What does it matter?" Crenna asked.

"There will be more—that is what matters," Yo answered. He rolled up the skin and put it away. "Now I will tell you why it matters, Crenna."

He settled himself near her, facing Crenna across the still-glowing coals of his medicine fire. The shadow of his brow hid Yo's eyes, and as he spoke, he did not gesture, hardly seemed to breathe.

"The prophecy has come down from Than, who was the first Oneida shaman in Grandfather Times. It was Than who was struck by the golden finger of a passing comet and was knocked into sleep. As he slept, the spirits of the future clustered around Than and whispered into his ears, awakening his soul. They lifted his soul from his body and flew him into the dark sky toward another time and Than saw it all from above as he floated among the stars.

"A ship came, from behind the moon, floating on spiderweb clouds. And he saw the men. Faces as white as skulls peered out of the ship, their eyes blue and mysterious and deadly. And when they reached the earth they built stone temples which stared across the land with jeweled eyes, and any Oneida who approached was struck down instantly at the sight of the temple. The people gathered in the forests, and the people called to Manitou to aid them, and they went out to battle.

"But Manitou slept, and their prayers did not awaken him, nor did the singing, the sound of their drums. Manitou slept, and they died, every one, and the forest wept and the grass turned black and the rivers ran red with their blood."

"You are not reading the prophecy correctly," Crenna said. Yo waved a limp hand and looked at her silently. "How could this happen? Manitou sleeping, not hearing the voice of his people?"

"It is what the prophecy says," Yo said wearily. Crenna realized suddenly that the old man was tired, that he had exhausted himself with his dancing. She rose and rested a hand on his knobby shoulder.

"I must be going, Yo. I only hope that the prophecy is fulfilled far in the future if it must be fulfilled. Let us live out our lives as my mother did."

The old man nodded, or Crenna thought he had. Then she realized that his chin had simply fallen forward onto his chest, and Yo was sleeping.

How old was he? she wondered. Despite his gray hair, he was spry. Despite his toothless mouth, he was exuberant and alert, knowing many mysterious things.

She left his hut and returned to the village, her arms crossed beneath her breasts to ward off the wind, which had chilled as evening came on. Below, the women were finishing their work. Tonight was the festival of planting, and there were preparations to be made.

An owl screeched at Crenna from out of the deep woods, and her head came around sharply. Old owl singing about death. It was not a cheering omen.

She walked through the timber, watching dusk collect in purple shadows beneath the trees, and she thought of Yo's prophecy. It seemed incredible. How could Manitou fail to answer his people's call? How could these white men— these Moon Men, these people from the bottom of the sea—invade their land and kill them? She chose not to believe in the prophecy, and she pushed the thought aside; yet it remained in some dark corner of her mind, nagging at her from time to time.

The shadows lay deep on the distant hills. Bonfires had been lighted, and the dancers, already painted, holding their instruments, gathered to drink from a common pot. The captive peoples stood at the edge of darkness, watching silently. Crenna passed Hawk, and the warrior, a Leni-Lenape, turned his eyes down. Hawk nurtured a hatred.

14

At times his eyes became defiant. Yet he was careful not to let it show often.

A captured warrior was not allowed to live unless he agreed to live like the women and children, planting, harvesting, being allowed no weapons or even a dog. Most warriors would fight to the death rather than submit to such a life in their enemy's camp, but this Leni-Lenape had accepted capture. Still, as Crenna passed, she felt his bulging eyes on her, heard a small hiss of breath as Hawk straightened from his submissive posture.

"You should never have spared that one," Ta-Tando said.

Crenna halted and turned to face her brother. Ta-Tando had been in the shadows in his corn-husk mask. "Am I late?"

"No. Nothing has started. We were waiting for the war party to return. Yushta has not yet dressed." He walked along with her toward the longhouse where cooking fires glowed.

"You should never have spared Hawk," Ta-Tando said again. He had to hurry to keep up with his sister. Ta-Tando had been born with a crooked foot. The old women, Raha-Sho, said that Crenna's mother must have stepped on a snake.

"Has he done anything?"

"I do not trust him."

Crenna nodded. Ta-Tando trusted no one. Hawk, for all his sullenness, had caused no trouble. He did his work and had not allowed his warrior's pride to flare up. He had been a prisoner for two years and had not violated his oath of submission.

"It goes against the law to condemn a warrior who has accepted the new life," Crenna said.

Ta-Tando, his face hidden behind his mask of woven corn husks, made a small disparaging noise.

Crenna was not concerned with Hawk just then, nor with the men from behind the moon. As they halted near the longhouse, she asked Ta-Tando, "Did you say the war party has not yet returned? They were only going to the river."

"Perhaps they will not return," Ta-Tando said with a shrug.

Ta-Tando enjoyed making such remarks. His brother

and Crenna's future husband were with that party, and he knew it, yet he could flippantly dismiss their absence. His resentments ran deep.

"They will return," Crenna said, kissing Ta-Tando's mask where its grotesque red mouth was painted. Then, leaving her brother to the darkness, she went into the long-house, where the women were preparing for the feast.

The longhouse, nearly eighty feet from one end to the other, was shared by numbers of families. Along each wall were sleeping platforms, and above these were storage areas for personal property. The most valuable objects were buried in pits beneath the owners' beds.

There were three fires burning in the fire pits, the smoke rising in lazy spirals to the open vents in the ceiling.

Crenna had been offered her own hut, and there were other headwomen she knew who accepted that privilege of rank, but she preferred to be with her brothers and sisters, with the tribe rather than apart from them. She found Kala slipping into a white beaded deerskin dress and she greeted her sister.

"Hello, Crenna," Kala answered, standing to straighten her dress, to tug it down over her ample hips. Even before her sister, Kala could not help her posturing; her loose-jointed, ripe figure was under complete control at all times, posing itself in sensual challenge. "Is Pawago back yet?" Kala asked.

"No," Crenna answered, ignoring the pouting smile, the barbed undertones of her sister's question. Someone should take this woman for his wife, she thought. A strong, jealous warrior who would beat her properly.

Sachim, who was already dressed, her hair braided into a single heavy strand, strolled toward them, a greeting for everyone she passed rising to her lips. Kala watched her approach with indifference. She snatched up her turkey-feather cape and strode out, her hips swaying fluidly from side to side in unconscious assertion.

"I believe they are waiting for you, Crenna," Sachim said.

"I'll be there soon," Crenna answered. She dressed hurriedly in her best dress, the one with the beaded eagle design. Sachim watched, her small hands folded in her lap, her large luminous eyes softly focused.

Already the others were trailing out of the longhouse.

16

Lepskha, Wakami's gangly daughter, tried to put on her moccasin as she hopped toward the door. Sachim laughed and then put her fingers over her mouth.

"You are happy tonight, Sachim."

"I am always happy, Crenna. Especially when I know the spirits are near to us, as they are tonight. I will dance and laugh for the Sisters, and in return they will smile on our efforts and the corn shall flourish."

Crenna was slipping on her moccasins. "Have you seen our brother Manto?" she asked casually.

"Not yet, nor Pawago," Sachim replied.

"Hurry up! Hurry up, children!" Yushta's voice came from near the eastern doorway. He was wearing his ceremonial headpiece and carrying the white wampum belt. He grinned and waved an arm. Outside, they could hear the rattles, the drums, and the flutes begin to play. The Huskface Society had begun its dance. Crenna hurriedly finished dressing, and smoothing down her turkey-feather cape, she took Sachim's small arm and they went out together.

The sky was bright with crimson fire. Golden sparks fountained up and were swallowed by the night. The dark moon floated through a starlit sky.

Crenna worked her way through the happy, chanting throng toward the stone where her father and the Turtle Clan headwoman, Wakami, waited.

The Huskface Society dancers moved in a circle around the fire, in perfect rhythm. She could see Ta-Tando, who was wearing the West Wind mask, shaking his rattle as he moved, his head thrown back and then forward, his knees lifting high as he sang. A child screamed, and Crenna knew that Long Nose was about. Old Lapsa took evil delight in sneaking up on the unsuspecting young ones and laying a hand on their shoulders.

Crenna reached the flat rock which served as a platform, and moments later a puffing Tachtathahuata, the headwoman of the Wolf Clan, arrived. She was a shriveled, sour woman who suffered from a variety of physical ailments—it was said out of her hearing that she had been stricken because she had once slept with a Susquehanna warrior.

Crenna watched the bright beacons of wavering fire, the aloof stars high above. She saw Sachim, hands folded together, standing apart from everyone, her face aglow with firelight. Kala walked among the people, smiling at everyone she met, a smile which lingered longer when she turned her attention to a warrior. Hawk, the Leni-Lenape, stood with the captured people, his face unreadable. Yushta's hand rested on Crenna's shoulder as the dancers, whirling and leaping, finished their dance. Tachtathahuata brought up an unhealthy noise from deep within her body. Rotund, cheerful Wakami, the Turtle Clan headwoman, moved nearer to Yushta, and the old warrior tried to ignore her without seeming rude. He wore the moccasins Wakami had made for him, Crenna noticed.

Then Crenna's eyes lifted beyond the camp, beyond the palisaded walls, to the empty marsh, the silent forest. But she saw no returning war party.

Yushta made a brief speech, and then he offered the white wampum belt.

"If there is any of you who has done wrong, who harbors an impure spirit which the Sisters may find offensive, come up now, and in the spirit of the festival, confess yourself."

A young warrior named Te-al-Pantha whom Crenna had grown up with bounded to the platform. He took the white wampum belt from Yushta and held it high overhead so that the spirits would see it and, remembering their vow to the Oneida, forgive him.

"I took my brother's dog hunting with me, but the dog did not return. I told my brother that a bear had killed his dog, but it was not true. I killed the dog because I was jealous of my brother. I ask the forgiveness of my brother and the spirits."

There was quite a bit of that sort of confession—it was meant to clear the air between friends and family members as well as purifying the tribe so that the corn crop could be blessed by the Sisters. Yet it was more than that; it was wonderful, exciting entertainment for the tribal members. On this night when nothing should be held back, all sorts of indiscretions were bared, and they enjoyed it to the fullest—although none of what was confessed could, by law, be mentioned again.

Crenna listened to the droning, sometimes excited voices, but her eyes were on the distant dark hills. What if he did not come back? Suppose she were never to feel his strong, hungry embrace again? She thought of his breath against her ear, of his hands gripping her waist as he threw back his head and laughed, his strong white teeth flashing, his dark eyes sparkling.

"Crenna?"

She realized it was not the first time her father had spoken to her. Wakami was just finishing her speech. Now, as headwoman of the moiety, superior to all of the individual clans' headwomen, it was Crenna's turn.

She took a step forward.

"We pray for the blessing of the Sisters upon this planting," she said. "We have lived according to the wishes of Manitou. We are Oneida, the greatest of the Iroquois people. Our men are valiant, our women comely and intelligent. We are compassionate in war. Savage tribes may butcher their enemies, but we adopt those who lay down their weapons. In this way we grow; in this way our enemies become friends; in this way mercy is served."

The firelight was bright in her eyes; her voice, resonant and magnetic, drew the attention of every tribal member. It had always been so—the eyes and the voice, gifts from Manitou used to fullest perfection. Even now, when her attention was wandering, when her thoughts went to the forests and the marshes, hers was a compelling presence.

"We are a strong people who will bow down to no invader . . . but only to the will of Manitou and to the will of the spirits who guide and aid us." She heard the sound of the gate being opened and saw the dark figures of warriors entering. She counted them and learned that all had returned. She could see Pawago, hands on hips watching her, grinning.

"Now"—she smiled suddenly, radiantly,—"let us dance to please the spirits! Let us dance and sing, and eat and drink, and let our happiness be a joyous prayer to Manitou!"

She lifted her hands high, and before she had lowered them again, the drums had begun. Dancers leaped before the fire, becoming exultant silhouettes. Crenna was already down from the stone platform, already rushing to meet Pawago.

He stood there still grinning, his strong arms outspread, and she had to slow herself, had to regain some of her stately composure. Still her heart was racing, her breath

19

was heated as she met him, was folded into those arms, as her cheek rested against his bronzed chest, as he whispered into her ear.

"So! You do love your warrior, my Crenna."

She lifted her face and he kissed her. A great log was burned through, and it collapsed into the nearby fire. Sparks shot into the sky in a brilliant golden shower; the dancers' voices rose to a chanting, passionate crescendo.

"Yes," she whispered, her fingers lingering on his throat, that powerful, laughing throat, "yes, Pawago, I do."

"My throat is parched. Let's drink something," he said, and with his arm around Crenna's waist, they walked across the clearing, friends greeting them.

"What happened at the river?" Crenna wanted to know. "Did you find them? Was there a battle?"

"We found them, and they ran. Rabbits. All Munsee are rabbits," Pawago said. They stopped at the huge clay pot which was filled with a drink made of the juice of choke-cherries and raspberries. Manto was already there, drinking deeply from a clay cup. He grinned as he saw his sister and Pawago, and he walked to them.

"I'm sorry we missed the confessions," Manto said with a smile, "I wondered what you have been doing all year, Sister." He looked at Pawago and smiled.

Crenna shook her head. Her eldest brother was a strong man now, his shoulders broad, his chest very deep. It seemed only yesterday that he had run and played child-hood games, sneaking up on his sisters to yank their hair. Now he was a warrior, and one day he would most cer-tainly be sachem. He was a big, outgoing man, so different from Ta-Tando.

"What's the matter, Crenna?" Manto asked, putting his hand on her head. "Don't tell me you were concerned about me? When I was with Pawago!"

"I am hurt when any of our men is wounded," Crenna answered.

"By the Munsee!" Manto laughed and exchanged an amused glance with Pawago. "They ran so fast we could not catch them. Excuse me. I see Taranta." Manto put his cup down on the peg which protruded from the side of the communal bowl and started weaving his way through the crowd toward a young, full-mouthed girl who stood wait-ing.

"Don't be surprised if there is another wedding in your house," Pawago said.

As they watched, Manto, receiving good-natured jostling and shouts of welcome, disappeared into the shadows. To one side stood the small man in the corn-husk mask. Ta-Tando, who had no woman he favored, who was favored by none.

"Let us walk," Crenna said, and Pawago, putting down his cup, nodded.

Together they left the palisade by the river gate. The starlight shone on the river, polishing it to faint silver. The trees stood in silent ranks; the dark moon sank slowly into them.

Pawago wanted to stop, to hold Crenna, to kiss her, but her mood was more sedate and she gently restrained him. They walked beside the river, listening to the quiet murmuring of the river spirits. An owl darted low, its silhouette dark against the dark moon. Upriver the frogs grumped in the reeds, complaining about the chill of the evening.

Pawago halted suddenly and lifted an arm. Crenna raised her eyes to the skies and saw the brief incandescent flare of a dying star streaking earthward. It fell in brilliant silence against the purple sky and then flashed brightly, a deep crimson, for only an instant before the night swallowed it up. There was only a wisp of pale smoke against the sky to mark its passing, and then that too was gone.

"A happy omen, Crenna," Pawago said. His hand tightened on her shoulder.

"An omen." Her voice was soft and distant.

"Is something troubling you?" the warrior asked, and she shook her head.

"Something has been, but it is something with no name. I believe it is only the dark of the moon. Something rises up within me and pecks at my consciousness, but before I can turn my thoughts to it, it is gone, leaving only a trail of smoke, as the star did."

"I don't understand you, Crenna." Pawago turned her by the shoulders and looked deeply into her eyes. "We are to be married. The long winter is gone. We are healthy and young. What can there be to worry you?"

She had no answer for him. It had no name, this vague apprehension which was a dark, furry, clinging creature. It

21

came and whispered words of no meaning, of ancient origins, and then was gone, leaving its tracks across her memory. It was a surging, primeval thing, like an animal long dormant stretching itself stiffly, moving beneath the snow, not quite revealing itself. It warned her of . . . What? It infuriated her at times.

And how do you explain such things to a man who wants to lie down with you on the night-frosted grass and cling to you, molding his body to yours?

She looked at Pawago and saw that he was scowling. Her hand still rested on his shoulder, and now she let it slip away.

"I'm sorry, Pawago. I need to be alone, I suppose. There will be other nights, a thousand of them."

"Yes." His answer was flat, his eyes dull, his thoughts obvious for all his attempts at hiding them. His hands too fell away, and he stared gloomily at the river, watching the winking of starlight on the flowing water. "I will join the festival," Pawago said. "And watch the others dance."

"Pawago . . ."

"It doesn't matter, Crenna," he said. He turned his back and strode away. She followed him a half-step, lifted her hand, and started to speak, but what was there to say? She loved him, or believed she did, but tonight was not Pawago's, it had to be hers alone, she had to walk until she was exhausted, to breathe the cold air in and out, cleansing her soul, to be alone in the darkness, forgetting the tribe, the political bargaining, Pawago.

Angry with herself, she turned, crossing her arms. For a minute she too stared at the river, at the mocking, half-visible eye of the dark moon above the serrated tips of the pines. Then she walked on, letting the solitude of night wrap itself around her, stretching her legs with each step, feeling the pull of tendon and muscle at the backs of her thighs, breathing in deeply until she was nearly dizzy, until the stars grew brighter and the murmur of the river became a muddle, a constant roaring of foreign words humming in her ears.

She stopped atop a low hill where there was a clearing occupied by a single lightning-struck cedar. There was no sound at all in all of the world but the pulsing of her blood, the hammering of her heart. She sat against the dew-frosted grass and then lay back, staring up at the infinite sky, asking it questions for which there were no answers—questions of no meaning, awkwardly framed. Wordless questions arising from the soul and not the mind. There was only silence in answer, and when the silence had gone on long enough, it seemed to be an answer in itself.

She rose and brushed herself off. She could see the village from the hill rise, see that the fires were burning down, dully glowing as a few shadowy, tiny figures clustered around the warmth.

Crenna took a deep slow breath, rubbed her hands back over her hair, and then slowly began to walk homeward.

She had crossed the river, using the stepping stones put there for that purpose, when she heard the low growl, the whimpering in the brush near the path. She halted, thinking of the three-footed bear which was prowling the area.

The sounds came again, low and mewling, and she was drawn toward them. The night seemed to grow warmer, the wind itself seemed to inhale and exhale rhythmically, and already Crenna knew.

She knew and did not want to know. She could not help herself; she was drawn to the sounds. Now a voice was raised in laughter, and she heard a murmured response.

She stopped dead, immobilized, embarrassed, angry, fascinated. The voice was Kala's, and the ragged breathing, the sounds of soft, rapid response, were unmistakable. Kala was with someone, and their mingled sounds were insistent, filled with smothered delight. Crenna hesitated. She believed for a moment that she had to know, that she must creep forward and see them.

And then suddenly she realized she did not want to know; it was better to leave the sounds to the night, the sight of it to the prowling beasts, and she hurried away down the path toward the Oneida village.

❀ 2 ❀

THE CORN GREW STRAIGHT AND tall. Summer approached and the days passed in peaceful progression. There had been an Algonquin raid against an Onondaga village, and the Iroquois had retaliated, but it was a small skirmish, inconsequential. Manto and Te-al-Pantha had encountered the three-footed bear, but although they had put four arrows into the great beast, it had escaped. On a lazy summer evening with the reluctant sun lowering itself toward the far hills, while streamers of frail crimson clouds hung in the sky, Pawago was made sachem.

Crenna approached him, and Pawago, unsmiling, his face and chest painted with yellow and red, listened as she spoke to him.

"Now you are a war chief, Pawago. Now the people of this village must rely upon you for their survival and protection. Now you are an Oneida chief; now you must be vigilant and brave. Now you must fulfill your duties with speed and faithfulness. Now you must strike down our enemies, show mercy to the weak and be fierce with the strong. Now we have placed our faith in you and your strong bow arm."

The sundown sky reddened Pawago's immobile face. Crenna turned and accepted the rack of deer antlers from Moa-Telah, one of the old sachems who had agreed to stand up for Pawago.

Moa-Telah's face was set grimly. This was a serious business. Crenna lifted the rack of antlers overhead, and the tips of the antlers seemed to glow momentarily with a ray of fading sunlight. She strode to Pawago and placed the antlers on his head. His hand brushed hers as he reached up to hold them there.

Only then did Crenna allow herself a smile of happiness. Pawago whispered to her, "Now I need only one thing to be completely satisfied."

24

"Soon," she whispered in return, but as she turned away, her smile faded.

Pawago made a brief speech, promising to be valorous and faithful. Then a drum started beating, and at its signal there was a cheer and the dancing began.

Manto and Ta-Tando went forward to congratulate Pawago. Te-al-Pantha shouted happily. Yushta had stepped up beside his daughter, and he studied her face in the dim velvet light of dusk.

"Are you happy?"

She nearly jumped; her concentration had been elsewhere. "Of course," Crenna said, and her father kissed her head. "What did you have to promise Wakami?"

"It was little," Yushta said, waving a hand. "Only marriage." Yushta smiled at his own joke. Crenna wondered when the joke would become reality. Her father was not so old, and when the winter settled in, a man used to a wife would be lonely.

Kala had wandered up, her eyes liquid and vaguely mocking. "What a fine-looking sachem we have," she said. Yushta shot a glance at his daughter. Crenna pretended not to hear.

"We are in the way of the dancers," Crenna said, moving deliberately away from her sister.

Yushta caught her arm after they had gone a way. "Kala means nothing by it. It is your sister's way."

"As it is a dog's way."

"It is the natural way. What is not natural is to do as you are doing, Crenna. You have been given breasts meant to sweeten and flow, to nourish babies. You have a strong, fine warrior who wishes to marry you. Now he is a man of position. You make him promises and then do not fulfill them."

"I do not tell you to marry Wakami," Crenna said angrily. She was immediately sorry. Yushta's face, lighted by the wavering firelight of the dancers' bonfire, seemed gaunt, much older. "I am sorry, Father." She placed a hand on his narrow wrist.

"I am the one who should apologize," Yushta said, looking beyond Crenna. "I who selfishly wish for grandchildren to brighten my old age. It is your business." He still stared across her shoulder into the distances. "I think I shall visit Yo," Yushta said. He kissed her forehead lightly and then was gone. Crenna folded her arms, started toward Pawago, and then stopped. Whirling away she walked toward the river gate, angry with her own indecisiveness—what *did* she want? To be alone, to wait until the juices of youth had been parched in the dry winds of time?

She could see her father ahead of her—a small, narrow shadow laboring up the hill toward Yo's hut.

"I should marry Pawago," she told herself sternly.

"When you wish it, if you wish it," a soft, familiar voice from out of the shadows said. Crenna turned to see Sachim by starlight. Her sister was sitting on a rock, watching the river, smiling at Crenna.

"I didn't even see you, Sachim," Crenna said with a false-sounding laugh.

"I am small," Sachim said. She got up as Crenna walked to her. "I sit in quiet places and listen—I sometimes hear things I should not hear. It is none of my business what you do."

"If I knew what I *wanted*!" Crenna said in frustration.

"Until you do know, do nothing," Sachim said. "Nature flows, the wind, the water, the stars. It is the way for us—to flow, and to do what is natural and right."

"But there is duty."

"Duty. Yes, I do not understand duty as you do, Crenna," Sachim replied. "But I suppose there is duty. To tribe, to family, to the spirits. Duty to husband. With all of these you have entered an agreement."

"I have an agreement with Pawago," Crenna said.

"I don't think it is the same," Sachim said. "But then, this is not my business. I'm only a small person who speaks from out of the shadows. It's only that I love you, my sister. I want you to be happy."

Crenna took her sister into her arms. So small and frail was this one, so loving and gentle. She hugged her tightly, amazed at the slightness of her frame, the lack of substance.

"I will leave you to your shadows, Sachim," she said, stepping back.

"I leave you to your duty," Sachim said, her words carrying a significance which Crenna did not care to question. Crenna walked on, feeling the night breeze against her face. Almost superstitiously she avoided the spot where she had overheard Kala and her lover. She walked on through the night, going to the lone cedar which stood upon the knoll, and there she watched the night stars blink on and glow with their blue-brightness across the timeless sky.

Moa-Telah, the Turtle sachen, walked among the celebrants, seeing Pawago, his face flushed and bright with firelight, accepting the congratulations of his friends. Ta-Tando, the little wretch, was standing in Pawago's shadow, his eyes as bright as a ferret's basking in reflected glory. What a strange, crooked child to have been born to such a warrior as Yushta! There was no understanding the ways of the gods.

He was tired of the dancing, and so the old sachem, his ceremonial eagle feathers still knotted in his scalp lock, walked to where a group of visting Onondaga warriors were speaking with some of the young Oneida braves. Te-lah-Shal, Moa-Telah's strong young son, was with them.

The young warriors' voices were raised excitedly, and Moa-Telah, smiling with anticipation, went up to them.

". . . Yotha," he heard one of the Onondaga say loudly.

"But Yotha is not here, so what good is such bragging?" Telah-Shal said, and the Oneida all laughed. "To say there is a man in the Onondaga camp who can outrace the wind means nothing. Where is this man?"

Telah-Shal spread his hands, and the Oneida laughed again.

Te-al-Pantha said, "Telah-Shal does not boast to hear his own voice. He can outrace any man alive. Why don't you Onondaga go home? Carry your tails between your legs. Admit that the Oneida have the best runners of all the Iroquois."

"You have not seen Yotha!" the Onondaga tried again.

"And we never will!" Te-al-Pantha laughed. "You boast of your fleet-footed Onondaga racers, and then, when we propose a race, you ask us to race against ghosts."

That brought another round of laughter, and the Onondaga, a tall, serious-looking man called Chaudha, stiffened. His tribal and personal honor were at stake. One of his own warriors goaded him on. "You are nearly as fast as Yotha, Chaudha. Race this spindly-legged Oneida. Who ever heard of an Oneida that could run?"

"Who has yet seen an Onondaga who *would* race?" Te-al-Pantha countered.

One of the Onondaga suddenly lost his temper. He reached for his war ax and had actually started to lift his arm before a grip of iron closed around his wrist. He turned to find an Oneida sachem standing before him.

"Put that down," Moa-Telah said coldly. "Will you make a feud over nothing? If you want to race, do so. If you want fight, go home and make your fights."

The Onondaga lowered his arm.

"I will race you," Chaudha said, stripping off his shirt. Honor seemed to demand it. He had started to remove his leggings as well when Te-al-Pantha asked, "What are the stakes? There must be stakes."

"I brought nothing but my bow and arrows," the Onondaga said.

Telah-Shal, who was also removing his shirt, stopped. He looked at the beautiful elmwood bow, the fringed elk-skin quiver, and said, "All of inferior Onondaga workmanship, but I will race for that. I will put up my ax."

The ax was shown to the Onondaga. Made of hickory, with a head of polished obsidian, it was a beautiful weapon, much coveted.

"If that is all you have," Chaudha said disparagingly.

"Where is the course?" an Onondaga, an older warrior with three fingers missing, asked.

"Around the palisade once," Te-al-Pantha said. He had taken upon himself the role of trainer and was now massaging Telah-Shal's heavily muscled long legs.

As one body they moved toward the river gate. Outside, they stood in two ranks flanking the path, the Oneida on one side, the Onondaga on the other. The warriors took up their position and Moa-Telah, who had been elected starter, lifted his hand.

When he lowered it, the two warriors took off at a dead run. The Onondaga was in front briefly as the two racing men funneled through the corridor of cheering spectators and disappeared around the corner of the palisade.

Telah-Shal could feel the rapid, cadenced pumping of his heart, feel the wild exhilaration swirling in his brain. His legs rose and fell as if there were wings on his heels as he dipped into the hollow and up the far side; the Onondaga warrior had been briefly ahead of him, but now he was a stride behind.

Telah-Shal gritted his teeth, throwing back his head. His arms cut at the night air; he seemed to float above the dark earth. When his toes touched the ground, he was able to bunch the muscles in thighs, calves, feet, and propel himself forward lightly, swiftly.

He could hear the wildly breathing Onondaga at his shoulder, hear the sound of his footfalls, but already as they rounded the southern corner of the palisade, Telah-Shal knew he would win.

He could see the face of Te-al-Pantha ahead of him, see his arms waving, see the Oneida beyond him leaping up and down as he ran toward them, as a gasping Chaudha labored at his heels.

And then he was around the last corner, and with his arms raised exultantly he passed the starting point, the cheering in his ears.

Te-al-Pantha locked his arms around his heaving chest and lifted him into the air, whirling him around as Chaudha, shamefaced, walked back and forth, holding his side with one hand, shaking his head.

"It was not a flat course," he heard the Onondaga complain. "The Oneida knew where the land fell, where it rose. I had no chance."

Telah-Shal tore Te-al-Pantha's hands from his chest and walked toward the Onondaga, shaking a finger. "You lost. You wagered and you lost!"

"I lost! Take the bow and quiver. But it was not fair."

"It was fair!" the Oneida insisted. "We started together."

"You knew the path!" Chaudha shouted back defiantly.

"And now you know it. Do you want to race again? Do you think the result would be any different!"

"I have nothing more to wager."

"I will take a warrior's wager," Telah-Shal said scornfully. The Onondaga hesitated. He looked at his hands, at his tribesmen, at the Oneida warrior before him. Sweat glistened on his chest. His eyes were sober.

"Well?" Telah-Shal was playing up to the Oneida men. "Is it a wager or not? Now you know the path. Your bow and quiver against your finger . . . a warrior's wager!"

The Onondaga wanted to turn, to stalk away, to go back to his village, but his honor was at stake. "All right," he said finally. "My finger against what you have stolen from me."

A chorus of cheers went up. "What I have stolen!" Telah-Shal laughed. "What you have *lost*, Stone Foot." He turned to his Oneida friends. "He should be called Stone Foot. His name does not suit him."

"Tell me when you are through bragging and are ready to race," the Onondaga said heatedly.

Telah-Shal turned to him and coldly said, "I am ready, Stone Foot."

Silently then they returned to their starting position. The faces of the Onondaga and of the Oneida were grim now. The game had turned serious.

Again Moa-Telah lifted his arm, and when he lowered it, the two warriors sprinted through the darkness between the two silent ranks of observers. Telah-Shal's face was a wooden mask, the tendons on his throat stood taut. Hot blood coursed through his veins. He was aware of every muscle, of the driving surge of his heart as he ran. The Onondaga was a stride ahead of him at the first corner, and he gained ground as they dipped into the hollow and scrambled up the far side.

Telah-Shal put his head down and ran on, stretching his stride as long as possible, putting the power of his thighs and buttocks behind each effort. His feet seemed far distant. The Onondaga was gradually pulling away from him, and there was nothing Telah-Shal could do about it. He willed his body to speed on, but now his legs were wild, somehow awkward machines rushing on at their own hectic pace, heedless of his brain's command.

Around the last corner Telah-Shal's lungs were burning. There were brilliant blue and red spots before his eyes. He could barely make out the Onondaga warrior before him. The man was going to beat him. He was three strides ahead. And then suddenly the Onondaga went down.

They were only ten yards from the finish. Telah-Shal could see the wooden faces peering at him; then he saw them brighten with glee.

Chaudha had stepped on a stone and it had rolled underfoot. The Onondaga went down hard, and Telah-Shal had to leap over him to keep from going down himself.

Suddenly he was clear of the fallen warrior and the Oneida men were crowding around him, holding him up as his heart banged against his ribs and his lungs ached, as his rubbery legs trembled.

"He would have won! He tripped on a stone," one of the Onondaga complained loudly. "He should not have to pay."

"He lost!" Te-al-Pantha said angrily, whirling around.

Chaudha had dragged himself to his feet and now he walked heavily toward the gathering. His face was bloody and dusty. His elbow dripped blood.

"I tripped," he panted. "We shall go again."

"No!" Now Telah-Shal was angry. "Twice we raced, twice I won. Moa-Telah?" he asked his father, who was unofficial judge, a sachem whose word must be respected.

"The Oneida has won. Forfeit the prize."

Chaudha's face was a mask of blood and hatred. His mouth was drawn into a fierce scowl, his eyelids were hooded. He nodded. "Take it and be damned, Oneida."

By torchlight they moved in a body to a nearby stone. The Onondaga's hand was placed flat against the stone and Telah-Shal offered him his knife.

"The small one," the Oneida said. "I would not take your bow fingers."

Chaudha glared up at the man. In his hand he held the knife, and for a minute Telah-Shal thought the Onondaga would leap at him. He braced himself for it, but Chaudha, wagging his head with resignation, turned the knife on himself. With a single stroke he severed his little finger. Blood flowed across the rock, and Chaudha, muttering a curse, flung the knife aside and wrapped his finger. Then he turned sharply, his eyes still flashing with anger, and with the Onondaga warriors he moved toward the river. The Oneida watched until their brother Iroquois were gone and then they shouted triumphantly.

Telah-Shal was given the Onondaga's bow and quiver and Te-al-Pantha tied the severed finger to a rawhide string.

"The victor's prize," Te-al-Pantha said, holding it aloft for a moment before tying it around Telah-Shal's neck. Telah-Shal fingered the grisly trophy and then held the bow aloft. He shouted across the river, "Tell Yotha, the great runner, that the Oneida send their greetings!"

That brought a laugh from the Oneida warriors, and together they turned and entered the palisade, dancing and singing, rejoining Pawago's celebration.

Only one man remained behind. He was not welcome among the warriors, for he was not a warrior any longer, but a woman.

Hawk walked to the riverbank and washed his face. Sitting down, he watched the wind in the trees and smiled, remembering his excitement when the Onondaga had fallen and Telah-Shal had flown across the line, the winner.

As if I were one of them, he thought ruefully.

But he was not one of them. He was Leni-Lenape, a coward, a woman, a dog. A man castrated as surely as if they had taken a knife to him. And yet he cheered his masters' victory.

Hawk spat and tossed a pebble against the still surface of the water.

"It is late," the voice behind him said, and Hawk stood. It was the young and pretty daughter of Yushta, the small one called Sachim.

"Very late," Hawk said, careful to keep his eyes lowered.

"Was there a race? I heard shouting and thought there was a race."

"There was!" Hawk's voice grew briefly excited as he described it, using his flat hand to demonstrate how the Onondaga had skidded on his face, how Telah-Shal had raced past him to win.

"It sounds very exciting," Sachim said when Hawk was finished. The Leni-Lenape's expression suddenly changed. Sachim could almost feel the heat go out of his body, feel him cool.

"I have seen better," Hawk said.

"Among your own people?" she asked gently.

"The Oneida are my people," he said stiffly. He had his eyes turned down submissively again.

"Perhaps now, but not always." Sachim looked closely at this strong young man, pity for him welling up inside. What was it like to lose your people, your identity?

"Not always," Hawk finally replied, "but it's better not to speak of it."

"Don't you think about them? The Leni-Lenape?"

"No. Why should I!" He was angry briefly, not at

Sachim, it seemed. At himself? "I can't talk to you. It doesn't look right. You are the daughter of a sachem, I am a slave."

"Not a slave! A captured warrior."

"It's the same. To you it seems merciful not to kill me. But do you know what it is like to live like I do?"

"No." Sachim smiled again as his eyes met hers. "That is what I am asking you."

He began to scoff, and then he looked, really looked, into her deep, large eyes, studied the slight, ingenuous smile, and he said, "I have already spoken too much."

Sachim ignored his argument. "What is it like to live as you do?" She touched his shoulder. "Would you walk a way with me and tell me?"

"It's not right," Hawk objected.

"No, it's all right. Honestly."

He shrugged and began walking with Sachim, his feet plodding as if he carried a burden on his broad shoulders.

"Where were you captured. Wasn't it at Sulfur Lake?"

"Yes—that's what the Oneida call it. I was very young."

"You aren't so old now."

"No? I feel old, tired, useless. I was captured by a war party your father led. I saw my brother killed, my cousins, my friends. The women and children huddled together in a copse. I saw blood on my hands, and I knew I didn't want to die. I was alone. I threw down my bow and groveled at your father's feet."

"You had no choice. You would have died for nothing. You did the right thing." They had paused in a cool glade.

Hawk leaned up against a mossy boulder which towered behind him. "In that moment I surrendered my manhood. It was the worst thing I have ever done."

"It couldn't have been better to die!"

"Far better. Far, far better. But I was young, I thought only life mattered. Now I know it is what your life *is*. What a man is. *How* he lives, *how* he dies."

"Still, you would have died for nothing. Your people were defeated." Sachim's hand stretched out, and to Hawk's astonishment, she took his hand briefly, her flesh cool against his.

"No. I would have died for the tribe. I would have died a warrior's death. Only the tribe matters, the tribe and a man's dignity. What is a man without a people?"

"There are other Leni-Lenape among us."

"Women and children. And the women will not look at me. They turn their heads when I walk by. No one will speak to me. The children hurl stones."

"They do not understand."

"They are right!" Hawk said, tearing his hand away from Sachim. "They are right. I am nothing. No warrior, no woman, no one at all. A coward, the children call me, and so I am. I am no one, not Oneida, not Leni-Lenape."

"You are someone. You are Hawk, the man," Sachim said with soft, eager encouragement.

"*Hawk!*" He laughed wildly for a minute. "Even my name changed because the Oneida could not pronounce my true name."

"Will you teach it to me?" Sachim asked.

"What is the use!"

"None, if you do not believe there is any point in it," Sachim replied calmly. "I thought you did not like your name. I did not wish to offend you."

"You do not offend me, Sachim," Hawk said, and his voice was quiet now. He darted a glance toward her and then looked away again. "My name does not offend me. I offend myself. I with my cowardice, with my dog's ways." He took a deep breath. "It is cold. Let us walk back to the village."

"Will you talk to me again?"

"I don't know. There are men who may not like it."

"And if they don't?"

"If they don't, Sachim," he answered, "they will kill me."

"But you will speak with me again?"

"Yes!" he said, sighing heavily. "Yes, I will speak to you again if you wish, small one. Brave one. Silly, beautiful one." And then he was grinning and Sachim was laughing. They stood facing one another in the darkness, the trees rising around them.

The scream of pain came from near the village. Hawk's head snapped around. Sachim stood, eyes wide, mouth open.

"What was . . . ?"

"Come on," Hawk said. "Hurry! Hurry, small one!"

They rushed through the oak and pine forest and found the river. Hawk held Sachim's hand, gripping it tightly as they raced toward the palisade, seeing men with torches streaming through the river gate, hearing the broken, pain-ridden cry rise up again and break off, falling silent in the night.

By the time they reached the body, there were already twenty men and women gathered around. Old Moa-Telah, wearing only his breechclout, was on his knees beside the river, holding his son's head on his knees.

Sachim saw Crenna and she shouted breathlessly, "What is it?" but Crenna did not reply.

Moving nearer, Sachim saw Moa-Telah, saw Telah-Shal, dead, his finger severed and stuffed in his mouth. She saw the tears in the old chief's eyes, saw Te-al-Pantha, his face a mask of fury, exhorting the other warriors.

"We must follow them. We must kill them!"

"Calm yourself, Te-al-Pantha." The voice was Crenna's. Soft, cool, composed.

"This was done by the Onondaga! They must be punished."

"Didn't you hear me, Te-al-Pantha!" Crenna responded. This time there was iron in her voice, fire in her eyes.

"My son," Moa-Telah moaned. "They have taken my son. My only son."

Yushta was coming on the run, Manto behind him. He sought out Crenna and asked, "What has happened?"

"The Onondaga returned and killed Telah-Shal."

Yushta glanced toward the grieving father, seeing Te-lah-Shal, the severed finger still in his mouth, his eyes open to the night sky.

"The dogs. The Onondaga dogs," Yushta breathed.

Crenna's hand gripped her father's arm at the elbow. "Father, we must be calm if we expect our young warriors to be calm. We must insist on lawful recourse if we expect the law to be adhered to."

"This is Telah-Shal!"

"This is a matter for Iroquois law!" Crenna said just as strongly. Yushta wiped his eyes; then slowly he nodded, and she felt her father's muscles relax.

"I shall speak to them," Yushta said heavily. He walked to where Moa-Telah, his old friend, still sat, holding his son's corpse. Crenna saw her father crouch down, rest a hand on Moa-Telah's shoulder, and whisper to him.

"No!" Moa-Telah's head swung around angrily. His

35

teeth were clenched. Yushta whispered to him again, hugging his friend's head to his chest. Then slowly Moa-Telah nodded, and he stood, leaving his only son to lie against the riverbank, his feet in the water, his eyes open to the drifting dark moon.

"Go to your beds," Yushta said to the gathered warriors. "Go home." Pawago stood apart, his face stony, unreadable. Manto and Te-al-Pantha held weapons in their hands. Ta-Tando hopped nervously from foot to foot, watching his sister, waiting for permission to pursue the Onondaga and kill them. Crenna looked away from her brother, was surprised to see Sachim clinging to the arm of an untouchable Leni-Lenape, and then briefly she closed her eyes before hearing the screams of Telah-Shal's mother.

The woman came rushing from the palisade, her hair a tangle, her eyes wild. She cradled Telah-Shal in her arms as if he were an infant and clawed at her own face, tearing deep crimson grooves in her mahogany flesh. Her sobs echoed to the skies, and Crenna was not the only one who had to turn away and walk back toward the village.

Yushta was beside her again. "This must be settled. Tonight! It is an insult, an attack upon our people." Lapsa, another of the Solitary Pine Tree sachems, was with Yushta. His face was equally grim.

"Send a runner to the Onondaga camp," Crenna said as she walked. "Advise Ka-Lo-Dzhe what has happened."

"And in the meantime," Lapsa said, "we shall—"

"In the meantime we shall go to bed and sleep," Crenna said. "What will you do? Start a war among the Iroquois? Attack your brothers over a warriors' feud, making an end to our great alliance over this incident? Cool your head, Lapsa. Act as becomes an Oneida sachem. Comfort Moa-Telah, but do not speak of war. Speaking of war makes war."

There were drums of mourning all night, and in the morning Telah-Shal received a warrior's burial. He was lowered into his grave with his weapons and personal belongings and the earth was heaped over him as his sisters and mother sang mourning songs.

Moa-Telah stood woodenly watching, his mouth grim, his eyes empty. He and the women of the family had taken a knife to their own faces, scarring themselves so that the spirit of Telah-Shal, returning, would not recognize them and take them away to the dark land.

Crenna stood on the knoll, listening to the rising and falling tones of the dirge, to the sobbing of the wind. There was nothing to be said to the family, no additional prayers she could offer to Manitou for Telah-Shal's safe passage to the Bright Land in the sky.

In the early afternoon the Onondaga arrived.

Ka-Lo-Dzhe led the party into the Oneida camp, and the face of this tall, horse-faced Onondaga headwoman was cold and spiritless. She greeted Crenna with a dry kiss.

Among the party was Pekoath, a white-haired, trembling ancient warrior. Chaudha was his son.

"Let us smoke and renew our friendship, the long friendship of the Oneida and the People of the Hill," Crenna said, and the Onondaga delegation silently followed her to the council lodge, where Yushta, Lapsa, Wakami, Tachtathahuata, a grim-faced Moa-Telah, and the newest Oneida sachem, Pawago, all waited.

Everyone was seated, and they smoked a pipe. Etiquette was observed and they spoke of many things, avoiding the true purpose of the meeting, leaving the most important topics until last.

"The Algonquin, bloody dogs, raided our women as they planted rice," Pekoath said as he took three ritual puffs of the pipe which burned mixed tobacco and birch bark.

"The Algonquin are dogs," Yushta agreed. "They fight only women."

"It is a wonder they had the courage to face Iroquois women," Moa-Telah put in. "The Onondaga women are a match for their cowardly warriors."

The old men began telling tales of Algonquin cowardice and everyone listened intently, adding other anecdotes. Food was brought in and served, and they ate, the Onondaga complimenting the food highly.

"A ship with Moon Men in it was captured by the Mohawks," Ka-Lo-Dzhe told them. "Nine men with faces like snow and long yellow hair. The Mohawks killed them all. No one can guess what these men want."

"They bring evil," Lapsa said. He glanced at Crenna. The tension in the council lodge was so heavy it was nearly visible. Harsh lines formed themselves around the eyes of the warriors and the lips of the headwomen. It was Crenna's place to broach the delicate subject, and she did so now.

"One of our young warriors has been killed."

"Oh?" Ka-Lo-Dzhe's eyebrow lifted as if this were the first she had heard of this. "Where does the blame lie, Crenna?"

"Who can say where the blame lies? There were young hot-blooded men contending with one another."

"Could any Onondaga men have been among them?" Pekoath asked in his trembling voice.

"It is possible." Crenna looked into the old man's eyes. "I have heard that this was so. I have heard that your son Chaudha was among them. Is this so, Lapsa?"

"It is so, I believe," the Oneida sachem said.

"My son?" Pekoath nodded his head thoughtfully. "I believe that I did hear that. And wasn't it he who ran the race with Telah-Shal, who is now gone to the spirit land?"

"Yes." Moa-Telah was unable to keep all of his bitterness out of his voice now.

Ka-Lo-Dzhe pushed to the heart of the matter. "A man was killed after that race," the Onondaga headwoman said. She shifted her glance to Crenna. "The law may have been broken. It is for us to decide what happened and who was to blame."

"The race was run by Moa-Telah's son and Chaudha," old Pekoath said, his hand trembling as he gestured. There was worry in the warrior's eyes now. All pretense was gone. "My son lost his bow and quiver. But he did not know the course, that is how he lost. Then Telah-Shal's friends goaded him into making a warrior's bet. Telah-Shal again won, but only because a stone was in my son's path, causing him to fall. The race should have been run again."

Pekoath went on. "My son forfeited his finger despite feeling cheated by the Oneida. Then, as he crossed the river, Telah-Shal hurled an insult after him. It made him angry. He returned and killed Telah-Shal."

Crenna was silent. There were only two options. The first of these called for Chaudha's death. Looking at the old man, she pitied him. These warriors and their games!

"Chaudha must die," Moa-Telah said, as if speaking of the weather. "It is the law, it is just."

38

"There is another way," Ka-Lo-Dzhe said, again letting her gaze shuttle to Crenna's eyes.

"It is not acceptable!" Moa-Telah said stubbornly. "An Onondaga has killed my son. Let the Onondaga pay with his life."

"He felt cheated," Pekoath said in a high, thin voice. "He tripped over a stone in the dark."

"The Oneida did not put the stone there."

"Perhaps your son tripped him."

"Everyone saw what happened! It was the stone. Chaudha should have been a man. He should have accepted defeat. Instead he sneaked back and committed murder."

"Some satisfaction must be given," Crenna said. "I believe Ka-Lo-Dzhe and I agree. But I believe we also agree that the payment should not be death. I want you to accept wampum belts, Moa-Telah."

"Wampum belts! For my son's life? It is not satisfactory, Crenna."

"Death for Chaudha accomplishes nothing."

"Wampum belts mean nothing to me. I am already a rich man."

The law was very clear. A murderer could buy absolution from the family of the murdered person with six wampum belts. If this was satisfactory to the family. If the wampum was refused, as Moa-Telah was refusing, the death penalty was then invoked.

"Come, Moa-Telah, think this through," Ka-Lo-Dzhe said. "You have been deprived of a son. Why inflict this pain on Pekoath?" The Onondaga woman looked into the bitter, scarred face of the Oneida sachem. "It was done, this murder, in the heat of anger. It was wrong, but you do another wrong in hurting Pekoath."

"No." Moa-Telah made a definitive gesture with his hand. "Blood demands blood. I insult the memory of my son by accepting wampum. That is it. I speak no more. Chaudha must die."

Yushta had not said a word; he was hesitant to speak against his old friend's wishes. Ka-Lo-Dzhe had no influence on Moa-Telah. She too was Onondaga, trying to protect her tribesman. It was up to Crenna to resolve this, and taking a slow breath, she rose in one supple movement.

"Come outside with me, Moa-Telah."

"You have nothing to say to me, Crenna."

"I have something to say to you," she said. Her voice, still soft, now became authoritative. "Come outside and listen to it."

Moa-Telah rose reluctantly; his battered face was set, his eyes hard. He followed Crenna from the lodge. Outside, the smells of summer were in the air. The scent of grass and dust and growing corn. The scent of the river and of corn soup.

Crenna walked a little way from the council lodge, Moa-Telah beside her. She stopped near the tanning racks, now empty, and whirled to face Moa-Telah.

"I am sorry Telah-Shal is dead," she said.

"I know you are, Crenna . . ."

"You are harming the tribe, Moa-Telah. You are harming the Oneida. You think only of your son. It is right to mourn him, but this—it is not right. I have to think of all the people. And in their name I must tell you that you are wrong."

"I don't understand you."

"You don't understand me because you haven't thought this through, Moa-Telah. You are in the grip of your grief. You cannot see past the funeral fire's smoke. You are harming my people, and I cannot allow it.

"What will happen now?" she demanded. "Chaudha will be killed. And then what will happen? His father will be angry. Perhaps his friends will come to the Oneida camp and kill another man. Then our men will respond—it has happened before, many times, and you know it. A feud with our neighbors, with our Iroquois brethren. I cannot allow it."

"They would not dare attack us," Moa-Telah said hesitantly.

"No, why not? If they do not, what then? We are left with rancor, with hatred between brothers. It has taken a hundred years to build the Iroquois nation, Moa-Telah. To develop a system of law."

"Killing my son was outside the law. Killing Chaudha is within the law," the old man said stubbornly.

"You don't violate the *law* by asking for Chaudha's death," Crenna said forcefully. "You violate common sense. You offend the people of our tribe. You place them

40

in danger, you breed bitterness. The tribe is important to me, Moa-Telah. I am headwoman, they are my responsibility. The tribe is more important than any one member. You are a sachem, a man of responsibility. You too owe the tribe a debt. You owe your son honor, you owe the law respect. But the tribe—the tribe which is all, which supports us and protects the weak, which nurtures the young, which provides for the old—the tribe you owe your service, your loyalty. You would harm the tribe and the well-being of everyone in it for the sake of your revenge, and that is a crime against us all, Moa-Telah. I can say no more. Do what your conscience dictates."

She turned and went back into the council lodge, seating herself beside Yushta. Pekoath looked up with hopefulness, but Crenna's expression offered no hope. The old man looked at his lined hands as if some answer were written there.

The doorway was suddenly blackened by the figure of a man, and he came forward, standing silently above them for a long minute.

"I will accept the wampum belts," Moa-Telah said quietly.

In the evening a runner reported that the Munsee were again fishing in the East River, in the Oneida hunting grounds, and a war party was formed.

With the dawn Pawago led his men out; among them were Te-al-Pantha and Manto. Ta-Tando followed them all the way to the gate, hobbling on his clubfoot, trying to appear uninterested in the activity, failing miserably.

Crenna watched her brother, and pity flooded her heart. It was time the boy became a man. Time he was allowed to go out with the war parties, impairment or none. He was always especially bitter after a group of warriors went out on some expedition, sullen and rude. It was time; she must speak to Pawago. By neglecting to initiate Ta-Tando, they were making him an outcast from society. His position was no better than that of a captured warrior like Hawk.

Thinking of Hawk recalled her father's irate words. "You must speak to her, Crenna. What is Sachim thinking of? She associates with that dog-warrior all the time now.

A Leni-Lenape! A coward, an untouchable! The daughter of a chief—it is unthinkable."

"Why don't you forbid it, Father? Why don't *you* speak to Sachim?"

"Ah, well," he had answered lamely. "You know Sachim—she does not even understand such things. I can deny her nothing."

Crenna had only smiled and kissed the old man's forehead in response. What he had said was true. Sachim made no distinction between classes. She was as unaware as a creature of the forest. It was also true that her father had never denied her a thing—Sachim asked for nothing. She was content to have food to eat, a blanket to sleep in. She was soft and gentle; scolding her produced only childish amazement in her eyes.

Crenna watched the women at work in the fields, noticing that the pumpkins were already large and flourishing, the sunflowers already nearly dead. The summer was nearly ended, and still she had not given Pawago his answer. Winter was coming on, and he would sleep alone. She wanted to answer him, to marry him, to sleep with him, but doubt lingered, and she could not understand it.

She walked the hillsides, seeing the hint of color in the leaves of the maple and oak. Soon the hills would be flooded with the fire and gold of autumn; the days were growing short.

She heard a voice calling her, and she saw old Lapsa waving his arm. Crenna had forgotten—she was the keeper of the masks for the False Face Society, and with Wakami ill, the men of the society needed their masks to make medicine. She turned and walked back that way, watching the wind drift the dust and rattle the long ranks of oak trees.

She was forgetting many things these days, and there was no reason for it. She was not sleeping well, either. In the night her head hummed with what seemed to be the sound of distant voices, as if she were being summoned by the spirits, or warned; as if some great knowledge were forthcoming, if only she would lie still enough, throttle her breathing, see beyond the stars. But the knowledge never revealed itself; the voices simply muttered away, leaving her feeling frustrated, tormented, and somehow quite lonely.

They jog-trotted through the woods, their moccasins silent as they leaped fallen trees and stones. They moved like the wind, and it was wildly exhilarating to be in such command of their bodies, to feel the fluid grace, to be soundless, sure, strong, and swift.

Manto could see the back of Pawago, and he noticed the way the muscles of his shoulders bunched, how those down his back rippled and swelled. He was a cat, a panther in the woods. Pawago's face was expressionless but for the gleaming eyes. He was hunting, and this time he would not be denied.

The Munsee had run, had sifted back into the forests and the marshes before; this time they would stand and fight or be captured.

Manto's heart surged with excitement. Te-al-Pantha was nearly at his shoulder, and he could see the savage joy on the young warrior's face. He too felt it. This raw, surging emotion like a loop thrown around all of them, joining their spirits. They were a pack of hunting wolves, the fingers of Manitou reaching out to clutch the enemy. They were wind and fire, their bodies only implements of the spirits' will.

Pawago forded the little creek, his feet splashing up tiny silver geysers. His head was thrown back exultantly. Their sachem was a man! A panther, a wolf, an eagle.

Manto splashed across the creek, feeling the round pebbles underfoot, feeling the wind in his face, the pumping of his heart. Then they were into the trees, the shadows changing so rapidly that they flickered in his eyes. The sunlight was brilliant through the dark, lacy foliage overhead. He leaped a fallen elm tree, followed Pawago into a brushy depression and up the far side. He could run all day, all night! Their bodies were not a part of them. They raced on, and his mind floated high above, watching the silhouettes of naked, fleet-footed warriors. They were a part of the shadows, a part of the forest, invisible and silent.

And then Pawago stopped and went to his belly. Without a signal, they followed his example, obeying orders which did not have to be communicated, but were felt, known almost before Pawago had finished thinking them.

No signals were necessary, no waving of arms or whistling, pointing of fingers or warning glances. Pawago had halted and gone to his belly. He would halt only if they were going no farther, so they had reached their destination. He would not go to his belly unless there was a reason to hide himself. Therefore he had sighted the enemy. All of that was communicated by the common, hunters' mind in the barest fragment of a second.

Manto crawled forward, carrying his bow in his right hand. He inched up beside Pawago, who was on the bank overlooking the slate-colored river. And then Manto saw them.

Munsee!

His facial muscles tightened. His lips drew back to form an unvoluntary grimace, exposing his teeth. His legs twitched with animal excitement. He glanced at Pawago. The war chief was utterly still, his breathing slow and gentle. Only his eyes moved.

There were the Munsee, and their straw baskets were filled with poached fish. They were deep within the Oneida hunting grounds and knew full well what they were doing—stealing food from Manto's tribe.

They could not run this time. They were caught and must pay. First they must be netted like the wriggling fish they had taken from the river.

Pawago was pressed against the earth; a leaf fluttered down from a black oak and settled against his back. His eyes shifted again to Manto, and he nodded. Manto crawled away from the edge of the bluff, and without signal his four men followed him, circling north, keeping to the river brush.

They splashed across the river a quarter of a mile upstream from Pawago's position and sifted through the trees, circling wide to come up behind the Munsee. Te-al-Pantha with his four men had circled south. Soon they would have the Munsee encircled, trapped, and at Pawago's signal they would trip the snare, swooping down upon the thieving Munsee before they could react.

Manto crept forward now, wriggling across the ground, which was littered with leaves and pine needles. The smell of decaying vegetation was ripe in his nostrils, and above that he could smell the dead fish, the water, the scent of his enemy.

He lay suddenly still. He wasn't twenty feet from the nearest Munsee brave. Only a thin screen of willow brush shielded him from their eyes. But the Munsee were stupid. They cleaned their fish and worked their nets and fish traps, not sensing the presence of an enemy.

Manto lay still, listening, watching. He could not see Pawago on the far side of the river, could not hear Te-al-Pantha's men creeping through the forest, but he knew where they were, knew that the moment of battle was near.

Let them fight, he thought. Manto did not want them to surrender, to stand quaking before the Iroquois. He wanted to test himself against them.

Manto had won an eagle feather already—against the Algonquin. That time, however, he had been with the old warriors, with his father, Yushta, and Lapsa. They had protected him, and although he had struck down two Algonquin warriors, he felt as if the eagle feather had been a gift.

This was his battle. His, and chiefly Pawago's. Pawago was the new sachem, the future war leader of the Oneida nation. It was their time to show they were men fully competent in war, that they no longer needed to stand in the shadows of their fathers.

A red ant raced across Manto's hand, twisting and retracing its tracks in confusion. A lone crow, dark against the blue sky, wheeled overhead, cawing hoarse warnings. Manto notched his arrow, testing the tension of his bowstring as he waited, his eyes alert. He seemed hardly to breathe. He stared unblinking for long minutes, his nerves prickling beneath his skin. A cold chill ran down his spine, like icy water.

He came to his feet as Pawago's war cry echoed across the river. Men were moving in every direction suddenly. Manto was aware of Pawago rushing across the river, sending up plumes of silver water, his men racing behind him. He could see a flash of color in the trees to the south, and he knew that was Te-al-Pantha. The Munsee turned and fled. A basket of fish fell from one Munsee's hands, the silver fish flopped against the sand of the riverbank. He saw the pinched, startled face of a Munsee brave as he reached toward the bow near his feet. Manto raised up, fired his arrow, and saw it bury itself in that enemy's back.

He saw the trickle of crimson blood, saw the sunlight

on the water, saw Pawago's war club rise and fall, cleaving the skull of a Munsee warrior.

He heard a fierce cry rise up in his throat, and he leaped from the underbrush, running up the sandy riverbank toward the Munsee who cowered there. He saw the dead warrior, his arrow still in his back, and he hurdled the body, his war cry shrill and triumphant.

Let them fight, Manto thought. Let them test their strength against mine. But already he saw that it was a forlorn wish. The Munsee crowded together, their hands above their heads. One warrior of eighteen or so groveled at Te-al-Pantha's feet. Their hands were empty, their eyes frightened.

Manto slowed his headlong rush and finally broke into a slow walk. He had his bow in one hand. His war ax swung loosely from the other.

Pawago circled the Munsee, taunting them. "Women! Thieves. Pick up your weapons. Fight like men. Cowards!"

The Munsee didn't move, didn't speak, did not look at their captors. Their heads were hung miserably. They had taken a chance and had failed. Now they would not see their families again. Women would wait by the lodge doors searching the hills for the returning men, but they would never come, and after a while their women would take other husbands, their children would grow up and forget they had lived.

"Cowards!" Pawago leaped forward, his face inches from that of a strong, flat-faced Munsee. The Munsee simply stared across Pawago's shoulder, watching the river wink in the sunlight. "Woman! Dog!"

Pawago shoved the man, and he fell to a sitting position. Still he did not move.

Te-al-Pantha spoke. "They know resistance is death," the warrior said. "We have won, Pawago. Our women will have much help at harvesttime. Let us take them to our village."

Pawago seemed not to hear him. His chest rose and fell slowly, his ax swung from his blood-smeared hand.

"Pawago?"

"Why feed them?" Pawago asked. "They are cowards, worthless dogs. Why feed them? They have come to steal our food, and so we feed them!"

Manto laughed. The wind was cold against his exer-

46

tion-heated muscles. Pawago just stood there. Manto thought that he had been making a joke, but he saw no amusement in Pawago's eyes.

"Cowards!" Pawago's voice was a roar. Without warning, he leaped forward. Manto saw his ax rise and fall, saw the Munsee go down, his head nearly severed.

"Pawago!" Manto shouted, but there was no stopping him. Pawago struck down another Munsee, and another. Screaming, a man tried to flee, but Te-al-Pantha caught him, knocked him to his face, and clubbed him savagely. Suddenly they were all striking at the Munsee. Manto saw anguished faces smeared with blood, saw Pawago's ax lifted time and again, saw Te-al-Pantha kill another man.

The Oneida swarmed over the prisoners, battering them, driving the heads of their axes into living flesh. And Manto was among them. He did not know why he was killing them. He simply joined in the massacre. He struck left and saw a man go down. Another tried to crawl away on hands and knees, and Manto killed him.

It was a dream, a nightmare. His war club swung in slow motion. He could see his victims' eyes in the moment before they died. A man lifted a hand to shield his face, and Manto cut the hand away. He was killing and he did not know why. Pawago's shrieks were loud and piercing. Bodies lay heaped at his feet. Blood clung to his chest.

He killed another man, desperately. A kind of fear made Manto strike, and strike again. He had to do his share. He was a member of the pack, and the pack was a killing thing. The sun spun in his eyes. The bright river seemed to tilt and flow toward the skies. Manto was killing, beating the man, until Te-al-Pantha's hand locked onto his arm and Manto realized the Munsee had been dead for a long while.

He stepped back, staggering. He felt bile rising in his throat. Te-al-Pantha looked sick, his eyes glazed. Pawago had broken into a triumphant dance. The others could only watch him, watch as he spun in a mad circle, his moccasined feet kicking up tiny puffs of dust.

Manto knew they were there—dead men lying in a jumble a few feet away; he could smell them. But he could not look that way. He did not want to see them. They had been the enemy, but now they were filth. He had broken the law, he had murdered, he had behaved as a savage coward. Why, why?

Manto glanced at Te-al-Pantha. Te-al-Pantha's eyes seemed to be fixed on the blood which ran down Manto's arm. Manto squatted down and scrubbed at his arm with dirt, rubbing until the skin on his forearm was raw. The stain would not wipe away. Te-al-Pantha turned and was sick. Pawago continued his mad dance, and the others only watched. They stood in a silent cluster, their backs to the dead, watching as their sachem leaped into the air, whirled, and panted a song. His tongue lolled about his mouth; a drop of spittle showed at the corner of his mouth. He was dusty and bloody, exultant.

Finally he stopped; he came up to them, panting. "It was what they deserved," Pawago said. He gripped Manto's arm tightly, his fingers digging into Manto's flesh. "It was what they deserved!

"We must make a pact. We must swear an oath." He still had difficulty speaking; his breath came in ragged gasps. "Do you hear me!"

They mutely shook their heads.

"It was what they deserved. They were our enemies, taking the food from our mouths. It was what they deserved. We must take a solemn oath." His eyes, fixed on Manto, were bright and slightly unfocused. "None of us can speak of this ever. To no one. Swear it!"

They made a pact then, standing on the riverbanks, the dead Munsee staining the sand with their blood. The warriors stood together and clasped hands, and they vowed never to speak of this. When they had done that, they dragged the bodies of the Munsee to the river's edge and threw them in. Some floated away, some lay sprawled on the sand bars, waiting for the water to carry them off, to take them southward, to their homes. Manto helped to drag the corpses to the river. They were very heavy, but they no longer seemed to have been men; you had only to avoid looking at their faces.

When they were finished, it was nearly dusk. Manto looked to the evening skies. Clouds billowed up against the dark northern horizon. It would rain—he could smell the moisture, the lightning in those clouds.

It would rain and the silver fingers would reach down from the skies and wash away the blood. The river would be swollen by quick-running freshets and the bodies would be carried away. There would be nothing at all to bear witness to their crime. Nothing but the stain in Manto's heart, which would not be rubbed away.

❀ 3 ❀

THE THUNDER BROUGHT HER HEAD around, and Crenna walked to the entranceway of the longhouse, looking out as the dark clouds rolled across the sundown skies, as the wind scattered the first heavy drops of rain. The wind gusted against her, lifting her dark hair, pressing her skirt against her legs, and she breathed in deeply, liking the clean scent of the air.

She watched until the clouds had roofed over the sky and the rain had become a steady patter on the roof of the longhouse, and then she turned back inside.

Returning to her living area, she opened the straw basket at her feet and began storing the masks away. The False Face Society had finished making its medicine. The men had gone to Wakami's sickbed and they had scattered ashes over her. Now she would get well. Crenna closed the lid to the basket and stored the masks away in the overhead bin. The women, driven in from their work, walked into the longhouse, dripping water, chattering, carrying complaining babies.

"They are coming, Crenna," Wa-Loka told her, and Crenna went back to the door. She watched the gate for a minute, and then, when the warriors were visible, she went out into the dark rain to greet them.

They were all well. Pawago had his head thrown back. The rain streamed down in convoluted sheets. He reached Crenna in minutes and threw his arms around her waist, spinning her off her feet.

"All well! No one is injured. We found the Munsee, but they ran away again." He kissed her roughly. There was an eagerness about Pawago, a savage joy. He kissed her again, so hard that he bruised her lips.

Manto and Te-al-Pantha walked past, their heads hung. They seemed weary, but Pawago was excited, wildly joyous. He kissed Crenna again, content to stand in the storm with her, the rain drumming down. Lightning flashed over-

50

head, forming a bone-white bridge across the skies.

"I must speak to Manto," Crenna said, pulling away. "Yushta is waiting to speak with him."

"Forget Manto, forget your father. You have me. Let us go out into the night, Crenna. Let's feel the rain on our bodies."

"We'll take a chill," she said, smiling hesitantly. He still clung to her, some strange exultation lighting his eyes. There was something highly charged about his expression, something frightening.

"I'll not be chilled. My blood is in a fever."

"My blood is not so hot as yours, Pawago," Crenna said, and she knew instantly that she had said the wrong thing. He still held her waist, but his arms were wooden. His lean dark face was fixed into a grin which reflected no humor.

"No," he said. The grin fell away. "No, I forget, it is not. I'll dry myself," he said, and he stalked away toward his longhouse, Crenna watching him through the rain.

He had a right to be angry, she thought, and then that emotion was replaced by momentary anger. At Pawago, at herself, she could not have said. She simply felt angry, felt like screaming. Thunder roared overhead and she turned to splash across the clearing to her bed.

That was when she saw Manto. She started to go up to him, to tell him that Yushta wanted to see him, but something held her back.

He simply stood there on one side of the longhouse, his face turned toward the dark skies. The rain washed down over him, but he did not seem to notice. It had grown cold and the rain was heavy, pelting the flesh, but Manto remained fixed, staring bleakly up at the cold, frothing skies.

"Manto!" she called out above the storm, but her brother did not respond. She took a hesitant step toward him and called again. "Manto?"

This time his head swiveled slowly toward her. He looked at Crenna, but did not see her. His eyes were large and quite empty. The rain ran in rivulets across his face and broad chest. In his hand was his war ax. Manto slowly looked away, and Crenna left him there, standing rigidly in the cold, driving rain, like a man without a spirit.

The storm rattled across the bay, chopping the waters to

51

whitecaps, and the rain fell steadily on New Netherlands. It was an ambitious name for the collection of slovenly huts which huddled together under lowering skies at the mouth of the Hudson; a tenuous toehold on this New World, indeed. The ship, an eighty-foot, three-hundred-ton, waterlogged, barnacle-laden flute, lay at anchor on the slate-gray, turgid sea. Pyramids of white foam lifted from the surface of the water, and driven by the wind, they scuttled shoreward to break against the crude earthern quay.

The lightning flashed overhead again, and a long re-sounding peal of savage thunder shivered the skies. Peter Van der Veghe walked toward the miserable hut at the end of the tiny rocky island which guarded the mouth of the Hudson River. The sea slapped at the quay, threatening to wash it away, as it would eventually, Van der Veghe knew. He was a man used to thinking in absolutes, in seeing the transitory nature of all things, and he could smile at the ambitions of the men around him.

He was a tall man, and his stride carried him swiftly across the open ground between the walls of the hastily built stockade and the quarters of the merchant general of the Dutch East India Company.

A dull light burned within the crude hut. The flickering yellow glow of it could be seen between the poorly fitting logs which formed the side of the hastily constructed shelter.

He tapped at the door, and without waiting for a response, stepped into Van Dyke's office. The big man sat in the corner, his ample belly straining against the buttons of his shabby vest. Van Dyke had a goblet of rum in his hand. His round face, marked with the broken veins of a drinker, lifted to Van der Veghe as he entered the smoky, cold room. The ship's captain stood near the fire, his clothing steaming.

Van Dyke introduced them lethargically, as if it were an effort to speak at all. Van Dyke was not the man for this venture, and he knew it; but his father, the powerful and quite wealthy tea merchant, had insisted.

"Captain Armgard, may I present Dr. Peter Van der Veghe, the naturalist I was telling you about."

Armgard, a robust, short man of forty, turned his sharp eyes toward the door. Van der Veghe, he saw, was tall,

52

blue-eyed, with a quick, intelligent smile. He reminded
Armgard very much of his son in Amsterdam, except that
Hans was not so tall.

The two men shook hands. Outside, the thunder echoed
once more and the rain cascaded down. Van Dyke lifted
his goblet to his lips and emptied it.

"So," Armgard said with a smile, "you have been here
for six months already."

"Yes," Van der Veghe answered. "Everything is new.
It's exciting for a naturalist. What an opportunity for me."

"Ah, the enthusiasm of youth!" Armgard said with a
smile. "I have been here three weeks, and already I wonder what ever caused me to go to sea. My men are
suffering from scurvy, my ship is infested with rot, the savages have stolen half our trade goods and killed two of my
sailors . . . and to you it's exciting, a great opportunity."

"It is, sir," Van der Veghe answered with quiet enthusiasm. "To a natural scientist it is a great adventure indeed.
This country is one gigantic botanical garden crowded
with rare and unknown species where undiscovered animals roam freely, waiting to be discovered. Even the mobs
of mosquitoes which plagued us until the rains came are
of immense interest."

"Fortunate scientists," Van Dyke said without amusement.

"I am most fortunate, sir," Van der Veghe replied.
"You can't imagine how important this is to me. My papers, when published, will cause a stir in Europe. My
academic career, if I may be so immodest, will assuredly
flourish."

"*You* at least will be happy to go upriver," Armgard
said sourly.

"Sir? I understood we were awaiting the arrival of the
colonists from the Netherlands."

"We were, Van der Veghe. But the ship is two months
overdue. High seas or pirates may have taken her." Van
Dyke refilled his cup with rum. "I have my orders. The
British, damn them, have already established a colony in
Massachusetts. The French are settled in New Burnswick.
Winter is upon us, Van der Veghe." He paused, listening
to the rain. "We must establish Dutch ownership, and to
do that we need colonists. We have none, or no voluntary

ones." He and Van Dyke exchanged a glance. "Captain Armgard has volunteered his men."

"Your sailors?" Van der Veghe's blue eyes reflected his surprise.

"Yes, my sailors," the sea captain told him. "I intend to construct an outpost upriver, using my men. When the colonists arrive in the spring, they will find a ready-made village. Then my men and I will return to New Netherlands."

"You have a site in mind?" Van der Veghe asked.

"Hudson thought that Albany fulfilled all of our requirements. Since he is the only man who has seen it, we're taking his word for it. Unfortunately, Hudson is no longer here to discuss it with."

Henry Hudson, the flamboyant Englishman who had sailed for the Dutch company, had never returned from upriver. It was assumed that the Indians had killed him after Hudson, his son; and eight of his crew had been thrown overboard by mutinous sailors.

"If you are therefore ready to pursue your adventures, Dr. Van der Veghe, I suggest that you gather your belongings and be ready to sail upriver when the weather breaks. It will mean spending all winter, of course."

"Nothing could suit me better," Van der Veghe replied. It would give him an opportunity to explore new areas of this savage land, and when winter settled, he would spend his time compiling his notes. "I'll be ready to sail when you are."

Van der Veghe went out smiling, a gust of wind hurling rain in through the open door. Captain Armgard turned his morose eyes on Van Dyke and muttered, "Ah, youth. Pour me a cup of grog, will you, Mr. Van Dyke? I may not be tasting any for a long while."

It rained for two days, and Peter Van der Veghe impatiently sat out the storm in his small log bunker, watching the water seep in across the earthen floor. On the third morning, an hour before sunrise, there was an insistent knocking at his door and he went out, seeing the stars shining brilliantly in a clear, cold sky.

The sailor with the red beard told him, "Captain says to notify you we're sailing, sir."

"Good, thank you. I'll be aboard in an hour."

"Captain wants I should wait for you, sir. I'll row you

out." The sailor delivered his message in a monotone. These sea-weary men had little enthusiasm for prolonging their stay in this strange and potentially deadly land.

Peter Van der Veghe collected his belongings quickly: a wooden box containing his notes and specimens, his duffel bag, and the folding chair he used for sketching in the woods. That was all there was; he had nothing else.

Van der Veghe was not a wealthy man. His inheritance had barely seen him through the university. This New World excursion, scientific interest aside, was certain to improve his position at home. He felt certain he would be offered a professorship upon his return. Then there would be nothing standing between himself and his marriage to Eloisa. He patted his coat pocket, ascertaining that her miniature portrait was there, snug and reassuring. He nodded to the sailor. "Ready."

The sailor turned without speaking and they walked across the dark settlement, watching the black pines sway in the wind, breathing in the tangy, bitterly cold air. The launch rocked violently at its mooring beside the quay, and Van der Veghe had to balance himself and time his boarding to the swell and fall of the sea.

Then he was aboard, his gear at the gunwales, the grim, red-bearded sailor facing him, putting his back to work as the oars cut at the choppy water. Ahead, the *Eindhoven* floated at anchor, a single lantern burning in the captain's cabin astern.

Van der Veghe was helped roughly up the boarding ladder and his belongings were stowed away below. The winch began to turn to the command of the boatswain, and the anchor chain lifted from the black waters.

Van der Veghe stood at the rail, watching the first flush of dawn out on the Atlantic. For a moment he had a clear view of the rotund Van Dyke standing before his hut, his fur hat pulled down over his ears, watching as the ship weighed anchor, and setting her fluttering sail, set out for the northern hinterlands, but when Van der Veghe looked again, the merchant was gone, and as the island receded from view, he felt suddenly and irretrievably cut off from all that was Europe.

The sailors clambered in the rigging like monkeys. The wind was heavy off the starboard quarter and the canvas popped in the breeze as it settled. The masts squeaked with protest as the lumbering, ungainly ship steadfastly began its upriver journey.

All around was forest, crowding to the very edge of the dark river. The sunrise flared brilliantly in the east, sending a fan of gold through the last of the storm clouds, painting their undersides deep violet. Geese winged past high above them, their numbers uncountable as they fled the coming winter.

The *Eindhoven* labored upriver throughout the morning. It was no easy matter fighting the current of the Hudson, which was heavy, following the rain, and the sailors muttered curses in four tongues as they worked.

The land was raw and empty. Frequently Van der Vegh saw deer drinking at the water's edge and an occasional moose. Beaver sat up and watched them with curious dark eyes as they sailed past. Once Van der Veghe spotted the dark shambling form of a black bear in the woods. Mystery, there was mystery all around. And somewhere out there lived thousands, perhaps millions of people. They were an unknown quantity and one which greatly interested Van der Veghe, despite the fact they were outside of his scholarly field.

The wind shifted and one of the *Eindhoven*'s booms came around with a creak and a thud. There was a low mist settling over the river. Van der Veghe turned to see the bowlegged figure of Captain Armgard crossing the damp deck.

" 'Morning, Dr. Van der Veghe," he said without cheerfulness. The seaman's face appeared puffy and there were rings around his melancholy eyes. "Enjoying the sights, are you?"

Van der Veghe laughed. "Immensely. I was feeling somewhat guilty about it. I am the only one who doesn't have to work his way upriver. But then, if there are any nature lovers among your men, they'll have the time this winter, won't they?"

"That's what I've come back to tell you, sir," Armgard replied. He leaned his massive forearms on the mist-dampened rail, and staring out across the foggy Hudson, said, "The men don't know yet."

"Sir?"

"The men don't know I've volunteered them to spend

the winter at Albany. They have the idea that we're just going to drop you off. And I'd appreciate it . . . nothing should be said to them, sir."

"I won't say anything if you request I don't, of course, Captain. Don't you think they should be told, though?"

"They will be, sir." Armgard winked at the tall, blond scientist. "When it's too late for them to balk."

"Isn't that leading up to trouble?"

"It's leading to trouble any way you care to look at it, sir. This way I've got 'em a step closer at least." Armgard sighed heavily. Van der Veghe looked across the captain's shoulder, seeing the dark, sullen faces of the crew. He was glad he would not be the one to tell them.

"Look!" Van der Veghe's head came around and his eyes narrowed. Above the ranks of pines and the gray oaks on the ridge a thin tendril of smoke could be seen, rising to merge with the gray of the skies.

"Can it be Indians?" Peter asked.

"Can it be anyone else?" Armgard asked with a dry smile. "After all, we are the only Europeans within fifty miles."

"Perhaps the British . . ."

"Not to our knowledge. No, sir, it's the Indians."

"What do they call themselves?" Van der Veghe asked.

"That's a difficult question." Armgard tilted his hat and scratched his cheek. "Most of their words can't be pronounced by us tongue-tied foreigners. Hudson called 'em Mohawks, though. I understand there's other tribes around near, but I don't know their names—no one does, I expect."

Van der Veghe watched the smoke until they were out of sight. "How do they live? Who are they, what do they do? Have they kings and queens, tax collectors, scientists and Masons, physicians . . . ? Who are these people? We don't even know that, do we? We are in their land and don't know a thing about them."

"I wouldn't expect there's much to know, sir," Armgard answered. "They're a poor savage lot. Live off roots and wild game, I expect. They're always half-naked. They lie, they steal, they have no Christian ethics. But then"—he shrugged—"neither do most of the Dutchmen I know."

"Can you speak to them?" Van der Veghe turned

toward the captain, gripping his sleeve. His blue eyes were intent as he studied Captain Armgard's face. The old sailor just shook his head.

"No one has learned their tongue, Doctor. Maybe we never will—I've heard 'em talk, and it's a devilish jabber, full of grunts and squeaks."

"Perhaps our good Dutch sounds the same to their ears."

"Perhaps it does." Armgard shrugged. "I do know one word, sir. Just one. But I'd use it with care."

"Oh?"

"Yes—I was told it meant 'friend' in the Mohawk tongue, and then one of our traders tried it out on a savage and got his head cut off for his trouble. Seems if you pronounce it wrong it's a terrible insult."

Van der Veghe smiled. "Perhaps I don't want to know it, sir."

The captain returned to his cabin, and Van der Veghe, watching him go, saw the eyes of the seamen shift toward their captain, saw the tight lips, the set jaws. What would they do when they had been told that Armgard's purpose was to land them at Albany to construct a town?

The fog curled past the ship and the river became a ghost river. The *Eindhoven* crept upriver now, feeling its way. A man at the bow called out as he spotted snags and sandbars. Finally it got so bad they could not travel. They were walled in with fog. There was no river, no land, no sky, but only damp, slowly shifting fog. Armgard ordered the anchor dropped, and men were posted as deck guards.

Van der Veghe went to his tiny, airless cabin and lit a candle, which wreathed his writing desk in smoky light. Taking the portrait of Eloisa from his pocket, he propped it up before him, gazing at her rosebud mouth, the sleek coiled blond hair, the fine lines of her face. He remembered the touch of her cool hand, her sparkling laugh, walks on the boulevard, a trip to Amsterdam in company with aunts and uncles, a dinner at that tiny restaurant which served French wine. He remembered a thousand small gestures, glances, pleasantries, promises—promises made with those glances, those gestures.

He withdrew a clean sheet of paper and he wrote his letter, not knowing when or how it would be delivered.

My dearest Eloisa,
Tonight finds me in a strange wilderness . . .

His pen hesitated and stopped. He gazed at her picture by the flickering candlelight, closed his eyes briefly, taking a slow, deep breath. Then again he began to write as the *Eindhoven* rocked at anchor, as the deep, concealing fog covered this savage river and night settled across the wilderness of America.

They were a week on the river, and if each day brought new excitement to Peter Van der Veghe, the sailors grew more morose and surly. Crossing the deck of the *Eindhoven* to study some otters on the starboard side of the ship, he was nearly knocked down by the impact of a passing sailor's shoulder. The man, a dark-eyed, heavily bearded Frenchman named Le Carre, never stopped to look back or apologize. Van der Veghe, rubbing his chest, watched the man go on his way. Then, shrugging, he turned away.

The boatswain was a thimble-nosed man with a fringe of white whiskers, called Kliik. He had seen it all, and Van der Veghe asked him, "What was that about? It was intentional, wasn't it?"

"They resent you, sir. Captain's told them we're making this voyage to drop you off in the interior. Winter's coming in, and the men know the time for sailing home is past."

"So, I'm a scapegoat, am I?" Van der Veghe laughed. His chest still hurt. "Why doesn't the captain tell them, Kliik?"

"He wants to get there." Kliik lifted a white eyebrow. Van der Veghe noticed for the first time that the boatswain was wearing a saber. "This ain't a naval frigate, sir," Kliik reminded him. "We're merchant, and although the mutiny statutes apply, the men don't take 'em a serious."

"Mutiny!" Van der Veghe laughed again, but the laugh broke off in his throat as he studied the bright, serious face of Kliik. "It's not possible, is it?"

"Happens every day somewhere, don't it?" Kliik asked, spitting across the rail into the Hudson. "Aye, it's possible. Our men have been two years gone from home. Weather's bad. The voyage makes no sense to them."

"If they understood that they are doing this for the Netherlands . . ."

"They're ordinary seamen, sir. They may be patriotic, but not to that extent, I don't believe. Besides, half our crew's not Dutch. Le Carre for example—you just met him."

"Yes. I suppose the ramifications of this voyage just hadn't hit me. Putting myself in their place, I'd feel the same."

"Yes." Kliik smiled, but it was a thin smile with very little warmth. "That's understanding of you, sir. The men, unfortunately, aren't that understanding. They're not considering men like yourself. They're men of action, aren't they? Were I you," the boatswain said with a friendly wink and a pat on the shoulder, "I might spend more time below until we reach Albany. I'd hate to find that you'd gone overboard somewhere on this stretch of river."

Then he winked again and was gone, a round, rolling-gaited figure walking the damp deck of the *Eindhoven*. Van der Veghe watched him go. The wind lifted the fine blond hair from his scalp, chilling him.

For a minute he was angry enough to feel a flush creeping up his neck, angry at Captain Armgard for using him as an excuse for this voyage. He was irritated and feeling stubborn. He was damned if he'd let this hooligan crew chase him below decks when there was so much to observe. It was all probably greatly exaggerated in Kliik's mind anyway.

Then he caught Le Carre's eyes on him and he was not so sure. The sailor was coiling a line, not watching his work, which his hands did automatically, but watching Van der Veghe, only Van der Veghe.

Peter felt like walking across to him, explaining: "Look here, sailor, it's not because of me you're going upriver. You're going to replace those colonists who never showed up, and build a Dutch settlement in this wilderness." But that didn't seem like much of an idea, upon consideration.

Van der Veghe watched the river for a moment, liking the glint of the water in the sunlight. Then, resigning himself, he walked astern and went down to his stuffy, rot-smelling cabin, and tried again to work on his letter to Eloisa.

It was a difficult task somehow. She had been expecting his return by the first of the year. How could he explain about this opportunity which was too enticing, too valuable to pass up?

How could he explain the strange bond he felt with this land, the enthrallment with the savage, unknown wilderness? Men had stepped onto a new continent, and they might as well have stepped onto the moon, for all they knew of it. Where did this land end? Who were the people? What was in the interior? There could be great civilizations, volcanoes, amazing, mythical-seeming beasts and terrible serpents. There could be vast plains or mountains covered with trees which bore fruit enough to feed all of the hungry in Europe. Who knew; who could guess until the interior was probed, until some light was shed on the vast, dark land of America?

That somehow must be explained.

"My dearest Eloisa," he began, and then there seemed no way to continue. He stared at the sheet of paper and slowly crumpled it, tossing it into the corner where the other unfinished letters lay.

He opened the locket and sat staring at her familiar face, and then, after a while, he put his hands to his face and sat at his desk, thinking of nothing as the ship sailed northward.

He had been asleep in his hammock when he was suddenly awakened. By what, he could not say. His eyes flickered open in the darkness and Van der Veghe felt it, recognizing it for what it was. The anchor chain was being fed out. The ship came up tight against its tether and strained briefly against it, the planking creaking.

Van der Veghe rubbed the sleep from his eyes. stamped into his boots, and climbed the gangway ladder. The morning was brilliant, blue and quite cold.

He found Kliik at the rail. "What is it?" Peter Van der Veghe asked, studying the bluffs along the shore, the dark blue-green ranks of pines.

"It is Albany, sir," Kliik said. There was no smile on his cherubic face. The wind rustled in the pines and slipped icy fingers beneath Van der Veghe's hastily buttoned blouse. The sails were being furled; the sailors scurried fore and aft, shouting to each other. Captain Armgard stood at the bow, and Van der Veghe strode forward.

"So this is it?"

Armgard's head came around slowly. His eyes were

deep; heavy bags hung beneath them. He smelled sour, but his voice was surprisingly mild. "This is it, Dr. Van der Veghe. And now I must tell them. Tell them that they have come home."

Kliik came hurring across the deck, his hand clenching the sword at his side. With him was the small shrew-faced mate named Leyden.

"All secured, sir," Kliik reported in a low voice. "Of course, they've got their rigging knives."

Armgard nodded his response. Kliik's words needed no explanation. They had taken the crew's weapons and locked them away somewhere. Van der Veghe was rocked; Armgard seriously expected rebellion.

"When the ship is secure, we'll go ashore in small groups, Kliik," the captain said. "You and Leyden will hold the ship. I'll wait until I have them on dry land before making my speech. If they . . . if there's trouble, unlimber the swivel gun, and if necessary, up anchor and away with you."

"Aye, sir," Kliik answered smartly.

"Sir," Van der Veghe began, "do you—?"

"Dr. Van der Veghe," Armgard said with surprising sharpness, "I advise you to assemble your belongings and prepare to disembark." With that Armgard turned his back and was silent, leaning heavily on the rail, his brooding eyes staring at the empty land.

Van der Veghe was on deck, his belongings packed, when the first boat was let down. The sailors, Le Carre among them, rowed strongly across the glassy river, and they touched ashore on a sandy beach below high-rising pine-clad bluffs.

Van der Veghe was the first ashore, and the sailors watched him with sarcastic approval.

Armgard, who was seated in the stern of the launch, spoke to his men. "I want a shore party mustered. Le Carre, you're in charge of that. Patrol the area, see that Dr. Van de Veghe is properly settled." Le Carre's eyes narrowed, and Armgard said with hollow joviality, "Stretch your legs, man! Enjoy the land beneath your feet."

"Aye, sir," Le Carre muttered. His eyes were dark and suspicious. Nevertheless he stepped from the beached boat. The sailors, excepting the two oarsmen, joined him. Armgard immediately ordered the launch back to the ship and Van der Veghe was left standing among the sailors, who scowled and looked around the sandy, driftwood-cluttered cove.

"And this is to be your home, *sir*?" Le Carre asked, giving the last word a peculiarly virulent inflection.

"So it appears," Van der Veghe answered mildly.

Le Carre merely shook his head. "Have a look up along the bluffs, boys," he told his sailors. He returned his gaze to Van der Veghe. "A man like you—where do you get the courage to stay alone in this bedeviled land? Or are you only a fool, Doctor?"

"Perhaps I am," Van der Veghe answered. Le Carre didn't even listen to his answer. The question he had asked was not the one which was gnawing at his mind, worrying him. Le Carre was no fool, and he sensed something.

The sailor looked toward the *Eindhoven* and seemed relieved to observe the launch returning with the remainder of the crew. Armgard sat at the stern still, his back rigid.

"I do not like this," Le Carre muttered, and he walked away from Van der Veghe, returning to the shore to meet the arriving boat.

Van der Veghe watched as the sailors returning from the wooded bluffs formed up behind their leader. Le Carre stood motionless on the windswept beach. Light sand drifted around his legs and lifted to sting their faces.

Armgard was ashore now, and Van der Veghe saw the captain gesture angrily, saw Le Carre take a step forward, his fists bunched. Now Armgard's voice, bent by the wind, reached Van der Veghe. ". . . for the glory of the Netherlands. You men will be richly rewarded by the company, I assure you. It is a matter of urgency, Le Carre."

Le Carre muttered something obscene in French.

"I have the ship and you can go nowhere anyway. Let us work together and achieve this worthwhile goal. Men!" Armgard pleaded with the others. There was no answer but bitter glances. The captain told them, "If this ship reappears at New Amsterdam without myself aboard, you will all undoubtedly be hanged as mutineers. Le Carre! Van Voorhis!" Armgard looked from one man to the next. "I am asking you to work for Holland, to earn yourselves a rich reward. Your other choice is to become criminals and very likely be hanged."

It was Van Voorhis who broke the long tension. He was

a wiry, red-bearded man with only a fringe of hair circling his narrow skull. "I will stay. Where would we sail? Winter is upon us, Le Carre! I will stay and work."

The assent was far from general, but begrudgingly most of the seamen agreed. Their choices were severely limited. If they could somehow take the ship, they would have to return to New Netherlands. From there they could not continue without fresh supplies; these could not be obtained.

Van der Veghe turned away from the angry knot of soldiers. He had gotten his wish—he had been brought deep into the American wilderness. But the circumstances were deeply disturbing.

Still, what did it matter to him? They had agreed to stay; let them be angry, they would not dampen his spirits. He left his belongings at the foot of the bluff on a weather-corroded boulder and climbed the bluff behind the cove.

Looking back, he saw that the boat had returned to the *Eindhoven*, probably to transport the sailors' possessions to shore.

The fog was returning. From the top of the windswept bluff he could see it creeping down the cold, rambling river, see its currents and feel its chilly fingers as it approached.

Beyond the river where the *Eindhoven*, looking small, squat, and somehow absurd rested at anchor, he could see nothing but an endless carpet of spruce and oak. Forest primeval stretching endlessly toward the distant sea.

To the west he could see the mountains rising blue and misted. All wilderness, only wilderness. Forest and hills, wild creatures and savage land. The wind was cold against Van der Veghe's face, the chill of the creeping fog was in his bones. He did not care!

It was cold, the sailors were violent and angry, the land was alien; Eloisa waited at home, and he did not care. He had come home!

He looked over the raw and ancient land, feeling a tingling along his spine. He felt suddenly quite young, and simultaneously, ancient and timeless. The wind drifted the fog downriver and it wound itself around him, staining his clothing with damp moisture, and still he stood there on the ragged bluff above Albany until the trembling of his muscles and the darkness of the hour forced him to the beach.

They began building the stockade in the morning. After the shivering cold night there was plenty of motivation. Van der Veghe labored with them—if he was going to spend the winter with these men, he didn't want them to resent him. He wasn't much help; he had never swung an ax or trimmed logs with an adz, but then, neither, apparently, had most of the sailors.

The old animosity seemed to be gone now that they realized Van der Veghe wasn't the cause of their winter voyage. They treated him coolly, however, spoke only grudgingly to him. He was an outsider, and he accepted that.

The stockade went up quickly, and by the third day they had begun construction on a low house where they would winter up. Van der Veghe was busy; his hands were blistered and raw, his shoulders ached. Still, there was time for his work, and he would walk through the forest, exploring the new land. He discovered a beaver run and he sat patiently by it for hours, watching the beaver drag their trees to the water to build their lodges, their own winter homes.

There were moose in the forest, porcupine, and twice, excitement raging in his heart, Van der Veghe caught sight of a prowling tawny lion.

There were smaller pleasures as well. He found a species of berry he was unfamiliar with, tentatively tried some, and found them delicious, if tart. He also found the tracks of a black bear near the tangle of vines. He found a large species of turtle hibernating in its muddy nest, nearly was struck by a six-foot-long rattlesnake, and in the evenings he returned exhausted, elated, and half-frozen to the camp.

There he sat by the fire, which they were still building outside, the fireplace not being completed, and he would record his observations in his journal.

"Having a dandy time, aren't you. Doctor?" Le Carre asked. Van der Veghe looked up to see the black-bearded Frenchman standing beside him, the flickering firelight painting his face weirdly, deepening the dark hollows around his eyes.

"I am trying to use this opportunity fully, Mr. Le

Carre," Peter responded, marking his place and putting his journal aside.

"Using the opportunity," Le Carre snarled. "I'll tell you what opportunity I'd like to use. The opportunity to split the captain's skull for him. It's cold, Van der Veghe, and there's nothing to eat but moldy ship's stores. There's nothing to drink to warm a man's belly. I'd like to get back to Marseilles, Doctor. Marseilles—that's where I was going to spend my winter. They've wine there, oceans of wine. And women . . . I know a lot of women in Marseilles."

Le Carre spoke as if entranced; Van der Veghe wasn't sure if the sailor was speaking to him or to himself. "What kind of man are you, Doctor?" Le Carre said, his attention focusing suddenly, completely on Van der Veghe. "Don't you like women? You spend the winter in some godforsaken place like this! Crazy. All Dutchmen are crazy!"

Le Carre had lifted his finger, ready to continue his bitter monologue, when a terrible, heart-stopping scream filled the night. Le Carre's head came around; Van der Veghe leaped to his feet, knocking his journal to the ground.

"What in God's name was that?" Peter whispered.

Le Carre didn't answer. He kicked dirt over the fire, smothering it, and they stood in the darkness for long minutes. The cry came again, and now Van der Veghe knew what it was; there was no mistaking the sound of a man in mortal pain. As they stood there shivering in the darkness, their eyes searching and finding nothing, the cry suddenly rose to a shrill, weaving scream, like that of some tortured banshee, and abruptly broke off.

"What was it?" Van Voorhis asked in a dry whisper.

"Who, you mean," Le Carre answered.

"There's someone hurt out there!" Van der Veghe shouted, gripping Le Carre's arm.

"No more." Le Carre shook Peter's hand away.

"We have to do something—go out and see what's happened!"

"Not me," Le Carre said in a muted voice. "You go out and see, if you want. I'm not going out those gates."

Peter Van der Veghe stood there numbly. Le Carre was right. A man had been killed, one of their men, but there was nothing to be done for him, nothing at all. The men huddled together in the darkness. With the fire out, it was freezing cold. They stood near the embers, which glowed warmly for a little while.

They spent the night without speaking, standing together in their primitive stockade, locked into the darkness, trembling with the cold, their heads filled with all sorts of panicked speculation. They had been transported to another time. They were cave dwellers cringing in their inadequate shelter, listening to the savage things outside devouring one of their own.

With the dawn they went out. Six men together, Van der Veghe among them. They carried clubs in their hands, and they moved with primitive caution, hunched forward as if to hear better, to see farther into the underbrush.

They found him in a tangled thicket, and Van der Veghe gagged at the sight of him. It was Kliik, scarcely recognizable. He had been mauled, torn apart, but it was not the work of beasts. He had been slashed with a knife, crushed by stones.

They crouched together around the body, their eyes meeting only fleetingly. Le Carre's mouth hung open, and he muttered inaudible throaty sounds which were meant to be words.

Kliik had come ashore after dark for some reason; it was a fatal mistake. "They must be out here every night," Van Voorhis said. His head swiveled as he looked slowly around.

"We'll have to bury him," Peter said.

"You bury him!" Le Carre explored. "I'm not staying out here to bury the boatswain. I'm not staying here at all. I mean to see the captain."

He stalked toward the beach, the others following. Van der Veghe hesitated and then went along. When he arrived, Le Carre was hailing the ship at the top of his lungs, his hands cupped to his mouth.

"Armgard! Captain Armgard!"

After a long minute the answer came. They could see the dark, tiny figure at the rail of the *Eindhoven*, hear the small voice: "What is it?"

"We've found Kliik. He's dead! We want our weapons, Armgard!"

After a baffled silence the captain shouted, "Kliik, you say? What's happened? Never mind, I'll come ashore."

The sailors clustered near the river's edge, all eyes intent on the *Eindhoven*. Van der Veghe sagged to the sand. He sat there with his knees drawn up, his long arms folded around his legs, watching the brilliant rose of sunset dry out the thin fog which crept along the Hudson, winding its way through the deep forest. After a time a boat was lowered and they saw Armgard, alone, making his way toward the beach.

When the boat touched ground, it was dragged ashore with sharp, angry movements. Armgard had to wait until they were through to step out. When he did, he was facing Le Carre, whose dark face was etched into a heavy scowl.

"What's this all about?" Armgard wanted to know. He shifted his eyes to the faces around him, reading the anger in their eyes, trying to gauge the violent feelings.

"Kliik is dead," Le Carre said, "Murdered. Savages done it. We want the hell out of here."

"I can't do that, Le Carre," Armgard said as if he genuinely would have liked to take them out of Albany.

"Then we have to have our weapons, dammit! Our swords, pistols!" Le Carre was nearly screaming. Armgard's answer was to shake his head slowly, heavily, from side to side. For a moment Van der Veghe thought Le Carre was going to hurl himself on Armgard and tear him apart. Instead the Frenchman replied in a reasonable tone, "We have *you* now, Captain."

"It will do no good to keep me, Le Carre." Armgard caught Van der Veghe's eye briefly and then returned his attention to the crew. "I have your weapons, I have the ship. Leyden is aboard, watching. Assault me and he'll sail away."

"He can't get under way, not alone!" Le Carre scoffed.

"If he cannot, then his orders are to scuttle her. He has the swivel gun upturned and loaded. It needs only to be touched off."

Le Carre growled and leaned nearer, gripping the captain's shirt tightly with his dark, scarred fist. "You bastard! A captain's supposed to watch out for his crew."

"And a crew is supposed to take orders!" Armgard shot back. Van der Veghe was surprised at the captain's mettle. He had seemed ready to fold, and now his spine had stiffened; he showed no fear at all. Le Carre's grip tightened and he drew Armgard's face to within inches of his own.

"Le Carre." It was Van Voorhis who spoke. The red-haired sailor stepped forward and put his hand on Le Carre's arm. "This is no good. You know Leyden—the fool will scuttle the ship."

"What are we supposed to do? Let ourselves be massacred?"

"It won't be like that," Armgard said quickly. "We'll keep the gun turned this way. If there's any sign of savages, we'll fire on them. They can't get into the stockade anyway, you're worried about nothing."

"My skin," Le Carre said, throwing the captain back. "To you my skin is nothing."

"We don't have a choice," Van Voorhis said. Most of the crew seemed to agree with him. They looked more resigned than angry now. Even Le Carre seemed to be cooling off. He turned to look at the other sailors, and read the resignation on their faces.

"All right. All right, dammit! What choice is there?"

That morning they returned to the building of their houses. No one went out of the stockade alone, and when the woodcutters had to go up along the slopes to work, four sailors went along to stand watch. That gave no one any false confidence. Twice tools had been stolen, and there was nearly a fight between two sailors before the truth, obvious and deflating, sank in—the Indians had done it.

There was no fire that night, and none the next. The temperature dropped steadily, and on the second morning following Kliik's death the skies darkened and bunched; the snow began to fall shortly after noon.

They worked frantically now, their fingers numb, their limbs frozen. Two of them already had frostbite on their toes by the time the storm broke three days later.

They had only a day of grace before a second storm, thunderheads mounting high into the sky, settled in and the snow began again. This time it was no light flurry. Lightning crackled all around them, dancing from peak to peak, and the thunder boomed, rolling down the Hudson. The snow fell in waves, and within eight hours it was two feet deep on the ground; noon was as dark as dusk, dusk as black as midnight. Midnight was an unspeakable wash of snow, a fierce wind tearing madly at the chinks of their rough shelter, blowing down pine trees up along the bluff, chopping the Hudson to a frothing fury.

Still, at daylight they went out to work. The buildings had to be completed if they were to survive. Van der Veghe was with the woodcutters. They moved like ghosts through the heavy, driving snow. He could barely see the three men in front of him. You had to.put your mouth next to another man's ear and shout to be heard above the constant shriek of the wind.

It happened before Van der Veghe could react. He saw nothing—only a blur of movement, a mad scrambling, a violent shadow, and then he saw the sailors go down. Two of them, their mouths wide open in shrieks which could not be heard above the wind.

Van der Veghe dropped his ax and ran. Someone was at his heels, and he didn't slow down to look back, to discover if it was an Indian or Van Voorhis. He only ran, falling twice in the heavy snow, which was to his knees even in the trees.

His breath was ragged, his lungs afire. His brain danced with bloody images. Then finally he saw the stockade looming up before him, dark and formless in the storm. He made it to the gates, panting, his heart beating wildly. He saw Van Voorhis come up beside him, and he noticed the crimson smear on the sailor's cheek. Together they pounded at the gate, pounded for what seemed like hours, until their hands were torn.

Finally the gate was flung open and they fell inside. "Close the gate! Damn you, man, close the gate!"

"Where's the rest of 'em?" the gate watch asked dully.

Van Voorhis got to his feet, and together he and Peter Van der Veghe closed the gate and barred it, the guard watching them stupidly.

They found Le Carre on his heels, sealing the wall with pine pitch. The sailor looked up, read it in their grim faces, and said, "How many?"

"We're the only ones they didn't get. They came out of the snow. Demons, they were," Van Voorhis said, "demons."

Le Carre didn't even move. His hand was still lifted, his crude brush in it. He nodded his head slowly. "All right— that's it. We're getting the hell out of here."

"Taking the ship?" Van Voorhis asked lamely.

"How else, you dumb bastard?" Le Carre asked.

"He'll scuttle it," Van Voorhis said, stepping nearer, his voice a taut whisper.

"They'll never even see us, not in this," Le Carre said, waving a hand beyond the walls, toward the storm, which raged on outside.

"How . . . ?"

"Swim. It'll be tough in that current, in this weather, but I've done it in worse. Then up the side and crack the bastard's head."

Van der Veghe was listening. It was all a dream. The massacre, and now these sailors plotting mutiny and murder. He caught Le Carre's eyes on him. His expression was dark and far from friendly.

"He'll scuttle her if he sees us," Van Voorhis protested again.

"Aye, and if we don't make our try, we'll all die here this winter. That's our choices, Voorhis. If the ship goes down, we'll try it in the launch. Most of us will fit in the boat. That's a chance, man! Can't you see it, that way we've at least got a chance!"

Van Voorhis, his head bowed, nodded. "They'll hang us if they find out, Le Carre. Hang us sure."

"They'll never find out. We'll tell them the savages got Armgard. If we all swear to it, who's to call us liars?" It was then that Le Carre's eyes returned to Van der Veghe, and the look he gave Peter was so feral and threatening that Van der Veghe took an involuntary half-step backward.

Le Carre went on, his eyes never leaving Van der Veghe's now. "We can trust the crew. We've been shipmates for two years, some of us for longer. We're all in this together, aren't we? The boys won't talk; they'd be hanging themselves."

Van der Veghe swallowed hard. His throat was dry; his tongue felt like a stick in his mouth. *They were going to kill him.*

He could read it in Le Carre's eyes. He could see slow understanding seep into the expression of Van Voorhis. None of the sailors would talk; they had all been together for years, sharing fortune and misfortune on the high seas. None of them would talk of the mutiny, but what about this young scholar? Perhaps he would be silent for a time, but when he was sure he was safe, what was to stop him from accusing Le Carre and the others? What indeed, but death?

With a rising sense of helplessness Van der Veghe watched the two men before him. Their minds were made up; he could see that now. Two other sailors had poked their heads in the door. Van der Veghe could see the snow drifting past behind them. They didn't even have to murder him, he realized. What chance would he have in this wilderness alone, without provisions? He couldn't walk out in this weather. A mile of exposure would be enough to kill him.

But Le Carre didn't want to take the chance. He didn't like Van der Veghe, never had. He would kill him, necessary or not.

Le Carre dropped the brush he had been holding. He stood and wiped his pitch-stained hands on his breeches. Then he came forward, his shoulders slightly hunched, his hooded eyes dark. Van der Veghe hesitated only a moment.

Then he kicked out savagely, with all of his strength behind it, knowing that if he did not fight he would surely die. The kick caught Le Carre in the stomach, and the Frenchman doubled up. Van Voorhis lunged for Van der Veghe, but Peter was already moving away. He felt the sailor's hand rake his back, and then he was to the door.

The two men there, stunned by the rapidity of events, stood immobile, their faces uncomprehending. Van der Veghe hit the doorway, and an arm came up to restrain him. He drove his forearm into the face of the sailor, broke away from the other, and stumbled out into the snow-covered yard. It was dark outside; the snow drove down relentlessly. Van der Veghe plunged on, the wind slapping him back.

He made it to the gate somehow, and as the guard came forward to question him, Van der Veghe slammed his fist into his face, feeling the impact of bone against gristle, the brief hot spattering of blood on his fist. Then, hurriedly, with numbed fingers, he drew the bar and swung the gate against the resisting snow.

He squeezed through, turning his head to catch a blurred glimpse of dark pursuing shadows, and then he was through the gate, running like a madman, blindly, through the snow, toward the shelter of the forest.

He ran deep into the pines, falling often, tearing his face and hands on brambles and twigs, running until his heart was a wild animal trying to tear itself free of the cage of his ribs, until the snow and the fury, the panic, had blended into a turmoil of confusion, flooding him alternately with hot rage and cold fear.

He ran until his legs were rubbery, until he no longer knew where he was or why he ran, and then, with the snow drifting softly past, he fell to his stomach in the shelter of a tangle of vines and brush. There he lay while the night passed, while the storm rumbled across the wildnerness. There he lay thinking tangled thoughts of home, of Eloisa, of the bloodied, barbaric face of Le Carre, until the numbing cold rocked him to an uncomfortable sleep.

Morning was gray. The snow had stopped, but the wind lifted the snow and shuttled it through the trees, drifting it along the windward side of the massive boulders down the gulley. Van der Veghe peered through swollen eyelids, trying to recall what had happened, trying to discover where he was.

His fingers and toes were stiff and nerveless. His head throbbed, and touching his forehead, he discovered scabbed blood and an egg-sized knot.

He sat up suddenly, completely aware. There below was the stockade, and on the river, the *Eindhoven* at anchor. It came back to him with a rush, and his jaw set grimly—he would die. They had given him two choices. To remain with them and die immediately or to run to the hills and slowly, dreadfully die.

He heard a footstep crunching on the snow, and he ducked his head. They had come searching.

"Van der Veghe?" The voice was mild, enticing. It belonged to Van Voorhis. Through the screen of brush, Van der Veghe could see other searchers below him, walking slowly through the snow which lay spread across the valley.

Peter pressed himself to the cold earth and watched as they worked their way upslope, carrying lengths of wood. Van Voorhis continued to call softly to him. What sort of fool did they think he was?

He crept away from the edge of the thicket, backing deeper into the thorny tangle. There was a lot of activity below. Le Carre was holding some sort of meeting. Behind the stockade, where they were out of sight of the *Eindhoven*, logs were being torn free of the structure. Probably Le Carre meant to use the logs as crude rafts when they tried to retake the ship.

Van der Veghe lay with his head on his forearms, trying to make his brain work, that so-logical mind of his. He could come to no conclusion as to what he ought to do. Run, fight, swim to the ship—all seemed folly. It was a time before he came to grips with himself and realized that the reason he could make no decision was simple: Le Carre had left him no choices.

He heard the movement in the brush behind him, and before he could move, the sailor was on top of him, his club uplifted. Van der Veghe threw a forearm out defensively and felt the shuddering impact as the club met his arm. Bone cracked and pain flared up hotly in his brain. Still, he had managed to deflect the blow, which would have crushed his skull—there was little sense of triumph in the thought.

He tried to twist free, and then, seeing the club rise again, he punched out as fiercely as possible, driving his fist into his attacker's face. It barely slowed the sailor down.

Van der Veghe tried to twist free, but the sailor was sitting across his chest. The club fell twice more before Van der Veghe could react. The first blow grazed his skull at the temple; the second fell solidly against his shoulder.

Writhing, fighting back with the fury of panic, Van der Veghe shoved the heel of his hand up against the sailor's chin. He pushed back hard, and the sailor was knocked back. Van der Veghe, panting, in deep pain, wriggled free and tried to crawl away in the snow.

The man, enraged now, leaped at him and dragged him down, swinging that club wildly. Twice Van der Veghe felt its savage impact. A rib cracked and the breath was driven out of his lungs.

Fighting back without method or science, Van der Veghe slammed his fist into his attacker's windpipe, and the sailor fell back, gasping, clutching his throat. Van der Veghe dragged himself to the base of a small spruce, and using it to brace himself, he got shakily to his feet in time to turn and face the fresh attack.

The sailor dived at him, a muffled growl in his throat,

and Van der Veghe kicked out again, catching the sailor in the groin. The club fell free as the man went to his knees, doubled up with pain.

Van der Veghe stood motionless for a long minute, his chest heaving, his head spinning through a maelstrom of confusion. Then his head seemed to clear and his eyes focused on the club lying inert in the snow.

The sailor saw it at the same time, and they dived for it simultaneously. Van der Veghe got his hand on the club and felt the sailor's hand claw at his, felt an arm go around his throat, strangling him.

But he would not let go of the club. He flailed wildly with it, felt it impact with something solid, felt the sailor's grip loosen.

Van der Veghe rolled free. The sailor moved as if to come to hands and knees, and he hit him again. There was a sickening, cracking sound, and the sailor moved no more. Van der Veghe backed away, the club in his bloody hand. The sailor's blood spread slowly against the snow, staining it incarnadine.

Van der Veghe felt his back come up against the pine, and he stood there on wobbly legs, watching the sailor with morbid fascination.

He was dead. The man lying there, his limbs grotesquely twisted, his skull showing a cratered indentation, was dead, and he, Peter Van der Veghe, had done it. *He had killed a man.*

For what? Why had it happened? He could form the logical chain of thoughts which told him that he had to kill or be killed, that that could as well be Peter Van der Veghe lying there dead in the snow—but it did no good. His stomach still knotted and twisted, and he knew he was going to be sick.

He clasped his head with both hands, moaning in a low, animal tone. He had not wanted to kill anyone! Ever! Blood trickled into his eyes, and he wiped it away. Van Voorhis was nearby, calling out still, and Peter ran off into the thicket, crashing through the brush, holding his head still, still moaning as he ran, stumbled, and fell to lie against the snow.

He lay there, his head throbbing with pain. Blood trickled from his cheek and made a small red stain against the snow, and Van der Veghe watched as it slowly spread and paled.

He worked his fingers, watching them move. His left arm . . . He tried it and found his fears realized. The sailor had broken it four inches above the wrist. Funny, he could not feel the pain.

No sooner had he thought that and carelessly moved his left hand than the fiery pain surged through his arm from wrist to shoulder. He blacked out momentarily. At least it seemed to be only momentary, but when he came around again, it was nearly dark. The lacy shadows had merged and pooled beneath the trees.

Van der Veghe stared at the shadows. There was hardly a wind. The trees around him stood in silent dark clusters. He did not want to move; he wasn't sure he could. There seemed to be no reason to move. And then he saw the smoke.

It cleared his senses, and he sat up suddenly, wincing as he unthinkingly put weight on his left arm. Smoke! He got to his knees and then shakily stood.

He hobbled forward, breaking through the brush. The smoke was coming from the river, or near it. He burst into a thicket and leaped back, the pulse pounding in his temples. The sailor Van der Veghe had killed lay there, his face still holding a crooked grin.

Grimacing, Van der Veghe stepped around the body and continued through the snow-heavy brush. Suddenly he could see the source of the smoke.

Fire glittered against the snow. Smoke billowed into the evening skies. Black, heavy smoke, forming itself into a dark, heavy column. They had fired the stockade.

He started forward and then stopped, falling to his knees, watching. It was nearly destroyed already, the weeks of work devoured by flames. Le Carre was pulling out. That meant he must have tried for the ship.

The ship. Van der Veghe came to his feet, stumbling forward for thirty yards before he gave it up. He could see the *Eindhoven* now, see her clearly.

She had her sail up and her bow was pointed downriver. Sailors stood at the rail, but he could see none of their faces at that distance. A body floated on the current, a dark, shapeless form. Armgard.

Van der Veghe moved forward, his arms dangling, his

lips working soundlessly, his blond hair falling into his eyes. He stood knee-deep in snow, watching dusk settle, watching as the *Eindhoven* sailed slowly down the broad Hudson, as the stockade fire burned lower, the smoke still drifting across the valley.

He watched in utter despair. The ship was far away now, a dark, purposeful dot disappearing around a wooded bend in the great river. And then it was gone.

It was gone—his only link with civilization, with New Amsterdam and Europe. Gone, like the dissipating smoke, like hope which had stirred in his heart, faltered, and then died.

He stood alone on the hillock, watching until there was nothing to watch, until there was no smoke, no *Eindhoven*, nothing but the ruined pile of ashes which had been the stockade, the empty river, and the purpling savage skies, and he knew already that he would never see the Netherlands again.

MORNING WAS BRILLIANT, CLEAR, AND cold. The early sun glossed the long snowfields, edged the tips of the dark ranks of pines with gold, and colored the few high clouds a brilliant crimson.

Van der Veghe was up and moving with the first light. He had passed a dreadful, sleepless night as the temperature plummeted to zero and below. He had tried to sleep, but closing his eyes had produced a tangle of violent, fiery images, dead faces, whirlpools which glowed and threatened to suck him down to unending blackness, bloodstained snowfields where a thousand Le Carres, only their dark, bearded heads showing above the snow, laughed as Eloisa wandered the empty land calling out to Peter.

The sun had chased away the bleak visions, but the terror in his heart remained. He was walking steadily inland now, the snow deep, his arm shot through with pain, his breath coming in icy needles. He knew not where he was going, only that the Indians were to the east of him, around the stockade, and he had no hope of evading them. They would certainly come back now, returning to see if the departing Dutch had left anything of use. If they found him, they would kill him as they had killed Kliik, as they had murdered Hudson himself.

He hoped vaguely to move inland and at some uncertain point to swing southward, trying to find the river again. With luck, somehow he might be able to build a crude raft and float to New Netherlands, although the hope was a flimsy one, and he knew it.

For now he simply moved, walking doggedly through the snow, trying not to think of Eloisa, of home, of Armgard and Kliik, of the savage Mohawks.

He walked, simply walked; his legs grew weary and knotted with the exertion of moving through the heavy snow, but still he walked on, his eyes seeing nothing but endless snow, endless forest.

He was aware of a ravening hunger, of the hot pain in his arm, of the weight of snow against his legs, of the cold, and of little else. There was no sense in thinking of other things, no point in remembering or planning.

Then suddenly there was no point in thinking, in walking; suddenly there was no hope at all.

He glanced up and saw them walking parallel to him. A long line of them, perhaps ten men, all carrying bows, all wearing furs and feathers, beads, their muscular bodies moving swiftly, easily through the snow. Van der Veghe simply stopped. He sagged to the earth and sat there in the snow, too exhausted to go on, knowing he could not fight.

There was a piercing, ululating scream, and the warriors ran down the long snowy slope, leaping exultantly into the air, the cold wind in their faces. Pawago was to the white man first, and his hand went to his yellow hair. He gripped it in his fist and yanked the man's head back, exposing his throat. Blue eyes looked up with blank acceptance into the face of Pawago.

Pawago's knife was in his free hand, and he touched it to the white man's throat.

"No!" It was Manto who called out, and Pawago's head came around in puzzlement.

"Why not? What's the matter with you, Manto?"

"Don't kill him. He's not fighting, is he? He's unarmed, Pawago." *As the Munsee had been.*

"He's not a man!" Pawago said harshly. He laughed and waved his knife hand in the air so that the blade caught the sunlight. "He's a devil. From behind the moon, or beneath the sea. You've heard what Yo says."

"He might be a man," Manto said, although he doubted it himself. A man with yellow hair and colorless eyes?

"He's come to spy on us, to find our camps so that the Moon Men might come upon us and kill us all."

"Well, then, he's failed," Manto said. It would have been easier to let Pawago have his way, to kill this white devil, but something compelled Manto to speak against his sachem's wishes, and he knew what it was—the memory of the Munsee slaughter had not let him sleep well for months.

Te-al-Pantha spoke up. "Let Crenna decide. And Yo.

Let the old chiefs decide what should be done with this man, this devil . . . whatever he is."

Pawago threw the white man's head backward, and he collapsed against the snow. The sachem had not yet sheathed his knife.

"What can they find out from him? He can't even talk. If they let him live, he's a burden on the tribe, a danger to us. Who knows what clever tricks he knows, what magic?"

Weshta, a young one-eyed warrior who had also been at the massacre of the Munsee, spoke up. "Let Crenna and the elders decide, Pawago. It may be that by killing this white man we shall bring the wrath of the Moon Men upon ourselves and our people."

Pawago's lips curled into an expression of disgust. He nodded slowly, knowing that these warriors were not so much arguing for the white man's life as reacting to what had happened that summer day along the East River. Manto shrugged his agreement; a war leader must be flexible, must have the support of his warriors. What did it matter if a single white man lived or died? The thing would amuse the women and children.

The white man was jerked to his feet, and as he was, a broken cry of anguish filled his throat. Manto frowned and only then saw the swollen, crooked forearm.

"He's broken his arm."

"So?"

"We should splint it up."

"Do what you want, Manto," Pawago said, turning his back to look out over the Mohawk land toward the far river.

Manto found two sticks and with a rawhide thong he wrapped the arm tightly. He looked into the white man's blue eyes, seeing human intelligence, fear, and mingled gratitude. His eyes were the color of the sky, and Manto wondered. He didn't seem to be alien, a man from the moon or from the bottom of the sea, although his skin was so colorless that it seemed he had never been in sunlight. He seemed nearly human. Very nearly.

"Are you ready, Manto?" Pawago asked. "We have a long way to go before we reach our camp."

"Ready," Manto said, rising. He put his arms under the white man's and lifted him to his feet. Pawago had already started toward the Oneida home camp, jogging easily through the heavy snow, his breath steaming from his nostrils.

"You must run too," Manto told the white man. "Run, or Pawago will leave you. Do you understand?"

He obviously didn't. Manto took him by the sleeve of his odd shirt and started out at a slow trot. The white man was dragged along beside him. He wasn't much of a runner, this Moon Man, Manto decided, but then, he was injured. Manto had been relieved to see the man's blood, to find it was red like his own; it made him feel that perhaps this thing was only some sort of undernourished, inferior human being.

They ran for an hour, across the long snowfields where the hummocks of snow made for difficult running, then up along a stony escarpment overlooking the river. They dipped low, crossed the white river, and were into the forest, still running.

The Moon Man was staggering, his face flushed red with exertion. His breathing was audible, rasping and labored. Manto and Te-al-Pantha had enough breath to speak as they ran, Te-al-Pantha occasionally assisting Manto in propping the white man up.

"Pawago wants him to drop, to die. He wants to leave him here."

"He's angry with us. He only wanted a yellow scalp to take back to the camp."

"Now what do you think of him?" Te-al-Pantha asked.

"What do you mean?" Manto knew full well what he meant.

"You were his greatest supporter. Everyone thought Pawago would make a great war chief. Now what do you think?"

They were in the spruce woods, the trees flying past them as they ran on, their lungs and hearts working efficiently, easily. They dipped into a hollow where the rocks were blanketed with snow, where the creek was fringed with ice, and then they angled up a game trail on the opposite slope where fire had killed some of the trees after a lightning storm. Manto could still smell the charred wood above the scent of pines, of cedar.

Manto finally answered, "I think he is not so good a war leader as I had believed."

"After last summer."

"After that."

They leaped a fallen tree together, practically dragging the white man, whose head lolled on his neck, his panting mouth open.

"I have spoken of that with Weshta," Te-al-Pantha admitted. He glanced ahead to where Pawago, far upslope, was winding through the trees. "We have thought of telling Crenna."

"We swore an oath!" Manto said with emphasis.

"And so did Pawago," Te-al-Pantha reminded him. His voice dropped to a steely whisper. He leaned his head nearer to Manto's as they trotted on. "He has broken the law, not once, but many times!"

"We swore an oath," Manto repeated quietly. "A man does not break his oath."

"Crenna should know. She should know that people have died because Pawago leads us. She should know that more people will die."

"She is going to marry him!"

"Then perhaps she will do nothing," Te-al-Pantha said, "but still she should know. I cannot sleep nights, Manto. Can you?"

At Manto's silence, Te-al-Pantha added, "I am proud to be an Oneida warrior. I am proud when we defeat our enemies. I am not proud of murder."

"Why tell me all this?" Manto demanded angrily.

"Crenna is your sister," Te-al-Pantha replied. Then Te-al-Pantha was gone, lengthening his stride to catch up with Weshta.

Manto realized then that Te-al-Pantha had been waiting for the opportunity to speak with him, that the others had discussed it before. They wanted him to speak to Crenna about Pawago. Perhaps they were afraid they wouldn't be believed and had decided that it must be Manto, her brother, who mentioned it. Fine! Manto thought bitterly. None of them shall have to break his solemn oath.

His dark mood returned. He had been trying for a long while to bury his memories of that massacre, and had nearly succeeded. Now Te-al-Pantha had brought it all back sharply. He could see the fallen Munsee in his mind's eyes, and the shame returned, the nausea. The white man stumbled, and Manto jerked at his arm angrily. Couldn't the man even run?

The Moon Man only glanced at him with hurt eyes, and Manto muttered an apology the thing couldn't even understand. They ran on through the snow-shrouded landscape, Manto's thoughts growing gloomier with each mile.

"Crenna!"

The Oneida headwoman had been in her longhouse. Seated on the edge of her bed, she had just finished mending a doll belonging to Wakami's youngest granddaughter. The little girl, all huge shining eyes and gratitude, skipped away as Ta-Tando called to his sister.

"They are returning!" Ta-Tando's eyes were extremely bright. He was making an attempt to conceal something very exciting to him, and failing utterly.

"Pawago?" Crenna asked, putting her porcupine-quill needles away.

"Yes, yes, they're coming across the marshes now."

Crenna frowned slightly, tossed her head, and stood, walking slowly to the doorway. Ta-Tando was practically bouncing with eagerness. What was it?

The skies were blue overhead, with a few chalk-white clouds over the distant mountains to mark the passing storm. The snow in the Oneida village had been trampled into mud. Across the compound women carried in the last of the pumpkins to be hung in the longhouses. Squinting into the white glare of the morning sun, Crenna could see the tiny dark figures of the returning men. Ta-Tando surprisingly gripped her arm just at the elbow. She looked at him with amazement—Ta-Tando disliked contact; he did not like touching or being touched. He looked as excited as he had that long-ago day when Crenna had given him his very first bow, when he had been no more than three years old, still chubby, his face still unformed. There had been snow on the ground that day too, and he had run about in the snow like an excited puppy, waiting for Crenna to take him to the river so that he could shoot his arrows.

"What is it?" Crenna asked, now smiling herself.

"You'll see. You'll see."

Crenna heard footsteps behind her, and she saw her father in his fur coat coming across the compound, his gait hurried. Behind him scuttled Yo. The shaman was shirtless despite the cold. Ta-Tando had spread his news quickly.

"Is it true?" Yushta asked, panting. Steam issued from his tight lips.

"Is what true?" Crenna asked. She had no idea what had caused the excitement. She was about to demand that Yushta tell her, when the gates swung wide, and by looking down the winding road beyond, she saw for herself.

She stared, took a step forward, then folded her arms and pursed her lips. She glanced at Ta-Tando, who was positively beaming; at Yushta, whose lips were tightly compressed; at Yo, who was scowling fiercely.

"They've come at last," the shaman said in a whispery voice.

And so they had. At least one of them. Crenna watched without expression as the hunting party passed through the gates, as the people began to gather around, following after them, chattering and shouting. The children ran and leaped, the women laughed and pointed. Yo stood muttering beneath his breath; Yushta scowled. Ta-Tando's eyes sparked.

He was there, between Manto and Te-al-Pantha. A tall Moon Man, pale as the snow, with sky-eyes, dressed in odd clothing. His hair was yellow and long, and his beard, perhaps a week's growth, was also yellow. He was injured, apparently, from the way Manto had to hold him up.

Pawago strode along ahead of the party, his head erect, looking competent and pleased with himself. He did not glance back or pay any attention to the shouted questions, as if he were above it all.

Manto had to elbow his way through the throng. People reached out and yanked at the yellow hair of the Moon Man—could it be real hair? They touched his garments, prodded his flesh, yelled excitedly to friends. Children danced in a tight circle around Manto and his prisoner. And Yo muttered almost soundlessly.

"Crenna," Pawago said, putting his arms around her as he reached her. "A thing we found along the way. Your brother wanted to bring it back." He nodded his head toward the Moon Man as if it were a matter of no importance.

Crenna looked across Pawago's shoulder at the sorry, dirty alien. The people continued to dance around it, shouting. She took a slow breath. Another problem to be handled. Let them look at him now, let them prod him and touch him, let them grab his hair. The sooner their curiosity was satisfied, the sooner they could get back to their routine.

"What will you do with it, Crenna?" Ta-Tando asked.

"I don't know." She shook her head and glanced again at the tattooed shaman, who was watching the Moon Man through the narrow slits of his eyelids. The clamor was terrific. People were still rushing toward the center of the yard, until it seemed that half the Oneida nation was dancing, shouting, milling around the strange white man.

Crenna looked at him again, wondering that such a ragged thing could cause such an outburst. He was white—because of that he was different. But everyone acted as if he had six legs. Yushta was angry, apparently; Yo almost fearful. Ta-Tando was beside himself with exultation. Only Pawago seemed to have things in their proper perspective. He had found this white man; he brought him to Crenna to see what should be done.

She looked into his calm, slightly arrogant black eyes, kissed him lightly, and said, "When they have finished playing with him, feed him."

"I'll do it," Ta-Tando volunteered. "I'll take him to the foreigners. He can sleep with Hawk—the Leni-Lenape lives alone."

"All right," Crenna agreed quickly. "Anything. Later we'll decide what to do. What a fuss they're making."

"You'd think it was a white *woman*," Pawago said teasingly. "Now, that would be a sight worth seeing." His arm tightened around Crenna's waist and she smiled halfheartedly. He had a knack of saying the wrong thing, her Pawago.

"I'm going inside. It's cold and I've seen what there is to see," Crenna announced.

Yo rushed up to her, his eyes holding an urgency. "We must speak of this, Crenna. It is important."

"Later, Yo. Later."

The shouts rang in Crenna's head, and she looked once more at the prisoner, looked at those pale eyes, shook her head, and turned away, Yo still calling after her, "You don't understand the importance of this!"

The uproar was loud even in the longhouse. Why had Manto brought this thing here? Weren't there enough problems? There had been a fight over a woman, and the fight had gone to bloodletting. A scout had seen Algon-quin hunters on this side of the boundary. Pawago de-manded his answer. Ta-Tando, in one of his moods, had burned down a corn crib, and his punishment was still in suspense. Yushta kept frantically asking Crenna to inter-vene for him: Sachim was continuing to associate with the untouchable Hawk. Moa-Telah, resentful over having been forced to accept wampum belts in exchange for his son's life, muttered vague threats about a reprisal against the Onondaga, their Iroquois neighbors. Crenna slipped into her sleeping cubicle, drawing the curtains. There the noise still reached her, and she was not escaping her worries, worries which she carried around with her, like burs which clung to her tenaciously; but a moment's respite, a mo-ment alone, perhaps an hour's sleep—she needed that just now, and she lay back on her mat, drawing her blanket over her, dozing as the hooting and raucous jeering, the whistling and laughing out in the yard, filtered through the heavy wooden walls of the Iroquois longhouse.

She slept, but it was a sleep plagued by bewildering dreams. Crenna stood atop a high, snowy peak. On her back she carried a heavy burden. She had not looked into the sack she carried, but somehow she knew it was filled with human heads. Now and then she could hear the faint whimpering cries. But here, atop the peak, she found the beginning of a long road which wound into the blue, blue sky, and she laid her burden down.

Starting out, she heard the cries from the sack grow louder and more insistent; she thought they were her chil-dren, crying out for her. Her breasts ached for them. Pawago appeared briefly, a floating head against the sky, and he laughed. "You have no children, Crenna; you never will," he said, and then he was gone, his laughter mingling with the roar of distant thunder.

She traveled on alone, up an endless road, between fiercely burning stars and mocking sky spirits, until she came to the Bright Land, where Manitou waited, his face obscured by clouds. His face was radiant, the glow from it shone like sunlight behind the clouds, and she ran as she approached it. And as she ran, the road behind her crumbled away. She ran faster, watching in panic as each step carried her nearer to Manitou, as the road behind her turned to dust. Finally she was there, stretching out her hands to the Great One, but the clouds, slowly parting, revealed his face. A face as pale as snow, with sky-blue eyes, and on his head was writhing golden hair. He laughed and laughed, and the road beneath Crenna's feet gave way.

She tumbled through the skies, the mock-Manitou's laughter following her until she fell to the earth, which was dark, empty, and silent. The earth opened beneath her and she fell into its depths. It closed up over her, and she had only a last glimpse of the bright, mocking Manitou head before the world went dark and there was no more motion, no sound, nothing but the slow beating of her heart.

Crenna awakened sharply, her heart pounding in the darkness. The dream had frightened her, but only briefly as she lay in that half-asleep, half-awake state where reality and unreality merge and the mind has difficulty sorting them.

Now she was fully awake. She could see the dark sleeping figure of Sachim, hear her soft breathing. Crenna sat awake, staring at the darkness. The dream meant something, since all dreams are visitations of the spirits. It meant something, but what? Was it significant, or a prank of Weenk, who brought sleep and dreams?

She turned the dream around in her mind and then tried to shut it out. She did not want to think about it. Crenna could not sleep again, and after an hour's tossing and twisting, she sat up again, pulled her dress over her head, found her fur-lined moccasins by feel, and slipped from the sleeping chamber.

Stepping out into the deserted corridor, she dressed, swept back her long, loose hair and went out. The moon was silver, brilliant on the long snowfields. There was no wind. All was still, frozen, silent.

Her first breath knifed at her lungs with icy daggers, but after a few steps she grew used to it. Wrapping her arms around herself, she walked to the river gate, opened it, and slipped out.

The valley was a sea of snow. The forest beyond was black and silent. The moon coasted high in the deep velvet sky. Beyond it, all the stars blinked in amazement. The river was a murmuring presence; the falls above, a fringe of ice.

Crenna walked swiftly, her feet crunching on the snow.

She noticed an old oak, broken with the weight of ice on its limbs. The willows along the river were sheathed in ice, Ka-tash-hauht had imprisoned the spirits which lived inside the trees. Now the trees could not bud, could not blossom. Winter was a foreshadowing of death, and now the land lay cold and dead.

She paused and looked to the frozen moon, shivering slightly. How had the Moon Man gotten here? Had he simply fallen off the moon? She saw a faint shadow, the smallest of movements, and lifted her eyes to the pine-clad ridge. It was only one of the sentries. With the Algonquin prowling, it had been decided to post scouts in all directions. Undoubtedly the man could see her from there and had wondered what the headwoman of the Oneida was doing wandering the cold night.

And what was she doing? Sachim had no trouble sleeping. She curled herself into a warm ball and slept, her face at peace. Kala, with whatever dreams she had, slept as well, though sometimes as she slept she made small pleasurable sounds. Kala. Crenna smiled and shook her head. Manitou had made her too much a creature of the body. She was a slave to it. She indulged herself and wondered what inhibitions could possibly restrain others. She was more of a child than Sachim, whom everyone termed a child.

Crenna walked along the riverbank, watching the river slink through its frozen channel. The man slipped up behind her silently. She turned sharply as his moon shadow crossed hers on the snow.

"Manto!" she said in surprise.

Her brother looked haggard. The moonlight cast dark shadows around his eyes. His cheeks were hollow. "I could not sleep," was all he said, and they walked a little way together in silence. They passed a tree where a white owl perched as still and colorless as an icy effigy of itself. Then its head swiveled and it blinked its yellow eyes.

Several times Manto had lifted a hand and leaned toward Crenna as if he were going to say something. Now he did. "It's about Pawago," he blurted out.

"What about Pawago?"

Crenna stopped, and Manto lifted a hand in a gesture of frustration. He shook his head. "It is difficult, Crenna. We swore an oath."

Crenna smiled encouragement. What was Manto going on about? "An oath, Manto?"

"Yes." He looked down at his feet and then across Crenna's shoulder. Suddenly his eyes met hers and she saw the deep worry in them, the conviction. "I have to tell you. I'm sorry."

Crenna, perplexed, said, "All right. If it is something that must be told, tell me, Manto."

He did, and she listened, no longer feeling the cold. A vagrant breeze lifted a strand of dark hair and twisted it across Crenna's eyes. She didn't lift a hand to draw it away.

Manto spoke awkwardly, haltingly at first, and then, as he described the massacre, his voice rushed on, one word running into the next. His eyes were almost feverish, and now he could not look at Crenna.

She felt a hot flush creep into her cheeks, she felt her facial muscles tense and her spine stiffen. When Manto was through, she shook her head slowly, definitely, from side to side. "It did not happen," she said hoarsely.

"It did," Manto answered in a soft voice. "It happened, and I was a part of it. It happened, and there's blood on my soul."

"It did not happen!" she said loudly, putting her hands on her brother's shoulders. Her thumbs dug into his flesh.

Manto let his unhappy gaze meet hers for a moment. "It happened, Crenna. I have done my duty." He shook free and was gone, a slender shadow moving across the snow, returning to the palisade.

Crenna stood watching, and the cold she felt now was not from the snow and ice Ka-tash-hauht had hurled from the skies. Why was Manto lying about this? He had to be lying. But her brother was no liar. Had he a sudden grudge against Pawago; did Manto perhaps wish to be sachem? She knew that was untrue as well—Manto was not a jealous man. Nor was he underhanded. If Manto had a grudge against Pawago, he was the sort of man who would walk up to the sachem and air his grievance. He was his father's son, and Yushta had trained him to be honorable and truthful.

If anyone else had brought her this news, she would have disbelieved him. Pawago had faults, but she could not believe he was a vicious murderer. Did he hate the

Munsee? He had never indicated that; nothing had ever happened to him which could be laid at the feet of the Munsee.

Why? If it were true . . . It had to be true. Had to be. Manto was above making such accusations falsely. One could read the truth of his words in his eyes; one could see the pain that the revelation cost him. Why?

Why, Pawago? She had battled for his appointment. She had trusted him, believed in his courage. Something stung her eye, and she wiped the tear away angrily. That smiling, laughing rogue . . . he was a murderer.

The wind had risen and she stood there watching it lift the light snow. She stood quietly, and quietly she brushed another tear away.

It could be ignored. In all likelihood it would not happen again. Why, Pawago? Being sachem had meant so much to him. To throw it all away . . . And what would their relationship be if Crenna accused him and took away the antlers? How could there be a relationship? He would be disgraced in the eyes of the tribe, Crenna would appear a foolish, infatuated woman. Perhaps they would believe Pawago had scorned her and so she had reacted in that way. Why, Pawago?

She placed the flat of her hand to her forehead and rubbed her brow. Manto was gone now, and it was easy to believe that she had imagined their conversation, that it had no more reality than her dream, but she knew she had not. She started walking swiftly toward the village, knowing what she would do.

She must speak to Te-al-Pantha and Weshta, the others who were there. They might lie, they might simply remain silent, keeping their dark oath, but she would know by their eyes; she would know.

She returned to the longhouse and tried to sleep. She had no fear of the dreams now; the waking nightmare was worse by far.

In the morning she managed to find Te-al-Pantha, working on a new bow. He polished the elmwood, turned it in his strong brown hands, and carefully evaded Crenna's eyes.

"I've heard a tale of Pawago and the Munsee you were pursuing, Te-al-Pantha."

"A tale?" He tried the supple wood, testing its resilience.

He did not look up from his sitting position to watch Crenna.

"A tale of murder, Te-al-Pantha. Someone has broken the law." She asked directly, "What do you know about it?"

"How would I know anything?" He shrugged.

"You were there."

"Perhaps I was not there."

Crenna's temper rose. Her voice was taut, brittle, as she spoke. "You were there. You broke the law. Now you haven't got the warrior's courage to admit it, any more than you had the courage of a warrior at the river."

"I took an oath."

"I am tired of hearing that! An oath is an honorable thing. Among criminals there are no oaths worth keeping."

He nodded, placed his bow aside, and looked up. "You already know, Crenna. It does no good for me to tell you what you know."

"Do I know the truth, Te-al-Pantha!"

"I think that it is likely," Te-al-Pantha said. He rose, his eyes carrying the same pained expression Manto's had. He looked deliberately away.

"I can't proceed with this on your guesses, Te-al-Pantha. You asked my brother to speak; someone did. I know that. You hadn't the courage to go against Pawago. You don't have the courage now to speak the truth." Her voice grew softer. "You asked Manto to speak for you all. Now you have left him alone. By your silence you side with Pawago."

"Pawago is sachem."

"Pawago has broken the law. Hasn't he?"

Te-al-Pantha's nod was barely discernible. "He has broken the law, and we with him." Te-al-Pantha kicked his bow. It bounced against the rock behind him, and there was a small snapping sound. Then the warrior was gone, tramping through the snow, each step an angry gesture.

Crenna stood in silence, watching him go. There was no longer any doubt. None at all. There never had been, really. The doubt she had felt was only a reluctance, a protest against events, a wish that things were not as they were.

"Good morning, Sister!"

Crenna turned at the cheerful greeting. It was Sachim, her cheeks aglow, her broad, animated mouth smiling.

Crenna put an arm around her sister's neck and hugged her. "Good morning, Sachim."

"Where are you bound?" Sachim asked.

"Nowhere just now. This afternoon there is a council."

"Concerning the Moon Man?"

"Yes. Something must be decided."

"You won't vote to kill him!" Sachim asked, her youthful face horrified.

"I haven't given it any thought, Sachim. None at all."

"That's what Yo wants." Sachim's voice was bright. She bounced as they walked toward the foreigners' compound. "Yo is a wise man, a man of magic, a man of the spirits, but he is wrong now, Crenna. I know he is wrong."

"How do you know, Sachim? How do you know anything about this white man?"

"I've spoken to . . . people who have observed him."

"Hawk?" Crenna asked, smiling.

Sachim laughed. "Yes, Hawk. He is living with the white man. Hawk says he is a man, that is all. Only different. Only a man in a strange land."

"As Hawk is." Hawk's sympathies were easily explained.

"Yes, as Hawk is. But there is sense to it. We would be as odd in a white land, would we not, Crenna?" Sachim touched her arm, but Crenna's thoughts were elsewhere. She had seen, or thought she had . . . "It is nothing to die for, being different."

Now Crenna was sure. She barely heard Sachim. She had seen, for a moment, the laughing face of Kala, seen the brown masculine hand on her breast, seen them disappear into the woods beyond the compound. The man she was with wore the feathers of a tribal sachem.

"Crenna? Are you listening? You won't vote to kill him, will you?"

"I don't know."

Now, what was wrong with Crenna? Always so sure and stately, these days Crenna was different somehow, abstracted. "Look," Sachim said, "here we are, let's see for ourselves."

"What?"

"Let's see the white man, shall we?" Sachim tugged at her sister's arm, kissing her cheek. "Come on, let's see this menace Pawago has captured."

This menace. Crenna smiled, but it was nearly painful. Her facial muscles stretched uncomfortably and she could imagine what sort of strained sardonic expression she had succeeded in forming.

Oddly, she could be angry with neither of them. It was their nature, as it was her own. But they were children, only children, who hadn't learned to discipline themselves. No, she was not angry, only regretful.

They were walking now through the open settlement where Leni-Lenape women stood smoking venison, cutting pumpkins into strips to be hung in their longhouses for winter provisions. Here and there a woman nursed an infant. They greeted Crenna and Sachim as affably as did the Oneida, but there was restraint beneath the surface of their voices, their happy waves.

But those nursing infants—when they grew to adulthood, they would be Oneida. They would be Iroquois through and through, and the Nation would be strengthened. That was the object of assimilating people, former enemies, strangers. The Nation was made stronger, those lost in battle were replaced. The tribe increased. One day there would be no other people in the world but Iroquois.

Pawago, apparently, understood none of that.

Crenna saw Munsee, Susquehanna, Leni-Lenape, Algonquin women and children. There were no men. The warriors had died fighting. All but one. Hawk, who was judged to be less than a man. Crenna saw Hawk standing over his steaming cooking pot. And beside him stood the other stranger, the battered, pale man who had fallen from the moon to complicate Crenna's existence.

Crenna had halted. She stood studying the two so-different men who shared a common fate. Hawk, dark, powerful, defiant. The white man, so tall and pale, his arms thin, his demeanor apologetic.

Sachim giggled with delight. She had hold of Crenna's arm. Her head rested on Crenna's shoulder.

While Hawk stirred his small pot, the white man was washing beans to add. He was saying something to Hawk, who kept shaking his head, glancing at the two approaching women. Nearer now, they could hear the white man repeating endlessly, "Beans, beans, beans . . ."

His head lifted at the sound of their footsteps and he smiled shyly, his cheeks flushing slightly. Hawk whispered

93

something to the white man, but it did no good. He could not understand. He continued to smile with what might have been embarrassment. This is a white warrior! Crenna thought.

Then, despite herself, she answered the man's smile. He looked so soft, so domesticated, and yet so amusing—pale and blue-eyed, his forehead lumpy. He must have been beaten up. She wondered momentarily if Pawago had done it.

"How are you getting along with your new friend, Hawk?"

The Leni-Lenape shrugged. He stopped his stirring and said cautiously, "We are doing all right. You see, I am teaching him the Iroquois tongue."

Hawk's voice was carefully modulated. He liked Sachim, of course, and he thought he could like Crenna, but he had never spoken to the Oneida headwoman. She had great power, it was said. Hawk wondered why she had come.

"And is he learning to speak?" Crenna asked. She looked again at the Moon Man, who was grinning still.

"Yes. But I'm afraid he will have my accent," Hawk answered.

"You see," Sachim said, gripping Crenna's arm again. "He is a man."

"Is that why you're here?" Hawk asked, throwing caution to the winds. "To see if he's human? Yes, he's human! Like me. You Oneida think anyone not of your tribe is subhuman! When you . . ." He shut his mouth abruptly and turned away.

"He meant nothing," Sachim said, apologizing for Hawk, but Crenna seemed unoffended. She moved next to where the white man stood.

"Where did you come from, Moon Man? Why are you here, and what shall we ever do with you?"

The Moon Man's eyes softened. He could not understand a word of what Crenna said, but he knew somehow that something grave was being decided. He looked at Hawk, and finding no help there, he bowed to Crenna and then stood before her solemnly, his hands at his side.

Crenna shook her head and turned away. The captured women and children had crept closer, curiously watching the scene. "Let's go, Sachim. Please."

"All right. Good-bye, Hawk." Then, turning back, Sachim said directly to the white man, "I don't think those beans are washed well enough."

"Beans!" he said, and he laughed, holding out the bowl of beans once again.

"You have to wash them better," Sachim said, making vigorous gestures with her hands. The white man's expression dulled and then brightened, his eyebrows lifting.

"Ah. Wash! Wash beans."

"That's right. Wash them better. Good-bye now, Hawk. Good-bye, Moon Man." She smiled and then joined Crenna, who stood watching the scene.

Walking away, Crenna said, "I wish I had your way with these people."

"You do, Crenna. Why, it wasn't for me the white man smiled. It was for you, didn't you see that?"

"I saw nothing of the sort," she said rather sharply.

"Well, it is true, Sister. And if you look at him just the right way," she whispered, "he's a fine-looking man."

"Sachim!"

"He is."

"He's thin as sticks."

"Lean."

"Blue-eyed!"

"Once you get used to it, they're rather handsome eyes. Blue like the sky, like the sea." Sachim was smiling, and Crenna jabbed her playfully.

"You're getting as bad as Kala."

"And if we don't watch her, she'll be visiting the Moon Man too."

"If he lives," Crenna said, shattering Sachim's smile.

"But that's up to you, isn't it?" Sachim walked in front of Crenna, facing her. Her brown eyes were wide, pleading.

"It's partly up to me. Partly."

"Then he won't die—I know you won't let him," Sachim said, influencing Crenna in her own subtle way.

It's up to me. Up to me whether the man dies, whether Pawago keeps his horns, whether to punish my own brother Ta-Tando for his vandalism, whether Moa-Telah should be censured for his war talk. It is up to me, she thought, and the thought was not entirely unpleasant. She prided herself on being fair; so far as she knew, the

95

council had never believed her otherwise. It was not entirely a burden, but there were times when a person did not know what was right. "What is your recommendation, Crenna? What are your feelings about this matter?" they would ask. And if you did not know? Worse, if you knew what was right and what was best for the tribe, and they did not coincide. It was not entirely unpleasant, but there were nights when a headwoman did not sleep well.

Glancing back, she saw the white man talking to Hawk, who gestured with his hands and spoke loudly. The white man nodded, repeated something, and Hawk clapped his hands together in appreciation. Perhaps those two outcasts were as happy as any of them in their way. For now.

She linked arms with Sachim, and they tramped through the snow and mud toward the longhouse. Fires were burning inside, and there was the chatter of women rising to meet them like the chatter of birds in a tree. Children scuttled along the floor, chasing a ball. They met Yushta, looking grim and weary.

"We are nearly late for council, Crenna."

"There's time, Father."

Yushta was biting his lip. He had heard something. She knew it suddenly. He had heard about Pawago. No sooner had she thought of him than the newest sachem, tall and powerful, competent and sure of himself, appeared in the doorway. He crossed the floor with long strides until he reached Crenna.

He drew her to him, kissed her neck, and stood back smiling. Across his shoulder she could see Yushta turn his head.

He's trying to buy me with kisses, Crenna thought with sudden amusement. For Pawago knew as well, knew that his secret was out in the open. But he wasn't worried; Crenna was to be his wife; Crenna was on his side; Crenna would protect him.

Sachim had slipped away, but Kala, still abed, peered out from behind the curtain which was draped in front of their sleeping chamber. She pouted, her sleepy, puffy face turned to Pawago. Crenna saw a tiny, darting look pass between them, and she turned away, taking her father's arm. "Let's go, or we will be late."

They went out by the southern door and walked toward

96

the council hut, Yushta and Crenna side by side, Pawago trailing.

"Are you angry with Pawago?" Yushta wanted to know.

"Angry?" She paused to think. "Yes. Disappointed."

"Kala knows no better. He is only a man long denied."

Crenna flushed. "That's not what I was talking about."

"But will that influence you, Crenna? You must not seek vengeance in this way."

He was serious. His tired eyes were extremely worried.

"I've never used my office for vengeance, Father. I will do what is right."

So that was what they thought. It was laughable, in a way. Still, it rankled—everyone in the camp knew about Kala and Pawago, it seemed.

"You must always think of the good of the tribe, Crenna," her father reminded her.

"I will, Father," she said, keeping her temper in check. "I will, always."

The interior of the council lodge was smoky and dark. Ta-Tando, shifting nervously from one foot to the other, stood just inside the doorway. Around the blanket on the floor sat Moa-Telah; Yo, the shaman; Wakami, and Lapsa. Crenna now joined them, followed by her father, who sat next to Lapsa. Pawago entered last, his chest puffed out, his glance flickering to Crenna, seeming to say: We have an understanding.

She slowly turned her head away. Her heart began thudding away and she couldn't repress its rapid beating. It was annoying. She liked always to have her emotions under control. But the full implications of this council meeting had suddenly come home to her. She might as well stand now and slap Pawago across the face. Yushta looked at her mournfully, and she knew what was going on in his mind: Grandchildren, Crenna. I have always wanted grandchildren.

Pawago sat opposite Crenna, his eyes dancing with messages, promises of fidelity, apologies, pleas for belief. . . . She turned her head away quite deliberately, angrily aware of the sharp stinging in her eyes. Casually she brushed the tears away. She looked up, finding Pawago's image blurred by the tears. She could no longer form a definite image of this man.

Do what is best for the tribe, Crenna. For my grand-children. Kala means nothing by it.

Begin it! she told herself sharply. Nothing was gained by delaying the inevitable.

She spoke up, her voice sounding oddly constricted to her own ears. "The first matter for our attention is the destruction of a corncrib and its contents by the brave Ta-Tando. The man is present." Ta-Tando, standing with his hands folded, his legs slightly bent, waited near the entranceway. "Did you do this thing, Ta-Tando?"

"Yes." He recoiled slightly, as if Crenna had poked a finger into his ribs.

"For what purpose?"

"For what . . . ?" He looked now at his father. "I don't know."

Yo helped him. "The man Ta-Tando," he explained, as if Crenna knew nothing about it, "has always had small visitations of evil spirits. I must at these times use magic to drive them away. His brain"—Yo tapped his own skull—"becomes red and he cannot stop himself. Then he is destructive until I work magic on him."

It was true. Crenna had seen these attacks often, since Ta-Tando was very young, beginning a year after their mother had passed on to the Bright Land. He would sit very quietly, mumbling to himself, sometimes sketching figures in the air. Spittle would appear at the corner of his mouth. Then he would hear no one, see nothing. His brain went red. He would rise screaming and begin to kick, to tear things apart. He had run through the longhouse throwing articles of clothing, food, everywhere. Usually it was only a matter of minutes before he recovered. Sometimes it took hours. Once it had lasted three days, while Yo chanted and sprinkled powders on him.

"You must rebuild the corncrib. The food is lost to the tribe, Ta-Tando. You cannot replace the corn; therefore you must hunt and fish until an equivalent weight of food is returned to our larders."

"Yes, Crenna," Ta-Tando replied.

She looked at the others, but no one had anything else to say, no additional punishment to mete out. You cannot punish a man for what the spirits make him do.

"You may go now."

Ta-Tando left, backing out, moving jerkily on his bad

foot. Crenna watched the curtain swing shut, closing out the blue light which had briefly flooded the council lodge.

Crenna proceeded to the next matter. "We have a man among us who is mourning the loss of a beloved son." Moa-Telah did not look up. "The law has been satisfied, but this man still demands vengeance, and he demands it against our brother Iroquois, the Onondaga. At night he speaks to other warriors, our young, impressionable men, and he asks them to go with him to raid the Onondaga, to find the man who has done him injury. What can we do about this?"

"The man must be spoken to," Yushta volunteered. Now Moa-Telah did look up, his scarred face obstinate, drawn. "The man must be made to see that he is injuring the tribe with this talk."

"The man is a leader of the tribe," Wakami said. "A powerful sachem."

"Then it is all the more important that he realize he may hurt the tribe," Yushta answered.

"Moa-Telah?" Crenna said softly, and the old man's implacable face turned to her. "Will you speak to this man?"

He nodded slowly and finally answered, "I will speak to him. He is a stubborn man, this old one, but I will speak to him."

"Make him understand that this is very serious," she said. "Make him understand that there will be no more warnings."

"I will make him understand, Crenna."

That aside, they discussed the Algonquin. Twice there had been raids. Three warriors had been injured and one killed.

"We must strike back unless we wish the raids to continue," Pawago said.

Strike back. Kill! Crenna watched Pawago, and she saw the narrowing of his eyes, the tilt of his mouth. There was more than courage and the willingness to fight in his eyes. Perhaps that was what they never saw. There was a ferocity, an animal need. The wild expression of a dog tearing a rabbit apart.

"Father?" Crenna prompted. She let the old warriors decide what measure they thought proper for defense. They considered doubling the guards again. Lapsa thought they should make a raid against the Algonquins, "So that they do not believe the Oneida have lost their heart. It might save a larger conflict later if they know that we will strike back, that we still have teeth and are willing to use them." Yushta agreed, as did Moa-Telah. Crenna deferred to their wisdom and experience. The matter was outside of Yo's realm of expertise, and he declined to vote.

The matter was carried: the Algonquin village must be raided and a toll exacted. Strength meant freedom, and the Algonquin must learn that the Oneida meant to remain strong and free.

"Now, then, for the form of it," Yushta went on, speaking confidently. "We do not want to launch a full-scale assault. We want them to know it is retaliatory. Two dozen men, I think?"

Lapsa nodded in agreement. "A quick strike and a quick return. Pawago can lead the party."

Crenna spoke up. "Perhaps the details should be discussed later."

"Why delay, Crenna?" her father asked. "Let's decide what we shall do and then go on to other business."

"Perhaps Crenna does not agree that a strike is necessary," Lapsa suggested.

"I agree with whatever the warriors decide is best for the tribe."

"Then the timing?"

"The timing," she said, closing her eyes as she bowed her head, "is your decision as well."

"Then to what do you object?" Wakami asked with a laugh. "Oh . . ." Her laugh trailed off. The Turtle Clan headwoman was looking at Pawago, and it all became quite clear. "Well, we can discuss the details later," Wakami said easily. "As long as we are agreed in principle, it does not matter when or how." *Or who.*

"The matter of the Moon Man," Yo said with agitation, using the lull in the meeting to remind them all of one of the main topics. "Something must be done. We have evil among us, and something must be done."

"It seems to me to be a religious matter," Wakami said. "Yo should decide what must be done."

Crenna glanced up sharply, caught Pawago's cold stare, and paused a moment, their eyes meeting, exchanging explanations, accusations. "I am not sure it is a matter for Yo to decide upon," Crenna said.

"Oh?" Wakami compressed her lips and shrugged. "I thought it was understood."

"Understood if the white man is a demon, a Moon Man, a beast, a thing," Crenna said more sharply than she had intended. "But he may be entitled to the protection of a captured warrior."

"He may be a man?" Lapsa shouted in sheer disbelief.

"Yes," Crenna answered. "Who can show that he is not a man?"

"He is white!" Yo shot back.

"A white man."

"A devil," Yo insisted. "The old tales—"

"Yo." Crenna leaned near to him, her expressive hands upraised, "this one is not from the old tales. He is here now. A man captured. A strange warrior, but still only a man."

"He is a magician—all of them are."

"Then how did we capture him? Why does he stay?"

"He is waiting for the others. Learning our secrets, Crenna."

"When I saw him last, he was only learning how to boil beans!"

Yushta gawked at his daughter, surprised that she was making such a strong effort to protect this alien. What was he, after all? Nothing.

"You do not understand what his arrival means, Crenna," Yo said with genuine sorrow. "It means . . . the end."

"Perhaps I don't understand. I judge him by what I see."

"Maybe," Wakami said, suggesting a compromise, "we should suspend a decision on the white man. Let us observe him. If he appears human, then let us treat him like a human being. If he appears evil, magical, then we shall strike him down."

"He does not belong here, no matter what he is," Yushta said slowly. "He is not like us. What is his tribe? What thoughts lurk in his mind? He does not belong here."

"Wakami's suggestion is a good one," Lapsa said. "Let

us observe the man, whatever he is. It is not right to kill a man who has not defied the laws."

"He is not a man," Yo said, shaking his head heavily. "Not a man." The shaman slapped his bare thighs and took in a breath. "Whatever you agree, I accept, but he is not human."

Crenna wasn't listening to the shaman. She should have been, knowing that Yo was wise, that he knew many things both through revelation and by studying the old prophecies and records. Yo, who spoke to the spirits, who knew the portents, who was the spiritual health of the tribe, wanted the white man dead, and simple courtesy demanded that his arguments be listened to, but Crenna could not. She could not! There was one item of business which had not yet been discussed, and now it had to be. Pawago, proud and erect, sat opposite her, his eyes haughty, sullen, his mouth set and vaguely sensual even as he challenged her. It was time to broach the subject, and she had no heart for it. He was to have been her man; he was to have been a leader.

"The last matter," Crenna began, "to be settled . . ." Her tongue stuck to the roof of her mouth, and the membranes of her throat and mouth were dry.

The others looked at her with expectant expressions. Lapsa, Wakami, and Yo had no idea what she was about to say. Yushta, who knew full well, seemed to shrink in his own skin. Pawago, still appearing confident, at ease, began to study her more closely, his eyes trying to strengthen the bond between them even as she spoke.

"It has been reported," Crenna said, taking resolution, "that a war party encountered some Munsee near the East River. It has been reported that although the Munsee were unarmed, and had, in fact, thrown themselves upon the mercy of this Oneida war party . . . they were savagely butchered, as if they had been animals."

Pawago clenched his fists. The tendons on his neck stood out. He glared at Crenna, not understanding this betrayal, for that was what it was, to his mind. A betrayal, a brutal attack. And then he thought he did understand. *Kala.* She knew.

"Can this be true?" Lapsa asked, looking from Crenna to Yushta and then to Pawago. He did not have to ask who had led the party. They all knew.

Wakami's face was immobile, but in her eyes a sort of triumph lurked. This would never have happened if the Turtle Clan warrior had been named sachem. But, no, Crenna had to have her man made chief. Now she was paying the bitter price.

"These tales," Yushta said feebly, "how are we to know they are true?"

"They aren't, they're lies!" Pawago said, coming halfway to his feet.

"Do you want the witnesses brought in one by one, Pawago?" Crenna asked. "Do you want to return with us to the site of the incident? Will you sit there and lie!"

"They are the enemy!" Pawago shouted.

"They were unarmed."

"They were stealing our people's food. They were taunting us, trespassing after they had been warned. They laughed in our faces!"

"And they surrendered to you," Crenna said, her voice a soft counterpoint to Pawago's ranting. "But you could not have them surrender; you wanted them to fight so that you might kill them, and when they would not fight, you struck anyway, in a frenzy, like a winter-crazed wolf."

"I . . ." His mouth worked soundlessly.

"You falter because you cannot deny it, Pawago. Can you? Tell me it is not true. Every man has the right to speak for himself, to defend himself. But don't tell me it was done because they were our enemies, don't tell me it was done because they were stealing our food. These are not excuses. There is only one defense—that you did not do it. Did you?"

Pawago, the small muscles in his cheeks clenching and unclenching, made no reply.

"We cannot have a sachem who cannot control his emotions, who falls into blood lust, who steps outside the law." Crenna looked at each of the other council members. "This is my fault. I looked at Pawago and did not see his heart. I forced his appointment upon the council. I apologize profoundly. I can only atone for my misguided act by taking back the horns. Pawago is not a suitable leader."

The council sat in stunned silence. The small gleam of triumph had faded from Wakami's eyes. She knew the embarrassment, the humiliation Crenna was suffering. They all knew, knew that she was not only repudiating the act but also turning her back on Pawago as a suitor.

"That is all, I think," Crenna said hurriedly. She got to her feet suddenly, looking at the floor, at the walls of the lodge, everywhere but into their eyes. "Excuse me, I have other business to attend to."

Her legs felt like they were made of stone. It took her hours to reach the entranceway to the lodge, to paw the curtain aside, to step out into the crisp, clean air outside. Finally she was outside, and she began walking, walking across the muddy compound, taking long, vigorous strides, breathing in deeply to cleanse her lungs of the stale air. A voice behind her called out her name, called it again, but she did not turn around, did not look back, and the voice faded into silence, belonging now to the past.

5

THE WEATHER WARMED BRIEFLY, AND a hard rain one night washed away the snow. Manto led a raiding party out against the Algonquin, and they returned triumphant. During that week the northern lights put on a fantastic display. In the evenings they watched the wavering curtains of light—deep violet, crimson, and orange—play against the northern skies, and Yo pronounced it a good omen.

Ta-Tando, working out his penance, spent his time hunting in the forests, and Pawago joined him. The two were growing closer. Ta-Tando had always admired the older man, and now they shared a grievance. Ta-Tando, always taciturn, moody, had turned positively surly with Crenna, and it worried her. Pawago was infecting the boy.

Yo cornered Crenna and tried again to drive his point home. "You must understand, Crenna. I beg you," he said as they walked toward the lake. "The prophecy is clear— the white Moon Men will come and there will be terrible bloodshed, destruction, fire, and disease. Now they are here and nothing is done. You condone this man's presence."

"I simply want him to be treated as we have always treated captured warriors, Yo."

"You have a good heart. You are a dear woman, Crenna, but you do not understand, you do not!"

They stood on the wooded slopes watching the men fishing from their reed boats out on the iron-gray lake. Crenna turned to Yo. "I do not understand, no. This man is doing us no harm."

"But he will. The harm will come. It is written, and it will be so." His bony finger came up, and he stood trembling, his small hunched figure tense, his eyes severe. "The harm will be done, and it will be because of this man."

The snows came again, soft heavy snows which fell endlessly, blanketing the world, closing out the skies. It seemed not a day passed when it did not snow. The young men played at snow snakes, sliding their long sticks along the grooves cut in the snow, and once a great lacrosse game was formed out on a snowy field. Fifty men on each team rushed toward the goals, trampling on one another, hurling the leather ball, shouting and swinging sticks mercilessly. Four men had to be carried from the field.

Crenna had stood watching the game, smiling at the raw energy, the wild enthusiasm. The wind was brisk, the day gray, threatening more snow. It was a time before she noticed the two men standing under the trees, watching the lacrosse game with hungry, longing expressions.

Glancing around, she saw no one else nearby. She started toward the two men, changed her mind, and then, with a surge of resolve, continued.

Hawk saw her first, and Crenna was surprised to see the anxiety in his eyes before he regained his composure and assumed his habitual wooden expression. The white man slowly turned his head as well, and he smiled. A boyish expression, it reached his pale eyes and caused them to sparkle.

A cheer went up from the field, and Crenna turned her head to see Te-al-Pantha breaking free with his stick, the ball well in front of him.

"Good day, Hawk," she said, and the Leni-Lenape bowed and turned his eyes down.

"Good day, Headwoman Crenna."

"Good day, Headwoman Crenna," the white man said. Crenna was astonished. He spoke almost perfectly, although there was an accent. Had he simply mimicked what Hawk had said? Very likely.

She complimented him, "Your greeting was almost perfect."

"I have always . . . good with tongues," he said, and then, knowing that he had mangled the sentence badly, he laughed again. "I will study more, Headwoman Crenna," he apologized, still smiling.

Crenna was staring at him in fascination despite herself. Tall, good-humored, he had none of that brooding quality which stained Hawk's personality. Hawk was overpolite, nearly fawning. The white man was polite as well, but his deference seemed only a matter of form. He would try to do what was right, yet he was not about to let himself be cowed by Crenna.

"Are you enjoying the game . . . ?" What was he called?

"Peter is my name," he said, and she nearly laughed out loud. *Peter!* And what sort of name was that? She tried it in her mind, turning it around. It seemed a merry name, a name for a sprite or a small animal. It was no man's name, no warrior's name. But then, he did not seem to care if he appeared strong, if people thought he was too weak to be a warrior. Yet, if one looked closely, there was a strength behind those eyes. It was an open strength, not devious, not magical or sinister. She could not take her eyes off him—such an altogether unique creature, he was. It was a pity they knew nothing about him.

But he could speak, he could learn. One day he would perhaps be able to speak their language well enough to tell them where he had come from, what his purpose was. She tried asking him now.

"Where are you from, Peter?"

"The sea," was all that he could say. He looked to Hawk, but Hawk could not help him. "The sea." He said it with quiet desperation, with a lost expression flooding his eyes. He said something else, quite rapid, in a tongue which was incomprehensible. The words bubbled from his lips, a crazed mélange of impossible sounds.

"You see," the white man said quietly. "You see." In his hand was a small oval-shaped, dully gleaming object. He snapped it open, and Crenna gasped. It contained the perfect image of a yellow-haired woman. She took the locket from this man who called himself Peter, and held it up to the light.

It was not possible. The artist had rendered a perfect portrait. The delicate strokes, the truth of the representation, were beyond the skills of even the finest of Oneida craftsmen.

The woman in the portrait looked out serenely at Crenna. A blond woman, her hair oddly twisted about her head, her eyes as blue as Peter's, she sat with her pale hands folded, wearing an impossible dress of blue and white. Crenna glanced up and saw the man gazing at her, his eyes distant, his smile bittersweet. "The sea," he said again, and Crenna handed the locket back to him.

She made her good-byes and turned to walk away. She was astonished at an emotion she felt rising in her breast. It had occurred when she had examined the portrait. Crenna had found herself annoyed. Annoyed! Why? The man meant nothing to her, the woman less. Yet she had felt annoyance that he had shown her the picture. Now, as she walked slowly downslope, she glanced across her shoulder and saw that he stood there, the locket dangling from his hand, his eyes fixed on her. She continued on, her thoughts twisting like leaves in a whirlwind. And as she walked she was careful to keep her back straight, her shoulders set. She knew his eyes were still on her, and again the annoyance rose. A cheer went up from the lacrosse field, and Crenna looked that way, brushing aside the childish confusion in her mind.

When she had looked back, she had seen Peter. Seen in that moment that he was only a man, tall, handsome, lonely, but good-humored. He was a man far from home, a prisoner of his adventure; she knew that now. Yo was wrong. All of her life she had trusted Yo's judgment, believed he knew the secret ways, and that among them all, he was the only one who could accurately know the future. But he was wrong; the prophecies were wrong when they predicted that the coming of a white man meant the destruction of the Oneida nation.

The man, Peter, had not come to destroy anything. He was a good-natured, intelligent man. Different from all of them, but still a man.

She had thought of all that in the brief moment when she had looked back to see him standing on the snowy hillside beside the forlorn Hawk. She had seen him there, his expression almost beseeching, his eyes bright, his lean body erect. Crenna had not seen the other man.

He slipped through the dark shadows beneath the pines, watching with black eyes which burned brightly with sullen anger. He had watched the meeting between Crenna and Peter, seen her laugh, seen her walk away with the white man's pale eyes following her every step, the sway of her hips, the set of her proud head, and Pawago's dark mood had grown darker yet, until no compassionate light at all could seep into his angry soul.

"What is it?" Ta-Tando asked. He was crouched against the snow, resting. The deer he had carried up from the river was heavy and the snowshoes he wore had made the going only a little easier. Pawago squatted down beside him, saying nothing for a moment.

"Well?" Ta-Tando said.

"It has all become clearer," Pawago replied slowly. He had a handful of snow and he rubbed it between his rough palms as he spoke. "I couldn't understand why Crenna turned against me. It was as if she believed the lies they told about me. Lies about what happened when we fought the Munsee. I thought she had some stupid idea that I cared for Kala."

"So did I," Ta-Tando answered. He hadn't been able to understand his sister's treatment of Pawago either.

"Now I know. I saw her." Pawago fell silent, and Ta-Tando had to prod him.

"What? What is it?"

"The white man," Pawago said. His face was as dark and rigid as a mask of bark with eyeslits. "I saw your sister with the white man."

Ta-Tando smiled crookedly. He cocked his head to one side and emitted a dry chuckle. "Crenna?" He shook his head. "Crenna with the white man!" It was unthinkable. Pawago, however, was not laughing. The big warrior continued to gaze steadily at Ta-Tando.

"She was with the white man," Pawago said, "speaking closely with him. I saw them." And at that moment Pawago's words were so convincing that he almost believed his own lies.

"No." Ta-Tando wagged his head. "No, no, no."

Not Crenna, Crenna the proud, the self-composed, the kind, the Oneida. Pawago was mistaken, had to be. *Crenna* with a dog?

"Why not?" Pawago said, reading Ta-Tando's thoughts. "Sachim with the Hawk; Crenna with the thing, the Moon Man. Why did she turn her back on me? Why did she take my antlers? You know, Ta-Tando," Pawago said in that coaxing tone which was most effective with Ta-Tando, "that I could never have done the things I am accused of."

"Manto . . ."

"Manto is influenced by Crenna," Pawago said with perfect logic. Ta-Tando continued to shake his head. He plucked tufts of hair from the deer at his feet. The animal stared at him with uncomplaining brown eyes.

"Yo has said he is our enemy. Yo has said he is the be-ginning of the end," Ta-Tando said, his voice stressful. Whom could a man believe in? He searched Pawago's face, seeing that strong, confident jaw, the proud eyes. Pawago a liar, a killer, a jealous trickster? *That* was not possible. Pawago was brave and strong, he was good, a proud Oneida warrior. Yet something had happened. Somehow he had lost his rank—there had to be an ex-planation. Ta-Tando rubbed his temples, his confusion ris-ing. For a moment he thought the terrible red veil would lower across his consciousness, and he felt panic growing, but it did not.

"He has cast a spell over your sister," Pawago said. He helped Ta-Tando lift the buck, grasping it by the antlers. "She is turning her back on her people. She consorts with the white man and condemns me for something I did not do."

When Ta-Tando didn't reply, Pawago said, "It worries me, Ta-Tando. I don't know—maybe this magician has been sent to disrupt us, and when the white army comes, we shall find ourselves in chaos."

That slowly sank into Ta-Tando's brain, its logic ringing true. He felt a moment's fluttering panic.

"Don't worry," Pawago said. "My friend, we know the truth, and Pawago shall not desert his people. They wish to make us weak, but Pawago is strong. I will destroy this white man and any who come into our land. I swear it!" His oath was a hiss between clenched teeth, and Ta-Tando smiled, almost with gratitude. Pawago was a man! He was, above them all, suited to be war leader. He trudged through the snow with Pawago, each of them gripping the buck's antlers with one hand.

Topping the hill rise, they could see the lacrosse game, and in response to a nod of Pawago's head, Ta-Tando looked to the west and saw Hawk and the white man standing alone, observing the game.

He felt sudden anger, and he fought it down, afraid of the red fog which sometimes followed sudden anger. They trudged through the village, and they could still see Crenna's tracks in the snow. She had gone to meet the white man, spoken, and then walked away. Ta-Tando looked at the tracks, proof of Pawago's words; then he closed his eyes.

"I must speak to my father. I must speak to Yo," the young warrior said, and Pawago nodded in response.

"Someone must. Crenna has gone too far. Her mind is clouded by the Moon Man's magic. Speak to your father, Ta-Tando. Speak to him before it is too late."

Pawago suddenly held up a hand. "Wait." Ta-Tando halted and then looked upslope. The game was over, and Hawk and his white friend were strolling toward the village. Ta-Tando felt his heartbeat accelerate; he saw the dark smile on Pawago's face.

He let go of the deer as Pawago did. Then they stood waiting. Ta-Tando watched the white face as the two outcasts approached. He felt a surge of fury. Hawk encourages him, he thought. Hawk, who has a deep grudge against the Oneida. Perhaps Hawk was directing the white man's magic. They were a dozen strides away now, and Pawago stepped into their path.

The white man nodded and started to step around Pawago. Hawk, his expression mirroring his anxiety, tried to grab the white man's arm and pull him back, but it was too late. The white man lifted a hand and said, "I greet you," and Pawago kicked him.

He drove his foot into the white man's groin, and the white man doubled up, falling on his side in the snow, vomiting up his breakfast. Pawago stepped in and kicked him again in the ribs, and the white man's head snapped back with the shock of impact.

Hawk started forward and then stopped, his mouth drawn down tragically. To attack an Oneida was to die—there was no excuse under the law. Hawk simply stood there trembling as Pawago kicked the white man in the head, splitting his scalp. Blood spattered the white snow, and Pawago kicked him again.

Ta-Tando stood hunched forward, his fists clenched reflexively. He wanted to attack too, to maul and kill, to destroy this white demon. With each kick, Ta-Tando's entire body trembled. He watched as Pawago, his face devoid of expression, aimed kick after kick at the white dog.

It seemed to be hours before he was through, and when he was, they lifted their deer and walked toward the village, leaving Hawk standing over the battered man.

"Why?" Peter Van der Veghe asked through the mouthful of warm blood. His entrails were on fire. Jagged pain

111

stabbed his side. His head thumped like festival drums. "Why?" He stretched out a hand toward Hawk, who was crouched over him. By the concern on Hawk's face he knew it had been a very bad beating. Just when he had thought he was learning the ways of these people, becoming accepted, if not a friend, this savage attack had come. He opened his mouth again to ask, but Hawk put a finger to his lips.

"Don't talk, Peter. Don't try to talk now." How could Hawk answer him? Peter didn't have the understanding yet to comprehend it all. Crenna had been engaged to marry this fiery young war chief, but then Pawago had been accused of slaughtering a band of unarmed Munsee men. Crenna had taken away Pawago's rank, and now Pawago, bitter and angry, was determined to regain his title, even if it required the discrediting of Crenna. It was all too much for Peter to understand at this point. He simply told him, "Don't talk, Peter," and watched the hurt blue eyes staring up at him in the misery of incomprehension. Hawk helped him to his feet, and together they walked down the long empty slope toward the village.

"Crenna." Yushta looked up, smiling, but his smile was only a gesture. Yo was beside him, appearing severe and tired. Manto had also been summoned to Yo's hut, and Crenna's brother rose to embrace her briefly.

"What is this?" she wanted to know. This was most unusual. Somehow, however, she knew, knew before Yushta put it into words.

"The white man. He must go."

"Go?" She looked into Yushta's dark eyes, then at Yo and Manto, who sat cross-legged on the mat beside Yo's flickering fire.

"Yes. We voted not to kill him, but we feel that for the good of the tribe—"

"This is a matter for council, Father, not to be discussed casually."

"If you would prefer to meet in council . . ." Yushta shrugged. "If you think you would find support for your position there, we will wait."

Briefly her thoughts flitted to Wakami, Lapsa, Tachtathahuata. Who among them would support her? "It may as well be here, Father."

"I think so. The man must go."

"He threatens our tribe, Crenna," Yo said with passion. His old face was deeply lined. The firelight illuminated the magic tattoos on his leathery body. "He is an evil thing. Why do we shelter him?"

"He has done us no harm," she argued. "Where would he go?" She gestured toward the entranceway. "It is snowing out there. I doubt the man can hunt or fish. It is the same as sentencing him to death to banish him at this time."

"Why do you protect him?" Manto asked. His voice was not challenging, but merely curious. Crenna looked at her brother. Without a fuss, without display, Manto was silently moving into the power circle. His status was slowly increasing. It was not mentioned, but everyone knew that Manto would replace Pawago eventually. "I apologize, Sister, but they are saying that you consort with the white man."

"Consort!" Crenna threw back her head and laughed. Yo stared at her in bewilderment. "I have spoken to the prisoner twice, three times perhaps. Consort! What a word. Does that mean we are planning rebellion or perhaps that we are lovers?"

Manto looked down, shamefaced.

"It is only what we have heard," Yushta said.

"I can imagine the source. Pawago, no doubt. Perhaps using poor deluded Ta-Tando as his voice."

"It doesn't matter who said it, Crenna," Manto said sincerely. "If you say it is not so, it is not."

"But that alters nothing," Yushta said. "We three and some others have spoken of this often. The white man must go. We will do no harm to him—although if he remains, I'm afraid there is more danger to him than the wilderness can offer."

"There have been threats?"

"I did not say that," Yushta said quickly.

"He has been beaten, Crenna," her brother said.

"When!"

"After the lacrosse game."

Then she knew who had done it, why it had been done. It had happened after she had met and spoken to Peter. She felt her facial muscles go hard, felt her nails biting into the palms of her hands.

"You see how it is," Yushta said weakly. "He is not wanted here. He will be killed."

"He is better off leaving, Crenna," Yo said. "Let him return to his own world, his own kind. It is best for him, best for us."

His own kind. Crenna thought incongruously of the portrait Peter carried, that of a young blue-eyed woman. Somehow she could picture it vividly in her mind. She could see the haughtiness in the painted eyes, the brittle smile, the demanding tilt of the chin. *She's not the one for you,* Crenna thought before her thoughts returned sharply to the matter at hand.

What they said was true. To remain here was certain death. He would be abused, possibly murdered. Yet out there . . . he had come from the land of the Mohawks. The name "Mohawk" means man-eaters, and the practice had not entirely died out. Crenna had always thought them the least civilized of the Iroquois. If Peter were to return to the sea, he would have to pass through the Mohawk lands again. They would kill him; he would have no chance at all.

She looked at Yo, at her father and brother, and it seemed that what they were saying was: We want him to die. If you will not send him away to die, we shall kill him ourselves.

"He might make it back to the sea. He might return to his own people and be happy there," Manto suggested, and Crenna knew that the comment was made only out of consideration for her. Manto could not have cared less. Yet what he said was true. If he made it, he might be able to return to his home at the bottom of the sea. What was life like there among the tangle of sea grass and ocean gardens? Among the raging sea spirits she had heard so much about but had never seen? His people must be strong or clever to outwit the hundred-ton fishes and the many-armed water witches. . . .

She imagined an undersea city where fish swam through the streets and waterfalls of air tumbled upward, where golden palaces housed pale-eyed women whose hair was decorated with sea grass. . . .

"In the spring," Crenna said without meeting their eyes. "No one can survive the winter out there. In the spring he shall be banished. It is best for the tribe, best for him."

She left them beaming with pleasure. A troublesome problem had been resolved. Crenna had capitulated. But then, what else was there to do? To argue that he had the lawful right to remain?

By winning that argument she would have sentenced him to death.

The snow was swirling, the wind out of the north heavy. The trees were gray, bowed with the weight of the snow. The land beyond the palisade was frozen and colorless.

What did she care what happened to that man? she asked herself angrily. He was a nuisance, more trouble than he was worth, an alien. A headwoman had more important things to think about.

She stopped suddenly, the snow drifting past, touching her cheek with a hundred wet kisses. She owed the man an apology.

It was a notion which would have produced laughter or stares of incomprehension, perhaps, but it was true. This white man had been brought here by Oneida, he had been attacked in defiance of Oneida law by Oneida. Now he would be banished by the Oneida when they knew full well that banishment was akin to murder. She tried to think of when another man had been banished, and could think of no instance in her life or in the tribal memory.

It seemed important to explain why this was being done. Perhaps he was not a man, but he was a creature of understanding. He was capable of feeling pain and pleasure—she thought of his winning smile. Perhaps . . . She looked toward the foreigners' compound, watching the snow slant down.

She wandered through the storm and came upon him unexpectedly. He was standing outside Hawk's bark hut in the blowing wind, simply watching the storm, his eyes far distant, but when he saw Crenna his pale eyes looked as if he had been expecting her, as if no one else could have come.

Crenna halted, felt a girlish flush creep into her cheeks, felt her mouth open wordlessly. They stood staring at each other in the snow. The storm whirled around them, screening off the rest of the world. Crenna took hold of her emotions angrily. What was she doing? She had come to apologize and now she stood gaping, staring at the man as the children had done on the day he had first arrived.

"Come into the hut," Peter said. "We'll both be down sick."

Crenna lifted an eyebrow. The man was learning their tongue rapidly. He walked ahead of her, smiling. She noticed that his beard was gone, noticed how the new buckskin shirt he wore fit his broad-shouldered, lean frame. She had never really appreciated how tall he was. She doubted there was a taller man in all the Oneida camp.

Inside, the wind was cut by the crude bark walls. It whined through the chinks in the roughly constructed shelter, making a curious sound. Crenna looked around; it was the first time she had been in Hawk's hut.

He had two old blankets on the floor. Two platforms where the men slept. And little else. But for the drawings on the wall.

Crenna stepped nearer, examining them. A lake trout, the most perfect replica she had ever seen, had been drawn there. Arrows and strange inscriptions decorated the picture. Below it there was a representation of its insides. Was he a magician after all? Why this interest in a fish's entrails?

She could not overcome her amazement. The hand which had drawn these pictures was masterful. They were exact in every detail. Plainly depicted were the fascicled needles of a blue spruce and its cones, the head of a moose, a terrapin; a tiny, delicate rendering of a lilac graced another wall. She turned, looking at him with wonder. "You did this?"

"It used to be my work." He shrugged. "Do you like them?"

"Is it magic?" she wanted to know, and Peter's face broke into a grin.

"No, Headwoman Crenna, not magic. I only want to know things better. To know the animals and the plants."

"For what purpose?"

"For the purpose of knowing," he said. He wanted to explain further, that was evident, but he did not have the words.

She looked at the sketches for a time longer, listening to the playful shriek of the wind. Snow drifted past the doorway. And he watched her. Watched her with those pale eyes. He examined her in different ways, she saw. Now his eyes would look at her intently, as if he meant to draw her. She could see him studying her dark hair, her eyes, the bones of her face. And then his gaze would become less specific. He would let his vision sweep over her; he was only a man looking at a woman, enjoying her.

"I have come for a purpose," Crenna said suddenly. "The tribe has decided that you must go."

"Go?" Peter was standing near the wall of the hut. Now he leaned against it, spreading his hands. "Go where, Headwoman Crenna?"

His expression was amused and concerned at once. He looked toward the doorway.

"Not until the spring," she said quickly. "It is understood that . . ."

He wasn't listening. He was looking into her eyes, that faint, quiet smile on his lips. "Go where?" he repeated.

"Back to the sea," she said, but she couldn't meet his eyes as she said it. Back to the sea through the Mohawk lands? The banishment was the same as an edict of death, except that the Mohawks would do the killing and the Oneida could stand aside with bloodless hands.

He ran his hands through his long yellow hair and laughed. He was not angry, not frustrated, but a sadness seemed to touch his eyes.

"Is it you, Headwoman Crenna? Is it you who has made this decision?"

"No." Her voice was small. She shook her head. "It wasn't my decision."

"I'm glad of that," he said. Suddenly he resumed his enthusiasm of a moment ago. "Do you see the lilac here? Can you tell me what colors you have seen?"

She watched him as he spoke. Now and then he forgot and lapsed into his own complicated tongue. She knew he was talking to keep from thinking of what must come with the spring, and she felt her heart go out to him. He was storing up knowledge which would never be shared, learning many things which would die with his death. He stopped suddenly and turned. He was only a few feet from Crenna, and she felt her heart thudding, felt an indefinable emotion swell in her throat and burst, trickling down into her heart. He towered over her. His eyes so soft, so unlike those of Pawago or of any man, smiled at her, forgave her.

Wrong. It was wrong, this emotion she felt, and she de-

117

liberately set her jaw and said stiffly, "I apologize for my people. Perhaps they do not understand you. Perhaps they are afraid of you. It is not our custom to turn a captive from our village. Do not hold it against us, please."

Do not hold your murder against us. Even to Crenna the words sounded bizarre, inane. But he smiled and stretched out a hand.

"I hold nothing against you. I would have been dead long ago if not for the Oneida. Perhaps I shall live; perhaps I shall see the ocean again."

His hand still floated before her, and without knowing why, she took it, feeling the warmth of his flesh, the sincerity of his light grip as his long fingers closed around her hand.

"I must go," she said, practically tearing her hand away. She turned toward the entranceway, and it was only as she passed out and stood in the storm once again that she dared to look back and study him. He still watched, still smiled, still held his outstretched hand toward her.

Crenna spun sharply around, wondering what in the world was the matter with her. Perhaps the man *was* a magician, for she felt tight loops of warm emotion encircling her breasts, her hips. She felt her heart beat more quickly, felt a warm surging of her blood and a deeper, slowly growing warmth as she walked through the drifting snow toward the longhouse.

Wrong. The thoughts she fought back were wild and wrong. He was nothing, and she was a leader of a proud people. She let the snow hurl itself against her burning cheeks, let it chill the sultry, pulsing warmth within her.

She slept restlessly that night, and exhausted herself with her tossing and turning. Finally she had to rise. It was hours yet until dawn, but she went outside.

The clouds, muted and frozen, clung to the horizons, but overhead it was clear, a silver moon beaming down placidly. The camp was still, the wind a whisper through the deep forest. Moonlight poured down like silver streaming from Manitou's cup. The snow was blue and silver, the shadows deep and soft. The stars flickered against the sky, describing a silent melody. Two darkly silhouetted nighthawks danced and wove against the stars, sketching unwritten poems of love.

There was an unreality to the night. In the midst of the

118

winter storm, a moment of calm; in the midst of darkness, light; in the midst of clinging, acid cold, a warm comfort. Unreality—the stars drifted past, laughing brightly. The moon beamed with soft approval.

Crenna walked across the crusted snow, her hands behind her back, the cold nipping at her nose and ears. Such things were not possible. It was self-delusion and showed a lack of self-discipline. One doesn't . . . She refused to name the emotion which darted about inside her brain, flying joyously down secret corridors, showing its bright face at unexpected intervals. One doesn't . . .

The shadows were deep around the stockade walls. Black pools against the blue-white snow. The nighthawks were gone; having fed, they sought the shelter of their secret nest. They lay together now, feathers and quickly beating hearts, warmth and surety. They had no need other than being, no responsibility for the others of their kind. Crenna turned her thoughts away. She was thinking without defining her thoughts, knowing that the moment she defined them they would be unthinkable. The warmth would be blown away by cold winter winds and the icy fingers of the season would tear her heart from her breast. All foolishness! She would not allow it. Hers was an ordered life, her mind methodical. These childish ramblings were for minds like Kala's.

The nighthawk screeched again, and she looked skyward, seeing nothing. The wind drifted her long hair across her face. Suddenly the warmth was gone. *The hawk.* Was she being foolish? And then she knew she was not. She saw a darting shadow, heard a cry of pain, and within moments the guard at the gate began to shout his warnings.

Crenna started back toward the longhouse, but it was too far. The Algonquin were already scaling the wall, and she saw three men leap to the ground inside the compound. The Oneida guard rushing that way was locked into momentary combat with the invading Algonquin. Then he was clubbed down as three enemy warriors converged upon him.

Another war cry pierced the stillness, and Crenna saw two more Algonquin leap from the walls. They rushed to the gate and swung it wide, and then they were swarming into the Oneida village, their screams challenging, bloodthirsty, their painted faces demonic in the silver moonlight.

Already the Oneida soldiers were emerging from the longhouses, running, weapons in hand to meet the challenge of the Algonquin. Some of them had not had time to dress, and they ran naked across the snow-covered yard, their answering cries filling the night.

Crenna ducked into a shadow, saw an Algonquin rush past so near that she could have touched him, and watched as two men collided in a violent, short-lived struggle. It was Te-al-Pantha, and the Algonquin he had met would never war again. Blood stained the silver snow, and the sounds of combat were a violent chorus echoing across the village.

Briefly Crenna saw Pawago emerge from his longhouse, saw his arm uplift, saw an Algonquin die beneath his war club, saw the exultation on Pawago's face as he strode naked into combat. Ta-Tando rushed around the corner of a building, carrying his bow and arrows, but he withdrew, and as Crenna watched him, he stood in the heavy shadows, his back pressed to the longhouse walls.

A woman screamed. An Algonquin howled with mortal pain. Arrows sang past. And then Crenna saw her. She was a child among the warriors, a lost and tiny creature loose in the world of death and destruction. Sachim stood in the center of the yard, looking this way and that helplessly, a sleepwalker on a battlefield. The one who never had understood violence was now surrounded by it, and it built to a savage crest, threatening to wash over her. Crenna leaped up, screaming. Sachim's head turned slowly toward her as the battle raged.

Old Lapsa had run an Algonquin through with his lance, and Pawago still fought, striking men down left and right. Te-al-Pantha had been hit with an arrow, and he dragged himself toward the longhouse. Manto had come rushing into the fray, and fighting with methodical confidence, struck down three Algonquin men. Yushta had appeared from nowhere, and the old chief was narrowly missed by a flying arrow. It never fazed Yushta. He went to his knee, and holding his own bow across his body, he fired time and again into the mob of onrushing enemy warriors.

Sachim still stood frozen in the center of the yard. Unable at first to decide which way to run, she was now left with nowhere to go as the Algonquin, still streaming into the village, flowed around her.

An Algonquin with black and yellow war paint gave a yelp and angled toward Sachim, his eyes glittering, and Crenna groped about her for a club, anything useful. They would not take Sachim.

She found nothing, nothing but a stone beneath the snow, and she started forward onto the battlefield. She was already too late. The Algonquin lunged toward Sachim and caught at her shoulder as one of his tribesmen fell behind him, an Oneida arrow through his throat.

Sachim backed away and tripped, going to her back, the Algonquin hovering over her. The arrow came from out of the darkness, and Crenna, glancing that way, saw Hawk leap over a tanning rack and rush to Sachim. He held a bow in his hand and his face was hard, feral. Another Algonquin turned toward them, and again Hawk shot an arrow. The Algonquin pawed at the shaft, which projected from his chest, and went down, writhing in pain.

Hawk had Sachim by the hand now and he led her through the wreckage of the camp toward the river. Crenna, satisfied that Sachim was safe, turned away and had nearly reached the shadows when she saw something that made her heart stop. Yushta was down, and an Algonquin stood over him with his club.

A shriek filled her throat and her hands went to her mouth even as she ran desperately toward her father. The Algonquin's arm lifted, but it never fell.

A panther-quick shadow lunged at the Algonquin from out of the darkness, and by moonlight Crenna saw the yellow hair. The Algonquin screamed with pain as Peter took him by the wrist, yanked the man's arm downward, and snapped it across his knee.

The Algonquin whirled in a mad frenzy, drew his belt knife, and then hesitated as he saw the yellow-haired man before him. The hesitation was deadly. Peter had hurled himself to the ground, snatching up the Algonquin's war club. Now he rolled to his feet, and the Algonquin, over the surprise, moved in, one arm dangling uselessly at his side. Crenna felt her heart stop. Peter had been lucky, she knew. She doubted he could take a trained Algonquin warrior in even combat. But then, perhaps she had underestimated the man.

She was never to find out. Yushta, dragging himself across the snow, recovered his bow and arrows. Coming to his knees, the old warrior notched an arrow, drew the bowstring, and shot into the Algonquin's back, the arrow embedding itself between the warrior's ribs.

The Algonquin's head jerked to one side as he tried to look across his shoulder. There was blood in his mouth and already the hint of death in his eyes. He slumped to the earth and slowly died.

Crenna was running. The battle around her was waning. The Algonquin were fleeing now, being pursued by the Oneida men. She noticed none of it. She ran across the snow, her loose hair streaming out behind her, her eyes stinging.

Yushta was to his feet when she reached him, and he gave his daughter a weak smile. "I am too old for this," he said. He was holding his shoulder. Blood leaked from between Yushta's fingers. "I'm all right," he told her, mock gruffness in his voice.

She saw the shadow on the snow before she turned. There he stood, his pale eyes concerned, his chest lifting and falling with exertion, the war club still in his hand.

Crenna was into his arms in two steps. She clung to him, laughing, looking up into his narrow, sober face. She leaned her head against Peter's chest, listening to his heartbeat. Then she squeezed him tightly again before realizing what she was doing.

Abruptly she stepped back, nearly staggering. The blood seemed to have drained from her head. Yushta was watching her, tight-lipped, his eyes grim. From somewhere Ta-Tando had appeared, and he too simply stared, looking from Yushta to Crenna and back.

"I want to see to my wound," Yushta said, his voice brittle. "Who is hurt, Ta-Tando?"

"Te-al-Pantha's leg is not good. I saw no one else injured," Ta-Tando answered. He spoke to Yushta, but his eyes, strangely defiant, were fixed on Peter Van der Veghe.

Together Yushta and his son hobbled back toward the longhouse. The compound was nearly deserted now. The Oneida men were off in pursuit. The Algonquin who had remained behind would never run again. They lay scattered against the snow. The silver moon was a beacon, lighting Van der Veghe's face.

"I tried to help," he said. "I hope I didn't make trouble."

"Trouble! You saved my father's life."

Van der Veghe said nothing. It seemed, however, that Yushta would rather have been dead than see the white man hold his daughter, however brief and unplanned the embrace was.

He looked at his own hand and seemed surprised to notice that he still held the war club. He opened his fingers and it fell soundlessly to the snow. "I'll go back to my own compound," he said.

Crenna hadn't moved, but her eyes were active, searching his face, trying to understand something which had no logic to it. She had run to him, held him—out of gratitude? That was the simple explanation, but it wasn't true.

She lifted her hand toward him, a gesture which was never quite completed. "I will walk down with you," she said, surprised at the words coming from her own lips. "Hawk took Sachim that way. I want to make sure she is all right."

If he noticed the discomfiture she was suffering, it wasn't reflected in his face. He nodded calmly, and Crenna led off toward the foreigners' compound. Only once did she glance back, and then she caught an expression on Van der Veghe's face, which was far from impassive. Their eyes met, only briefly, and Crenna turned away, walking steadily onward across the frozen snow.

Sachim was waving. A slender figure backlighted by the pale moon. Hawk stood submissively to one side. It touched Crenna somehow, seeing him like that. A warrior, a brave man who had saved Sachim's life out of friendship. It was enough to make her pause and examine the Oneida attitude toward captured men. She realized that it was not the first time she had examined their policy lately. Unconsciously she had been doing it all along, finding Hawk and Peter disturbing. How much penance was due?

The idea behind the law was to allow the captured men to pose no threat to the Oneida, but did Hawk and Van der Veghe form a threat?

Sachim rushed to her, laughing, and the sisters embraced. Crenna stroked Sachim's hair, then held her off at arm's length, examining that large-eyed, delicate face.

"Thank you, Hawk," Crenna said. "Thank you for saving my baby from the Algonquin." Hawk murmured something and continued to look down at the snow.

"It's cold," Peter said. "Maybe we should return to our hut, Hawk."

Crenna looked at him and saw that Peter Van der Veghe was intensely aware of the awkward situation. These men should not have been alone with these women of high rank. They should not speak to them unless spoken to—no matter that they had just saved Sachim's life, and that of Yushta.

Hawk was in an agony of discomfort. Had he been threatened too, beaten? By moonlight now she could see that her guess was correct.

Hawk's face was swollen, his lips split. They were healing wounds, not injuries suffered during tonight's battle. Van der Veghe still had the scratch on his cheek, the bruises on his jaw. What other injuries that were not apparent? She felt humiliation. This was how they now treated their prisoners.

She looked at the men again, again thanked them, and watched as they walked away, Van der Veghe limping slightly.

"A very exciting evening," Sachim said with a sigh and a toss of her head. "Too exciting for me. Will there be a war now, Crenna?"

"I do not know," Crenna replied. "Sachim—what happened to Hawk? Do you know?"

"Yes, I know. He told me about it." She hesitated a moment and said, "Pawago beat him for speaking to me."

"Pawago!" Crenna was furious. "What right does he have to beat a man, foreigner or not? Why wasn't I told?"

"They didn't wish to say anything. They expected no protection, Crenna. To say what had happened would invite another beating."

"Don't they know we have laws to prevent things like this?" They were walking along the river toward the camp, where smoke now rose from the longhouses. There would be no more sleep this night.

"They didn't imagine anyone would care, Crenna."

"But I do care! We can't have this sort of behavior. Have you seen Peter's face? The way he walks! It was a savage attack. Hawk looks unwell too," she added belatedly.

Sachim was smiling tenderly, and Crenna halted, demanding to know the cause of her amusement.

"I am only happy, Sister," Sachim said. "Happy for you."

"For me?"

"Yes, Crenna."

"What are you talking about, Sachim? You can be exasperating at times, you know."

"I am happy," Sachim said simply, "that you have found a man you care for."

"A man I . . . Peter!" She laughed, fooling not even herself. "I only want to see the laws obeyed. I was angry because of these incidents, not because Peter Van der Veghe was involved!" She waved a hand in a gesture of denial. Sachim smiled again, infuriatingly. "You can't think it, Sachim! I—with a savage like this Moon Man?"

"Perhaps I was mistaken," Sachim said. They turned and walked on. "I am mistaken about many things. I am not too clever sometimes. I only thought that you cared for the man. It was just the way your eyes shone, the way you became uncertain when you were near him, losing the composure you are known for, your command of yourself. Forgive me, Sister, if I have offended you. Sachim can be a silly woman at times."

There was a glimmer of amusement in Sachim's eyes, however, as she made her profuse apology. Crenna felt her cheeks grow hot. She recalled the beating of his heart beneath her ear, the calm strength of his body, the cool appraisal of his eyes. Silly! If Sachim was being silly, what did that make Crenna? A woman of responsibility, of high position, growing flustered around this . . . Moon Man. Savage.

The very strength of her annoyance supported Sachim's statements. Crenna sighed audibly. Even the highborn can have their infatuations. Even sensible women can be foolish.

All right. Admit it. Admit you like the man. Recognize that it is only a silly infatuation, Crenna. It will pass. She glanced at Sachim, saw that her sister was still smiling, and felt the urge to choke Sachim. For she knew—she knew!

Yushta was lying on his mat in the longhouse. Wakami was hovering over him, clucking her tongue as if this proved exactly how much Yushta needed a new wife. She had applied herbs to his wound and was now bandaging the old man's shoulder tightly.

"How is it, Wakami?" Crenna asked.

It was only then that Yushta seemed aware of his daughters' presence, and he looked up at Sachim and Crenna, the pain in his eyes deepening.

"Fine, fine. No problems. The Algonquin have tried to kill this old Solitary Pine Tree more than once, eh, Yushta? More than once."

Yushta nodded. Ta-Tando stood nearby, his expression cynical as he watched his sisters.

"How is Te-al-Pantha?" Crenna asked. "Does anyone know?"

"Well enough. He will hunt in the spring," Wakami said.

"Good." She looked at Ta-Tando, noticing the accusation in his eyes. Briefly she was angry, and she almost spoke up, asking why a man who had not fought, but who had hidden in the shadows during the Algonquin attack, should be angry with those who did. But she said nothing. It would have crushed Ta-Tando, and he could no more help being what he was than Peter Van der Veghe could.

"We must hold a council meeting, Crenna," Yushta said. His eyes fixed on his daughters.

"Yes, Father. As soon as you are well we shall hold a council."

"Tomorrow," Yushta said sternly. "With first light."

"Don't worry about things," she said. Perhaps the wound wasn't serious, but it was painful certainly. She could read the suffering in his eyes. Beneath the suffering, however, was a stronger, less self-explanatory emotion. "Manto and I with Lapsa can handle the war plans. The Algonquin will be punished."

"It's not about the Algonquin, Crenna." He looked at Wakami, who held a blank expression, her lips pursed. "It's something else."

"All right." Crenna's voice was casual, but she knew exactly what it was about. She didn't dare glance at Sachim. "Whenever you wish, Father. I shall notify the others."

"At sunrise," he said weakly, closing his eyes until only a thin band of dark brown showed between his eyelids.

"At sunrise," she agreed.

Wakami touched Crenna's shoulder. "He is tired now, Crenna. The wound has weakened him. Let your father sleep."

Crenna nodded and turned away, finding Ta-Tando's eyes still on her. And who had been poisoning *his* mind? The answer was obvious, and Crenna felt anger growing within her as she turned away.

All this trouble over one white man. They should be planning retaliatory measures against the Algonquin, taking care of a hundred necessary matters, but instead, they worried about this single man, this disruptive and annoying, captivating man from the sea.

Crenna stood in the doorway of the longhouse, watching the moon sink into the timbered hills, listening as the wind stirred the spirits in the forest and nudged them to quiet murmuring. She started to stroll toward the river, but halted. There was no point in it. The thoughts could not be left behind. They followed her everywhere, tangling themselves in her hair, clinging to her back, working their way under her very skin. Angrily she turned and went to her bed, knowing that it was useless, that she would never sleep that night.

She lay awake, listening to the breathing in and breathing out of her people, knowing that somewhere in the forest or in the marshes, other Oneida fought and perhaps died. And somewhere across the camp a blue-eyed man slept while others plotted his destruction.

⚙ 6 ⚙

THE COUNCIL MEETING WAS HELD at sunrise. The coming
sun stained the snowfields orange and deep purple. The
wind had risen with the dawn, and it whined across the
long valleys, lifting the fallen snow, pummeling the deep
stands of timber.

Moa-Telah looked up as Crenna entered. He wore a ban-
dage around his head from last night's fighting. Tachtathahuata and Wakami sat together in one corner, Yushta
and Lapsa in the other.

They wasted no time in getting to the point. "The law
has been broken by two foreigners."

"What law?" Crenna asked.

Lapsa apparently had been chosen spokesman; he told
Crenna, "Two foreigners who had agreed never to touch
weapons again entered the compound last night armed."

"The penalty is death," Yushta reminded Crenna, and
she whirled at him in frustration.

"Those two men saved my sister's life and that of my
father, Yushta!"

"They are banned from touching any weapons," Lapsa
said.

"Under *any* circumstances," Wakami put in. "Next time
they may decide to turn their weapons on the Oneida."

"This is foolishness; I won't listen to these accusations,"
Crenna said hotly.

"It is not foolishness, it is the law. A law our tribe has
always lived by."

"The law is wrong this time," Crenna said.

"It is your duty to enforce the law."

"It is my duty to do what is right for the tribe. Killing
two men who have proven themselves to be friends to the
Oneida is not right."

"We have voted—" Yushta began.

"I don't care!" Crenna said, and she stood. Her face
was determined. As headwoman she had the power to veto

128

a council decision, but she had never before gone against the will of the council members. Now she stood there and told them quite coldly, "These men will not be harmed. What have they done to us? There are people among us who do not want the white man and Hawk here. There are those who want them dead. And so they wish to distort the laws to kill them. I will not have it! These men have done nothing."

"Crenna . . ." Yushta began in a coaxing tone, but she didn't listen. She was already out the entranceway, walking across the snow, her stride defiant. Yushta looked to the others. Nothing was said, but pitying glances were heaped upon Yushta. The poor man, a good father and strong warrior. His daughters being driven mad by magic.

Lapsa muttered, "My head hurts," and that signaled the end of the meeting. One by one they rose and departed, Wakami going last. Yushta was left to sit alone in the council hut, wondering what had caused the world to take a sudden deceptive turn toward evil. Crenna, that strong woman, the best of them all, she who cared only for the tribe—Yo had warned that white magic would cloud her thoughts. And now it had come to pass. Yushta rose. He would go to Yo's hut and ask the shaman to make dance magic. Perhaps there was still time to save his daughters from the evil spells of the Moon Man.

Crenna, standing on the snowy hill rise in the deep, cold shadows of the pines, watched as her father labored up the slope toward Yo's hut. She suffered through mingled anger and pity as she watched.

He could not understand—nor could she, really. Crenna knew what they were thinking: for Pawago the law had been strictly enforced, for the white man Crenna had put herself above the law.

How could Yushta believe all of that? Believe that she was jealous of Kala and Pawago, believe that she was in love with this white man?

"In love with Peter?" she said with disgust, and it was at that moment she heard the footsteps on the snow and turned, her heart in her throat, to find him behind her.

He couldn't have heard, she thought anxiously. He couldn't have understood.

There was no indication on his face. He had stopped within two paces of her and he stood watching silently.

The wind lifted the fringes of his buckskin jacket and ran dancing fingers through his pale hair.

"Peter!" Crenna said with a laugh. "I'm surprised to . . ."

And then she went to him, not knowing why, not bothering to ask herself why. She went to him and clung to Peter Van der Veghe, and he was, at that moment, a rock in a turbulent world. A warm, secure resting place. He demanded no explanation; he took her as she was, his hand stroking her hair, resting on the small of her back.

Warm comfort surged up in Crenna's breast, and her blood raced through her veins. She told herself to step back, to examine what she was doing, to deny love, but she could not, and finally she quit trying.

She did not think. They held each other tightly, listening to the concert the wind played in the trees. It must have been cold out there, on the hill rise, but they felt none of it. They were speaking rapidly to each other, not hearing what the other said, not caring.

He was a man, gentle and thoughtful. And he cared for her, giving no thought to what she could do for him, what her skills or powers were, who she was. She was there and he was with her and the wind could blow, Ka-tash-hauht could hurl snow against them, bury them in snow, and it could do nothing to chill her.

His breath was against her ear and on her neck and she felt her legs tremble, felt an answering weakness in Peter. He was magical! His magic, soft and gentle, wreathed her, prickled the skin, set the heart to hammering, blurred the vision with hot tears, started the legs to quaking, drove away all worry and concern, shut out the world. A thousand people could be watching—it did not matter. She had fallen into a deep warm pit. Quite voluntarily she had taken that last small step which plunged her into its depths, and now there was no escaping. She could only fall deeper, into its unending heart.

His lips brushed her throat, and she tilted her head back, feeling the skin burn with pleasure where his mouth had touched her. Her hands went around his neck, her fingers winding themselves in his long yellow hair.

She looked up at him, finding his eyes blue and beautiful, his face pale and astonishingly handsome. The strangeness was gone in that moment, and as her lips met his, he became more than familiar, he became necessary, and his magic, tightening its grip on her heart, overwhelmed all reluctance and she knew that he had won, that there was no way this Oneida woman could defeat this tall, gentle sorcerer from beneath the sea.

She drew away from him, looking into his face, searching it minutely, wondering how this could be happening. He smiled, understanding her. His hand touched her forehead, and he kissed her eyebrow.

"I can't explain it," he said. "I don't know how or why. It's wrong, perhaps, but I feel as if it were destined. I came around the world to find you, and find you I did. It could have been no other way."

"It can't be *this* way . . ." The objections were returning, the logical reluctance, the unsureness. Until he drew her close once more, held her so that she could not breathe, until the lights began twinkling in her head and she was afraid at once that he would not let go, and that he would and she would sag to the earth, unable to stand on her own feet.

"I have to go," she said suddenly. She drew back, looking at the ground, the sky, the long wooded slopes, anywhere but into those patient blue eyes.

"All right." His hand still rested on her shoulder, its pressure so slight, so reassuring. He nodded, and his hand fell away. "I know it must be difficult. Maybe impossible, I don't know. All I do know is that I want you, Crenna, and I'm not suitable for you. But if you—"

"Sh." She silenced him. She could not think about it now. Thinking only brought confusion. She looked at him for one lingering moment more and then turned and walked quickly away, not daring to look back at the tall man who stood alone in the snow, watching her go.

"My sister always leaves her men like that," the voice behind Van der Veghe said, and he spun around to find Kala walking toward him, her hands behind her back, her hips swaying, her lush, overripe mouth curled upward into a challenging smile.

"Hello, Kala," Van der Veghe said. He had seen this woman before, knew who she was, but he had never spoken to her. Neither had Kala shown the slightest interest in him.

Now she laughed as she moved toward him, her eyes

131

teasing, her abundant breasts moving beneath the buckskin dress she wore.

"I couldn't understand why my sister threw Pawago away. Now I can see." She sucked in her lower lip and moved even nearer to Peter. "Crenna is the intelligent one, you know. She saw the possibilities."

Van der Veghe, taken aback by the forwardness of Kala, looked down the wooded hill in the direction Crenna had gone, as if for help.

Kala laughed again, a burbling, lusty laugh. She stepped against Peter Van der Veghe, her breasts against his chest, and taking his hand, she placed it on her thigh, pressing it there as she stood against him, swaying slightly.

He could smell the soap she had used to wash her hair, and the fainter, more earthy scent which was Kala. Her hand had slipped around his waist, and she smiled up at him.

"I won't leave you wanting more, Van der Veghe," she said, and her eyes made a promise of it. Van der Veghe moved back sharply.

"Please go away," he said, and her eyes narrowed.

"All right." Kala moved closer again, however, letting her fingers trace sinuous lines down his shirt front. "I'll leave for now. And when you lie awake on your bed tonight, you'll think of Kala. Then it will be too late."

"Please go," Van der Veghe repeated. Her fingers had hooked themselves in the waistband of his trousers.

This time she drew away sharply, stung by his tone of voice. "You men are crazy! Why do you prefer that dried-up sister of mine! You may be sorry about this, Van der Veghe," she said, a sullen little smile forming on her mouth. "You may be sorry you turned me away."

Then she was gone, winding her way through the trees. Van der Veghe fingered his forehead nervously. That one was trouble. Explosive, demanding, mocking. She said she couldn't understand why men preferred Crenna—no, he thought, she wouldn't be able to understand that at all.

Taking in a deep icy breath of the clear winter air, Van der Veghe started walking down the snow-clogged gully to the south, angling toward camp and away from Kala.

He dipped into a water-cut gorge where gigantic gray boulders topped with snow dominated the rugged slopes, and he leaned up against one of these boulders, thinking.

Only thinking. *Crenna.* He had to have her, he knew that now, but was it in the realm of possibility at all? Would she be willing if it came down to that?

He didn't understand the Oneida political structure well, but well enough to realize that he was lower than the lowest peasant in the streets and she was a princess, aloof, respected, admired.

But she seemed to—she must—really care for him, to want to be with him. She was no feather tossed about in the wind, no changeable, flirting imp like Kala. She wouldn't engage in an idle flirtation—at least, that is what he told himself.

It was all too much, really. He knew nothing of these people. Oh, he could use their language well enough now, perhaps at the level of a twelve-year-old, but there were always nuances which escaped him.

He left off thinking about that and thought of her. So erect, her eyes intelligent and thoughtful, her raven-black hair glinting in the cold sunlight. The hesitant smile, the uncertain hands stretching out to touch him.

He halted suddenly, his heart going cold. How could it be? Where could they go? The Oneida had banished him; with the spring flowers Peter Van der Veghe would leave, and how could she come? How could she?

He closed his eyes tightly, feeling bitterness, a sense of frustration. It seemed, as he had told Crenna, that all of time and the cosmos had conjoined to bring him to this land, to find this woman to love. Now he was here, now he had found her, and it seemed that those same great vague forces had combined to prevent their happiness. How could this work? How could it? Where could they go, what would they do?

"Crenna," he whispered to the empty air. "It must be."

His hand was in his pocket and now Van der Veghe touched an object which was too familiar and yet alien. He drew the gold locket out and opened it, looking into the painted representation of a woman's eyes, a woman who had no reality any longer, whose mouth seemed harsh, who seemed a cool, distant memory.

He looked for a long while at the portrait of Eloisa before he continued on down the slope, clambering over the snowy rocks, through the dead gray willow brush. Somewhere up above, the locket lay lost against the snow.

Winter settled. Long gray days when the Oneida remained in the comfortable longhouses while the wind blustered outside and the lightning-laden skies exploded with elemental joy.

The old men yarned and the women did their handiwork, sewing beads onto the finest buckskin shirts or decorating moccasins with flattened porcupine quills. There was no concern about survival; the larder was full. They had dried venison, fish, squash, corn, and beans enough for a long winter. Neither were they concerned about the Algonquin—war would have to wait for spring.

Kala lounged abed, only half-dressing for days on end. She settled her languorous gaze on Crenna, half-smiling, as if they shared a ribald secret.

"Now, what in the world's gotten into her?" Crenna asked Sachim, who sat cross-legged, making a beautiful necklace of polished shells.

"Kala?" Sachim looked up. "I don't know. It should be easy to guess—her mind runs in only a few channels. You do know just how jealous of you she is, don't you, Crenna?"

"Jealous?" She supposed she did know, vaguely. There were always little barbed remarks, sullen pouts. "What has that to do with anything?"

"It was Pawago she wanted, Crenna. Because you had Pawago, because Pawago was a war chief."

"Yes?"

"Now she does not want Pawago," Sachim said enigmatically.

Crenna shrugged, slipped from their sleeping chamber, and walked through the longhouse, pausing to chat with some of the women, getting briefly involved, involuntarily, in a ball game several of the children were pursuing raucously.

Sachim's meaning struck her suddenly as she stopped to scoop up the sand-filled leather ball which had rolled against her foot. She stood there motionlessly while the children, hands wriggling in impatient supplication, waited for their ball. She handed it to the nearest boy and stood frowning.

Van der Veghe. Sachim could only have meant Van der Veghe. The thought infuriated her. It wasn't beyond Kala to shift her aggressive energies to the white man, but how could she! To want something only because Crenna did, or because she thought Crenna might, was not only devious, it was alarmingly unhealthy.

She turned her head slowly, and from where she stood she could see Kala's pretty, childish face poking out from behind the deerskin curtain of their compartment, watching Crenna, and she knew that Sachim was right.

Damn the woman! Crenna had to fight back an impulse to walk back and slap her face until it was crimson. Kala is a destructive thing, she thought. Not merely childishly predatory, but evil. Had she already been with Peter? The thought was unbearable, and the pain she felt when she thought it caused her to realize how deeply she felt about the white man.

Swallowing her anger, she went to the door of the longhouse and peered out. Great heaped clouds rolled past, darkening the world. Thunder rattled across the valley. The snow fell in heavy waves. Crenna leaned her forehead against the door frame and watched the storm for a long minute, its icy breath in her face.

With sudden resolution Crenna returned to her compartment, unfolded her heavy fur-lined jacket, and slipped into it under Kala's haughty gaze. Crenna could feel pinpoints of fire burning on her cheeks. Without saying a word, she returned to the door and went out into the storm.

It was a furious, malignant thing. The winds tore at her, booming thunder mocked her as she struggled through the heavy drifts. She did not pause to think about what she was doing. She would have decided it was foolish, childish, mad. She fought her way through the storm, lifting her head once as a fierce bridge of lightning arced overhead, brilliantly illuminating the skies briefly, revealing the awesome tangle of clouds, the snowy tide rolling across the earth, washing out the warmth, the reality of her world.

She came suddenly upon the hut, and she burst in without knocking, knowing a knock could not have been heard above the howl of the storm.

He was there, and her heart began to beat rapidly, happily. He was there and well, a tall blond man with kind blue eyes. He had been working at some project, sketching she now saw, on thin, pale bark. Now he stood, his eyes

135

questioning but warm with welcome, and she rushed to him from out of the storm.

The night was cold and angry, but Van der Veghe was warm and gentle. She went to him and placed her arms around his neck, kissing him deeply, his lips searing against her winter-touched mouth.

She kissed him again, felt a trickle of melting snow run down across her cheek and mingle with a warm unashamed tear.

Hawk was there, sitting on the edge of his bunk. His eyes were wide, his jaw had dropped foolishly. He gawked at them stupidly, unbelievingly. Crenna did not care. She had eyes only for the tall, pale man who had bundled her up in his arms, holding her away from the tug of winter winds.

"I love you, Crenna," Van der Veghe said, and his eyes held a desperate sincerity.

"I love you, Peter," she said shyly, softly. She repeated it louder. Hawk recoiled at the loudness, and she laughed. "I love you, Peter!"

Then they fell into a fit of relieved laughter. Peter clung to her, repeating over and over that he loved her, while Hawk watched the two of them as if they were mad—or he was.

"Come with me then," Peter said suddenly, and it sobered Crenna. She drew away a little. He held her hands in his. "Come with me, then, in the spring, Crenna."

In that moment the preposterousness of their situation came back to Crenna. The confusion began again. Go with him? Where? How would they live? Leave the tribe, her position, her family?

He sensed the change in her immediately, and he drew her close again, stroking her snow-damp hair, her back. They stood together silently, the wind shrieking past outside, their hearts thudding together. Peter pulled back with a smile.

"Let me show you something," he said.

He led her to his bed and showed her what he had done. By taking reeds and pounding them flat, weaving them and pounding them again, he had made a very thin barky tissue of them. Paper, he termed it. "Very crude, but I'll get better as I learn." He showed her what he intended to do. By binding the paper together, he had made a book, and each page was illustrated and annotated. "So that the men in Europe—across the sea—can learn about the animals and plants which flourish here."

It was remarkable; again Crenna was awed at his skill in representing familiar animals, fish, insects, and plants. Yet her thoughts would not focus on the sketches he showed her. Her hand trembled, her vision blurred. *Come with me, Crenna. Come with me.*

They sat for hours after that, saying nothing. Crenna rested her head against Van der Veghe's shoulder. His arm was around her and from time to time he gave her an affectionate squeeze. He did not repeat his request, but it rang in her mind. *Come with me.*

Hawk shifted on his bed, watching the doorway constantly, expecting the worst. This time it would be no beating if they were caught, but death. Crenna was sensitive to Hawk's concern, but she was unable to draw herself away from Peter, to rise and leave.

This was right—this was where she belonged, next to this tall, gentle man. Out there . . . all was winter.

Hours later she lay awake in her own bed listening to the constant warfare in the sky. Her feelings would not remain constant. At times Van der Veghe's suggestion seemed far away, dreamlike, impossible, a child's dream; then her emotions would focus his appeal sharply, and she could see no other way life could go on. She had to be with him, to live with him, to be his wife, to spend the winter nights with that man and no other, to suffer childbirth for him, to do for him.

"A maiden's foolish dreams," she told herself out loud.

"And they are the very best kind," Sachim whispered.

Crenna's heart raced. She had spoken aloud without knowing it. She must have her love etched into her face, her eyes must sparkle with it. She must stagger about and gaze dreamily upon people, not hearing them, seeing them. It was no way to behave. It simply wasn't done.

She gave up sleep as an impossibility and rose from her bed again—when had she last slept a night? She walked the longhouse, hearing nothing but the gentle sounds of sleeping. Once an infant cried out loudly, but it was almost instantly silenced, finding its mouth filled with its mother's comfort and nourishment.

They slept, all of them, content, and nourished by Manitou, by the tribe, the family. There was only one among them who ran through the winter night, who stalked the longhouse floor, who tossed and turned in her bed all night, who could not decide what was right, what was necessary, whether she was a woman or a leader; a daughter, a lover, or an aloof overseer.

There was only one who found no comfort in what had always been the warm, completely fulfilling embrace of the tribe, that life-sustaining, perfect unit.

She opened the door a crack and looked out at a storm-tossed winter night. How long she stood there, she did not know. Her thoughts were as tangled as the frothing skies. She did not even hear Sachim come up behind her on soft, gliding feet.

Crenna turned sharply, abruptly aware of the presence of her sister. Sachim, unsmiling, her eyes imperturbable looked past Crenna into the phantasm of the storm.

"What can I do, Sachim?" Crenna asked. Her lips barely parted as she spoke. She did not look at her sister, but studied the whirl and toss of the storm as if it were all-important, as if an answer were sketched there by the random winds of winter. "He wants me with him; what can I do?"

"Only you can answer that, Sister," Sachim replied. "Only you know. Only your heart."

"My heart *knows*, Sachim! But the tribe! How can I even consider leaving the tribe?"

"Crenna, my wiser sister, the tribe has always been. It has survived good leaders and bad. It has endured and will endure until Manitou wishes otherwise. When a headwoman is no more, she is replaced, that is all. None of us is indispensable to the tribe. We are only indispensable to people, to those people who are close to our hearts. And it is better to fail the tribe than to fail the heart, Crenna. The heart, abandoned, grows sour and old and dry. Then there is nothing left to serve the individual or the tribe."

Her words, spoken softly, yet with conviction, ended, and when Crenna turned to face Sachim, she found her sister gone. There was nothing left. Nothing but the howl of the winter wind, the constant snow, and the slow, determined beating of her heart.

"Father?" Yushta looked up from his meal. His eldest daughter stood at his doorway, appearing younger than he usually thought of her. Something else had changed. Her demeanor was not that of an equal; it was that of a daughter. She was not wearing her rank in her eyes; she was only a young, beautiful woman.

"What is it, Crenna?" Yushta put his bowl aside.

"Go on eating, please." She slipped through the curtain and sat opposite her father, watching silently as he ate. His hands were growing old, she noticed. The knuckles appeared prominently; the veins were great blue ridges. At times, in cold weather, his hands curled up like claws with arthritis. The skin sagged beneath Yushta's chin now, and his eyes were not as bright as they once had been.

Still, he was her father, every gesture and word reminding her of other days, of growing up under his wing, of fishing through the ice in winter, of tobagganing under his laughing eyes, of watching with quiet pride as Yushta returned from a hunt with a brace of turkeys or a fat deer.

"What is it, Crenna?" Yushta asked finally. His voice was softer now, perhaps affected by her reflective mood.

"Father . . . I want the white man to stay. I don't want anything to happen to him. I want him to stay and be allowed to live as a free man, as our guest."

"No!" Yushta's voice was sharp and final. The softness had gone from his eyes.

"Yushta. Father, I ask that the white man might stay . . ." the words did not come easily, "so that I might stay. Because if he is driven from the camp, I am going with him."

Yushta's jaw clenched. He opened his mouth, said nothing, closed it again, and shook his head. He looked at Crenna as if he were afraid she had gone mad; and then he looked at her as if he were afraid she had *not*.

"Crenna." That was all he said. He did not argue—his daughter was no impetuous, immature creature of impulses. If she said that, then she meant it. But how could she mean it? Yushta's eyes reflected all the arguments which Crenna had hurled against herself, but nothing was said. Nothing could be said.

"He is disruptive. If he stays, someone will die," Yushta said finally.

"Why? It need not be so." Crenna tried to laugh, but her laugh was a mockery of joy.

"Someone will die. And someone else, and another man, until we are divided, brother against brother—this Yo has said, this I believe."

"Father." Crenna got to her knees. She took Yushta's hand and held it tightly, gazing into his tired old eyes. "For me, for the sake of your daughter, Crenna, please consider it. Please."

But Yushta looked away, watching his skies crumble. There was nothing to consider, nothing to say. His mouth was too dry to speak. He only nodded slowly, meaninglessly.

"Thank you." Crenna put his hand to her cheek, kissed his fingers, and then rose, sweeping out of the room leaving Yushta feeling ancient, withered, devoid of understanding. The arrival of one white man, and the world had turned upside down. Yo was right; the shaman knew. Yet what could he do now? To lose Crenna was to lose a bit of his heart.

He sagged to his blanket and sat for a long while, his hands to his face, asking the guiding spirits to come to him.

The weather cleared briefly in the morning and then the snows came again and the world went dark, closing out all promise. People became shadows, words were muffled wind sounds, life crept past, a ghostly unreality. In the longhouses children shivered and hid their heads beneath their blankets as the elders told tales of the three-legged ghost and of the blood-eyed spirit bear who prowled the winter storm. Specters and dark spirits crept across the camp, keeping to the shadows, moving with the rustle of the wind.

And Ta-Tando stood alone, watching the slow, heavy movements of the rolling clouds, the snow as it fell. He should have been cold, but he was not. The snow which fell stroked him lovingly, gently feeding the rage which churned within him. Ta-Tando waited, fingering the haft of his long knife, his eyes on the foreigners' compound, on that certain hut which appeared intermittently through the gaps in the advancing storm.

The camp was silent, bludgeoned to unconsciousness by

the constant weight of the freezing storm. Only Ta-Tando moved in all of the winter darkness. Only he who held his own warming, demanding fire in his heart. Only he who knew the demon and knew what must be done.

He waited while the hours crept past and the world was silent and dark. He couldn't see his own hand held out before him in the storm, nor the knife in it. He crept down the gully, where the snow was waist-deep, and came out near the riverbank. The river wound its way past secretly, hidden beneath the mounds of engulfing snow.

Ta-Tando waited, panting with the exertion and cold. Taking his bearings, he turned toward the hut, the wind caressing him, tearing at his clothing, urging him on. The door opened silently. The room was dark and the man lay sleeping on his bed.

Ta-Tando stood there in the silence. Snow dripped from his body and splashed against the floor. The wind raged and the spirits whispered in his ear. The whispering built to a roar and he could feel the red curtain lowering, feel the tangled thoughts yield to the slinking red fog which overcame all doubt and built to a white-hot, vengeful certainty. Then Ta-Tando seemed to be no longer in his body. He floated free, a child drifting higher, his mouth open, making no sound as he tried to cry out. The other Ta-Tando, the one below him, the one who held the knife, slipped forward across the floor of the hut and stood over the sleeping foreigner.

Ta-Tando saw the knife lift, poise, and then strike down with the violent fury of a cougar's slashing fangs. *Once.* Once is not enough, he may live. *Twice.* Twice is not enough. The knife sank to the haft, and he had to twist and yank to free it so that he could strike again. *Three times.* That was not enough. Nothing was enough until he was hacked to bloody meat which no magic could make human again, and Ta-Tando brought his knife down again. Again. It was a methodical tool of destruction, a weapon of vengeance which cut down again and again until his arm was weary with the bloody work.

Abruptly the red fog cleared, and he came to himself, finding himself standing over the mutilated foreigner. He was awed, not afraid or ashamed, but awed at his own power.

He crept from the hut, staggering as he went, his breath

coming jerkily, his hand stained with blood. Outside, he ran. Ran as far and as fast as possible through the deep snow. He plunged his arm into the snow, wiping it clean, wiping the jagged blade of his knife clean. He stayed on his knees for a moment, trembling with the exultation. Then he rose, looked around once to assure himself no one had seen him, and ran on home. Reaching the long-house, he was aware of a change in himself, in his soul, which seemed purified. But there was something else. Looking up through the tears, Ta-Tando saw that the skies were clearing again. It was a sign of happiness, and he went into his bedchamber, slipping beneath his blanket, to lie there happily, sleeplessly, until morning.

Crenna awoke to the hand on her shoulder. It was Wak-ami who had awakened her, and she drifted up from her cottony land of dreams slowly, irritably. She had dreamed—dreams she could no longer recall, dreams which fell to nothing as she tried to grasp them now, to save them to be savored again.

"What is it, Wakami?"

"Rise quickly, Crenna. A terrible thing has happened." The old woman's face was weighted down with unhap-piness.

"The Algonquin?" she asked, sitting up, her eyes search-ing Wakami's face.

"Rise up quickly, Crenna," she repeated. She would say no more.

"What is it?" Sachim asked sleepily. Crenna shook her head.

"I don't know." She was already slipping into her dress. Sachim was watching her, and there was a terrible intelli-gence in Sachim's dark eyes.

"What are you looking at, Sachim?" Crenna asked, still irritated at having been shaken from her dreams. Sachim got to her knees and came to Crenna, looking deeply into her sister's eyes. She clenched Crenna's hand.

"I dreamed . . . It was a bad dream. I dreamed . . ."

"Dreamed what, Sachim?" Crenna asked, pulling her jacket on.

"Wait for me, Crenna. I want to come with you!"

Sachim dressed hurriedly as Crenna watched. Then to-gether they went out into the compound yard. Sachim

142

gripped Crenna's hand tightly, saying, "I know what has happened, I know it," in a broken voice.

The sun had not yet risen. There was a golden promise of sunrise to the east. The sky was clear, the morning exceptionally cold. The men and women stood together near the council hut. All of them: Yushta, Yo, half-dressed, Wakami, squeezing herself to keep warm, Moa-Telah, Tachtathahuata, Lapsa, and Pawago. Ta-Tando hung near the group, his eyes bright. He leaned forward wolfishly as Crenna and Sachim walked past him, but he didn't answer their greeting.

"What is it?" Crenna demanded immediately, and then she saw him. Weshta and Te-al-Pantha had Peter Van der Veghe between them. He stood looking around him with uncomprehending eyes, eyes which brightened as they settled on Crenna. She felt like rushing to him, embracing him, but this was not the time and place. Yushta was grave, Pawago's eyes glazed by one of his dark moods.

Ta-Tando had come rushing up suddenly. He leaped into the air, made an odd sound, and then backed away a few feet, muttering to himself. Crenna heard him say something about "magic," but she paid no attention.

"What is it?" she asked briskly.

"Murder." It was Pawago who answered. His chest was puffed out proudly "And we have the killer."

"Crenna . . ." Peter Van der Veghe began. Pawago turned and without a warning kicked Peter in the kneecap. Van der Veghe went down into the snow. Ta-Tando let out a pleased murmur.

"What is this!" Crenna was angry now. She walked to Pawago, ordering him brittily, "Stay away from this man! What is this? Someone tell me."

She spread her arms and turned in a circle, looking from face to face. No one would speak, and then they all spoke at once.

"A man was murdered. The foreigner Hawk," Wakami told her.

"The white man must have done it," Moa-Telah said.

"Who else, Crenna?" Yo asked. He stepped nearer to her.

"They shared the hut."

Crenna held up her hands, her head buzzing. Van der

143

Veghe was struggling to rise. No one helped him. "What is this? Are you accusing this man of murder?"

"It *was* murder!" Pawago's dark face appeared nearly in front of Crenna's. His lips were curled back. His eyes were darkly triumphant.

"You are not a council member, Pawago. Let someone speak for the council." Her voice shook as she fought for control. Control over the anger, fear, and confusion which mingled in her mind. "Yushta! Father?"

"The Leni-Lenape Hawk was found dead in his hut, Crenna. He had been stabbed many times. The white man was not there. It is obvious what has happened."

"Obvious!" Crenna laughed in disbelief. She looked at Van der Veghe with deep compassion, and he managed a smile for her.

"It's all right, Crenna. They want to kill me—" Peter began. Pawago reached out a hand, grabbed Van der Veghe's hair, and yanked him forward, throwing him to the ground.

"Te-al-Pantha!" Crenna said, leveling her finger at Pawago. "If this man harms the prisoner again, I want you to kill him."

"Crenna . . ." Te-al-Pantha laughed uneasily.

"Did you hear me, Te-al-Pantha?"

"Yes, Headwoman Crenna," Te-al-Pantha said with a sidelong glance at Pawago, who stood, arms akimbo, his eyes hooded.

"There will be death," Yo said, his eyes turned down. "Death where the white man goes."

"Be still, Yo!" Crenna said. The old shaman, shaken by the tone of her voice, looked up, his face reflecting astonishment.

"Crenna!" Yushta shouted. "How can you speak to Yo like that?"

"Is that what we are here for? Yushta, Father. Wakami, Lapsa. Why are we here?" No one answered, so she supplied her own answer. "To punish the murderer of Hawk, the Leni-Lenape."

Pawago smiled thinly. Peter, still on his knees, cocked his head as if he had not heard her properly.

She went on. "Who is the killer? Who saw this man do it? Let him now speak."

No one came forward. "No one saw it, Crenna," Wak-

144

ami told her, "but they share a hut. None of us would kill the foreigner. Why would it be done?"

"I don't know. Peter," she said, turning her attention to Van der Veghe. "What happened?"

"I have no idea. Crenna, I didn't do it," he said emphatically.

"I know it, Peter."

"*She* is the inquisitor?" Pawago exploded. "She loves this thing!" His crooked finger pointed at Van der Veghe.

"Pawago," Crenna said tensely. "Must I remind you again that you are no longer a chief. You have no right to offer your opinions. Be quiet or I shall have you taken away."

Ta-Tando had crept closer now, and he stood behind Crenna as she turned back toward Van der Veghe. His fists were clenched tightly.

"What do you know about this, Peter?"

"Practically nothing. Yesterday morning was clear, as you know. I went up into the forest to sketch. Before I could return to camp, it had started to snow. I know nothing about what happened to Hawk—I was not there last night. But I don't think it was Hawk they meant to kill."

"Why not?"

"Hawk was in my bed. He had given it to me. His bed was on the windward side, and the hut is not tight. The cold comes through the walls. Last night it was very cold and I wasn't there, so Hawk slept in my bed. That is where they found him murdered. The killer was after me."

"Who knows you were in the woods?" Lapsa demanded. "How did you survive the night? Who saw you? How do we know you were not in your hut?" His thin arm moved jerkily as he asked these questions.

Van der Veghe's response was calm. "I was with another man. An Oneida warrior. The storm came in heavily. Still, I would have tried to return to the camp, but the warrior convinced me to stay with him. He had built a shelter of pine boughs. We sat up smoking and talking most of the night."

"What warrior!" Pawago shouted, unable to restrain himself. "What lie is this?"

"Show us the man," Yushta said. He looked around him in mockery, and abruptly the mockery fell from his face.

Manto had come forward, and Crenna's brother said, "I

was the man, Father. The white man was with me last night. It is as he says." Manto looked from Crenna to Van der Veghe expressionlessly. Then he turned and walked away through the snow without saying another word. He did not have to defend what he had said. It was Manto, and no one would challenge his honesty or his strength.

Then one by one the others left, Ta-Tando slinking away silently, Pawago striding off angrily, Yushta wearing a mask of stone. They were gone, the vultures who had gathered to feast on Van der Veghe, and Crenna knew in that moment that it was ended. It could never be the same again. They had tried to kill Van der Veghe; failing that, they had tried to execute him for the murder.

It was over, and she felt no sadness just then, only a moment of bitter resolution, and then Van der Veghe was beside her, his arm around her shoulder as they stood together, watching the bright sun coast through the empty sky.

"Have you thought about where you will go when you leave, Peter? Have you thought of what you might do?"

"Yes, I have an idea now," he answered.

"Have you thought of what I might do?" She looked up at him, her eyes shining.

"You . . . Crenna!" He stared at her, fighting back the raw emotion which welled up in his throat. He was laughing and crying at once.

"I shall go," she said. She let her gaze sweep across the familiar hills, run over the village where the cooking fires now curled smoke into the pale sky. Abruptly her eyes returned to his, and she nodded, smiling ever so faintly. "I shall go wherever you go."

She had vacillated, not able to come to a decision. To leave all that was familiar was not easy. But they had forced a decision upon her; they had made it for her this morning. The decision, once made, left no lingering doubts. She decided, and she knew it was right, that there could be no other way, that happiness lay only with this man, that the rest, important as it was, would mean nothing if she did not have Peter Van der Veghe.

She would go. It was done.

7

THEY WALKED THE LONG, PEACEFUL valleys eastward. Patches of snow still lay in the shade cast by the forests of elm and ash. The skies were clear, and the earth, just stirring beneath the patient, warm prodding of the springtime sun, was reawakening slowly. Purple lilac already dotted the young grass with color, and rhododendron flourished in the hollows. Here and there they found violets beginning to flower, and just-budding wild roses.

For day upon day the geese and ducks winged northward overhead, casting swift shadows against the meadow grass. Bear with fuzzy new cubs roamed the woods, startling the bluebirds which flocked there.

They walked the long valleys, this tall yellow-haired man and his Oneida wife, and it seemed they were alone in the world. They drank sweet, icy water from the creeks and breathed in the clean cold air. When the midday sun made them drowsy they napped together in the cool shade, their legs intertwined, their arms wound around each other, their breathing soft and untroubled.

"We are alone," Van der Veghe said, sitting up to chew on a tender blade of grass. "Can we really do this, Crenna?"

"The first people did it," she answered. She rubbed his neck and shoulders, bending forward once to kiss his back between the shoulder blades. "I have always lived here, Van der Veghe."

"But there was always the tribe. The tribe had great hunters, carpenters, fishermen . . . I am none of those."

"But you will be, because you have to be now. I will help you, Peter. This is no time to lose confidence."

"I haven't, really, it's just that I want to do right, do what is right for you, Crenna."

"Then love me." She laughed and lay back against the grass, her raven hair spread against the deep green, her eyes sparkling, her lips parting slightly in anticipation.

She lay there on the sun-dappled grass looking up at her husband, and he came to her, lying beside her, his lips meeting hers, moving with deftness and then with hunger as his arms encircled her. Crenna laughed softly, squeezing him will all her might for one minute, looking into those blue eyes.

He rolled aside, his hand lingering on her shoulder, and she slipped from her dress, Van der Veghe's appreciative eyes on her. She spread her dress on the grass and lay back, her forearm over her eyes to shield them from the glitter of sunlight through the elms.

He stood, and the sun was blocked out. Crenna watched as he undressed, liking the form of the man, the definition of his long muscles beneath the pale skin. Then he was with her again, and their bodies met, the sensation-filled, quiet greeting of flesh to flesh.

His hands were confident, eager. His kisses traced patterns across her throat and breasts, and Crenna laughed with the joy of love. It had always been that way between them. There was only a brief, nervous tension, the anticipation of nerve endings crying out for fulfillment; but that passed quickly, and their loving became a joyous, merry undertaking.

Her hands were pressed against his muscular thighs, her abdomen was pressed to his, their bodies coming together in a natural, easy configuration. Their legs tangled together and their lips met. Crenna laughed deep in her throat and Van der Veghe smiled in return, nuzzling her dark hair, tracing the whorl of her ear with his lips, whispering unintelligible endearments.

The sun was dazzling through the foliage overhead, the day filled with a thousand sparkling diamonds. He was warmth and goodness, sensation and happiness, and he lay pressed against her, his hands following the tapered line of her thigh, running across the swell of her hips in tender amazement. His eyes, deep with passion, winked with the flickering sunlight, and Crenna's body responded with a surge of joy.

There was no wild rush toward fulfillment, no frantic pursuit of completion; it was enjoyed moment by moment, a touch, a beginning, a lingering kiss, a slow inhaling, a hesitation. Each moment for the moment, knowing that fulfillment was inevitable, inevitably sweet and rewarding, and when it did come, Crenna flushed with excitement, feeling his man-strength, the searching of his mouth, the clenching of his hands as they clung together, the day spinning past, their nostrils filled with the sweet scent of spring grass, their eyes love-dazzled, their bodies only extensions of their souls as their spirits met, flared brightly, intertwined, and became one pulsing, sparkling entity.

There was no moment when the lovemaking was over, when they would step back and say, "We are finished." There was only the long flow of the day, the constant touch of flesh against eager flesh, the pulsing and swaying together, soft murmuring, needful clasping, quiet urging, and gentle release.

"We are alone, Crenna," Peter said, lifting himself on one elbow, letting his fingers laze on her breasts. "I was worried about that—the two of us alone in the wilderness." He leaned forward, stroking her hair as he whispered into her ear, "But now I know that it is enough. There are the two of us, and we are enough."

They entered the Mohawk camp at sundown. Their coming was no surprise. They had seen Mohawk runners in the forests all afternoon as they walked northward and eastward toward the village.

Wechakapi himself met them at the gateway to the Mohawk camp. Wechakapi was old and grizzled. Three fingers were missing from his right hand; his face was scarred with the marks of mourning and of warfare.

Wechakapi was a legend among the Mohawk. Although the Mohawk, like the other Iroquois, had their head-women, it was Wechakapi who dominated their tribal councils through sheer physical strength and personality. He was a war leader, a politician, and some said a hater of women since his young bride had run away with a trusted warrior—Crenna did not know if it was true. She did know that Wechakapi hated white men. He had already killed many, his land bordering the river which seemed to spawn the pale Moon Men.

"Say nothing at all," Crenna cautioned Peter. It was unnecessary; he could not speak the language, and had no intention of trying to manage the hatchet-faced war chief.

Wechakapi had a blanket around his shoulders and a scowl on his dark, leathery face. He carried a pipe in one hand, a hatchet in the other, his arms crossed.

"Crenna, daughter of my friend Yushta, headwoman of the Oneida, our Iroquois brothers, I greet you." The dark eyes of the old one clawed at Van der Veghe's. There was a sizeable gathering near the gate. A hundred or more Mohawk of all ages, both sexes, watched with incomprehension, fear, and loathing as the white man shifted uncomfortably.

"What brings you to our land, Headwoman Crenna?"

That was an abrupt plunge into things for an Indian, and Crenna knew that the Mohawk was deeply displeased to see Peter Van der Veghe.

"I come hoping to share your hospitality, to bring you the greetings of my father and my people, and to request a gift of your renowned kindness."

"Come in," Wechakapi said after a long pause. "Come into my village, Headwoman Crenna. Bring your things with you if you prefer." That was a reference to Van der Veghe and not to the bundles they carried.

Wechakapi was generous with his food. He sat watching Crenna eat—Van der Veghe was not offered food; one doesn't feed dogs in the lodge—and the Mohawk smoked.

"You are the most generous of men," Crenna said when she was finished.

"There is more."

"My poor Oneida stomach is not used to such quantities of food. The Mohawk indeed prosper under your leadership, Wechakapi."

"We do prosper," he said, accepting the compliment as if it were said in all sincerity and not as a matter of form. He asked then about Yushta, about Lapsa and Manto. He asked if anyone had seen Crenna's mother's spirit lately, asked if Yo had seen the firefall in the night sky, and what the Oneida shaman thought.

Finally the purpose of Crenna's visit was approached again. "I am surprised to find you alone in the Mohawk land, Sister Crenna. Is there a purpose for this honor you do us?"

"Yes, Wechakapi," she replied. "I wish to dwell in your land."

Wechakapi's eyes narrowed; his white eyebrows drew together inquisitively. He gestured with a gnarled hand. "Here? But why, Crenna? I cannot understand this."

"I wish to live here with my husband."

150

"You married!" His mouth opened in a toothless smile. Then his eyes darkened. His gaze shifted to Van der Veghe, who sat silently in the shadows. The smile dropped from his lips. "You wish to live in the Mohawk village?" he asked dryly.

"No, Wechakapi. Not here." Crenna reached into her bag and removed three beautiful wampum belts. She laid them across her lap, smoothing them. "What I would like to do, with your indulgence, is to live on the site where the white men built their stockade. The stockade which your people burned when the whites were driven away. I know you cannot sell tribal land, even to another Iroquois; I do not ask that. Simply to be able to live upon that land with your blessing. In trade for that right, I offer you wampum and my friendship."

Wechakapi rubbed his forehead roughly, as if it itched. "I cannot comprehend this. Is *that* your husband?" He nodded at Peter.

"Yes."

Wechakapi's frown deepened. "And you wish to live by the river? For what purpose?"

"To fish, to hunt, to trade, to raise children."

"Are you sure you are not deceived, Crenna?" the old chief asked.

"What do you mean?"

"Are you sure this land is not being taken for the coming of white warriors?"

"It is not," she said definitely. "My husband is not a warrior, he had no friends among the warriors, he does not do their bidding."

"So he says. I think I have seen this man—was he there before, at the stockade?"

"He was there," Crenna admitted.

"As a soldier!" Wechakapi slapped his thighs.

"No. He is a craftsman. Peter, let me see your notebook, please."

Van der Veghe removed it from his bag and handed it silently to Crenna. She passed it to Wechakapi, who opened the book, astonished at the images of animals and plants there. He turned the pages, wagging his head. "This is his work?"

"Yes."

"Then he is a sorcerer," Wechakapi said with finality, handing the notebook back.

Crenna did not argue with Wechakapi. A sorcerer he could understand. That would explain why a headwoman would marry such a creature. It was excusable, whereas living with a white warrior would not have been.

"I do not like having this man here, Crenna," he said honestly. "But I give my word you shall not be harmed; you may live upon the river. I do this for Yushta and for you, Crenna, not for the wampum," he said, although he stretched out his hand and took the wampum even as he spoke. "I give you the land—until there is trouble."

"There will be no trouble."

"No. There will be no trouble. If there is trouble, Crenna, it is ended, you must go."

"We will leave when you say we must, Wechakapi."

"I do not understand this," he muttered as if to himself. Then he sighed, and smiling, told her, "I shall have one of the three belts rewoven into a deed of peace. You shall take it with you to the river, and if anyone asks why you are on Mohawk land, you shall have the wampum treaty to show them."

"You are kind, Wechakapi," Crenna said. Then she rose and took the Mohawk's hand briefly. Peter waited until Crenna gestured to him, and then he stood, shouldering the packs. Wechakapi continued to stare at him, still not comprehending how such a thing had happened. Perhaps it was as his own shaman had told him—when the white man came, the world would turn upside down and strange creatures would roam the land; women would go mad and strong men would shrink away from their pale faces. Wechakapi looked into the face of Van der Veghe by torchlight. That, at least was laughable. It would do no harm to give the man a lesson, however.

"Come with me," Wechakapi said, gripping the sleeve of Van der Veghe's shirt. The language was near enough to that spoken by the Oneida that Peter understood it. If that were not enough, the insistent tugging was.

Leaving the bundles near the entranceway to the council lodge, Van der Veghe crossed the yard with Wechakapi, Crenna following. It was already dark outside; the moon had not yet risen, and they nearly bumped into the building before seeing it.

"In here," Wechakapi said, and Peter, ducking, followed him into a mud-and-timber hut unlike any he had seen in the lands of the Iroquois.

Wechakapi let go of his sleeve, leaving Peter alone in the darkness. Then flint struck flint and the sparks ignited a torch of shredded birch bark and resin. The torch flared up and the wavering shadows twisted across the walls of the hut. Peter recoiled.

Wechakapi chuckled. "Good, you do not like, huh, sorcerer?"

No, Van der Veghe did not like it. Before him were bits of armor, including one entire breastplate. Two helmets, one badly crushed, hung on the wall. They were all of Dutch manufacture. That was hardly the worst of it.

In tiny alcoves cut into the wall of the hut, ivory gleamed in the flickering firelight—the skulls of dead men, each in its own cubbyhole, blank eyes staring out at Van der Veghe, bared teeth grinning evilly. In one larger alcove, leg and arm bones were stacked like tinder.

"All white bones, sorcerer," Wechakapi whispered, leaning close to Van der Veghe. Then the war chief of the Mohawk laughed, and Peter felt Crenna's hand slip beneath his arm and squeeze him.

"What is the purpose of this, Wechakapi?" she asked.

"Purpose? There is no purpose," Wechakapi said as the torch guttered and went out, leaving them in the acrid darkness. "I only thought the white man might like to visit his friends' spirits. We honor the bones of our enemies, you see. That is the way of the Mohawk."

There was another short laugh, and then Peter felt the old chief move past him toward the door. Wechakapi paused. "Crenna, if you do not wish to wait, I will have the wampum treaty sent to you. Perhaps you are in a hurry to leave the Mohawk camp and reach your new home."

And then he was gone, his silhouette briefly blacking out the glittering stars visible through the doorway of the medicine hut.

Peter let out the breath he had been holding and put his arms around Crenna. "I think perhaps we had better not wait for that wampum belt."

"Wechakapi *might* prefer us to go," she answered wryly. "But his attitude doesn't matter, does it? He gave us what we asked for. We shall have our land and we shall be left alone. We have each other. Come, husband, let's go *home*."

It was at sunrise that they reached the Hudson. The river was a tarnished mirror set between dark ranks of weary pines. Haze drifted through the treetops, and the sun was reddening the tips of the tallest trees.

Albany lay a heap of ashes and burned timbers, squat and useless, primitive and empty. The old stockade had not a timber standing. Wechakapi's people had taken it apart piece by piece.

"A dismal sight," Peter said, but even as he said that, he did not feel dismal. He was eager, elated, happy. The burned timbers were a defeat for the Dutch; but for Van der Veghe and Crenna they marked a victory, a promise, a beginning.

"Home," she said, sharing his thoughts. Crenna placed her head against his shoulder, and her dark eyes took in the bluffs, the forest, the far striving river. She pressed his hand in hers and said brightly, "Are we going to stand dreaming all day?"

They were at work an hour later. They had no tools, but Crenna showed Van der Veghe how her people felled trees and sectioned them, cutting into the bark and burning the logs through. They had done little by nightfall. The work was slow and wearying. Neither of them felt tired, neither felt as if it were labor. They were building a home.

"We won't need a stockade," Van der Veghe said. "That'll be a help."

"No, and we shouldn't build one. We haven't come to fight anyone—why build fortifications and make them doubt our motives?"

Van der Veghe agreed. He lay back against a small cedar, his eyes on the sundown sky. Crenna's head was against his chest. The sunset flushed Van der Veghe's skin, burnished it to a soft gold. His hand rested on her breast, and she held it there, feeling a quick response growing.

"I still wasn't sure," Crenna admitted. "Not sure until we reached this spot, until we began to build."

"A slow beginning," Van der Veghe laughed. There were four logs in place for the foundation.

"It was only one day; there will be many, my husband," she said, turning to throw her arm across his chest. The evening was warm. Frogs grumped in the reeds along the river. A nighthawk darted and swooped low across the water, pursuing insects.

"What more could there be?" Van der Veghe said softly. His eyes were on the distances.

"What more?" Crenna responded. She could think of nothing. Her man, her home, fair weather, a beautiful land. There was nothing else. "You have made me happy, my husband."

"Me!" Van der Veghe laughed, squeezing her tightly as the sky fell to a deep crimson and pale orange. "You have given me everything, Crenna. I was barely alive and didn't know it. I was a slave to my mind, to my ambitions. I would have been dead before I had learned to live."

"And what about Eloisa?" Crenna asked teasingly. "Didn't she make you feel alive, Peter?"

"Eloisa? Eloisa? I've heard the name somewhere, in a dream, or perhaps I was told about her by another man. A man who lived long ago and far away."

Crenna smiled contentedly and curled up in his arms. A moment's melancholy touched her as her own thoughts sped away to the tribe, to family and friends. In thought she tested the memory, like dipping a toe into icy water, and she found it insubstantial, unreal compared to the strong warmth of the man beside her. This new adventure had nearly erased her old longings, her old concerns, and she knew that as the days passed, as the nights drifted past in quiet joy, there would be little left of the old way. It brought her a brief pang of regretfulness, a sense of loss, and a tear stood in her eye.

Van der Veghe noticed it and asked, "Is it all right? Will it be all right, Crenna?"

"You have made me happy, my husband. It will be all right."

In the morning Crenna fished for their breakfast, astonishing Van der Veghe with the ease with which she hooked four fine fish. She broiled them over a low fire, and they ate, planning the next steps of their building, their home.

"Later I'll build a second structure," Van der Veghe said. "For the trading post."

Crenna nodded. They had discussed it and agreed it was a good plan for earning a living. The white men would come—after talking with Van der Veghe, she understood that now. They would come into this land and they would bring goods to trade. Van der Veghe would make his living in that way; he was no hunter.

"Wechakapi will not like seeing more whites come," she told him.

"No, he won't like it." Peter shook his head in agreement, "but he will have to get used to it. Believe me, Crenna, they will come, and he shall either have to make war on all of them or accept it. We told Wechakapi we would trade here. He is no fool, he must have realized that I meant with the whites too if they came."

"I just don't want there to be trouble," Crenna said, and she knew there could always be trouble where Wechakapi was involved.

"He wouldn't violate his treaty, would he?" Van der Veghe asked, propping his head up with one arm.

"No, he would not do that."

"And neither shall we. If there is trouble, it will be with Wechakapi and others. We shall remain neutral."

"Even if it involves your own people, Peter?"

"I have no people but you, Crenna," he said, and he was serious. His finger lifted her chin, and he kissed her. His lips, now familiar, so stirring, met hers, and her vague uncertainties faded away to blend with the falling purple dusk. The world was a quiet place, a warm place, and nothing could harm them ever.

Day by day the house went up. Van der Veghe was not a skilled craftsman, but his abilities grew by leaps and bounds with practice. The house, already waist-high, would be completed before autumn.

Crenna, who knew how to snare game and how to fish, spent much of her time stocking the larder. She had built a drying rack, and there fish hung by the dozens. Sometimes Van der Veghe went with her, learning to find game trails, to creep close to dozing fish, to be silent in the woods, but he was impatient to have the house done, and most often Crenna hunted alone.

"When the house is done, I will do the hunting," Van der Veghe promised.

Crenna looked into those sober blue eyes and asked impishly, "Will you have us starve this winter?"

"I'll learn enough," Van der Veghe promised. "It's a

warrior's job, isn't it? Man's work to hunt? I don't want to disappoint you; I want to do whatever I should."

"And you are, Peter. You are making me happy. In time, you will learn. For now, let's divide our duties sensibly. I can hunt better than you. The logs are too heavy for me."

"Yes," he said, rubbing his chin thoughtfully, "I suppose that's so. I only want to be a proper Indian husband."

"Just be Van der Veghe; I ask for no more."

He had begun on the roof, and it was a complicated job. Still, his new confidence guided him surely as he worked. Crenna, wandering toward the river to check her fish traps, heard him suddenly call out. "Look at this, Crenna! What is it? It's a handsome beast."

She turned back toward the house, wondering what Van der Veghe had found. He could not suppress his naturalist's curiosity and was forever asking her what this animal or that insect was, inquiring into its habits.

Crenna, smiling fondly, strode toward the house.

"Crenna! What is this? Handsome devil. Look at that coat. Beautifully striped. And not shy at all, are you?"

Crenna had a sudden unhappy premonition. She broke into a run, lifting her buckskin skirt high, her long legs rushing her toward the house.

Too late. She burst through the open doorway just as Van der Veghe made a grab for the skunk. She was too late to call out as the skunk lifted its tail, poised itself in the deliberate manner of its clan, and let loose a noxious spray.

"God!" Van der Veghe fell back, pawing at his eyes and nose. "What in the devil's name!" He spun away, his eyes watering, gasping. The skunk waddled off, unperturbed.

"Peter!" Crenna started forward and then collapsed, laughing. She went to the ground, and she sat there, the vapor drifting around her, Van der Veghe coughing and wiping at his eyes.

"This is funny?" he asked, and then he started laughing too. "This is . . . funny?" He staggered toward her, and picking her up, he carried her from the house into the fresh air. "What was that?"

"A skunk, as any five-year-old Iroquois could have told you."

Van der Veghe could only wish that he had had a five-year-old Iroquois with him. He looked at Crenna and announced, "You stink, beautiful wife. That is"—he scratched his head—"I think you must. I can't smell you above myself. And I know I stink."

His eyes were still watering, his nose burning. They hurried to the river and stripped off their clothes. Plunging in, they swam out fifty feet, where Crenna, treading water, laughed as Van der Veghe tried to rub the smell off his skin.

"It won't work, Peter."

"Damnable little beasts, aren't they?"

She laughed again, and he swam menacingly toward her, wrapping his arms around her. He kissed her, and they temporarily forgot about swimming, sinking slowly under the water, to rise gasping moments later. Crenna wiped back her hair and turned to swim toward the shore, feeling Van der Veghe's pursuing hand slip over her buttocks. She was an otter in the water and knew it, and so she slowed and Van der Veghe caught her nearer the shore, where they could stand, their bodies pressed together, his hands on her hips, drawing her against him. She clung to his shoulders, her lips parting to meet his. The river was cool, but she did not feel it. Her blood raced warmly through her veins.

He was hard, insistent against her. Her hands slid down across his abdomen, her eyes sparkling. "You smell so bad, Peter," she said.

"Yes." He wasn't thinking about that, and neither was she. He kissed her neck, her ears, each eyelid, responding to the touch of her hands.

"I haven't checked my fish traps yet."

"No." He clung to her, his hands sketching circles on her sleek back, his mouth tasting hers.

"And there is the house, Peter Van der Veghe."

"It stinks in the house," he reminded her.

His hands rested against her thighs, his mouth worked along her shoulders to her breasts, and she shivered and it was not with the cold. She quit her teasing. Her man was too serious, and so, suddenly, was she.

He lifted her in his arms and walked from the river, the water raining off their naked bodies. He carried her into the trees, where the falling sun had warmed a patch of grass. Gently he placed her down and gently he came to her, and the day wasted away in a flood of kisses, soft touches, urgent pleadings, the brush of flesh against flesh, fragmented, drowsy conversation, honeyed, luxuriant completion.

"I love you, Peter," she said. He had fallen asleep, his head against her breasts.

He stirred and muttered, "I'll work tomorrow. I promise I'll work tomorrow."

"You do smell bad," she told him. Her fingertips explored his body, the hard thighs, the slim hips, the lean shoulders taut with new muscle.

"Yes." His voice was muffled. His lips were against her breast. He was exhausted, and not only with the lovemaking. She realized that he had been working hard, probably harder than he had in his entire life. He had been a scholar, something he had tried to explain to her—it seemed vague still, but it had something to do with making books and reading other men's books. Hardly a sort of work to harden hands, to broaden shoulders, to deepen a man's chest.

Yet he was working now, trying as hard as he knew how. He was unfamiliar with carpentry, with the ways of this land, with work, and yet he carried on, all for the sake of her love, and it could only make her love him more.

Now that she thought of it, she realized that he was exhausted at night. He needed more afternoons like this, when there was nothing to be done but to doze in the warm sun, to pluck the blades of grass, and to speak softly of things which didn't matter; after all, the house would be done soon enough, long before winter had settled in.

The house was finished eventually. It was far from beautiful to look at, but to Crenna and Van der Veghe it was a monument to love, a promise of a rich future. They stood together at sunset, simply staring at the house, admiring the rough-barked logs, the uneven roof, as if it were an architectural landmark.

"And that," Van der Veghe said, "is that." There was a touch of wistfulness to his voice, and Crenna wondered if he was thinking of the permanence the house represented.

Perhaps he was, but he shook the mood aside. He turned, hoisted her, and spun her laughing in a circle.

"Now for the rest of it. The trading post, the tanning racks, the corncrib, the garden!"

It was too late for a garden, but that meant nothing to Van der Veghe's eagerly projecting mind. Thunder boomed once in the distance. A low bank of clouds had been hanging near the horizon throughout the day.

"Oh, no! Something must be done about that," Crenna said, and Van der Veghe, hands on hips, watched as she went into the house and returned with a handful of tobacco. Frowning, he studied her as she placed the tobacco down and struck fire to it.

"It is Hinu growling at us," Crenna said. "The thunder god must be placated, Van der Veghe!" He was smiling, and she became angry. "He must be given tobacco when he approaches, rumbling with anger."

Van der Veghe tried to wipe the smile from his lips. He watched as Crenna industriously fanned the flames, as tobacco smoke rose into the skies. He turned and looked to the north, toward the clouds, perspiration cooling on his body.

After a time he felt Crenna's arm slip under his, and he held her. Silently they turned to go into the house and eat. There was nothing inside the house. Van der Veghe intended eventually to make some furniture, but that was a secondary consideration. For now there was nothing but a packed-earth floor, the raw log walls chinked with river mud, and a wealth of love.

"You never speak of your old land," Crenna told him as they lay beneath the furs that night. Her breath was soft against his chest. His hand ran lightly over her arm and shoulder.

"It seems I can't remember it well," he replied.

"But you can," Crenna said, smiling. She lifted herself on an elbow to look into Van der Veghe's face. "Don't you miss it, any of it?"

"I suppose so."

"What is it like?" she prodded.

"Like this. People and the land. Living, growing, dying."

"Tonight you are philosophical."

Van der Veghe laughed. For one thing, the Iroquois equivalent of "philosophical" was, roughly, "gazing at the moon," an equivalent he found revealing.

"Philosophical," he agreed. "I used to wish to be a philosopher, Crenna. Yes, in Europe there are men who can earn their living by gazing at the moon! But I found I was spending most of my time thinking about life and very little living it."

"When was that?" she asked.

"Long ago."

"Where?"

"You're curious tonight," he said, stroking her hair, thumbing an errant strand of it back from her forehead. "What's come over you?"

"I only want to know you."

"You know all that is important. The rest was trappings, posturing, all costume and pretense."

"I don't believe you."

"Do. It's true."

"Then it was an unhappy way to live, Peter. I am glad you came away from it."

"So am I." He fell silent, meditative. "Now I am alive, only now. With you. With the sun burning my skin, with my hands raw and callused, with you to bring me my meals and to lie down with me in the night. Nothing else matters."

"But sometimes you moon-gaze."

He didn't answer for a minute. "Sometimes."

"And then what do you think of?"

"You are persistent tonight, aren't you, Crenna?"

She kissed him on the lips. Once, twice, three times, each kiss a little longer. "What did you think of? Of Eloisa?"

"No!" He laughed out loud. "Only with relief—I think of the formal dinners I'm missing out on, of the pompous professors at the university doing their best to outshine each other with their pointless papers. I think of taxes and . . ."

"Of what?"

"Taxes." It took a long while to explain that, and still Crenna could not understand taxes.

"But you didn't tell me what you thought of when you moon-gazed," she said.

He thought of his philosophy and wondered what he had thought about exactly. The names of scholars he had read raced through his mind—all their names meaningless

161

to Crenna; in this place, in this time, having no meaning at all, perhaps. "I can't explain it," he said finally. "There are things in Europe which you would not believe or understand."

"Oh?" Her eyes closed halfway.

"I mean, Crenna, you would have to have been raised in that culture to understand them . . . well, taxes for instance. Philosophy. Certain things are difficult to understand for an outsider, impossible perhaps."

"But still they are important?" she asked with a touch of slyness.

"Yes," Van der Veghe answered. "Still they are important."

"Like my burning tobacco for Hinu," she said.

Van der Veghe laughed out loud. "Yes!" he said, gripping her shoulders and pinning her to the bed, where he smothered her with kisses. "Like burning tobacco to Hinu. You took me all the way around that just to make the point? I laughed; I'm sorry. I'll never laugh again, even if I do not understand, even if what you do seems bizarre, outlandish! Never. What a mind you have, woman," Van der Veghe said. "What lips . . ."

Winter settled in quietly, and they were warm in the house at Albany. The wampum-belt treaty hung prominently on the wall of their house, a visible symbol of the peace they dwelt in.

There were long days when they could not go out of the house at all, when Hinu the thunder god raged around the house. And those were the best of days. The fire burned brightly and they lay beneath their furs, sharing the timelessness of love.

Other days were brilliant and clear, and together they wandered the snowy hills, gathering firewood or simply walking in silence over the glistening land, the breath steaming from their lips, Van der Veghe's cheeks flushed apple red with the cold.

"How could we be happier?" he yelled once. He stood on a hill rise, overlooking the forest beyond, the empty, snowbound land, and he shouted, his arms wide, "I could not be happier! I have Crenna and I love her! I am as happy as a man can be."

Crenna doubled up with laughter, watching as Van der Veghe began an impromptu dance in the snow, leaping

162

and twisting, shouting at the top of his lungs. He gathered her up in his arms and swung her around, forcing her to join in his madly exultant jig, until, exhausted, they both fell to the snow and lay there panting.

Crenna laughed until her side hurt, until her stomach ached. Van der Veghe held her hand, and they lay on their backs in the snow, watching the cold, crystal-blue sky.

"Oh," she said, holding her belly.

Van der Veghe glanced at her, saw she was wincing slightly, and sat up, dusting the snow from his shoulders and hair. "Are you all right?"

"Yes," she answered, but she still held her stomach.

"What is it, then?"

"Nothing." She looked into his concerned blue eyes. "Are you really happy, Peter? Can nothing make you happier?" There was a light in her dark eyes, and Van der Veghe tensed. He leaned near to her.

"Why? What is it, Crenna?"

She didn't answer, did not have to. She simply held her hands against her abdomen and smiled. The slow understanding crept into his eyes, and his face lit up.

"A child? You mean it?"

"It happens."

"Yes, but to us! A child, Crenna!"

She nodded. He was himself a child at that moment. He looked away, picking up a handful of snow, and she watched him. Then suddenly he hurled the snow away, leaped up, and went bounding across the snowfields.

Crenna stood to watch. He was dancing and leaping, his legs flying in all directions, his arms waving triumphantly. He was running down the hill, yelling from the bottom of his lungs, wildly screaming, springing high into the air. "Crenna is going to have my baby!"

Then he leaped high into the air, too high, and he came down in a tangle of limbs, cartwheeling down the slope, snow flying everywhere as his last loud cheer faded away.

She took a dozen steps toward him. Shielding her eyes, Crenna peered down the slope. Had that great foolish man hurt himself?

No sooner had she thought that than he scrambled to his feet and was running up the slope, legs and arms flying, his hair streaming out behind him, his jacket covered with snow, laughter echoing down the slopes.

"Crenna!" He reached her panting, tried to speak, and fell to his knees. He clung to her legs, and she stroked his snow-frosted hair. "Crenna . . . happy," he managed to pant, and then he simply held her, his face against her abdomen, and she laughed out loud.

She knew how he felt, could not believe that two people could share such joy. Her own heart was full with it. Her joy ran and leaped and laughed and cartwheeled through her heart. There was nothing more she could ask for. Nothing.

He stood, and together, silently, they walked down the long snowy hillside toward the log house where a fire burned, where their child would be born.

Van der Veghe's joy was unconfined for months. In the evenings Crenna would sit near the fire, doing her bead-work, listening as Peter rambled on. "If it's a boy . . . if it's a girl," and he would quite seriously plan for its education, an education which would combine the best of two worlds' knowledge. At any odd moment he was apt to leap up, come to Crenna and kiss her, let his hands rest with wonder on the growing swell of her abdomen.

At those moments they were silent; there were no words fit to express such deep love, that love which produces another human being to enfold in love. The fire would burn low as Van der Veghe's head rested on her shoulder, and Crenna would lift a hand to stroke his head, to hold him.

"Those are little. . . ." He picked up the tiny moccasins Crenna had made and turned them over, his eyes flooding with tears. "Crenna." He said nothing else, but sat on the floor next to her leg, watching as she methodically cut two holes in the soles of the moccasins and then, holding them out, cocked her head with satisfaction.

Winter had gone, and the baby had not come. Crenna waddled around the house, holding her back, which ached in the mornings, watching Van der Veghe, who didn't laugh at her ungainly gait, but viewed it with excessive concern.

"I'm all right, Peter. It's simply a part of the price we women pay. Swelling up and moving about like a duck . . . a small part of the price we pay so that we may bring new life into the world."

Van der Veghe looked unconvinced. "Isn't it late, shouldn't it be here?" He rubbed his forehead, looking much more weary than Crenna felt. He glanced at the cradle he had lovingly made out of whole logs, and then back at his wife.

"I'm not good at this, Crenna. There hasn't been enough practice."

She had to smile, but at times his concern was wearing, and more than once she simply sent him out of the house. "Go see to the fish traps, Peter. I think I forgot to check them." Or, "It may rain. Perhaps you should bring some dry wood in."

He would go then, but never for long. He would return with his arms loaded down with wood, and he would peer at her expectantly, his eyes concerned, until Crenna would laugh, and laughing, cause her abdomen to ache, and wincing from that, cause his concern to deepen.

"What will I do?" he asked as they lay in bed, his hand on her swollen abdomen, feeling the slight stirrings beneath the taut, stretched skin. "I don't know anything about birthing a child. What will I do? Will I become terribly incompetent? I won't know what to do."

"The child will come, Peter. It will come whether you are competent or not, whether I am or not. There will be pain and a little more worry, and then it will come. There is nothing that can prevent it."

Her eyelids flickered open. It was the middle of the night, and the room was icy. Beside her her husband lay sleeping, his face at peace. Inside, the new life stirred uneasily, and Crenna touched her stomach.

No, it was not his legs and strong tiny arms. It was her body, a body grown weary of carrying another, who was now large enough to be expelled, who must be expelled before her womb burst.

It was time. The realization came to her sharply. She was excited, apprehensive, and happy at once. She lay still, hand on her stomach, feeling the changes within. A small cramping, a shifting of her muscles, and then a sharp motion somewhere within, as if her stomach would tear apart and the infant emerge. But he would not come that swiftly.

She lay back, afraid because this was her first child. She had seen women die in childbirth; if the same happened to her, where would that leave Van der Veghe? She bludgeoned that thought down and lay back, her breath coming in sharp intakes and slow, leaking exhalations.

She glanced at Peter, deciding to let him sleep. The hours straggled past, the time marked only by the occasional meaningful pain. Her abdomen seemed alive. It writhed and clenched itself, angry at being distended for these long months.

It was well past midnight when the pain, which had seemed bad enough before, collected itself and flared up angrily in Crenna's stomach. Was that right? She tried to recall. Had others had such pain just then? She couldn't think properly. Was everything right? Her stomach knotted and her spine seemed touched by fire.

She waited still, counting the contractions, which seemed to come one after the other. The first child comes slowly, she remembered; but perhaps this eager young one did not know that.

It was time. She closed her eyes tightly as a contraction swept through her. She stretched out a hand toward Peter, suddenly wanting him awake, but she restrained herself in time. She placed the blanket between her teeth and bit down hard.

It was time. One after the other, ripples of spasms swept across her abdomen, which felt torn and twisted. It was time—she had to get up, knew she had to get up, but she could not do it.

Crenna threw the blanket off her, swung her feet slowly to the floor, the cold floor, and then she sat there, her head thrown back, perspiration glistening on her face. She started to cry out, and bit her finger so that she would not.

Her legs seemed far distant, lost beneath the fecund, massive belly. Bracing herself, she waited until the spasm passed, and then she stood.

She hobbled toward the doorway, her feet dragging. She held her stomach and breathed in tiny puffs. She chanted to herself and fought back the tears which were accumulating in her eyes.

Finally Crenna made it to the doorway. She stripped off her nightdress and stood naked before the wide-flung door. Cold night air swept into the room. The stars winked questioningly at her. The river flowed past. She could see the dark crowns of the oaks along the river.

She found the apron which had been left by the door, and she tied it around her waist. There was a sudden contraction, and she nearly fainted from it. Her breasts leaked as she fought back a cry of pain; her loins trembled. Her abdomen tightened into a hard, wooden knot, and then, long moments later, finally relaxed.

Crenna stood trembling in the doorway, her hands braced against the frame. She looked across her shoulder, assuring herself that Van der Veghe still slept. She did not want him awake to see her like this, hair in a tangle, face slick with perspiration, body swollen and naked, tears standing in her eyes. She did not want him to see . . . A sharp contraction like an iron fist reaching into her womb and closing tightly came, and then another, and another on its heels.

But the first one should be slow in coming! She knew already that it would not be. The child was eager to come into the sunlight, to learn to stand, to laugh, to run across the grassy meadows, to be swung high into the air by its strong, laughing father, to watch the sunlight on the glittering river, to learn the quiet ways of the woods, to sleep beside its mother through the long winter night . . . Another contraction, and Crenna readied herself. She tied the apron between her legs like a hammock and threw her head back again, wiping her eyes.

She was frightened, and it angered her that it should be so. "Every woman has done this. It is nothing. How can I be afraid. I am Iroquois, I am Oneida, the strongest of the Iroquois, the strongest of Manitou's children. I am Crenna, daughter of the warrior Yushta, headwoman of my people. I will not be afraid!" These thoughts, half-muttered, half-thought, did little to fight back the fear, but they took her mind from the pain, which was intense now. Her insides were on fire and were being stripped from her by the tearing talons of eagles.

It did not matter—*I am Crenna*—there would be a child. Van der Veghe would laugh out loud with pleasure. Yushta would smile fondly.

It came again and again, and Crenna squatted down in the doorway still bracing herself, watching the thousands of diamond stars through the blur of vision. The stars swam past, peered earthward, blinked with faint interest, and went dark. Briefly dark as the world spun crazily under Crenna's feet. She was crouched low, straining now, trying to gut her body, to spew out a hundred children, a nation of Oneida. And she would be left a flaccid skin upon the ground, her breasts leaking milk.

She fought off the dizziness and threw back her head again, gazing skyward. The stars were haughty, mocking, impervious.

"But you do not live!" Crenna said angrily. "You are *nothing*. Nothing because you do not live and you are angry because I can make life." She pushed down. "Angry because Van der Veghe's love for me can make life. We can exist and you can only *be*." She pushed again, thighs trembling, womb burning, teeth grating against teeth, and then it happened.

It could not. It was too miraculous, but it happened. The child, the earth, all of the universe, seemed to drop from her womb, and she became light, victorious, a conquering warrior queen.

She could not look, but she did, as an atavistic compulsion swept over her. She found it in the apron, wrapped in a blanket of her own making. She cleansed the child almost frantically, murmuring small, soothing sounds. The knife she had kept at hand was there, and the rawhide strings.

She laid the child on its back on the table. It did not cry out, and for a moment Crenna thought it was dead. But the tiny, perfect fingers groped for her breasts, the tiny feet kicked.

She wrapped it quickly in a blanket, her legs still trembling, her heart pounding with exertion and exultation, her hands uncertain, and the baby cried out. Once. A dry, piercing cry, and Crenna's breasts responded with a flowing of milk.

She laughed and placed the infant to her breast. She looked at Van der Veghe—he still slept, his brow furrowed slightly, as if the cry had reached him in his dreams.

Crenna walked stiffly to the doorway and then across the yard. The stars were flashing blue-white beacons in the sky. The river muttered as it pushed on toward the sea. Crenna reached the riverbank and went heavily to her knees.

She unfolded the blanket from her tiny parcel, and the

baby kicked and then began to cry strongly, fiercely. She would be a strong woman, this little girl, Crenna thought. She touched her daughter, let the angry infant hold her finger. Then, taking resolution, she did what must be done. She placed the baby in the icy river, washing her clean. The baby squalled in terror and tiny anger. To come from its mother's warm womb to this icy water was a violent shock.

"I am sorry, little one, my lovely one, my dear one, but it is the way. It must be done."

The infant was washed and then taken from the river and held aloft. Crenna held the baby high overhead, her face triumphant, the pain temporarily forgotten. The night was dark, the skies cold, but her heart was warm with the moment.

"Manitou, I show you your newest daughter, I show you an Oneida woman! Bless her life as you have blessed all of your chosen people. Remember her face, and when it is turned up to you in prayer, do not turn a deaf ear. She is my daughter, Manitou; she is Oneida."

Then the warmth left and Crenna lowered the child. The baby was carefully wrapped in her blanket, and Crenna let it nurse, feeling the outflow of the milk which had been stored in her breasts, anxiously awaiting the birth. She swayed from side to side as the baby nursed. The air was cold against Crenna, who still stood naked in the night. The infant girl, warm and exhausted now, fell asleep, tiny unformed mouth half-open.

The weariness returned, and Crenna walked stiffly back toward the house. The house where Van der Veghe slept and she was happy with herself, pleased and proud that she had not awakened him, proud that she had brought this child into the world.

She crept into her bed, the tiny living thing next to her breast. Once she heard a small exhausted sigh come from its lips, and she smiled. She was so tired.

Crenna's eyelids were heavy. She looked once more at Van der Veghe, and closed her eyes, feeling the pulsing of her own heart, the smaller, fainter beating of the infant's heart against her breast, and she was content, utterly content.

She was happy that she had not awakened her husband. She tried to imagine the look on his face when he awakened in the morning, turned to kiss Crenna, and found the baby, their baby, beside her, and with that pleasing thought in her mind, Crenna fell asleep, a smile of relief and gratitude, of complete joy, on her lips.

8

CARA—THAT WAS THE BABY'S name—was sitting at
Crenna's feet, poking at the stream of ants which wound
its way across the porch of the trading post, when the ship
rounded the bend in the river and sailed into view, white
sails bulging in the wind, its masts above the forest pines.
Crenna stood suddenly, and she stared, simply stared.

Van der Veghe had described these ships before, but
now that one was nearly upon them, it seemed incredible.
Huge, purposeful, other-worldly.

"Peter!"

She scooped up baby Cara, who laughed, thinking it a
game, and turned anxiously toward the door to the trading
post. Van der Veghe came out, still holding the copper
bowl brought by a wandering Cayuga who had traded it
for Mohawk blankets.

Van der Veghe nearly dropped the bowl. "Good God!"
he exclaimed.

He stepped onto the porch, staring at the sun-bright
river. The Dutch ship swung ponderously toward shore,
and Van der Veghe returned to the trading post, putting
down the bowl, removing his apron.

By the time he emerged again from the building to
stand beside Crenna and Cara, who tugged at his pants leg
until he picked her up, the ship had launched a boat. Four
oarsmen rowed toward the shore, and Van der Veghe
could make out a rotund gentleman in a blue suit sitting
in the stern, watching him with questioning eyes.

"What will we do?" Crenna asked.

"Do? Nothing. They're Dutch."

"They're white," Crenna reminded him.

"Wechakapi?"

"Yes." Her eyes were serious. "Whatever they want,
they mustn't stop here."

"No. I'll tell them," Peter promised, but his eyes were

far away, happy. Perhaps he had missed his own kind more than he had admitted, or known himself.

Peter kissed Crenna and then Cara, who pulled at his nose and giggled as he handed her to her mother. Then Van der Veghe stepped down off the porch and walked toward the Hudson.

The sailors stared at him in astonishment, and Crenna saw the fat man in the odd suit step forward and shake her husband's hand.

"Sir? Excuse me," the fat man said, "I hardly expected . . . Who are you, in God's name?"

"Peter Van der Veghe."

"Van der Veghe! My God, man, you're supposed to be dead. You mean you survived two years in the wilderness alone . . ." He looked to the trading post and saw that Van der Veghe clearly had not been alone.

There was a striking tall Indian woman who at this moment wore her dark hair down, flowing across shoulders and breasts, and a tiny cherubic girl with the same raven hair framing her unformed face. Van der Veghe himself was dressed in buckskin clothing, fringed and beaded. His blond hair, quite long, was gathered in the back with a rawhide tie. He looked hale and hearty, as the entire family did.

"I managed to stay alive," Van der Veghe said. "I was fortunate enough to be befriended"—if that was the word, he thought with a smile—"by the Indians."

"Incredible. Simply incredible!" The gentleman stuck out a hand. "The name is Linden. Organizer and president of the Dutch Colony Company."

"Pleased to meet you," Van der Veghe said. "Can you tell me, by the way, what became of Le Carre? He was a mate of the—"

"I know who Le Carre was," Linden replied. "He was hanged. I don't know what those men had in mind. There was only one place to go after they left here, of course, back to New Netherlands, and there . . . well, Van Dyke was not the fool these men apparently thought he was. They confessed after an interrogation of some length."

"I'd wondered," Peter said. "Come into the post, won't you. Have something to drink."

"It would please me," Linden said. He waved a hand at the captain of his boat crew and followed Van der Veghe to the trading post. The Indian woman, he noticed, was watching him with what bordered on anger. Perhaps it was only the way of these savages.

"Crenna, this is Linden, a Dutchman," Peter said.

"What does he want?" Crenna's arms were folded. The baby clung to her skirt.

"Let's find out," he suggested mildly. "We can at least be hospitable."

"It's trouble, Peter. I don't like it. I'm sorry, but I don't like this at all."

"What's she say, Van der Veghe?"

"She asks if you would like some tea," Van der Veghe lied, and as he did, he wondered why. But it was a heady experience, to actually speak to someone who knew Dutch, to touch the outside world again. He was somewhat ashamed, and kept his face turned from Crenna, who went to the fireplace and stoked it until the fire was burning hotly, too hotly.

"Build this all yourself, did you?" Linden asked, looking around.

"All ourselves. Such as it is," Van der Veghe said.

"Don't deprecate it. It's one of the finest structures in America." Linden laughed at his own mild humor.

"May I ask . . ." He moved his elbows as Crenna set two cups of elderberry tea before the men. "May I ask why you are here."

"Why?" Linden only now removed his hat, wiped his freckled brow, and nodded. "To establish Dutch ownership, of course. The very same task you yourself were involved in. My settlers—"

"You have settlers on your ship!"

"Yes." Linden stared at Van der Veghe as if he were afraid the wilderness living had touched the man's mind. "Sixteen families. More will follow, of course." He sipped at the weak tea.

"What does he say, Peter?" Crenna asked, resting a hand on her husband's shoulder.

"He says he's brought Dutch settlers with him."

"Settlers? Families? Women and children?"

"Apparently."

"But he can't!" Her hand tightened on Van der Veghe's shoulder; her black eyes flickered to those of Linden. "He mustn't!"

"I'm afraid he has. There's nothing to be done about it, Crenna."

"Tell him about Wechakapi, Peter."

Van der Veghe nodded. Turning back to Linden, he began to speak in Dutch. "This is a hostile environment, sir. The local Indians are Mohawk. Their chief is a man named Wechakapi. He is hostile toward the whites, very hostile."

"But he's let you live here!"

"Only because of my wife. She has blood ties with the Mohawk. It is Wechakapi who killed some of the *Eindhoven's* crew and destroyed the stockade they had built here."

"Surely the man can be reasoned with."

"He won't speak to whites. He mistrusts us. There is a long association of white men with their superstitious lore, sir. They react as we might if a party of people with long tails and horns on their heads tried to settle in Amsterdam."

"Can't the man be bought?" Linden asked, his tone one of annoyance.

"I couldn't say. You would have to bargain with him."

"Would your wife act as interpreter?"

"I doubt it. No, she wouldn't."

"You could ask."

Van der Veghe did, and Crenna's answer, given thoughtfully, was what Peter expected. "I have settled here with you, Peter, and we live in peace. Wechakapi has given us this land. He does not want other whites on his land, however, and for us to associate with these Dutchmen or take their part is bad for us. For me to speak the requests of these people is not good."

"She won't?" Linden asked angrily.

"No, and I agree with her," Van der Veghe said. "We can't risk our peace in order to speak on your behalf."

"Then it's on your head, isn't it?" Linden asked. He shoved his teacup across the table, placing both meaty hands flat on its surface.

"What is on our heads, sir?" Van der Veghe asked, the heat rising in his veins as well.

"The safety of these people. They're going to stay, you understand, no matter what. Where else can they go? They've sold what property they had in Holland, come to the New World to settle. They'll not return, and if they wished it, I wouldn't transport then, sir." He rose sharply. "You have it in your power to negotiate peacefully with the Indians, to tell them that we mean them no harm, that these are hardworking honest farmers who only wish for a little of this land."

"I tell you, Linden, we have no influence on the man, none whatever. It would endanger our situation to speak to Wechakapi on your behalf. And 'A little of this land!' What does that mean? It's Wechakapi's land."

"*You* are living here."

"I only live here; I don't own the land. We have a treaty with the Mohawk."

"There seems to be little left to say, Van der Veghe. I was pleased to find you here—someone familiar with the land, who knew the Indians, someone to help our countrymen. Now I see that I assumed too much."

"Yes," Van der Veghe said through tight lips. "I think you did. You have brought these people here to suffer and perhaps to die. I must tell you now, I won't have them on my land. I won't have war brought to my family."

"The other side of the river. Is that yours?"

Van der Veghe shook his head mutely.

"Then it will be ours. And damn the Indian that tries to drive us from it!"

With that, Linden turned and stalked from the trading post, leaving the door open. They could see his stiff-backed, blue-clad figure striding toward the boat, where the sailors looked up expectantly. They saw Linden shake his head, and then Van der Veghe closed the door. With a sigh he turned to Crenna.

"Will you tell me now what that was about?" she asked.

He did, and Crenna listened thoughtfully, her eyes narrowing as Van der Veghe made it clear that the Dutch intended to stay despite Wechakapi.

She turned then, picked up the cups from the table, and stood before the fire, watching the flames. Cara cried out with delight at something she had found on the floor.

"There is only one thing to do then, Peter. I must see Wechakapi. If I do not, not a single Dutchman will live to see the spring."

It was two days before Crenna reached the camp of the Mohawk. Children were at play throughout the camp. A hunting party was just going out, the men carrying their food in their war bags. An old woman recognized Crenna and lifted a hand in warm greeting. Suddenly she saw Wechakapi himself, and his greeting was far from warm.

His eyes were frozen fire, his jaw tight. He knows, she thought. Still she managed to smile and greet the war chief of the Mohawk nation respectfully.

There were no preliminaries to their conversation, no smoking of the pipe, no eating, no polite inquiring as to the health of relatives.

"You have come for the white men," Wechakapi said, and it was an accusation. "I knew it would come to this, Crenna. Your sorcerer has blinded you."

"He did not want me to come," Crenna said honestly. "This is my decision."

"He is a sorcerer—you think it is your decision, but it is not. He plants these seeds in your thoughts while the moon is bright."

She knew she would get no further with that argument, so she changed tacks, coming directly to the point. "Wechakapi, I have come to ask you to let the whites settle on your land."

"To give them my land!" Wechakapi was rigid with emotion.

"To sell it to them."

"No one has offered to buy it."

"I will speak to them. A fair price."

"The council would not agree."

"If you asked them, the council would agree to sell that land."

"Crenna." He ran a hand across his hair and leaned slightly forward. "You ask too much, my Oneida cousin. Give them Oneida land if you wish. I will not have my land overrun by white devils."

"They are not devils, Wechakapi," Crenna said softly. She had lowered her voice, hoping that it would soothe Wechakapi. "They are only farmers, simple people."

"Who will multiply."

"They harm no one. They are far from your camp."

"Are you sure they are not soldiers, Crenna? Warriors in disguise?"

"I am certain. If they were, you could crush them, could you not? If you sell them the land and they violate whatever terms you choose to lay down, you can kill them, can you not? Wechakapi is great, your army is strong. What can it harm to indulge a woman and let these people remain for a time? They can be friends, Wechakapi."

"I am uncertain, Crenna. I do not like the whites. Their looks, their very smell. But it is as you say," he had to admit. "If they violate a treaty, I could crush them."

"Certainly."

The Mohawk chief was silent, and Crenna knew he was thinking of the wealth such a treaty could bring him. How many wampum belts and rich goods the whites must have!

He wasn't convinced then, but hours later, when the darkness had settled, when Crenna had gone repetitiously through her arguments until her throat was dry and her head bobbed with weariness, Wechakapi finally clapped his hands together and said, "I agree to this.

"They may not own the land, Crenna. Tell them that. They may live there—no more than fifty families. They may not have warriors among them. They must pay me thirty wampum belts or its equivalent every year. If I should tell them to go, they must be away from my land within one month. If they agree to this, they may stay. If they do not, I will kill them."

Crenna left while the moon was high, before Wechakapi could change his mind. She had done it, then—built fragile peace. The Dutch could live without fear on that land if they agreed to Wechakapi's terms. Why, then, did she feel as if she had committed a great crime?

She had saved many lives, made Peter happy—for although he wouldn't admit it, he must wish others of his kind to live around him. She had pacified Wechakapi, done nothing but convinced him a few farmers should be allowed to live upon the land. Why this guilt, then?

She stopped, staring up at the haloed moon which dangled on silken threads from the vault of heaven. *Mocking thing, terrible pock-faced moon.* She could feel the pulse throbbing in her throat, feel her heart beating too fast. *What have I done?*

The answer, of course, was that she had opened the door, she and she alone. She had let in a few weary, optimistic, honest people. A few more men like Van der

Veghe, a few pale women, a few yellow-haired children. But how many more would follow?

She thought of Yo's nearly hysterical prophecies, of the hordes of blood-soaked white men he saw in his visions, of his dark anticipations. Briefly she thought of that, was able to visualize it all. And then she cast those thoughts away, convincing herself that they were childish fears given life by the darkness.

She walked homeward, stretching her legs, the yellow moon still mockingly pursuing her. She did not look up, but only watched the long moon shadow at her feet as it flitted across the dark and sullen earth.

The town across the river grew and withstood the first hard winter, when it was most likely to wither and die. By spring, fields had been cleared and corn had been planted, the seeds purchased from Van der Veghe's trading post, traded happily by some Mohawk men who took away Dutch-made blankets and iron kettles.

The Van der Veghe trading post had become vigorous with the coming of the Dutch. Not only Mohawk, but Munsee and Susquehanna, and occasionally, to Crenna's joy, Oneida came there, bringing furs and foodstuffs. Once every three months a ponderous Dutch ship fought its way upriver to the settlement, bringing supplies from Europe, taking away holds filled with valuable furs.

Wechakapi was becoming a very wealthy man and he found he had fewer objections to the white men living on his land as his horde of manufactured blankets, pots, cloth, steel knives, glass beads, mirrors, and innumerable oddities grew.

Van der Veghe too was making money. The Dutch wanted to trade on a large scale; Europe was hungry for furs. Van der Veghe's post, located on the river as it was, became an outlet for Dutch goods and Indian furs, with the traffic flourishing in both directions, making both the Europeans and the red man wealthy in their own lands.

"Each laughs at the other," Crenna remarked. "The Mohawk has many furs—how many can a man use?—and when he gives a few to the Dutchman and is rewarded with beautiful beads and steel fishing hooks, he thinks what a fool this man is. The Dutchman, greedily eyeing the mink and ermine, the beaver and fox, thinks: These savages are stupid. And what is the truth, Van der Veghe?"

"There is no truth. Whatever is rare is valuable. A man's time and place declare what has worth."

"You are rare, Peter," she said, "and the most valuable of all that exists on this earth."

"Then at least you don't intend to trade me for glass beads." He laughed.

Crenna laughed as well, as she laughed frequently. These were good times, so different from her life in the Oneida world, but good times. She watched the smoke across the river curling into the skies from the chimneys of the Dutch houses, watched Cara at play, her dark head bobbing and weaving among the heads of the pale-haired Dutch children; she felt the weight in her womb, listened to the cheerful voice of Van der Veghe across the room as he bargained with a visiting Cayuga warrior who had come a hundred miles with his otter pelts, and she knew she should be completely at ease, utterly content. But she was not.

It wasn't that there was anything missing in her life. She had warmth, food, love. But there was an uneasiness which visited itself upon her in the nights, a dark, muddled conviction that danger hovered overhead like an ax waiting to descend.

Sometimes she awoke in near-panic, her heart thudding, her eyes wide. Then she would lie there, watching the ceiling until her heart stilled, until Cara stirred and she held the baby to her breast, scooting nearer to Van der Veghe. *Silly woman*, she would scold herself, but it didn't help matters any to believe she was only being foolish. The danger, the fear, the sense of impending calamity, were real.

In the early summer Crenna's second child was born. A bawling, leather-lunged, red-faced boy who seemed ready to reach out and grasp the world, to charge after his destiny and devour it. Van der Veghe was mad with ecstasy. He named the boy William, and Crenna did not argue, although it seemed a strange choice.

It was apt, however, by the time William could crawl. His hair had turned pale, and his eyes, a muddy blue at birth, had turned to the color of cornflowers. He was a strong, good-natured, winning baby, and no one doted on him more than Cara, who was now nearly four and considered herself quite grown-up.

Crenna stood behind the counter of the trading post, the baby playing at her feet as she shifted the bales of furs on the shelf behind her. She hummed to herself as she worked, concentrating so busily on what she was doing that she didn't hear the door open, hear the soft footsteps cross the floor. What caused her to turn, she did not know, but turn she did.

"Sachim!"

"Hello, Sister," Sachim said. Then she thrust out her arms, and they hugged across the countertop, Crenna's eyes filling with tears.

"What are you doing here? Who is with you? Father, Manto? How is everyone."

Sachim, overwhelmed, laughed, hugged Crenna, laughed again, and stepped back to examine her at arm's length. "You grow more beautiful, Crenna. How do you do it?"

"*Is* everyone all right, Sachim? I thought when I saw you that maybe . . ."

"Everyone is well, Crenna," Sachim assured her.

"Come over to my lodge . . . my house," Crenna invited. She stepped from behind the counter, gathering up the blue-eyed, yellow-haired baby.

Sachim laughed in astonished joy and put her hands out to take William, who, surprisingly, went to her willingly. "Such a boy! Look at him. Yellow-haired, can you believe it! Did you ever think you would have a son like this?" She kissed his cheek, and he gurgled. Sachim laughed, hugged the boy, and handed him back.

"Come along, we have much to talk about."

"But can you leave your work?" Sachim asked, looking around.

Crenna nodded toward the wiry, silent Mohawk who had been working in the corner. "Turlock will watch things."

"He works for you?" Sachim shook her head in wonder. Looking around the store, she said, "Such wealth, Crenna. It's amazing."

"The furs do not belong to us. Peter buys them and keeps them for the Dutch. He is the agent of what is called the Dutch-American Company. He is given a certain percentage for every fur he purchases."

"It sounds very complicated."

"Not so complicated at all, not so complicated as life used to be. Peter makes the decisions, examines the furs, takes care of the money."

"Then you don't miss it." They had reached the door to Crenna's house. "Being headwoman?"

"I shall always miss it," Crenna said honestly. "But never enough to go back," she added.

Cara ran up to the woman, was greeted and admired, and went back to her playing. Sachim watched her go, saw her meet two towheaded children who were stepping out of a boat from the settlement across the river, and she said, "They were wrong, weren't they? They said the white would bring doom. Yo and Yushta. They said they were savages. They were wrong."

The sisters had tea together, and Crenna asked about the tribe, trying not to reveal how much she did miss the Oneida. "Wakami and Father, surely they are married by now."

"Not yet." Sachim laughed. She folded her hands on the rough wooden table. "But Manto is, you know."

"To Taranta!"

"Yes." Both of them had always liked Taranta, an over-ripe, full-mouthed, happy woman.

"And you, Sachim?" Crenna asked. Sachim shook her head, but there was an elusive gleam in her dark eyes.

"A man has asked me, but I am not a wife in my heart."

"But you have given it thought."

Sachim turned her eyes downward. "Sometimes."

"Who is it, Sachim?"

"Kinpo," she answered. Crenna remembered him only as a thin, uncertain warrior who spoke to practically no one.

"Do you ever remember Hawk?" Sachim asked suddenly, and Crenna, looking up, surprised a look of tenderness in her sister's eyes.

"Sometimes."

"Yes, so do I, sometimes." Sachim smiled, but it was a worn expression.

Crenna's forehead wrinkled briefly. Had Sachim loved Hawk? She had never thought of that before, even considered it. But, looking back, she saw it was possible. She now hurriedly changed the subject. "Father's health is good?"

"It is fine. He will outlive us all. Manto is a great bull of a man now, and Ta-Tando . . ." Her voice faltered, trying to find the words to describe their younger brother. "He is also healthy," she said, resorting to that trivial observation.

"His mind?" Crenna asked, leaning her elbows on the table.

"He is not a boy any longer, Crenna. Nor is he so shy as he once was. He swaggers and hints that . . ."

"What, Sachim?"

When her sister looked up again, her eyes were flooded with tears. "Crenna . . . I think Ta-Tando killed Hawk. I think he did it meaning to kill Van der Veghe."

"He has admitted this?"

"No, but there are hints. Smirking looks, veiled boasts whenever the subject is brought up. I believe it, Crenna! I do believe it."

Thinking on it now, Crenna could also believe it. It caused a churning in her stomach, to realize that it could very well be so, it could very well have been Ta-Tando, and only the merest chance had kept it from being Van der Veghe who was murdered. She did not wish to dwell upon it. She realized she had been silent too long. Quickly she said to Sachim, "It's probably nothing more than empty boasting. Ta-Tando always wished to make himself appear larger."

"Yes," Sachim said, as unconvinced as her sister, "that is probably it." She blurted out, "I wish you were with us, Crenna! As happy as I am for you, I wish you were still headwoman.

"It is Kala who has succeeded you, and she does not lead, but acts on whim and fancy. She parades around the camp in her finery, liking the feeling of power. Her decisions are capricious. She is a woman without morals, our Kala. She was headwoman for only a week before she reinstated Pawago."

"Pawago!"

"Yes. She is indifferent to his crimes—maybe she doesn't believe he was guilty, but I think she knows he is, and does not care. She likes him, and so she has given him back his antlers. She does whatever she likes, caring noth-

182

ing for the good of the tribe. I wish you were with us, Crenna, although I see you are happy here, and I am happy for you."

Crenna covered Sachim's hand with her own. "You are welcome to stay here too, Sachim."

"No. I thank you, but I can't. I am not so strong as you, Crenna. I have no man such as Van der Veghe. I am Oneida, and I need the tribe."

"I too am Oneida, Sachim," Crenna reminded her softly.

"Yes, I know that, Crenna."

"And if there were any way I could help, I would return. But I have given up my position; even if I wanted to come back, I have no voice, no vote, no status. And I do not want to come back. You simply miss me, perhaps you miss your youth. You have Kinpo, don't you. Smile. Things are good in the Oneida camp. Let Kala strut—we see through her. Ta-Tando is just a youth, a small man who wants above all to be big. Pawago is simply a bully. All of that has little to do with your happiness."

"You are right," Sachim agreed, but her words sounded false even to herself. "It is just that sometimes I miss the way it was. I miss you, my sister." Sachim stood and embraced Crenna again, kissing her gently on the lips, her fingers brushing back the hair from Crenna's eyes as her own eyes shed tears.

The door opened behind them, and Van der Veghe, striding in, asked, "Is there a kiss left for me, Sachim?" His arms stretched out to her, and she rushed to him, clinging to Peter with a fervor which surprised him.

"We are honored—" Van der Veghe looked at Crenna, whose smile was bittersweet, puzzling him— "thrilled to have you with us. Stay a lifetime, Sachim, a year at least. Please."

"I can stay but a few days," Sachim said, stepping back, her wraithlike body withdrawing from Peter's arms. She looked up at him with luminous gratitude, with love.

"Crenna, please tell her she must stay the summer, a month at the least. We have missed our small sister."

Again, briefly, Sachim hugged Van der Veghe, leaning her head against his chest.

"Do stay, Sachim," Crenna said.

"No. A few days, no more." The sisters' expressions worried and puzzled him.

"Is everything all right?" Van der Veghe asked.

"She has a man she misses already," Crenna said quickly, and Van der Veghe smiled, nearly believing his wife.

Van der Veghe kidded Sachim, pressing for the details, and to Crenna's surprise, Peter seemed to know more about Kinpo than she did. He went out of his way to praise Kinpo as a swift runner, a great hunter, a kind and stalwart man, but Crenna could read the questions in his eyes when he looked up at her. Something was wrong; he could sense it, as Crenna had.

Sachim ate with them, helping to prepare the meal while Van der Veghe lay on the floor playing with the two children. The dark-haired, black-eyed girl and the blond baby boy. He laughed and they giggled, crawling over him as he tickled them, hoisted them high in the air, and gurgled at them, bringing forth gales of childish laughter.

"He loves them so," Sachim said quietly. "How lucky you are, Crenna, how lucky. Your life is peaceful, happy. I envy you."

Crenna beamed, yet at the same time, even as she watched Van der Veghe and the children play, listened to Sachim, who watched with ill-concealed admiration, she felt the old uneasiness gnawing at her, clutching her heart.

It is absurd, she told herself. Nevertheless she felt as if she were dancing on ice, walking a long bridge made of straw. All of her hopes seemed doomed; her happiness seemed to be only a moment's reprieve from the crushing resolve of imminent destruction.

Silly woman.

It was nothing, only the unsettling undercurrents Sachim's tales had produced beneath the placid pond of her existence. You feel too deeply, she told herself, worry too much. The world is young, golden, aglow with health and well-being.

But there were dark clouds in her soul, and they would not be banished by sunshine or by the warmth of her hearth.

Winter was harsh and long; the ships no longer came, nor the Indian traders. There were weeks on end when the world was dark at all hours, when the shrieking wind flung itself against their house, challenging them with its might. It bothered them not at all.

They had firewood and food and each other. Crenna taught Cara how to make moccasins. Although her first efforts were slightly misshapen, still they praised her highly.

During the long winter evenings Crenna told tales of Goweh, the echo god, who was called on when the Oneida wished to enter battle. If Goweh did not answer their summons, then the battle was put off; she spoke of Hinu, who rid the earth of giant creatures so that the Iroquois could come to this land; of the Great Heads who had no bodies, but were huge long-haired, large-eyed spirits who were very malicious; of the Stone Giants, who came from far to the west to kill all the eastern Indians, but were defeated by Manitou. Van der Veghe did not laugh once.

The children did, with delight, at times. Their favorite tale was that of the forest pygmies who were responsible for carving the caves and hollows in rocks one saw. They had destroyed great monsters by dropping pine cones on their heads—the one spot unprotected by armor.

Van der Veghe simply listened, smoking his pipe. The longer he and Crenna were married, the more he understood the Indian culture; the more he understood it, the better he knew his wife. He listened, warmed by the fire, soothed by his pipe, recognizing that the tales the Indians told were not so different from those he had heard as a boy—tales which explained nature and the ways of men.

Her voice was mellow and her eyes intent as she sat before the fire, gesturing with her hands as she spoke to the children.

"This is how the first man was born: The great Manitou once took the form of a giant eagle. The eagle lived among the pipestone rocks in the Land of Peace. When the Manitou-Eagle wished to eat, it swept across the distant plains to find a buffalo, which it would snatch up in its talons and carry off to its nest.

"The pipestone rocks are red; that was caused by the blood of the buffalo Manitou took to its nest."

"Where are the pipestone rocks?" Cara asked.

"Far to the west. A hundred days' journey. One day I shall show you. Now, once while Manitou was away searching for a fat buffalo the great Serpent, ageless, timeless, found Manitou's nest. There was one egg in the nest, and as the Serpent came near, the egg began to move with fright. Now, the Manitou could hear the egg move, and he swooped down on the Serpent with a great boulder in his talons.

"Manitou crushed the Serpent's head with the rock, but the egg was also broken open and a full-grown man stepped from the egg."

William, fascinated, but exhausted, crawled up onto his father's lap. He snuggled in, his face aglow with firelight.

"The man was unable to move the great boulder which had pinned him down, and he cried out to the Manitou, 'Set me free, O Great One!' But the Manitou would not set him free just then. The man was born too early, and he could not take care of himself. He had to be instructed before he could be set loose on his own, and Manitou was to be his teacher.

"He taught the man how to hunt, how to make a bow and arrow, how to make clothes from a deer's hide, and how to be a thinking, moral creature, different from the animals in the forest.

"When Manitou was satisfied that the man had learned his lessons, he placed his wing across the man's face and the man fell instantly to sleep. When he awoke, there was a woman standing beside him, and as Manitou removed the rock, the first two people ran off into the forest to become the mother and father of all the Indian nations."

Later Crenna noticed that Peter was awake in the darkness. "What are you thinking of, my husband?" she asked.

"Your tale about Manitou and the first people. It seems so similar in ways to a tale we are told at home, in Europe. The longer I live with you, Crenna, I wonder—are we all so different, or all so very much alike?"

"And what have you decided?"

He laughed, drawing her near. "I have decided only that you and I, man and woman, are different, and it pleases me."

She closed her eyes again and scooted closer to him, while the embers burned low. "It pleases me as well, Peter Van der Veghe."

It was in the spring that they came. Two dozen hard-faced bearded men carrying weapons in their hands. They straggled out of the forest, and Cara, who had seen them first, came running to the trading post.

"White men, Father!" she shouted, leaping into his arms.

Frowning, Van der Veghe went to the door. They were whites, and by their dress he took them to be French. Two dozen men, three dogs, and the first horse Van der Veghe had seen since leaving Holland.

They came directly to the trading post, some of them still holding swords in their hands—against what menace, Van der Veghe had no idea. He sent Cara running home with a loving swat on her bottom.

"Gentlemen," Van der Veghe greeted them. His French, always poor, was execrable with disuse; nevertheless, he was understood.

"We want food and gunpowder."

"Gunpowder?" Van der Veghe laughed. "I've seen none yet in America. Food I have. Come in, please."

Their leader, a sullen, scarred man with a black mustache, followed Van der Veghe into the post, gesturing to another man, who began untying the furs from the back of the gaunt, pale horse.

Entering the post, he began looking around himself, to Peter's annoyance. Turlock took one look and ducked out the rear door.

"What are you doing?" Van der Veghe asked.

"Looking for gunpowder."

"I told you I haven't any."

"I don't believe anything a Dutchman tells me."

One of the other Frenchmen had toppled a bale of furs, and Van der Veghe spun that way angrily. "Keep your hands off my goods!"

They paid no attention to him, and he could only stand and watch while they virtually ransacked his store. Satisfied that Van der Veghe had been telling the truth, the Frenchman, without apology, set about making a bargain.

"I have fifty otter pelts, forty fox, thirty beaver. This is what I want—"

"I'll have to have a look at them first," Peter interrupted.

"Top quality," the man said, leaning closer so that he was nearly in Van der Veghe's face. "I want salt, five pounds, flour—"

"I have to see the furs first," Van der Veghe repeated.

The Frenchman's hand shot out before Van der Veghe could back away or react in any way. It gathered in the front of Van der Veghe's shirt, and Peter was lifted to his toes.

"Dutchman, you trade for what we want, or we take it, do you understand? We have a long way to go, and we need supplies. If we kill you, who will know or care? Who will punish us?" He released Van der Veghe, throwing him away from his own bulky, musty body with a sharp thrust of that massive arm. "I want five pounds of salt, twenty pounds of flour . . ."

Van der Veghe stood shaking with repressed rage for a moment. Instinct told him to lash out, to slam his fist into the Frenchman's face, but logic cautioned him. There were ten men in the room, all watching. He shrugged and turned away, filling a sack with the supplies the Frenchman demanded.

It was then that Crenna burst in the doorway, halted abruptly, and stood looking at the bearded faces. "What do they want?" she asked in rapid Iroquois.

Briefly Van der Veghe explained. "Go back to the house, Crenna. Take the children and go into the woods."

"What are you saying, Dutchman?" the leader of the trappers demanded.

"Nothing."

"Peter . . ." Crenna hesitated, felt the probing eyes of the Frenchmen on her, and turned, hurrying back to the house, knowing that Van der Veghe was right. Picking William up and leading Cara after her, Crenna went into the woods. There she held the children against the earth, instructing them to be silent.

Her heart swelled in her throat, and she felt the flush of shame and anger heat her cheeks. To run from such as those! The Oneida never would have run. Never! But Peter was alone, there were no other warriors to help him, to protect Crenna.

"Who are they, Mother?" Cara asked, but Crenna shushed her.

The girl's face was frightened, and so Crenna forced herself to smile. "Friends of your father's. He is pretending he has no wife and children." It was a barely satisfactory answer, and Cara accepted it with obvious misgivings. Nevertheless, she was still, as was William, who seemed to accept it all as a game—not a very amusing game, but still a game.

It seemed hours before they left. Crenna watched the river, hoping some of their Dutch neighbors might visit the outpost, but it seemed today was not a day for shopping. Finally they did leave, and Crenna, holding back the fear she felt, the anger, watched as the Frenchmen tied their purchases onto the horse and headed off upriver.

"What is that, Mother?" Cara asked, jabbing a chubby finger at the horse. "What is that?"

Crenna didn't answer. She waited until the French were gone around the river bend, and then she stood, her heart driving against her ribs. Van der Veghe mercifully appeared, seeming unharmed. He stepped from the outpost and waved a hand in their general direction—it was obvious they had hidden well enough to conceal themselves from casual eyes, since Van der Veghe never did see them until Crenna emerged from the forest, Cara's hand firmly in hers, William in her arms.

"Well?" She was breathless. Van der Veghe looked calm enough, introspective in fact. As if he had had a revelation.

"It's nothing. They took what they wanted and left. But I wonder—"

"If you hadn't traded with them, what they would have done?"

"Yes, just what they would have done."

"But it's over, they've gone." She released a squirming Cara's hand, put William to his feet to totter after his sister, and she clung to her husband, the anger, the fear, gone, replaced by vast, warm relief. "You don't think they'll be back?" she asked, sensing some reserve in Van der Veghe.

"Yes." He smiled distantly. "They'll be back. Maybe not these men, but others, many more like them. Something has happened. The wilderness is changing; it's as if we've come to a point where our innocence must be lost."

"Van der Veghe?" Crenna asked, touching his chin with her finger. "Moon-gazing?"

He laughed. "I suppose." They walked arm in arm to the store. He told her what he had discovered. "Do you remember what you showed me once? A Munsee had brought some fox pelts, and you said, 'Look, Peter, these are Algonquin pelts—the ears have all been cut off to make medicine.' "

"Yes, I recall that."

"These men—all the fox pelts had been mutilated like that. They didn't trap for those furs, they got them from the Algonquin. I noticed the moccasins one man wore, recalled what you had told me about Algonquin moccasins, how you can read moccasins as we read race in a man's face. They were Algonquin as well. Crenna, these men are living with the Algonquin, I'm sure of it."

"They said nothing?"

"No, and I didn't ask—there's no telling what their reaction would have been. But I am sure of it, the French are friendly with the Algonquin, and if they are friendly, it can be for only one reason—they wish to make this wilderness a French colony."

"Does that matter to us?"

"Doesn't it? We represent the Dutch interests in America." Van der Veghe was silent, and so was Crenna. Turlock had returned to the trading post, and he set about his work with a wooden expression. What was he thinking? Crenna wondered. Did he too see the Algonquin sign? Turlock was Mohawk, Iroquois, and as such, a bloody enemy of the Algonquin. When the Frenchmen had looked at Crenna with dark, appraising eyes, she had taken their looks for those a man gives a woman; perhaps she had been wrong. Perhaps they had seen the stamp of an Iroquois and were examining their enemy.

She was thinking too much, as Van der Veghe did. Making much out of a small incident. A handful of rude Frenchmen insisting on their way had made their trade and gone on their way. They would not be back; the episode was ended.

She walked out alone, moving through the shadows of the trees, watching sunlight glint on the lazy, rambling river. She wanted to believe her own logic, her own lies, but could not. Van der Veghe was right. She could feel it as well. The Dutch had come, the French. Men were growing greedy for the land, for dominance. Old animosities had been transported from the Old World to the New. They had never lived at peace in Europe; why should they be expected to here?

She wanted to disbelieve it. All had been peacefulness, warmth, contentment—but did things ever remain that way? She knew they did not. Terrible things had happened among the Oneida. Crimes were committed, men murdered, savage wars begun. It was the way of man, it seemed. They had lived here on the river in peace for a while, perhaps only because they were away from all of the others, because they lived in love.

She looked up into the blue sky, seen through the dark curtain of pine boughs, and breathed in deeply, slowly. *It's as if we've come to a point where our innocence must be lost.*

That was what he had said, her moon-gazer. And Peter had believed it, at least at that moment. Some foreboding touched him, like the dark, smothering wings of Crenna's own vague uneasiness. Something had taken him and whispered into Peter Van der Veghe's ear: *You must lose your innocence.* Crenna had heard the same voices, although the words had not been so clear. Now they were, given meaning by Van der Veghe. Now it was all clear, and she stood shivering in the deep forest, although the day was not cold; she stood unhappy and alone in the midst of happiness and love.

She would not have it! She would have no more of these dark thoughts, no interference from these small spirits who carried whispered malice. She threw back her shoulders and angrily set off toward the river. She would bathe and return to her husband. She would hold him, and they would laugh together at their foolishness. But the whispering followed her to the river, the wind mocking her resolve as it soughed through the dark pines, and Crenna had to walk quickly to outdistance the small tormenting voices.

THE WINTER WAS SILENT AND somber, and the dark imaginings were buried beneath brilliant white coverlets of snow. The fire burned as warmly as ever, and there were no Frenchmen to disturb the tranquil times.

In the spring they came once, but their leader was not with them and Van der Veghe did not want to ask what had happened to him. They were brusque but not impolite. They traded their Algonquin furs for supplies and left, their conversation limited to the business at hand.

"Perhaps," Crenna told Van der Veghe, "we have painted our villains too darkly."

He agreed with her, but his eyes held the same doubts she harbored. The French were not their enemies, perhaps, but the fact remained that they were in the way. Their trading post had become a Dutch community, and it was a challenge to France.

When the first scheduled ship failed to arrive, they thought little of it. There were always delays. But no trader arrived until June, and when it rounded the bend in the river, they saw instantly that something was wrong. The Dutch ship was missing a mast. The hull was blackened with fire, the railings torn away.

"The British," they were informed. "They've started construction on a fort five miles south. They've cannon in place, and by God, they showed little compunction about using them."

There were seven Dutch sailors to be buried.

"How can there be a British fort?" Van der Veghe asked. "Wechakapi would not allow it."

"He would allow it for a price," Crenna argued. "He has learned that the white man has wealth. Yes, he would allow it."

Leaving the trading post in Turlock's hands, they traveled south together one afternoon. They could see the smoke from a mile away, and cresting a wooded knoll they could see the stockade under construction. British soldiers in scarlet tunics patrolled the perimeter of the settlement. There were no farmers to be seen, no tradesmen, only armed soldiers.

"If Wechakapi saw this . . ." Crenna began. Then, holding Van der Veghe's arm tightly, she fell silent. Van der Veghe nodded. They shared a common thought.

"Let's go down and take a look," he suggested.

"Isn't it dangerous?" Crenna asked. One didn't walk into the enemy's camp.

"No. At least, I don't think so."

He knew the Europeans better than she, and so Crenna, holding his hand, walked with him as they approached the British fort. They could tell by the foundation plans, which were marked off clearly, that this was to be a permanent and large settlement. Van der Veghe was frowning heavily, not liking what he saw any more than Crenna did.

A British soldier with his high-peaked hat spun toward them, but he did not try to stop them as they walked up to the uncompleted gate of the stockade.

"There," Crenna said, and Van der Veghe nodded. They had both expected it in their hearts, although they had tried to subdue the notion.

It hung from the cross-member above their heads, a red-and-white wampum belt, of Mohawk manufacture, a deed of trust and of title.

"They have bought the land," Crenna said softly, with a shadow of doubt, although the evidence, hanging before them, was incontrovertible. "They have given Wechakapi his price."

The tall man had dark eyes, dark hair, and a drooping reddish mustache. Van der Veghe was unfamiliar with the British insignia of rank, but the man moved with the confident, somewhat stiff motions of the upper classes, carried in his eyes the vaguely haughty sheen of high rank.

"May I inquire who you are, what you are doing here?" the Englishman asked.

Van der Veghe, whose English was even worse than his French, managed to comprehend enough of the sentence to respond with his name and that of his wife, "an Oneida headwoman," he added although it was not strictly true.

"Oneida!" The Englishman was pleased. "Sir Charles will be sorry to have missed your visit. He is deeply interested in an Iroquois alliance." The soldier's eyes narrowed, his brow furrowed. "But aren't you the man who runs the trading post upriver?"

"Yes."

Crenna, watching the officer, saw his mood, reflected in those dark eyes, shift. She glanced at Van der Veghe, who nodded in reply to some question.

Quickly Van der Veghe told her, "He's pleased you're Oneida; not so pleased that I am Dutch."

"I understand there is quite a Dutch force at Albany," the officer said offhandedly.

"No," Van der Veghe answered quickly.

"But I have heard—"

"There are no soldiers at all."

The Englishman either didn't understand Van der Veghe's terse words or chose to ignore them. "And the Dutch soldiers are friendly with the French—is that not so?"

"We have no soldiers among us."

"Won't you stay awhile?" the British soldier asked, gesturing toward the fort, where a hundred carpenters labored. Their sawing and hammering made a continuous cacophonous noise. The scent of pine sawdust was heavy in the air. "Sir Charles will be back soon—my commander—he would be happy to speak with you, offer you tea, perhaps, and a few delicacies you have not tasted for a while."

"I have left my trading post unattended," Van der Veghe said uneasily.

"Who are these men; what do they want?" Crenna asked.

"I don't know. They are British; I know nothing else," he told her as the Englishman watched them with faint contempt, faint interest.

"Please stay. I know the commander would be overjoyed to speak with you," the officer said again, his mustache lifting as he smiled quite unconvincingly.

"Sorry. We have to get back," Van der Veghe said. Before the officer could say another word, they had turned and were walking swiftly toward the forest across a field of freshly cut stumps.

"What is this?" Crenna kept asking, raising her hands in frustration and then letting them drop. "Wechakapi must be going mad! These soldiers—and they're not friendly to you, are they, Peter?"

"They're not unfriendly at the moment," he said rather weakly.

She stopped, putting her arms around his waist. Her eyes searched his with tender concern. "You know what I mean."

"Yes, I do, Crenna."

"British. And the French living with the Algonquin. What do they all want?"

"Only this, I'm afraid. Only all of this." Peter had halted again. His eyes swept the forest, the hills.

"Do you mean it? You know them, Peter, do you really mean it? They want it all?"

"In pieces. They want a little now, some later. Purchased or taken by force of arms. Yes, I mean it. After all, it's quite precedented, isn't it? It's the way of the world, and always has been. How did your people get the land from the Algonquin? How did the French? The British, the Mongols, for God's sake!" Peter was angry. It was a deep frustration, and he said to her, "For a time I forgot. Perhaps I thought things were more civilized here."

"All of it?" Crenna had barely heard Van der Veghe. She stood, hands clenched, lower lip drawn in, staring toward the Catskills to the south. "It's laughable. It won't happen. They'll be driven back to the sea, I can tell you that. They might be able to buy Wechakapi, to fool the Algonquin, but the Oneida leaders . . ." Her voice faded away. What about the Oneida leaders? She realized Peter had been talking simultaneously; neither had heard the other. It didn't matter, they had been expressing the same thought in different languages. Now they stood together on the brow of the hill, the thought returning over and over, a theme in the windsong, a muddled note sung by the river, screeched by a sullen jay in the deep pines, throbbing in their echoing hearts. *We have lost our innocence.*

When he came, he was resplendent in armor; his dark hair was carefully brushed, his long mustache meticulously waxed. His tall, haughty figure cut a dashing silhouette against the pale blue sky behind the rise where he stood with sixteen armed men.

He wore a scarlet-and-gold doublet beneath his breastplate, and its sleeves billowed in the wind. His eyes were a sea green, flecked with gold. His face, lean without being long, was punctuated by a slightly ambitious straight nose.

Already the Indians were gathering around this strange visitor. Some held bows menacingly, but Sir Charles Pyle studiously ignored them. He was a representative of the Crown, and his contempt for the savages was equaled only by his raw, rather primitive courage. He was a throwback to his Norman forebears, an adventurer by nature, restless in the confines of his manor at Kent, constricted by the fashions and forms of London society and court life. He was a raw man, as sinewy of soul and heart as any savage Indian who stood before him. Pyle's civilization was only trappings and stage sets.

Perhaps his men knew it, for his soldiers were fantastically loyal to him, knowing that Pyle would hurl himself onto the enemy's lances if it came to that. They sensed some deeply male, deeply pagan strength in the man, and they followed him with the devotion of primitive tribesmen to their war chief.

All of this could be read in his face, in the mocking green eyes, in the casual, poised stance of the man, in the confident, slightly deprecating smile.

Women could appraise his character instantly; some of them, recognizing the brutality inherent in such a man, recoiled from Sir Pyle's advances; others, transfixed by the sheer savage magnetism, fell at his feet. Pyle treated them all with contempt. Women were used to erase boredom or to fight off winter's chill, no more.

"On down, then, Briggs," Pyle told his lieutenant. "They've had their look at us. Steady on, men. Briggs, hold that wampum belt aloft!"

Pyle's tone was electric with subdued excitement. Briggs glanced at his colonel, seeing the open enjoyment in his eyes. He loved this, damn the man. Pyle, he was sure, would have regarded a pitched battle and a warrior's death as a welcome adventure. Briggs was not such a savage. The stony faces, the black, unsmiling eyes of the Indians, sent a chill racing up his spine. He tried not to show it, held the wampum belt up where it could be plainly seen, and fell in behind Sir Charles Pyle.

"Where are your leaders?" Pyle was calling out. "Where are they? Tell them I have come."

The language was that of the Mohawk, but Wechakapi had assured Pyle that his brothers, the Oneida, would understand his words.

Perhaps they did, but Pyle saw no spark of understanding in the Indians' eyes. No one ran to summon the Oneida leaders.

"Come on now," he shouted in English, "don't stand gawking, you bloody savages!" Then, in Iroquois, "Where are your leaders?"

Not until he was at the gate to the stockade itself did certain representatives appear. Pyle took them for leaders by the way the crowd parted for them, by the questioning glances the Indians shot at them.

The first man to confront Pyle directly was one of these. A broad-shouldered, sharp-faced warrior with deadly hooded eyes wearing his hair in a thin brush which stood up from his mahogany skull.

"What do you want here?" the man asked. Pyle smiled thinly. He recognized this man—not that he had seen him before, but he knew the type. It was his own type, savage, shrewd, powerful, and quite cold.

"I want to speak to you. About wealth and war and the Algonquin," Pyle answered, hoping he had gotten the words right, not caring entirely. The man understood him. Their eyes met, and an understanding passed between them. Pawago had recognized a brother.

"I still don't understand what it is you wish," Yushta said as they smoked in the council hut. The Englishman accepted the pipe with distaste.

"Then I will explain again," Pyle said. He glanced across the blanket to see Kala still studying him, her eyes filled with liquid warmth, her every movement a subtle sexual signal which Pyle read very well.

He was a god, this one, Kala thought. In silks and plumes, armor and leather. A white god. She thought briefly, bitterly of Crenna and her Van der Veghe. Van der Veghe was nothing beside this man. Van der Veghe was weak; Pyle was strong—you could see that in his face. Strong and obviously wealthy, a powerful man, a man of position, whereas Van der Veghe had had none. And that weakling had rejected her! Rejected Kala and taken up with her stiff-backed sister Crenna, who probably still did

197

not understand the joy of rolling on the grass with a lusty man. Pyle was speaking, but she was barely listening.

"The Frenchmen, other men from over the sea. Another tribe. They have formed an alliance with the Algonquin, your enemies."

"We do not fear the Algonquin," Lapsa put in.

Pyle glanced at him with sour pity. "I know that. The Oneida are brave. The Mohawk are brave. All Iroquois are brave." Manto, his arms crossed, made a small disgusted noise. He had heard flattery before. Pyle shot him a glance. "But soon thousands of French will come with great war machines—thunder guns which can destroy an entire village."

"There is no such weapon!" Tachtathahuata insisted.

"But there is." Pyle, sitting cross-legged, bent forward, his eyes sharp. "The French have many weapons, and they will turn them on the Oneida."

"We are not their enemy," Yushta protested, not comprehending still what the white man meant. An army of these Frenchmen had come to their land to destroy the Iroquois? Why? What did he mean? Where were the French?

Pyle studied him and said with infinite patience, "They are your enemy because the French have allied themselves with the Algonquin. The Algonquin want you to die; the French want your land."

"And what do you want, Pyle?" Manto asked shrewdly.

"Only to survive," Pyle said in response. He smiled, but it was a razor-thin expression which Manto mistrusted. "The French are our enemies. They hope to drive us into the sea."

"He has come to beg for Oneida warriors," Pawago said, cutting to the heart of the matter. Pyle was toppled slightly off-balance by the remark, but he continued to smile. He shifted his glance to Kala, who returned the smile willingly. Briefly Pyle was not a warrior, not His Majesty's envoy, but a man, and he let his eyes sweep over Kala's lush body, studying the shapely bronzed legs that disappeared into her elkskin skirt, the loose fullness of her breasts, the ripe, slack mouth, the wide, inviting eyes which met his and smiled in implicit understanding.

"To beg for nothing," Pyle resumed, picking up the thread, "but to propose a mutually beneficial alliance."

"To ask for warriors," Pawago said again. He pursed his lips and shook his head.

"You seem to mistrust me. Look,"—he spread the wampum belt before him on the rug—"Wechakapi trusts me. He knows me."

"What did you give him to trust you?" Yushta asked dryly.

"I give all of my friends gifts."

"What sort of gifts?" Kala asked with frank interest. Lapsa looked away with disgust. This headwoman was a greedy child.

"Whatever you can imagine," Pyle said. "I have brought gifts with me. There will be more."

"Let us look at the gifts," Kala said eagerly.

"Let us find out what the man wants," Manto shot back. Pawago's head slowly swiveled toward Manto. What was Manto doing here? He was no sachem, but Pawago knew what they whispered: Give Manto Pawago's antlers.

"He has told you what he wants, Manto," Kala said angrily. She pouted petulantly, and Pyle smiled.

"Only to ally ourselves with you for our mutual protection."

"We cannot do this without an Iroquois council," Yushta said. "It is a matter for the League, not for the Oneida alone."

"Then call an Iroquois council," Pyle insisted.

"I cannot see the need of it," Yushta said. His words were brittle now. "I do not see the French; I do not see the Algonquin. I only hear you—asking us to fight for you."

"You misunderstand me, friend," Pyle said.

"I think not."

"Father!" Kala's voice had dropped to a purr. "Are we to be rude and shortsighted? Let us consider what the man asks, let us discuss it and consult the spirits. Let the man stay and visit us; let us learn of him"—she looked levelly at Pyle—"and he of us."

"I cannot see the good of it," Yushta said wearily.

"There is no harm." It was Pawago who spoke. "It may be true, old man," he said, using the slighting term he had adopted recently in speaking to Kala's father. "It could be that the Algonquin are ready to attack us. We should not dismiss such information with a shrug and a clap of the hands."

Pyle looked from one face to the next. There was a tension between certain members of this council, and it could work to his advantage. Already he had sized up the situation. The tall, dark warrior was with him, probably because he wanted war and plunder. The woman, the young one with the exuberant body and hungry lips, was with him; and surprisingly, this bundle of warm flesh and juices, of childish petulance, of sulking mouth and eyes, of womanly magnetism, was the one who held the supreme rank.

She was the one he needed, then—she who now looked deeply into his eyes, she who offered herself plainly. Pyle smiled and nodded his head, his confidence in the success of his mission growing by the moment.

"But what *does* he want?"

It was dark and silent on the fringe of the golden glow cast by the campfire. Pawago stretched, leaned back, propping himself up on his elbow, and answered the lean, crooked man beside him. "War, Ta-Tando. The man wants war. Yushta knows it. The others pretend it is not so, but it is war he wants."

"Against the French?"

"And the Algonquin. Is that so bad?" Pawago was chewing thoughtfully on a strip of jerked venison. "You recall the attack on our village by the Algonquin. What was done about that?"

"Manto led a party . . ."

"Retribution. They attacked us and killed three men. Yushta says: Go, and be careful you do not harm too many Algonquin, my son."

Ta-Tando became briefly angry. Pawago was attacking his father and brother. But his anger subsided. It was true, after all, and it was difficult to be angry with the Oneida war leader—he, above all of the others, thought always of the tribe.

"Five Algonquin were killed," Ta-Tando said almost apologetically.

"Yes. Perhaps. Five." Pawago was darkly silent. "And so they will return one day—we all know that. They will return, and six Iroquois will be killed. Six friends, six family members. Yushta will throw up his hands and wail. Yo will bless us, and we will go out with orders to kill seven Algonquin. Do not make the enemy angry, they have only killed us!" Pawago spat disgustedly.

"Your father grows old, Ta-Tando. It is not his fault, but he grows more cautious with age. He wears his title, Solitary Pine Tree, proudly, with honor. But what is past courage worth?"

Ta-Tando had no answer for that. "I don't trust the Englishman," he said.

"Nor do I!" Pawago laughed. "That doesn't matter. He is offering soldiers. When we are through using him, we shall run him into the sea!" Pawago paused and added, "At least that would be my plan if I were allowed to proceed with it."

"You are war leader!" Ta-Tando objected.

"Have the Oneida ever had a war leader so shackled?" Pawago demanded. "Kill six, kill seven. It all grows out of Crenna's accusations, you know." Ta-Tando stiffened; he did not like Crenna's name to be sullied. "Not that it was her fault, of course," Pawago went on fluidly.

"What do you mean?"

"Well, it was the Dutchman all along, Ta-Tando. Didn't you even recognize that? The Dutchman who wanted her, who tricked her, made her accuse me of crimes."

Ta-Tando *had* thought of that, but the argument seemed flimsy. Now, once Pawago had spoken it, it returned to him and took on solidity.

"There's nothing to be done about that now," Ta-Tando said morosely. He shifted his position, sitting up to stare at the campfire.

"No?" Pawago's voice was insinuating. Ta-Tando looked slowly toward the Oneida war chief. "Do you think the British love the Dutch? Do you think Pyle would allow Van der Veghe to live?" Pawago asked.

Ta-Tando's eyes narrowed. His heartbeat picked up slightly. He had tried to kill Van der Veghe, and Pawago, alone among the tribe, knew it. Pawago alone among the tribe, shared his violent hatred of the Dutchman who had deprived them both of Crenna.

"I suppose they would not," Ta-Tando said, and when he turned his head to Pawago, the Oneida war chief was grinning. He stretched out a hand and gripped Ta-Tando's shoulder so tightly that it hurt.

"No. Nor would I."

"But the others . . . the council—"

"Only one person needs to be convinced," Pawago interrupted.

"Kala!"

"Yes, Kala. She is headwoman."

"Then we shall have to talk to her, make her see that war is imminent, that an alliance with the British is not to be disregarded. It is up to us, Pawago!"

"Yes," Pawago replied. "We must be the ones to convince her." Pawago rolled away from Ta-Tando. *We must convince her*! He laughed silently. How little you know your sisters, Ta-Tando. For Pawago had seen them earlier, strolling toward the river, and he knew that Pyle, if he had not yet convinced Kala that an alliance was necessary, was close to a settlement.

The night was warm and the crickets along the riverbank chirped in primitive rhythm. Her heart was warm beneath her breast. She had difficulty catching her breath as his lips crept along her throat.

"It tickles." The mustache tickled and his lips were fiery. She tried to laugh but could not. When Kala made love, it was a merry experiment, a joke at times, to the infuriation of men. This was no joke.

His hands were deft, sure, his lean body hard and supple.

"Why did you come to our land?" she asked. Why was she talking? It was unusual for her. Nervousness? She laughed inwardly at the thought, but there was substance to it. This man made love as if he were making war. Callused hands attacked her breasts, flanked her hips, and seized her trembling thighs.

He lifted her hips higher, drew her head roughly toward him, pressing his mouth to hers, his tongue hard and darting.

"Kala," he whispered, giving her beleaguered lips a moment's respite. His savage kisses had bruised her lips against her teeth. "Such a lovely name, my princess," Pyle said. His voice was sincere, his mouth smiled at Kala from

202

out of the darkness, but his eyes, lighted by the glimmering starlight, did not smile. This was not love; it was war, and there was no humor in it.

He rolled to his side, drawing Kala with him, his hand on her hip. Roughly he lifted her leg and thrust his between her thighs before settling, holding her naked body in the iron bands of his arms.

"We must be one. One thought, one body. You and I, the white man and the Indian princess."

His words were low, throaty, his eyes surveyed her with obvious need, his hands drifted over her legs and hips, floating tender voyagers.

"We are together, we are one," Kala said, placing her fingertips on his jawline, fingering his mustache.

"We must remain one," Pyle answered. "Brother and sister, father and daughter, man and woman."

He turned her roughly, placing her on her back against the dew of the grass. The starlight was in her eyes, and his kisses searched her, urging her to blossom, to flow. Her body seemed to become heavier, sweeter, softer. His kisses twisted and broke her mouth. It became slack, a useless tool, incapable of speech, useful only as a receptacle for him. She became a thing which existed only for his use. A toy to batter and to probe, to manipulate and discard.

She felt a quivering hesitation and a moment of shock as he took her. It was time to laugh—didn't Kala always laugh at moments like this, revealing her mastery of men, their foolishness?

But she could not laugh. Her mouth gaped, her throat constricted. She shoved a knuckle between her teeth and bit down hard. Her hair lay in a tangle across her face, her breasts. Somewhere beneath her breast a slow thudding began, a chorus repeated by her rhythmic body, a deepening, richening beat.

"We will remain together. We must," she said suddenly, half sitting up before his weight shoved her back and pinned her to the dew-frosted, yielding earth. The starlight was molten silver flowing from out of a deep, glittering sky. It flowed across her body, down her thighs in hot rivulets, and she was lost in time and space, knowing only that she must hold him tightly so that he could not escape, so that they might always be together.

Crenna lay quietly watching a single star. Her breast rose and fell with the soft inhaling. "What are you thinking of?" Peter asked.

It was a time before she answered him. For a moment she simply held his hand, that familiar, supporting hand. "Just of life. Of time. It passes so quickly. Events you cannot control sweep by. All of time like a great whirlpool which captures our moments and swallows them. Irretrievably. The moments are gone, the decisions we made. You can't snatch a moment back. Not a single moment. It's all gone."

"Yes, I know." His hand squeezed hers.

"And it's only luck which causes us to make the proper decision at the proper time, to seize the moment before it too slides away into that whirlpool."

"Yes?" Peter yawned, turned his face toward her, and smiled.

"I don't know why my thoughts run this way on this night. I simply awakened and felt the tug of the currents. I felt: *This* is all of my time, and it is slipping away. And so, dear Peter, I felt most fortunate that Manitou presented you to me, that I came to the right decision, that our love did not vanish as it could have so easily."

He kissed her lightly and then fell off to sleep. Still Crenna lay awake. She had not explained things properly to him. What kept her awake, nagged at her thoughts, prodded her? Odd, tangled feelings. Life, each hour so long, was fleeting. The years became like minutes. Events raced past. Before a person could grasp them, touch them, they were gone and you were left pounding your skull, trying to remember exactly how it had been. They were all in that whirlpool, spinning away, being sucked down. Faces appeared and then vanished beneath the water. Hands were held out, touched, and lost. She gripped Peter's hand again, gripped it tightly, and finally, happily, she fell asleep, her dreams untroubled.

The man Creighton arrived a week later.

Crenna heard the cadenced drumming of feet against the earth, and her head came up. It was a moment before Van der Veghe, rearranging his trade goods on the shelves, heard the sound. Then he slowly frowned and turned toward her, their eyes meeting.

Still holding a steel ax, Van der Veghe walked toward

the door, Crenna beside him. Turlock, as was his habit when the unexpected occurred, had slipped out the side door.

They were in the yard before the outpost. Cara and William stood watching them, their eyes wide. Sixteen scarlet-clad soldiers in a neat file, and at their head, facing Van der Veghe and Crenna, a white-mustached man with cold blue eyes and a flattened reddish nose.

"Van der Veghe?" he asked.

"I'm Peter Van der Veghe, yes. This is my wife—"

"I'm General Reginald Creighton," the Englishman said with evident pride. He took three steps toward them, stood rocking on his heels a moment, spared a dry smile for the children, and went on. "I've come to give you official warning. You are operating a foreign-owned concession on British soil. Please vacate this land within thirty days."

Van der Veghe couldn't answer for a moment. He cocked his head, quickly translated for Crenna at her impatient tugging of his arm, and stiffly took one step toward the pompous British officer.

"Are you mad!" he exploded.

The general didn't even blink. "You are operating this trading post under the auspices of the Dutch-American Company, an agency of the Dutch government. As such you are no longer welcome here. This land is British property."

"This land is mine!" Van der Veghe retorted. "Not Dutch, not the company's. But mine. Mine and my wife's."

"From whom did you purchase it?" Creighton asked, lifting a white eyebrow. He had stretched out a hand to pat William's hair, a gesture which infuriated Van der Veghe unreasonably.

"It is leased from the Mohawk Wechakapi."

"That is what I understood." Creighton nodded to himself. "Wechakapi has abrogated that lease."

"What is he saying?" Crenna demanded. Her English was not much worse than Van der Veghe's; he had been slowly teaching her both Dutch and English, as she taught him her own tongue, but what she understood of Creighton's remarks made no sense.

"He says Wechakapi's terminated our lease."

"He wouldn't!"

"He might. If they paid the old miser enough. Look here, Creighton," Van der Veghe went on, reverting to English. "What's this about?"

At that moment the movements and sounds on the opposite bank of the river caught his attention. Now he could see a group of Dutch settlers gathered around men in red coats. He returned his gaze to Creighton.

"This is British territory now, Van der Veghe, through a treaty of purchase signed between the Crown and the Mohawk Wechakapi. Your lease has therefore been terminated, and you are advised to leave. As an agent of the Dutch government—"

"I am no one's agent," Van der Veghe said. He ran harried fingers through his hair. "My wife and I simply operate a trading post, that is all. We are not Dutch agents. We harm no one. We will speak to Wechakapi ourselves—*he* must be the one to tell us our treaty is no good."

"As you like, sir. You have thirty days."

"And if I do not move?" Van der Veghe asked. His jaw was clenched so that it was hard to speak. He realized fully the implications of this. And just where would they go if the British did evict them? Not to the Oneida camp, nor to Holland. Where? This was their life, this post built with their hands.

"If you do not move?" Creighton shrugged. "There will be little profit in staying here, sir. I assure you your countrymen across the river will leave. We will tolerate no Dutch colony on British soil. Of course there will be no more trading ships allowed up the Hudson. Our fort is situated in such a way and armed specifically to prevent that."

"What does he mean?" Crenna asked in a whisper.

"He means they'll blow from the water any ship that's not British."

"Your trading days, as you see, are over."

"No. I can trade among the Indians—we survived that way before."

"Not with the Mohawk, I don't think," Creighton said, and his smile was a particularly nasty expression. "We have asked Wechakapi to prevent that."

"What are we hurting!" Crenna shouted at the man in

her halting English. "What are we doing to you? We do not make war!"

Creighton smiled, finding her amusing. "It is British soil, madam."

"It is Iroquois land!" she flared up. "And I am Iroquois, Not you."

Creighton was undisturbed by Crenna's excitement. He nodded and reached out his hand to pat William's head again. Van der Veghe drew his son away.

Creighton's expression darkened. "The Iroquois are our friends," the general said to Crenna, using the tone he might have used with a child. "Your chiefs and head women know that we are their friends and a strong ally. They have given us certain lands for our own. The Mohawk, the Oneida—"

"That is a lie!" Crenna said. "The Oneida do not sell their lands."

Creighton smiled with pity. "They have, madam, I assure you. You are Oneida? Your headwoman has approved a sale of land to us."

"No!"

"Yes. I assure you. Now, can't you see that it is necessary? Your headwomen are wiser than you. They are your leaders—"

Crenna had burst into harsh laughter, and Creighton, the muscles in his jaw twitching, could only stare in amazement. Van der Veghe looked grim.

"What did I say?" Creighton asked.

"The Oneida headwoman is my wife's sister," Van der Veghe explained.

The general's ruddy face brightened. "Then we are practically related," he told Crenna. She stopped laughing and peered questioningly at the soldier.

"What do you mean?"

"The Oneida headwoman—Kala, is it?—has married one of my officers."

"Has . . ." Crenna had to lean against the awning pole beside her. She couldn't speak for a moment.

"What did you say?" Van der Veghe asked, his words slow in coming.

"I say she has married one of my officers. Kala has married Colonel Charles Pyle in a very pretty Oneida ceremony. Weren't you invited?"

"No." Van der Veghe shook his head slowly.

Crenna could only stare at the British general. Kala, dear Kala, had married an Englishman? *Why*, dear Kala, little, voluptuous one? The question should more properly have been phrased: Why did a British soldier marry Kala? The answer to that was more easily discerned. Kala was a flighty, emotional, frivolous thing likely to do whatever entered her mind. But a British officer had to have a reason—true love? Crenna, hoping she was not growing cynical, doubted it. There was only one other reason. For the sake of this grand alliance, for Oneida land and Oneida arms.

"Where is she?" Crenna asked quietly.

"At the fort. With her husband, of course." Creighton, mistakenly thinking he had achieved a breakthrough, pressed his point inanely. "Now you see—Kala trusts us, listens to us. Won't you? You will not be safe here any longer. The French will be coming, with their Algonquin allies. You hate the Algonquin, don't you?" His tone was insufferably patronizing, and Crenna shouted at him.

"Be silent, fool! Kala is a fool, you are a fool. I am a fool for wasting my time speaking with you."

Creighton's slack face suddenly became stony. Van der Veghe saw the warrior's gleam in his eyes. This man was used to commanding; he did not suffer such remarks gallantly.

"Be off this land in thirty days."

"When Wechakapi tells us to leave, we will leave," Van der Veghe answered.

"I will be back." Creighton's voice was brittle, measured, "I will be back in thirty days. If you have not gone, I shall remove you, sir."

"Will you!" Crenna said, jabbing a finger at the man. "Do it and see how long the Oneida remain friendly with you. You think I am no one, a child, a savage. I am Crenna, and I was once headwoman of the Oneida. It is my sister who now decides what the Oneida will do. It is my father who leads the warrior clan. You will be making a mistake, Mr. General Creighton, if you try to remove my husband and me from this land. You have built an alliance—very well. But to remove me will be to crush that alliance, I promise you that!"

Crenna spoke with confidence, and Creighton looked

temporarily cowed, but inside, Crenna was not sure of herself. Would Kala lift a finger to help her? Possibly not; and if she did, would the British listen to her? Despite their pose of friendliness and equality, Crenna could sense the contempt the British had for the Indian.

That was not what worried her most intensely, however; after Creighton had gone, she and her husband stood on the porch of the outpost, watching the Dutch across the river congregating in confusion, anger, and despair. "It is the drift of things," she told Peter. "The feeling that events are moving now of their own impetus."

"The whirlpool," he said with a thin smile. He squeezed her shoulder.

"Exactly. What do the British want? Land alone?"

"I don't think so." Van der Veghe had to be honest. "They are quarreling with the French, as they have for hundreds of years. The land is the prize—neither side concedes the Indian any right to this land." Crenna was angered by his words, but he held up a hand to calm her. "It's true. Harsh, but true. As you have reminded me, we still see things from a different perspective, you and I. I can assure you, Crenna, to the European the Indian is someone to be dealt with when he is strong, used when he is willing, dispensed with when he becomes unnecessary."

"Your condemnation for your own kind is strong."

"My kind?" He shrugged. "Maybe. Your kind, all kinds. This is the way the world has always been, Crenna. Everywhere. And so it will be here."

"The Oneida must not participate," she replied. The wind off the river was in their faces. Far away, the Dutch, in confusion, wandered their colony. "There will be a war. We always thought: Well, there cannot come enough whites to matter. When there are too many, we shall slaughter them. But now there are many. Ships must cross each month, laden with soldiers, only soldiers. And now the tribes are being seduced by white wealth, like Wechakapi, trapped by his own greed. The white man plays upon our ancient animosities."

"That is how I see it," Peter told her. "Believe me, Crenna, they will not leave until they have what they want, and what they want is all you possess."

"We are strong." Her fists clenched as if to show how strong she was. Her eyes gleamed dully. "We do not have

209

to fight their wars. We must not, Peter Van der Veghe. We must not!"

With those two concerns—the probable eviction of Van der Veghe and the possibility that the Oneida might become involved in a European conflict—Crenna resolved a course of action. She had to speak to Kala. Creighton had said she was still headwoman of the Oneida; that could not be right.

Perhaps the Englishman did not understand Oneida law. Crenna had given up her rank when she elected to leave the tribe. Kala, living at the British fort, must certainly have done the same. In that case, the position would have fallen to Sachim, and had it done so, they had no worry about being driven from their land by the British—although, she reflected, Wechakapi, at his British allies' urging, could still do just that.

If Sachim were headwoman, then Crenna felt sure she could convince her youngest sister that Oneida lands must not be sold to the British for any price, that war with the French-Algonquin armies must be avoided if possible.

This was all speculation—she would know nothing until she had spoken to Kala or Yushta. Kala, according to Creighton, was at the British fort only five miles south. Therefore, that was the first order of business.

She and Van der Veghe barely discussed it. She had told him she must go, and he had nodded his head. He had said little, but his eyes showed deep understanding. Knowing the man as she did, she knew that he was not so concerned with losing the outpost as with the greater implications of a British-Iroquois alliance. War clouds were shadowing the land, a war of European manufacture, and if those clouds began to rain, it would be a long, hard storm which would wash away civilization as Crenna knew it, peace as they knew it, life as they hoped it would be for Cara and for William.

The children did not ask many questions; perhaps they sensed the importance of the moment. At any rate, they stood silently beside Van der Veghe as Crenna, walking swiftly southward, disappeared from view, passing into the deep forest.

The shadows were deep and cooling, the scent of pine and cedar heavy and pleasant. The forest was as it always had been; walking through it brought back intense, pleasant memories of other times. A squirrel jabbered at her from a pine bough, and oddly that jarred Crenna's thoughts, bringing her back to the present.

Her heart was heavy, her stomach felt empty and knotted. Through the trees she could see the fort now. It had grown in the short time since she last visited it. A great blockhouse had been raised near the river, and all the land had been cleared on the remaining three sides. Cannon lifted their ugly black snouts above the ramparts.

She had never seen a cannon fired, and prayed she never would, but Van der Veghe had explained them—an explanation she found elusive, but which filled her with discomfort.

The soldier at the gate let her through without questioning her, and she halted, looking around. Wagons were lined along one wall, beside them other cannon, these on wheels. A group of red-coated men in perfect unison drilled on the parade ground, their sergeant's voice echoing across the fort. There were four low buildings inside the fort, one of them as yet uncompleted. Each was constructed to withstand assault, the windows being only slits in the log walls. Above it all a red-white-and-blue flag fluttered in the wind.

Crenna walked toward the buildings, her mouth drawn down. The first person she tried, a young red-haired soldier, had no time to listen to her. The second, an older man in civilian clothes, looked her up and down with delight and bobbed his head. "Mrs. Pyle that would be. The colonel's wife?" he asked in an overloud voice. "You want Mrs. Pyle, another Indian lady?"

Did he think she was deaf? "Yes, Mrs. Pyle," she replied. The man lifted a hand and got back to his work, which was stitching harness leather with a long curved needle.

She walked in the direction the harness maker had indicated, looking with some amazement at the dozen horses standing in a rough paddock. They watched her with an equal curiosity, their ears pricked.

Crenna studied the rows of closed doors, walking in a slow half-circle. She was nearly past one door when she heard a familiar childish laugh.

Pausing, she went up to the door, listened until she was sure, and then, opening the door, she went in.

The room was dark, although four candles burned on a low mantel above a stone fireplace. Kala was sitting in a chair, and her eyes came around, bright at first, growing cold and challenging as she recognized her sister.

"Crenna," she said as if unsurprised. She did not rise. A white woman, bulky and doughy, stood behind Kala, arranging her hair. Crenna's sister wore a long, dark blue dress which had lace on the sleeves and the collar. Kala touched her throat, to emphasize her finery, Crenna thought, and then asked sharply, "What is it?"

"I need to talk to you, Kala."

"I am busy, Sister."

The white woman, after an initial glance of curiosity, paid them no heed, but continued braiding and pinning Kala's long blue-black hair.

"You can't be too busy to discuss the well-being of the tribe."

There was something of the old tone of command in Crenna's voice, and Kala, recognizing it, smiled thinly. "The tribe is wealthier, stronger now than ever it was when you were headwoman, Crenna, Sister," she spat back.

"You are following a dangerous course."

"What is it!" Kala rose suddenly, nearly knocking her hairdresser aside. "Now that you see what I have, do you want your position back? You think that because I am here the tribe lacks a headwoman? Now that you see what a wealthy white husband can mean, you have come crawling! Van der Veghe does not shine so brightly, does he? Look at you. Dressed in buckskins. Can your husband spare you from your labors today, or did you sneak away to talk to me, Crenna? Don't you have to look after your brats? What!" Her hands were flung out in a contemptuous, demanding gesture. "What do you want of me?"

"I want to speak to you about the tribe," Crenna said slowly, her words coming between barely parted teeth.

"In what capacity? I mean, what is your position, Crenna? Sister, tribeswoman? You have none. Petition the council." She turned her back deliberately. The white woman, as if on cue, held up a mirror, ornate and gilded, and Kala touched her hair with satisfaction.

"I never knew you hated me so much," Crenna said

slowly, meaning it. Kala's eyes, reflected in the mirror, caught hers.

"I don't hate you, Sister. I pity you. I am wealthy and powerful, loved by a courageous, well-situated husband. You are nothing. Soon you will not even have a piece of land to squat on."

"Kala—"

"No, wait! I know what you are going to say. Creighton spoke to my husband. You do not want a British alliance—why not? They are strong, friendly. Our tribes, the Oneida and British, are bonded by marriage. They do not like the French or Algonquin. We also hate the Algonquin, and we must prepare for our defense."

"This is how you presented your argument to the council?" Crenna asked.

Kala waved a hand, and her hairdresser disappeared. "Yes. And I was right. I have made us wealthy." She had circled a small round table of deep red wood, and now she leaned across it, hands braced against its surface. "I was, am, a better headwoman than you—that is what nettles, isn't it? That I, Kala, could do your job better than you."

"It's not that at all, Kala," Crenna replied, fighting back the anger which had collected in her throat. "You have sold Oneida land—"

"Land we have no use for. Our hunting grounds are to the north."

"It is land other Oneida fought for, died for."

"They lived in their time, we in ours," Kala said with a gesture of dismissal. She straightened up, smoothed her dress over her hips, and smiled. "We need an ally, we need steel axes, we need iron pots. We must live for now!"

"And forfeit the future?" Crenna's anger was seeping out.

"You won't bait me. I decided; I will continue to decide. You left Oneida soil and abandoned your role as headwoman. I remained on Oneida soil. I married an ally of the tribe. I am headwoman!" She tapped her breast so roughly that it must have hurt.

"The council should have been informed of the possibilities of war."

"There is always the possibility of war." Kala had walked to a bureau; now she fastened a pearl necklace

213

around her throat, careful to display it prominently to Crenna.

"Not like this war will be if it comes, Kala. You must listen!" She was to Kala in three steps. Taking her arm at the elbow, she jerked her sister around, and Kala's face turned to stone.

"Get out of here! You are nothing," Kala said, prying her sister's fingers from her arm. "It was discussed, decided. We all agreed to sell land. Pawago, Yushta, Moa-Telah, Ta-Tando—"

"Ta-Tando!" Crenna's eyes became slits. "Why Ta-Tando? How could he vote in council?"

"Simply." Kala laughed. "He is sachem now. Lapsa died, you know. I gave Ta-Tando Lapsa's horns."

"Ta-Tando is not suited for any position of such importance!"

"*You* did not think so. I do. He is my brother—he was so grateful," she simpered, "he told me, 'My sister Crenna would never have done this for me.' "

"Kala . . ." There were no words for this. Her idea of the headwoman's position was childish, lacking utterly in responsibility. When did she think of the *tribe*, of the tribe and not of Kala? When she sold Oneida lands, when she appointed Pawago and then Ta-Tando to responsible positions?

"I have to know, Kala. Have we voted to go to war with the British?"

"The matter is undecided," Kala said offhandedly. "Yushta cannot make up his mind. Tachtathahuata is against it. Wakami waits for our father to decide. Moa-Telah, Pawago, and Ta-Tando are in favor of striking a blow against the Algonquin before they can attack us."

"And you, Kala? What are your feelings?"

"I do not concern myself with war—that is a sachem's affair." She shrugged, and Crenna despised her sister for it. "But they will vote to fight beside the British. My husband, Sir Charles, is not here at the moment. Why? Because he has visited all the Iroquois in council. The Onondaga, the Mohawk, the Seneca have all voted to fight with the British. Only the Cayuga and the Oneida procrastinate."

"Kala, can't you see any of this from a distance!" Crenna moved to stand directly before her shorter sister.

"Don't you see that this is going to be no battle for hunting grounds, no short battle of retaliation. This is going to be a war which can crush the tribes!"

"Oh, I don't think so," she said whimsically. Crenna could only stare. Kala had turned away to fasten a bracelet.

"Please go with me to the village, Kala. Let me tell you what is happening, according to Van der Veghe."

Crenna had said the wrong thing. "Van der Veghe! That effeminate thing!" Kala mocked.

"You would not know a man if you walked into him, Sister," Crenna replied. Strangely, she was not angry. You cannot be angry at someone who insists the sky is pink, a rock soft, a raven white. "Come with me to the village. You are headwoman—help me prevent this."

"Prevent what?" she asked with blank innocence. "Besides, I must prepare to leave. When Pyle gets back, we are leaving."

"Leaving?" Crenna could only stare.

"Yes, he has his orders."

"But where are you going, Kala? Where could you go?"

"He is taking me home! He is not ashamed of me, as Peter is apparently ashamed of you. Or perhaps Peter has no great estate, no fine house to take you to. Yes, don't look at me so, Crenna. Sir Charles is taking me home. I am going to England to live."

To England! And what of the tribe, what of her duty, what of her people who must die in battle if this was not stopped now, now before the British could lead them into this war? There was no point in speaking to Kala any more. She did not hear, and when she thought, her mind was shadowed with rancor; when she spoke, her words were twisted venomously. Poor, proud Kala, thinking only of Kala. Now she believed she had defeated Crenna in some complicated game of souls; she had only defeated herself, and for the first time Crenna could see the hollow, sad husk of a woman that was Kala—a woman of flesh. A woman of fleshly appetites, because there was nothing inside of her. Absolutely nothing.

Crenna discussed it with Van der Veghe that evening, and he agreed with her. "You must go back, must try to halt this madness. Will they listen?"

"I don't know. At one time . . ." She smiled weakly.

The firelight was dancing on her cheeks. "I don't know. If they are undecided, there is hope. If there is hope, it must be done. I must speak in council."

"I'll go with you," Peter said.

"You cannot help."

"Perhaps I can." He shrugged. "I want to go. The children are no longer babies. They can stay with Turlock's family. It is a long way, Crenna, but I think I can purchase two horses from the settlers. They are leaving, they have no choice. Two or three of them have horses."

She looked at her man. Her man who saw the trouble of her people and wanted to help. Her man who felt the urgency of it, whose face reflected his concern. She thought of Kala's words, of her scorn, and she could feel only a deep pity for Kala. Kala, who would never know what a man was, what love there could be between a man and a woman. *Here was a man.* Her hand crept across the table and rested on his, and they talked as the fire burned low in the hearth.

IT RAINED THROUGHOUT THE DAY, the low clouds rolling down the long valleys. The birch along the cold, quick-running river were lacquered with rainwater, shuddering before the cold wind.

Crenna lifted her eyes to the sky and then glanced at her husband. Water streamed from Van der Veghe's hat and stained his buckskins. His face in profile revealed his concern. He felt her eyes on him, turned, and smiled.

"It will be all right," he said, and she let her horse walk near enough to his so that she could briefly lean her head against his shoulder.

She was weary and cold and knew he must be as well. Thunder rumbled distantly, the wind rattled in the trees. The rain streamed down in silver ribbons. They forded a small brook where red fern and rhododendron grew in a profuse tangle, and climbed the grassy knolls beyond.

Crenna lifted her head suddenly, her nostrils flaring. Van der Veghe had smelled it as well, and now, through the clearing curtain of mist, they could see a long, pale streamer of smoke curling into the gray skies.

"Almost there," Van der Veghe said, and again he attempted a reassuring smile.

"Almost." Crenna's heart began to pound faster, quite ridiculously she thought. And yet she was an outsider now, and her mission seemed impossibly large. She had taken their trust and cast it away for the love of the Dutchman. To return now and attempt to influence them was a formidable task. She had no right at all to speak to the council.

Again she briefly tormented herself. If this war came about, it would be because Crenna had not been there when the Oneida needed her. Yet she never regretted her decision—life with Van der Veghe had been good, she had been happy.

But deep within her, old training, old roads of thought, led to guilt. *The tribe, Crenna, the tribe matters above all else. Without the tribe we are nothing. The tribe nourishes, the tribe protects and comforts.*

Yet she had turned her back on the tribe.

Cold rain trickled down her neck and the wind caused her to draw her blanket more tightly around her shoulders. Now she could see three campfires and hear, through the muffling rain, the sound of a dog yapping.

Briefly she was angry—she did love the tribe, and always would! It was Kala, Pawago, and those like them, those who would rush madly into this war, who did not consider the tribe. If Van der Veghe was right, the tribe would not survive this war. That thought deepened her chill. It was an incomprehensible thought which overwhelmed her with intensity. Her eyes seemed unfocused for a moment; her bones, her blood, seemed to belong to another body far away, and Crenna hovered above that sheath of flesh which had been her.

The Oneida vanished, buried without a trace. . . . She did not choose to think about it any longer. Her hand stretched out unsteadily and touched Van der Veghe's arm. He patted her hand and smiled, but she could see the tension etched into his face.

"It can be done, my darling Crenna, and it is you who must do it."

She only nodded. The lodges were clearly visible now through the iron mesh of rain. A gust of wind caught her dark hair and twisted it. She took in deep, icy breaths and heeled her lazy pony forward a little faster. Then she slowed, relaxed again. She could see the women laying strips of venison on the smoke racks, see children fighting in the fields, see a hunter returning with a buck across his shoulders, a frantic gabble of children at his heels.

They were there, alive, well. The Oneida survived. She shook aside her strange desolate mood, her childish apprehension, and rode on, the mist parting to allow them passage.

A pointing finger lifted toward them, and Crenna heard a shout. People emerged from their lodges and stood squinting into the rain.

A small, frail figure appeared, leaped into the air, and

started running toward them, and Crenna felt her heart warm.

"Crenna! Crenna!" Sachim called until she was breathless, running toward them as the Oneida stood and watched. Crenna got down from her horse and held her arms out to embrace her sister, who rushed into her arms.

Van der Veghe had gotten down as well, and he stood holding the reins to their horses. Sachim turned to him in the drizzle and hugged him tightly, still holding her sister's hand.

Together they turned and walked arm in arm into the camp.

In the milling throng Crenna saw them all—like people returned from the land of the dead, like a dream come to life. Her people, the Oneida! She felt the cold sting of tears in her eyes.

The old man shouldered his way through the crowd, looking stooped and weary. But his eyes were bright, his face glowing as he held out his arms to his daughter.

"Crenna!"

"Father." She went to him, holding him tightly.

"I thought you would never return." He held her at arm's length, searching her lovely face, noticing the few fine lines engraved by the passage of time. Then, a little woodenly, Yushta turned to Van der Veghe and thrust out a hand, which the Dutchman took.

"Yushta, it gives me pleasure to see you well," Peter said quietly.

"Everything is well with you?" Yushta asked, and Van der Veghe nodded. The old man looked beyond them hopefully. He lifted a quizzical eyebrow.

"We did not bring Cara and William, Father. It is a long journey."

"Yes, yes," he said a little heavily. He had obviously wanted to see his grandchildren, despite his pose of indifference. "William," Yushta said, nearly to himself, shaking his head. "That is no name for a warrior."

"In my native land," Peter said, "it was the name of one of the greatest of all warriors. A man who built a great nation."

"Oh?" Yushta brightened at that. "You must tell me about this other William sometime. And you, Crenna, you must tell me all about our small William."

"Of course I will. We didn't think . . ."

"I know. I was disappointed when you left. Angry. But time, age I suppose, have left me with a sense of my own foolishness. I want my daughter back, I wish to see the babies."

"Then you shall," Van der Veghe said immediately. "Soon."

"Come into my lodge," Yushta said, nodding toward the longhouse. "Tell me why you have come."

They followed the old man into the longhouse, Crenna and Sachim whispering together, Van der Veghe striding silently behind them. It was then that they saw him. Standing arrogantly to one side of the longhouse, shirtless in this downpour, his massive chest inflated, arms crossed, haughty black eyes surveying them.

"Good day, Pawago," Crenna said, but the war leader of the Oneida did not answer. He turned sharply away and walked toward his own lodge.

"At least he did not kick me," Van der Veghe whispered, and Crenna laughed out loud.

"He has never forgotten," Yushta said, his old eyes suddenly sharp, warning. "He will never forgive you for taking Crenna."

"No," Peter said, watching the broad back of Pawago vanish through the mist, "I suppose not."

They ducked into Yushta's warm lodge, where a fire burned brightly, and removed their blankets and coats. They steamed by the fire, sipping blackberry tea while Yushta filled a pipe.

"Where is Ta-Tando? And Manto?" Crenna asked.

"Fishing. Both of your brothers are fishing. Winter approaches again, Crenna."

She nodded, only half-hearing the answer. She looked around the lodge at the blankets, the straw baskets, the old bearskin which still hung on the wall. All of it should have seemed so familiar, but did not. Being there brought a rush of disconnected memories. The winter the bear was killed, the disastrous supper Sachim made when she was only seven. But they were fragments only, half-remembered, half-imagined. Even Yushta somehow seemed different.

She recalled vividly how his hands had worked when he used to tuck her beneath the blankets and furs on a winter night, how he would laugh with old Lapsa those times when, pretending to be asleep, Crenna would lie awake listening to the old hunting tales, the blood-curdling stories of war. But this man who sat cross-legged on the floor now, puffing on his clay pipe, seemed not to be the same man. She supposed living with Van der Veghe had changed all of that.

Perhaps she could never again be one of the tribe, no matter how she longed for it. Perhaps she already was no longer Oneida, but half-white, her patterns of thought, her perceptions altered by her tall, yellow-haired man.

"What brings you home, Crenna?" Yushta asked, and she glanced up sharply, hesitant now that the moment had come.

She sat beside her father as Van der Veghe, pretending to be interested in the weather, peered out through the curtain which hung across the doorway.

"I want to speak in council, Father," she said as plainly as he had asked,

The old man's eyebrows folded together. He shook his head. "I don't understand."

"Yes, you do. I want to speak to the council when it gathers."

"In what capacity? You hold no rank, Crenna."

"I am still your daughter."

Yushta was silent for a long while, staring into the fire. The flames twisted themselves into crimson and copper arabesques; the dancing firelight deepened the hollows of Yushta's eyes, and Crenna thought: He looks very old, very weary. Suddenly she wished she had brought the children with her.

"I will ask," he consented. "That is all I can do."

"Thank you, Father." She touched his cheek with the back of her hand, and he took her hand, kissing it.

"I love you, Crenna. I am sorry for . . . before."

"I'm sorry too, Father. Sorry we could not understand each other."

He placed her hand gently aside as if it were something valuable and quite fragile. "What is it you wish to say to the council?"

"I will plead for peace," Crenna said thoughtfully. "This war that is building, it must not be."

"Pyle says that if we do not fight with the English, the Algonquin and French will overrun us."

"Pyle says many things," Crenna answered shortly.

The old man was silent. Then, "Have you seen Kala?"

"Yes. We quarreled. She has told me she is leaving."

Yushta nodded wearily. "What does she say about this war?"

"She echoes Pyle," Crenna said.

Van der Veghe, watching the slow gray drizzle, the drifting of the low, dark clouds above the meadows, heard his wife's soft, coaxing voice find and project a subtle power, and in that moment he understood the sort of headwoman she had been—capable, convincing, inspiring.

"The war," he heard her say, "is a war between the whites. They are using us to their own advantage. The French are using the Algonquin, the British the Iroquois. They are aware of our ancient animosities, and they play upon them. But they have no thought for what is best for the Oneida. We are bodies to them, people to die so that the French must not die, so that the British must not bleed."

"The Great Council does not think so," Yushta objected. "The headwomen of the Onondaga and Seneca do not hold this view. The Iroquois League, even the contrary Mohawk, agree that this war must be fought."

"The Oneida must not fight!" Crenna's voice was soft, but it crackled like the fire at her back. Her eyes were bright with fire. "How do *you* feel, Father? Moa-Telah, the other old sachems?"

"I am not certain. . . ." Yushta's face was glossed with doubt. His face was scored with lines of age and of worry, nearly of pain. "Pawago is war leader," he said with a resigned shrug.

"And craves the gifts of the British, the honors of war."

"Yes, yes," Yushta said miserably. "I do not understand these modern times, Crenna. The war does not seem honorable, yet if we do not fight and the Algonquin come with their French allies . . . I do not know." He sagged as if deflated.

"Will you keep an open mind, Father?" She took his gnarled, leathery hand between both of her own. "Will you listen when I speak at council? Will Moa-Telah and the others?"

He was silent. For a long moment there was no sound but the crackling of the weaving flames, the drumming of rain on the roof of the longhouse.

"Yes," he said finally. "Of course I will listen, but I am afraid this decision is already written in stone, Crenna. I do not think it can be changed now."

"If it cannot, then I fear for us, Father. If it cannot, then I fear we shall be enveloped by storm clouds, and the rain which falls shall be as hard as iron and as deadly."

And it could be, she thought, that there would be no dawn following such a storm. The clouds which approached them were ominous, dark as night, and there was no shelter from the bluster and death-dealing rain of such a storm.

The rain pattered down and the wind tugged at the curtain, but beneath the furs and new blankets, Crenna was warm; beside Peter she was safe from the storm which raged outside. She wrapped herself in forgetfulness.

There was no place on earth so untroubled; nowhere was there shelter to match Van der Veghe's love. His arms were woven around her and his long, muscular thigh was warm against her leg. His breath was gentle on her cheek as he kissed her, and her heart began to hammer as he lowered his lips to her breasts, loving her, driving the world away.

She clung to him as if in desperation, returning two kisses for every one of his, touching his broad chest, his small, whorled ear. Her fingers ran down the knuckles of his spine, and she laughed silently as he pressed against her, being Peter Van der Veghe, the man who could drive away the night.

The rain became a panting, urgent series of exhalations, the thunder a trembling which racked her body, and the rain turned hot, became a part of her, a portion of Peter's love.

He was warm and close in the night, and he took her in his cradling arms and vaulted into the skies, where above the writhing masses of gray clouds, red and yellow, deep blue and violet stars twinkled brightly and they sailed across the oceans, touching mountaintops, viewing exotic cities of gold and of jade before they tumbled earthward, unafraid, clinging to each other, landing softly in deep,

deep clover as they knew they would. And then the sweet summer-warm grass closed over them and they were able to laugh like children before yawning heavily, still clinging to each other; they were able to fall into a deep, heavy sleep, the golden warmth surrounding them like the comforting arms of Manitou.

Dawn arrived with a flourish of color. Crimson arrows pierced the low clouds; a fan of gold sprayed downward, glittering off the lake, which had lain slate gray, silent, moments before.

The sun touched the lake, and it stirred. Fish rose to feed at its polished surface. The maple trees, fresh with rain, stirred and reflected the red of the sky with their autumnal foliage. Frogs grumbled in the cattails, and Manto cast his straw fish traps into the water from the sandy spit where he had made his night camp.

With the traps set, he squatted and chewed on his jerky and pemmican, watching morning flare up, paint the lake and the sky with color, and settle to a dull gray, its life exhausted.

Yesterday's catch was drying on the framework of sticks Manto had constructed, and he walked along the spit to his drying rack, noticing that a raccoon had raided his fish. Its tracks were clearly visible in the soft gray sand.

Manto stretched, yawned sleepily, and glanced toward the woods. He had heard something and thought it must be Ta-Tando, but he saw no one.

Returning to his traps, he squatted on his heels and drew in the sand with a crooked stick. One more day, and he would return home to Taranta. They had three deer now, many fish, and Ta-Tando's bear of which he was inordinately proud.

He looked to the mottled skies, smelling more rain. Winter was not far away, and it would be a hard winter, he thought. Manto thought about his wife, Taranta, for a time, visualizing the heavy, comforting breasts, the sway of her broad, capable hips, her pleasant laugh, and he realized that he was lonely. One more day.

Again he heard the sound, and he stood, peering toward the southern shore. And then he saw them.

Algonquin.

But Manto thought nothing of it. The Algonquin were

his blood enemies, but this was a neutral hunting ground. A necessary convention if both tribes were to survive. It was unlawful to fight in the hunting grounds, and the punishment was severe for any man who did so.

Manto glanced at the Algonquin again, hearing strange words, seeing a flash of brilliant color. Silk it was, like Pyle wore. There was a Frenchman with the Algonquin, and Manto spat on the sand. He did not like the French at all.

The Frenchman was showing something to the Algonquin, whom Manto recognized now. It was Caspa, a young war leader, a broken-nosed, filthy man.

What was it? Manto saw a long bronze funnel attached to a polished section of wood. He frowned, wondering what it could be. As he watched, the Frenchman pointed at him and yanked at a small attachment to the device. He heard Caspa laugh, and Manto felt irritation rising. If it weren't for the laws . . .

The Frenchman lifted the strange device to his shoulder, peering along its length. Manto saw him smile. He saw the puff of black smoke. And then his ears filled with the roar of thunder and he felt fiery rain tear at his body. His eyes—he could not see; and his face was smeared with blood. The Frenchman laughed, Caspa laughed, and Manto felt his legs go rubbery, felt a searing pain writhing in his abdomen, and he knew he was dying.

But how . . . ? He went to his knees, trying to hold his belly together with his hands, but it was useless. The sunrise had returned, fiercely red, dazzlingly bright, and Manto was puzzled by that.

And then he was puzzled by nothing more. He fell through the deep storm clouds beneath him, and his face slammed against the soft gray sand. He lay unmoving beneath the leaden skies while a fine silver fish flapped furiously in his straw net, trying to escape.

The skies paled and then went dark. Storm clouds stood heaped in a jumbled stack against the setting sun. Crenna stood in her father's lodge with Van der Veghe beside her. This, then, was the moment, and she wondered where the old confidence was.

"I'm nervous as a child," she said, and he silently placed a hand on her shoulder. She spun, clung to him for a moment, kissed his lips lightly, and then walked out into the Oneida camp, passing the long rows of houses, the curious black eyes of the children.

There was light from the huge council lodge lying in a damp wedge against the sodden earth, the sound of a man's low, hurried voice.

Crenna swept the curtain aside and stepped into the lodge, and their eyes came up to meet her. They were all there, the old warriors and the young, the headwomen of the clans. There were the faces of those she had comforted, those she had disciplined, advised, and encouraged. They were all different now, seeming alien, and she was a stranger among them. Her resolve faltered, but she took a deep breath, forming her face to reflect confidence, and she took her ceremonial position to her father's right.

Te-al-Pantha stood in one corner. Across from Crenna sat Moa-Telah. He had painted his craggy face. A single white band ran from his forehead down his arched, prominent nose to his chin. He had knotted feathers into his hair. He was not alone in displaying these war signs.

Yet, Crenna thought, they were intelligent people, open to the arguments of logic. She would convince them, she must.

Her buoying confidence was destroyed by the entrance of Pawago. His face and chest were painted wildly, and he carried his war ax; he leaped into the council lodge, waving his ax, cursing the Algonquin profusely. He drew a response—excited agreement, as he had anticipated.

He glared at Crenna as if to say: And what can you answer to that? He knew, somehow he knew why she was there, and his theatrical entrance had been planned to smother her arguments before they had even been presented. There was a war mood in the air, as in the old days, a mood, Crenna thought grimly, which she had once encouraged.

They ate first, and then the pipe was smoked, and eventually the subject was broached. It was Pawago, the supreme Oneida war leader, whose place it was to speak in the absence of Kala, and he came to his feet.

"The Algonquin have been our enemies since before the mountains were thrust up by Manitou in his rage. Since the first man who called himself Oneida fished the long river and sang his hunting songs. We all have fought the

Algonquin. Look, Winneka, where is your arm? The Algonquin took it. And Wakami, who stole your daughter? Who does all evil, is bloody and a shame to Manitou? The Algonquin."

Pawago moved around the lodge restlessly. "It is only a few days to the next Great Council of the Iroquois. The Mohawk, the Seneca, the Onondaga have already voted to war—they know the treachery and evil of the Algonquin. When I go, may I say that all of the Oneida are with our brother Iroquois at this hour?"

There was a chorus of raucous assent, and Pawago grinned. "The snake Algonquin do not have the courage to face us alone. Now they have the Frenchmen with them, many of them. The British, our friends and kinsmen, hate the French—they have warred many times in their own lands. Now the English are here to help us squash these insects.

"Some people say that the English are not our friends." He stopped directly in front of Crenna without looking down at her. "How can that be? They have asked nothing from us but a little land, and to fight at our side. Sir Charles Pyle—is he not our friend? He brought us blankets and knives, he married an Oneida woman. Who can speak against the English? They have not murdered our sons and daughters, killed our warriors, burned our houses—it is the Algonquin who have done that! And the French who have encouraged them. Who," he asked, this time looking directly at Crenna, "can deny this?"

There was a brief silence and then a wild chorus of fervent agreement. Tossing his head, Pawago resumed his seat.

There was little argument, but each person present took the time to make a speech, few of them differing from Pawago's. Crenna waited patiently; old Moa-Telah had begun recounting every battle against the Algonquin he had participated in since boyhood, digressing to hunts and other occurrences as the notion struck him.

Finally he fell silent, leaving one pitched battle at its climax, his old eyes distant, glazed with nostalgia. Crenna saw her father stir, and she felt her pulse quicken. Deliberately she calmed herself.

"My daughter Crenna, who was once our headwoman,

has come with me. She wishes to speak to the council," Yushta announced.

"Let her speak, then," Winneka said, relighting the pipe.

"Yes," Te-al-Pantha agreed. "Let us hear her."

"What business has she here?" Pawago demanded. "She is not headwoman, she is not Oneida."

"I am Oneida," Crenna said to Pawago, meeting his harsh gaze. "You and I have had differences, Pawago, but may I not be allowed to speak for the benefit of the Oneida? I am concerned for my people."

"Concerned?" Moa-Telah asked with surprise.

"Yes," Crenna answered, warming to her task now. "Concerned about this war you propose. Whom does it benefit? The white man. What do they want from us? Our weapons and strong arms first of all, then our land, every inch of it. Why else are they here?"

"She speaks of the French."

"I speak of both sides, French and English!"

"Her husband deals with the French," Moa-Telah said, to Pawago's intense satisfaction.

"Van der Veghe deals with all people."

That thought didn't go down well with the Oneida. Van der Veghe traded with the French, did he? Crenna brushed it aside. "That has nothing to do with war.

"Can't you see what is happening here?" she asked, looking at each warrior and headwoman in turn, her eyes pleading. "If the British win this war, where will they turn next?"

"You speak foolishness, woman," Pawago shouted, not even deigning to use her name. "If the British and Iroquois do not win, we shall be slaughtered by our enemies. We must fight!"

"You must let the Europeans fight their own wars," Crenna said. "Are the Oneida fools, to be used in such a way? What should be done is not being done because of pride and prejudice. What should be done is to council with the Algonquin, to make peace while the whites fight their battles. And battle for what? *For your land.*"

"We can spare a little land," Wakami said. "We have already given some to the English as a peace token. More than they can ever use."

"Ever? They are coming, Wakami, by the hundreds, by the thousands, each day. While we fight and kill each other, they will step over our bodies and claim the land soaked with our blood."

"Only a fool could suggest a council with the Algonquin!" Pawago snorted. "Things have gone too far."

"Only a fool would plunge blindly into this abyss. That, Pawago, is what you would have our people do. You cannot understand the vast implications of this war. The world is moving, traveling across the seas. War is no longer the same. It is not as it used to be when we raided the Algonquin and they raided us. This will be a war of annihilation, a terrible, sweeping war which will not be fought for a time and then forgotten as we return to our winter lodges, but a war which will destroy the Oneida for all time. To win will only be to become lackeys of the British."

"If we can defeat the French, we can defeat the English if that time comes. But why try to see that far into the future? Now is the time we must consider. And now is when we must fight the Algonquin and their French allies to survive!"

There was a murmur of agreement to Pawago's speech, but Crenna began to see doubt on some of the faces around her. She began again, but Pawago interrupted her harshly.

"What right has this woman to speak! Who is she? A Dutchman's woman. She speaks for him."

"I speak for myself and the Oneida!" Crenna shot back.

"Van der Veghe does not want war because he is weak and knows his outpost will be destroyed; he hates the British because they have purchased his land from Wechakapi. He has convinced his woman to speak for him, hoping to save his property."

"This is not true, Pawago. Drop your resentment for a moment and listen to me with your mind! Yes," she said, waving her hands, "Van der Veghe would be destroyed by war, but I don't speak for him, nor has he asked me to. I speak to you because so much more will be destroyed. Our way of life, our race! For what? False valor, manhood, pride! These things do not matter, only our survival matters, and by selling ourselves to the British, we are signing away our right to exist."

She rose and slowly circled the room, her eyes glittering, her fine dark hair reflecting the glow of the low fire. The old intentness was there, but not the old power. How she wished for it for this one moment!

"Already the British speak of the forts they will build at the great lake at Yo-ma-avo. Of the roads they will carve across our land, of the wheat they will grow, of the thousands of whites who will live upon our land! I have heard them at the outpost! *This* is what they war for. For the interest of the *English*! And their interests and ours, Pawago, are not the same. Their interests will bury us, my people."

"Woman's foolishness!" Pawago spat, waving a disgusted hand. He burped a disparaging sound, smirking at Crenna. Moa-Telah sat shaking his head worriedly, in the slow fashion of the old.

Yushta, who had been silent, now spoke. "When things are seen in this light . . . perhaps we should not be too hasty in our decision to fight."

"We don't have the time to listen to each silly woman!" Pawago said. The cords of his throat were taut with anger.

"There is no sense in rushing toward death, Pawago," Moa-Telah said firmly, and Crenna silently blessed the old war chief. "Let us debate until each of us is certain. I suggest we speak again tomorrow, when we are fresh. I am tired now, and would like to sleep."

He had started to rise and Pawago had opened his mouth to object again when the curtain to the council lodge swung open and a blast of cold wind crossed the room, guttering the fire.

Crenna's head spun around. Ta-Tando stood at the door, his body washed with rain, his jaw clenched, his eyes oddly empty.

"Ta-Tando?" Yushta rose and started toward his son. "What is it?"

"Manto, Father. Manto. A Frenchman killed my brother, Manto." He blurted the story out. Returning from his hunting, he had seen a Frenchman with an odd weapon, and Caspa, the Algonquin subchief.

"I paid no attention to them. We were on the neutral hunting grounds, protected by Manitou's laws. And then I saw my brother, Manto, standing hands on hips, watching them. I heard the Frenchman laugh and I saw his weapon explode like thunder. Flame spewed from it, and my brother . . . my brother lay dead."

Then Ta-Tando was silent. His head hung heavily, his narrow shoulders trembled. Crenna glanced at her father, knowing what she would see. The old warrior's face was drawn down with anguish; his fists were clenched tightly. He ground his teeth together and then slowly began cursing, calling for Manitou's wrath to fall upon the French and Algonquin. And she knew, knew that there would be no more talk of peace. The Frenchman had killed her brother; he had also killed any hope there might have been for peace.

She went to her father and held him, and across his shoulder she saw Pawago, despicably smiling. She could have killed him at that moment. She wondered how she could ever have felt love for the Oneida war leader, this sly, devious man.

"I must sleep," Moa-Telah said. He finally rose and came to Yushta, resting a hand briefly on his old friend's shoulder. "We shall find the man, Yushta. Find him and kill him. We will honor Manto."

Yushta shook away from Crenna, and with Ta-Tando at his shoulder, he went out into the darkness, where a heavy rain had again begun to fall.

With a last glance at the smirking Pawago, Crenna followed them. The rain rushed down, slanting across the sky. The wind drifted her hair across her face, chilling her.

The clouds were very low and she moved through them silently, her shawl wrapped around her shoulders. Suddenly Van der Veghe had found her. He knew somehow, already knew, and he held her close to his chest.

From across the camp came the sounds of Yushta's mourning song, and she listened motionlessly to that sound, mingled with the rain, with the soft murmuring of Peter Van der Veghe, who held her, stroking her damp hair while the rain washed down. But it was not enough. Not even Van der Veghe could protect her from this storm; nothing could. It would roll on like a dark, angry behemoth, destroying all in its path, and there was nothing to be done about it. Nothing at all.

❀ 11 ❀

THE ORDERLY, A NARROWLY BUILT corporal with a heavy North Country accent, was packing the last trunk. Sir Charles Pyle, at his desk, was finishing an entry in his journal, which he hoped to publish in London. At the tap on the door he rose, closed the leather-bound journal, and crossed the room.

"Sir Charles."

"Come in, sir," Pyle said warmly. He opened the door wide, and his superior officer entered. General Creighton stood in the center of the room, watching the orderly fold Pyle's dress tunic.

"Nearly ready, are we?" Creighton asked.

"Nearly so."

"I've been down to the ship. The captain's ready to sail when you are. About dusk, I guessed."

"That should be ample time."

"I hate to lose you, Charles, you know that. You've done wonders with the natives. I hate to think what sort of position we'd have been in if you hadn't swung the Iroquois our way." Creighton cleared his throat and asked in a lowered voice, "Has that all been worked out?" He lifted his chin significantly toward the adjoining room.

"No problem there, sir," Pyle replied.

"Good!" Creighton rubbed his hands together and beamed a smile at Sir Charles. "You won't forget to drop in at Kew and see Hattie?"

"No, sir. I'll be sure to visit your wife."

"I appreciate it, sir. Well . . ." Creighton shoved out a red hand. "Take care, Charles. I can assure you that my report will be a glowing account. You'll go far, sir. Doubtless you'll hold rank on me when we next meet."

Pyle laughed and shook Creighton's hand. Then, touching his cap in a two-fingered salute, Creighton left. The orderly had only to fasten the wide leather straps of the trunk, and Pyle told him, "I'll finish up, Corporal."

232

"Very good, sir."

Pyle watched as the man went to the door and passed out; then he approached the adjoining room, hesitating at the door. It wouldn't be easy, but dammit, it had to be done. She was a bouncy little thing, and it was a shame, but what was there to do about it?

Taking resolution and a deep breath, Pyle tapped at the door.

"Come in," Kala said eagerly.

She looked up from her packing to see Pyle in the doorway. He was leaning against the jamb, just studying her with those sea-green eyes.

"Almost ready," Kala said. "I can't wait to get started. Though I'm nervous about the ship and all, when we—"

"You can't go, Kala."

She couldn't believe she had heard him right. She half-smiled, and stood looking at him, trying to make sense out of the words.

"You can't go to England with me. I already have a wife, you see." He smiled with bitterness or perhaps regret. "It wouldn't do at all for me to show up with another."

Kala couldn't answer; she couldn't move. Someone had torn her insides out. The world, firm and familiar beneath her feet moments ago, had simply vanished. She stood staring.

"You'll be better off here, Kala, honestly. Among your own kind. You wouldn't understand England, nor would it understand you. Look here, take everything." He waved his hand magnanimously. "Dresses, jewelry, it's all still yours. Go back to your people."

"Why?" Her voice issued from her throat in a strangled croak. "Why?"

"I'll be frank with you, Kala," Pyle said breezily. "I want you to stay here, among the Oneida. If you leave, there will be a new headwoman, won't there? Your sister—what is that little one's name? Never mind. But the British need a strong friend among the Oneida . . ."

His voice droned on, and Kala, still standing rigidly in the center of the room, overwhelmed by humiliation, said nothing. She barely heard him.

What had happened? Moments ago she was set to travel to England with her husband, to live in his manor house, to wear jewelry and meet his friends, to raise his children. . . . A slow, solemn anger began to build in Kala's breast. She realized only now what had happened.

He had planned this from the first! He had never loved her, but only used her to forge an alliance. He had sacrificed himself for the king!

"It must have been terrible for you," she said, stepping nearer. "Having to sleep with a savage. And did you laugh when you told the other Englishmen about it? Did you have your dirty little jokes?"

"Kala, be reasonable." His voice had become stern, parental. "You've had other men. We gave each other pleasure, and incidentally helped our people. I've left you with quite a lot, things you never could have seen or even dreamed of in your entire life! Diamonds, for God's sakes, pearls! You are undoubtedly the richest woman on this continent right now. What else could you want! Grow up, for God's sake. You think I could present you to the king! I'd be a mockery. It can't work."

"I love you." Her voice was soft, her eyes beseeching. She stepped even nearer, so that her face was only inches from his chest. She looked up into his eyes, her fingers touching his tunic.

"For heaven's sake, woman. You couldn't have believed . . . not deep in your heart!" He laughed again, and Kala could not stand it. The cruelty, yes, the insults. But not the mocking laughter.

"I love you!" she screamed. She hurled her arms around his neck, and Pyle stepped back, prying her loose. Kala's hand struck out, meeting his cheek with a resounding slap. She struck him again and again, but he didn't even respond. She clung to him, tearing at his clothes, the hot tears welling up in her eyes.

She had hold of his neck with one hand, and now he deliberately, casually removed her hand. He was smiling, damn him! Smiling. The tears wouldn't stop, and that angered Kala. She wanted to tear his throat out, to kill him.

"Kala!" He had both of her wrists now, and he shook her violently until her head snapped back and forth. "You're being foolish. Go home, Kala. You'll see that I'm right when you've cooled off."

Then, as if she weighed nothing, he flung her away. Losing her balance, she crashed to the floor, banging the small of her back on one of the trunks. A strand of carefully arranged hair fell free to droop across one eye. She sat staring at the door. He had gone, simply gone. Thrown her away and departed, still smiling.

She got to hands and knees, and panting, crawled toward the door. Rising, she gripped the latch and yanked, but he had bolted the door from the other side. She pounded the flats of her hands against the rough wooden door. "Pyle!" she screamed. "Pyle!"

But there was no answer. The man was gone. He was filth, he was a devil! She loved him.

Go home. Go home and tell Yushta, tell everyone that her British husband had discarded her, that he already, in fact, had a wife in England! Go home? She sagged to the floor, her back to the locked door, and began to laugh. She laughed until the tears began to flow again; then she buried her face in her hands.

Her nose was running, and that irritated her. Rising, she staggered across the room, throwing a drawer from the bureau as she looked for a handkerchief. All of them had been packed.

Kala wiped her nose on the sleeve of her new blue velvet gown and threw back her head, snuffling and coughing. Her hair was already in disarray; now she tore the pins from it and let it fall free.

She sat on her trunk and looked around at the empty room. She was trembling now, and so she went to the sideboard and removed a decanter of whiskey. Pyle had introduced her to liquor, and she was fond of it. It numbed the senses, blurred reality, and when you were in high spirits, it made the world bright with sparkling gaiety. She poured herself a glass of whiskey, downed it, and then threw the glass angrily against the wall, where it shattered.

Sitting on the trunk once more, she drank directly from the decanter, feeling her heart slow and thud away heavily with deliberate, slow cadence. She sniffed again and wiped her eyes.

The whiskey burned her throat and bubbled up in her nose. Her stomach started to turn over and then relaxed, and almost instantly she felt a golden haze surround her. She relaxed slightly, and still sniffing, turned her eyes to the doorway again.

It could not have happened! He loved her; he had told

her so many times. *Go home, Kala.* Go home and leave your pulsing, bleeding heart lying on the floor, and when I have time, I shall come back and step on it once again.

She took another drink, noticing the small whirring sounds beginning in her ears. Outside, it was growing dark. Twilight shadows fell through the narrow slits in the walls of the log house.

Go home, Kala, and tell them it was all a joke. Say, "Look he has given me jewels, it's all right. He has paid me for my favors, what else can I want?" *Crenna.* Oh, would she laugh. She and Van der Veghe together in their bed, laughing through the night: poor, dear Kala.

She took another drink. The room was a blur now. Was it the darkness or the liquor? And where, for that matter, was the joy which came in the bottle? Where were the laughter and the tingling, uplifting warmth.

This whiskey's spirit had gone cold, had deserted the bottle. Pyle had taken the spirit with him, as he took all. All of it! Sailing away with it, crossing that sea Kala had never yet viewed. Back to England. Let me tell you about my savage Indian lover!

Kala's head fell forward. She was extremely dizzy. Her eyes, at cross-purposes, let things drift in and out of focus. She saw a scattering of hairpins, a few shards of crystal. The shadows merged in the center of the floor, forming a dark pool, and she watched them leadenly.

She heard a shout outside the house, and it was a moment before she could react, could lurch to her feet and with the decanter dangling from her hand make her way to the window.

She leaned her head heavily against the wall and squinted into the dusky light outside. She saw the sails being unfurled, saw a sailor in the rigging, saw low fog creeping lazily down the river.

Pyle. "Don't leave me," she said, rolling her head from side to side. Abruptly that mood passed. She looked at the nearly empty decanter and dropped it, letting it roll around the floor, the last of its amber contents staining the wood. She crossed quite deliberately to her trunk, fumbled with the straps with wooden fingers, and finally flung it open.

She began digging, strewing her dresses, her petticoats, her scarves and hats about the room. There it lay. Kala's hand closed around the handle of the carving knife. Pretty, ebony-handled, deadly knife. She straightened up with alarm, but there was no one there. Only spirits, dark and tormenting, flitting across the deeply shadowed room. Her hair hung in her eyes; she wobbled as she made her way to the door, slipped the knife between the badly fitted door and the jamb, and lifted, freeing the latch.

Pyle's room was dark and cold, smelling faintly of him, of bay rum and tobacco, of leather. It was a cold room, barren and dead.

Kala crossed the room, fumbling for the latch to the outside door. Slipping out onto the porch, she moved quietly, swiftly through the shadows, the whiskey hot in her veins, the spirits whispering bloody thoughts in her ears. She slipped once and went down, slashing her own hand with the long-bladed knife.

She sucked at the cut and stumbled on, her heart pounding, her ears ringing, her vision blurred. The ship seemed impossibly distant. Her legs were miles away, futile, churning, childish appendages.

The stockade gate was unguarded—the river gate opened only from the inside. Kala could see the sailors walking around the capstan, bringing the anchor up, and she hurried even more. Her lungs were fiery with the exertion, the knife in her hand was cool, her eyes were unfocused.

She was suddenly there. The river lapped at the rocks along the bank. The ship towered above her, creaking and groaning, impatient to begin its journey.

Kala stood panting for a moment. Then, holding her breast over her heart, she rushed to the dock. Clambering up, she walked its length, feeling the give of the sodden planks underfoot, smelling the river, the lingering salt scent of the ship itself.

Pyle. There he stood, alone at the rail, and he seemed hardly surprised as Kala, breaking again into a run, sprinted toward the ship, holding her long skirts high.

She saw the dark figures of monkeylike sailors in the rigging, heard a shouted command. A star, glimpsed through the masts of the ship, blinked mockingly. She reached the ship and threw herself onto the rope ladder which dangled from the rail.

Clawing her way up, she whispered over and over,

"Pyle. Pyle." Then she was on deck. None too soon. The ship slipped away from the dock and drifted on the slow tide of the Hudson, sailing seaward, the dark, squat fort being left behind as the sails overhead caught the wind and impelled the ungainly craft southward.

He was there—there at the rail—and although she could not see his face in this light, she knew he was smiling. That old hateful, spellbinding smile.

He had his back to the rail. The crosshatched shadow of a rigging ladder barred his face and torso. His eyes caught the faint gleam of a lantern astern. Kala staggered as the ship rolled, changing tack slightly, and she had to grab hold of the rail to steady herself.

"Kala." His voice was flat. No surprise registered.

She loved him. She hated him. She wanted to cut his heart out, to die in his arms.

"Kala?"

She moved along the railing, a dark, whispery shadow in the night.

"What are you doing here?" he demanded. "I told you to go home, why didn't you go?"

In response she held the knife up, and it too caught the faint glimmer of light from the swinging lantern. She held it poised overhead, ready to strike downward instantly. Yet her heart was pounding and she could decide nothing—love, hate? To kill or let live, to throw herself at his feet, to spit in that magnificent, supercilious face. The tears began again, and she damned them for giving her away.

"Ah, now, Kala, It's hardly worth this, is it? I'm a rogue and a scoundrel, not worth the killing, nor the tears of a pretty woman. I was sent to do a job, and I did it to the best of my ability; I am sorry, really, that you had to be a tool in this bit of work . . . but then"—he sighed—"that is a woman's lot anyway, isn't it? Likely always will be, in the last analysis.

"But I'm not worth the loving, dear girl, and certainly not worth the killing."

She was wagging her head, agreeing with him despite herself. Still the knife hovered overhead. Pyle, unflinching, unmoving, watched it. Then, damn him, he had to smile, and Kala lunged at him, the knife flashing in the feeble lantern light.

She drove it at his heart, felt her arm come up short as his forearm blocked her downstroke. She screamed and tried to twist free, but he had her wrist in his grip and he bent her hand back upon itself until her fingers opened involuntarily and the knife clattered to the deck.

"Kala . . ." He was panting now too, but his eyes were cold. Kala twisted out of his grasp, swung out at him with all the strength she possessed. She hit his temple, and he shoved her away angrily. Now for the first time his smile fell away, and Kala, through the haze of liquor and rage, was gratified. She dived for the knife, and he kicked it, sending it spinning away into the shadows.

Kala hit the deck hard in a headlong, futile dive. Slowly she got to her feet, and the face she now saw was not that of the Pyle she knew. It was neither mocking nor amused; he was angry and deadly serious, his hooded eyes glaring at her. For a moment she was too afraid to move, but then she leaped at him, trying to claw his eyes, to knee him in the groin.

She saw his fist descend, felt it club her skull, and the dizziness of the whiskey was nothing compared to the violent vertigo which overwhelmed her now.

"Damn you," he breathed into her face, "why couldn't you have let it alone!" His fist fell again, and Kala felt blood spew from her nose. She staggered backward until her waist met the railing. Still Pyle came at her. She lifted up her hands to protect her face, but that did no good. He mauled her savagely like a big cat, beating her, battering her until she felt her feet go out from under her, felt herself slip over the railing and tumble through space.

Her head struck something hard, and her mind was flooded with red lights. Then she was in the water, the dark, sucking water, going down into its icy grip, her eyes seeing nothing, her body unable to respond to her commands. She saw the lantern through the fathoms of water, saw the dark bulk of the ship, and then Kala saw no more. There was nothing more to fight for, and so she gave it up, feeling the dark grasping hands of the river spirits claw at her breasts and tug her gently, inexorably to the depths of their dark watery home.

"Everything all right, Sir Charles?"

"What?" Pyle turned from the rail to see the ship's captain, a squat, red-bearded man, standing before him, his eyes narrow with puzzlement.

"Yes, Captain," Pyle said. He smiled graciously. "Quite all right."

"I thought I heard . . ."

"Quite all right, sir. No problem at all. Nice night for sailing, eh?"

"Good weather, sir," the captain answered uncertainly. "If you're sure . . . ?"

"Quite sure, sir. It's all been taken care of, you see. Nothing to worry about. It's all over now."

With a moan she came swimming out of the darkness and sat straight up in bed. The night was cold; Van der Veghe slept. What was it?

Crenna shuddered, looked slowly around once more, and lay back, eyes open to the night. It had come from out of the depths of a dream, a cry for help, a hand reaching toward her from out of infinite darkness, a mortal, muffled scream.

Crenna felt her heart skip. She ran her tongue around her dry mouth and closed her eyes tightly, trying to piece together an explanation of the event. There was no answer. The night had simply grown weary of its lethargy, and growing malicious, it had roughly prodded Crenna awake.

Awakened now, she could not go back to sleep. The world outside was awake, plotting, hating, preparing to bleed itself upon the earth.

She thought of a dozen impossible schemes. She would visit the Algonquin. Plead for peace. It was absurd, even in this half-dreaming state. They would likely murder her on sight. If she talked, they would not believe her. If the impossible were to happen and the Algonquin agreed to meet the Iroquois, what then—would the Oneida listen to her? No. The war had been hatched in private meetings, nurtured by hatred, and now it was a walking, squalling child of destruction; soon it would grow into a bloody giant, spreading destruction, overwhelming even those who had conceived it.

She lay back again; the night throbbed on.

It was a week after that that Sachim arrived. A rainstorm had passed in the night and the trees were speckled with jewels of water in the morning sunlight. High clouds drifted past overhead. She came out of the forest carrying a sack across her shoulder. Her hair was loose down her back, and she moved so tentatively that at first Crenna thought her sister was injured. But she was not; she was simply uncertain, approaching the outpost like some wild creature afraid of rejection, prepared for a rapid retreat.

"Sachim." Crenna held her tightly, smelling the familiar scent of her hair, looking into those wide, open eyes.

Sachim smiled weakly. "May I stay with you?" she asked, and Crenna was too astonished to reply at first.

"Certainly," she said finally.

"But Peter . . ."

"He has told you before you are always welcome here, Sachim. You know that. Come in by the fire. Tell me what this is about."

Sachim nodded almost with gratitude. But before they entered the outpost, Sachim halted, and gripping Crenna's arm, said, "You know Kala is dead, don't you?"

"Dead?" Crenna laughed. "She's gone away with her husband, I know that."

"I don't mean that. She is dead, Crenna."

"How? What do you mena?"

"I don't know how. When or where. I only know she is dead. I saw her face in a dream, and it was the face of the dead. She smiled as if to say she was not in pain and reached a hand toward me. Then I saw her no more. She is dead, Crenna. I thought maybe you had seen her as well."

"I'm sure she's not dead," Crenna said, embracing Sachim once again. She was aware of Van der Veghe standing in the outpost door, watching them. "She's happy, having the time of her life in England." All the same, she remembered her own visitation, and deep within her she knew that Sachim was right.

Van der Veghe greeted Sachim, asking Crenna a question with his eyes. She could only shrug. They had tea and ate, waiting until Sachim was ready to tell them.

"With Kala gone," she told them hesitantly, "I am headwoman of the Oneida. It is mine by birthright, this position for which I am fantastically unsuited." Crenna objected, and Sachim, smiling sweetly, took her hand across the table. "It's true—everyone knows it. I haven't my sister Crenna's intelligence and power of persuasion; I haven't even my sister Kala's magnetism and raw energy. Nevertheless, I am headwoman."

Sachim lifted her hair back over her shoulders and looked at them with bright, wide eyes. Crenna waited patiently.

"My first act was to speak to the council, speak against the war. They did not laugh out loud," she said ironically, "but my words meant nothing."

"You are headwoman!"

"In their minds it is a title only. I tried to argue with Pawago. He simply mauled me and cast me aside. I am, as I say, unsuited."

Crenna watched her sister closely now, knowing that she was holding something back. There were deep shadows in her eyes.

"I could do nothing, you see. Nothing but watch them go out to war, watch them return. There are battles constantly now. The camp has been attacked once, although the warriors beat them back before the Algonquin could cause much damage.

"I watched them go out," she repeated with a sigh, "and I watched them come back . . . until I could not watch anymore. I have come here. I was impressed with the peace of this place, with the peace of your love. I would not be an imposition," she promised.

"Of course not," Crenna said, feeling a dampness in her eyes.

"I only regret that we cannot promise that our peace will continue," Van der Veghe said.

"But what about Kinpo?" Crenna asked. "I thought you were to marry him."

"Kinpo." She repeated it softly. "Yes, he and I married. Then I watched him go out to war. He did not return, Crenna."

They sat silently for a minute, and then Crenna rose, walked around the table and held her sister, bending her head to her back. "Stay with us, Sachim. Stay and share what peace we can offer you."

Van der Veghe heard them arriving before they emerged from the forest. Twenty British soldiers led by two mounted officers. Glancing toward the river, he saw

Crenna at her washing, saw Sachim leading the children in some dancing game. Then his eyes shifted back to the crimson-clad soldiers.

One of the officers he recognized, although he did not know his name. He heard a small sound behind him and saw Turlock slip out the side door. One day Turlock would not return.

"Good morning, Van der Veghe."

Van der Veghe nodded as the officer swung down from his horse. There was something about the soldiers . . . And then it hit him. A dozen of these uniformed men were Indians! Mohawk. The incongruity of it was enough to make Van der Veghe think he was imagining it; but there they stood, not as rigid as their British counterparts as they waited at attention, their uniforms not fitting so well, but they were there. Van der Veghe had time to notice they were barefoot before the British officer spoke again.

"You were notified that this land was British soil and advised to move from it, Mr. Van der Veghe." He spoke as if he were reading from a scroll. Crenna, Peter saw, was hurrying toward the outpost.

"Yes, I was advised," Van der Veghe said. "But I explained to General Creighton that I have this property through my wife on a lifetime lease from the Mohawk chieftain Wechakapi. I have the treaty inside, if you would care to—"

"I assure you that it would mean nothing to me, nor would it prevent me from acting upon my orders, which were issued by General Creighton . . ."

Damn, couldn't the man talk like a human being?

"What is this!" Crenna had Van der Veghe's arm, and she spoke fiercely, eyeing the young Mohawk in uniform. "This is my land. Given me by Wechakapi. We are supposed to be allies—the British and the Oneida. What right have you to come here and try to force us off our land!"

"Madam. I have my orders."

"You are no warrior. You are a coward. Twenty men to force the rightful owners of this property from it. Who do you think you are?"

"Lieutenant James Briggs, madam."

"And I am Crenna. An Oneida woman. This is my land. Get off it!"

Briggs had developed a tic under his left eye. Each time it twitched, his reddish mustache lifted at the corner. "I understand that this argument has been presented to General Creighton already. I understand that the argument is unsatisfactory. I understand that you have no official position with the Oneida council, madam, that in fact you are not Oneida, according to your tribal laws."

"But *I* am." The interrupting voice was more timid than strident, but there was an inflexible resolve in it. "I am Sachim, the headwoman of the Oneida people. What are you doing, you who are supposed to be our allies?"

Briggs was hardly at a loss for words. "Madam, whoever you are, I assure you that according to the stipulations of the treaty signed by General Creighton and the leaders of your nation—"

"*I* am the leader of the Oneida nation," Sachim said, and her voice was as forceful as Crenna had ever heard it. "If you dare trespass on my sister's land, dare try to bully her and her husband, I can assure you there will be no treaty between Creighton and the Oneida."

Briggs faltered for the first time. Who in hell was this reedy woman with the huge dark eyes? His orders had been most definite—dispatch the Dutchman—yet he might be damaging the Iroquois alliance if he moved at this point, ignoring Sachim's claims. He would have to talk to Creighton; that was all there was to it. Damnation!

"I shall return, Van der Veghe," Briggs assured him, and Van der Veghe did not doubt it. They stood together, the three of them, watching the soldiers disappear again into the deep green forest.

"You did it!" Van der Veghe said to Sachim, whirling her around. Sachim smiled briefly, tentatively.

"And you said you had no strength. It was magnificent!" Crenna added.

"He angered me, that's all," Sachim said. "It doesn't matter in the end, does it? He'll be back. There will be no peace here. There is no peace left anywhere in our land. Our people hunger for excitement, for the thunder of war. There will be no peace for any of us."

Sachim was right, and they knew it. Still, they dared hope.

It was three nights more before they came. Van der Veghe sat up in bed, seeing Crenna already at the window.

Sachim was rubbing her eyes, sitting in her own bed. Peter vaulted from the blankets and went to the window.

"What is it?"

Before Crenna could answer, Van der Veghe saw it for himself. There were a dozen men swarming over his outpost. His furs were stacked in the yard, his goods strewn across the earth. The raiders were Indians, wearing paint. They moved silently, swiftly.

Van der Veghe's hand was on the door latch before Crenna could stop him. "No," she said, pleading with her eyes. "It's no good. What can you do to stop them?"

"I can't let them ruin the place!" Van der Veghe was frantic. He tried to tear free of Crenna's grip, but she held on, clinging to his wrist and shoulder.

"Don't go. They will kill you! What are a few furs? What are all of them?"

"Our life!" Van der Veghe shot back.

"*We* are our life. Not a pile of animal skins. Don't go, Peter! There's nothing to be done."

They were simultaneously aware of the glare of the fire. Flinging open the door, Crenna still clutching his arm, Van der Veghe saw the flames begin to leap and dance against the purple sky. Great golden fountains of sparks shot up, and the writhing, greedy flames were gnawing at the walls of the outpost. Crenna felt the tension go out of Van der Veghe, felt him surrender to inevitability.

The fire lit the skies, and a few of the Indians broke into an impromptu dance. A war whoop shattered the stillness, and the flames roared in response.

They wasted nothing—the furs were taken away, along with the food supplies. But the outpost was only ashes and ruined timbers by morning when Crenna and Van der Veghe went out into the frosty yard.

They stood together staring at the ruin of their work, at their hopes, at the ashes of their peace. Van der Veghe said nothing for a long while. He leaned heavily against Crenna's shoulder, and then finally with a smile he said, "Well, we'll have to work out of the house for a time."

"You mean to stay?" she asked.

"Yes." His words were slow, his tone heavy. "We will stay. Who are they to drive us out? This is our home. Let them take their war someplace else. We shall endure." He lifted Crenna's face to his and asked with quiet concern, "Or do you think it is wrong?"

"Wrong? For us to keep what is ours, to live our lives in peace while they wage war? It is not wrong, Peter. It is what must be done."

While it could be done. War was stretching its massive arms, striding across the land, darkening the skies, and the iron-hard rain had already begun.

Turlock never came back after that day. After all, he was Mohawk too, and there was no store to work in. Crenna and Van der Veghe gave little thought to trading and rebuilding the outpost that fall. Winter was coming on quickly, and they were without provisions. And so, as Crenna's people had always done, they hunted and fished, and with Sachim's help they prepared for the hard weather.

Van der Veghe went once to the British post to lodge a complaint, but Creighton told him, "The Crown can hardly be held accountable for the actions of certain unidentified savages." The sarcasm and hypocrisy were so heavy that Van der Veghe was happy just to leave the fort and breathe the clean air outside once more.

"I asked about Kala," he told Crenna, "but he knows nothing. Another savage—'Who knows what motivates these people?' No, he didn't know if Pyle took her, they had never discussed it."

"And this," Crenna said so quietly that Van der Veghe could barely hear her, "is the savior of my people. Why can't they see what is happening? Why can't they see who these men are, what they want?"

There was no answer to her question, and so Van der Veghe did not try to respond. He knew how she felt. If Van der Veghe could see his life crumbling away, his dreams burned to ashes, Crenna, he knew, was wise enough to see the way of her people, their very existence, being swept away by the same forces. And they eagerly came up to meet the forces of destruction. They embraced the Giant and smiled as it devoured them. And there was nothing to be done about it, nothing. The world had gone dark and cold, and they could only suffer it.

12

THE FIRST SCOUT FOUND THE blue-clad French army and its Algonquin allies at sunrise, camped along the upper Hudson, fifty miles north of Albany. The runner turned and began the long journey back toward the Oneida war camp. It took him most of the morning, and on exhausted legs, his body raining perspiration, he made his report.

The supreme Oneida war chief looked up and smiled thinly, praising the runner. "Now," Pawago said to the narrow warrior beside him, "we have them."

Ta-Tando wrapped his gray blanket more tightly around his shoulders. "Are we ready to attack, Pawago?" His voice was tight, thin.

"Not until Creighton is with us."

"What help has he been up to now?" Ta-Tando asked sharply.

"Little," Pawago admitted. "But it is what the British can provide from now on that matters. The French have given up their tactics of concealment. Now they march side by side with the Algonquin. Now the British must come forward as well."

"We do not need the British." Ta-Tando leaned forward. His face, striped with yellow and red paint, was strained, shaded with anger. Pawago hoped he was not going to fall into one of his fits as he had at Beaver Creek before the battle.

"The British have cannon. So do the French. We do not want to face the French cannon. Let the Europeans battle each other; let the Algonquin scalps hang from our leggings. It is the way this war must be fought, Ta-Tando," Pawago said, explaining carefully to his lieutenant. "There are in fact two wars: the European war being fought on our land and our war with the Algonquin. Creighton has explained this; did you not listen?"

"I listen to nothing the white bastard says."

"Then you are making a grave mistake," Pawago

snapped, the humor going out of his eyes. "He is our ally. Why abandon your strength? If we have cannon and British soldiers available, why not use them to our advantage? You are a poor tactician, Ta-Tando."

"Give me the chance to lead," Ta-Tando said, "and I will show you what kind of tactician I am. Why does Te-al-Pantha have command of the second unit? I am supposed to be your lieutenant."

"Te-al-Pantha has more experience." Pawago smiled again, and there was no warmth in it. Ta-Tando seemed not to notice. "Your time is coming, Ta-Tando. Soon. Be patient, little warrior, be patient."

The following day Ta-Tando and Pawago went to the fort on the Hudson, and there they conferred with Creighton. The British general had learned a few things in his short stay in America. He no longer spoke condescendingly to the Oneida; he treated them like equals. Yet Ta-Tando could see the mockery lurking in Creighton's eyes as he outlined the battle plan. Ta-Tando mentioned this to Pawago.

"You see scorn everywhere, Ta-Tando." Pawago put his hands on Ta-Tando's shoulders. "You are my great friend, but this is the truth—you are too ready to take offense, and always have been."

"Perhaps. Yet I don't like this ally of ours, I don't like the battle plan."

"It is a good plan. We will assault the French-Algonquin force, striking quickly and from cover. Killing all we can, we will retreat before our own casualties can be heavy. Retreat and lead the enemy behind us into Creighton's cannon. What is wrong with that?"

"We risk too much; Creighton risks too little."

"We are mobile, Ta-Tando. It must be our force which strikes."

"I don't like it," Ta-Tando repeated, and now Pawago's face stiffened.

"It is the way it will be, Ta-Tando."

"Yes. All must be as Pawago says." With that Ta-Tando turned and went back to the fire to squat on his heels beside old Moa-Telah, who had insisted on fighting. Ta-Tando said something to the old man, and both sets of eyes shifted to Pawago, who spun on his heel and stalked away, wondering why he had put up with this sulky, unpredictable warrior for so long.

Their anger at Crenna, their hatred of Van der Veghe, had united them; their war aspirations kept them bound. Yet Ta-Tando was too timid. His caution was a tether on his freedom of action.

Pawago stood on a wooded hill rise overlooking the valley of the Mohawk. He could see all the way to the Hudson and beyond, and he thought: I am the master of this land. Creighton believes it is his, old Wechakapi still thinks it is the Mohawk who control the valleys. But I am the conqueror, the defender. Far to the north, through the purple haze of twilight, Pawago could see other campfires burning. Many of them, and he smiled thinly, knowing that they were the fires of his enemy. In a matter of days they would all be dead or dispersed, and Pawago would stand as supreme warlord of the Iroquois nation, the greatest warrior who had ever lived. So it would be; so it must be, it was his destiny.

Van der Veghe carried water to the two horses, pausing to examine the hock of the roan. It had nicked itself somehow, but the wound was healing. He patted the horse's neck and stood silently in the corral for a minute, in no hurry to get on with his other business.

What business? He had to smile. The British had ransacked his outpost. His furs had been stolen. No Dutch trader would ever come again, and if the armies of the French came, they would not be coming to trade. The Mohawk were up in arms—something was brewing out there, they heard runners in the night, many runners, and sometimes saw them flitting through the woods, as swift and ghostly as shadows. None of the other neighboring tribes dared to come to the outpost; the Munsee, the Susquehanna, the Leni-Lenape, were staying close to their lodges, knowing that the great nations were warring. If they did come, Van der Veghe had nothing left to trade.

It was discouraging. He could only wait and hope that times would get better. At times he felt useless now, beaten, ineffectual, and his spirits drooped.

He lifted his head, his hand still on the roan's shoulder. There she was—he smiled warmly—the reason he did not give in to despondency, the reason he hoped, the reason he lived.

"Peter!"

She waved a hand and ran across the yard. Peter watched her, still, after all this time, fascinated by the sway and rhythm of her agile body, by the oval face framed in black hair. That face which was at once serious and amused, ready to laugh, to enjoy life, but which reflected an awareness of the deeper seriousness of existence. That face which beamed when it turned to the children, which could warm his own heart more than any winter fire.

"What is it?" he asked. She slipped beneath the corral rail and stood beside him. Peter put a hand on her shoulder, lightly stroking her sleek neck.

"They're here."

"Who's here?" His eyes lifted to the outpost. He saw no one but Sachim and the children.

"Not at the post, but a few miles distant. I met a runner at the river. We spoke while he drank. He was Mohawk, carrying word to Pawago."

"Pawago!" Van der Veghe frowned, his eyebrows drawing together. "I thought this was a Mohawk war."

"It is not, Peter. It is an Iroquois war. The gathered tribes are moving eastward to join the Mohawk. The Oneida, being the closest, are already here." She held his shirt sleeves tightly and said, "Don't you see what this means? Yushta is up there, Ta-Tando, all of them. And they will come down to fight beside the British."

"We expected it. Eventually."

"But not this soon."

There was something on Crenna's mind, and he had a foreboding of what it was. He was hesitant to ask, but finally he did. "What will you do?"

"Go to them."

"It's useless, Crenna!" He felt real fear growing in his heart. He held her by the shoulders, looking into that implacable face. "Useless and quite dangerous."

"I have to go."

"Why?"

"To speak to them, to beg them to stop before it's too late."

"It won't do any good. You know it. I know it. They're determined to have their war."

"I know." Her eyes pleaded with his, asking for understanding. "But as long as there's a chance, Peter . . . as long as there's any hope . . . The fighting hasn't begun, I must speak to them."

He ran a harried hand through his hair and shook his head slowly. "It's too dangerous."

"They won't hurt me."

"Not even Pawago?"

"No, not even Pawago. I know it's futile, I know that the massed weight of the Oneida force is moving toward war, gaining inertia, gathering strength. They have decided to fight, to bleed. I know it is futile!" Her voice softened. "But it has not yet been done, and up until the moment the first arrow has been loosed, there is still a chance that it might not happen. A chance."

"Damned slim chance."

"But a chance."

He nodded slowly. The woman would have her way. She loved her people, and that was that. She had been a leader for them. A great leader; at times, despite himself, Van der Veghe felt guilty about taking her from them. They needed her, or someone like her now, at this time of war. The war, they both felt, would be the end of the old way. The war, when it came, would upset tradition and crush the Indians' independence. New allies brought new restrictions, new obligations, new treachery, new dangers subtle and more menacing than the Oneida could comprehend.

"All right." Peter kissed her cheek. The wind teased a strand of her hair, placing it briefly against his lips. "Go to them, Crenna, and if there is a way . . . may Manitou let you find it."

She did not look at him again. Slipping under the rail, she disappeared into the forest, becoming one with it. She walked on, her thoughts somber, until she suddenly stopped and smiled, looking back. *May Manitou let you find a way.*

They had lived together a long while, this Dutchman and Crenna. They were interested in each other's ways, wanting to learn in order to grow closer. Peter had not been thinking about what he was going to say; the Iroquois saying, a familiar expression with Crenna, had slipped from his lips unbidden.

She could only repeat the thought and hurry on. The wind was cold; the barren trees shivered before it. Soon it would snow. If the war did not begin soon, perhaps it would not begin this year. Perhaps if the Oneida had a winter to ponder this, their determination would fade. . . . Meager hopes, but she fed herself on them as she walked the long slopes, rushing to head off destruction.

She found the camp at noon. Five hundred Oneida warriors at rest on the wooded hill. At rest, their thoughts, their eager souls poised, alert, ready to go into combat, to cover themselves with glory, to fight and die.

Their faces were painted, their chests covered with totem signs and spirit symbols. They worked on their weapons or sat in wooden silence around the dead campfires. Crenna walked among them, through them, past eyes which recognized her yet gave no indication of it. No voice was lifted in greeting; perhaps her reputation had been so tarnished that they despised her; she could not tell. There had been a time when she could read their thoughts, when she knew their tendencies, how to cajole and soothe and inspire each warrior. Now she had forgotten.

Her time had gone, and she was a stranger among them. Te-al-Pantha was the first of the leaders she encountered. He was still a tall, handsome man, but the years had added lines to his face. His mouth was downturned, his face leathery and still as she approached him.

"I greet you, Te-al-Pantha."

"You should not be here."

"But I am. Where is Pawago? Where is Yushta?"

"Together." Te-al-Pantha inclined his head toward the south. "Go home, Crenna," he said as she started that way. "We do not want you among us anymore."

Stung, she turned, a harsh reply on her lips, but Te-al-Pantha had risen, and now he walked away, his back rigid. There was no point in hurling words after him.

Did they all feel that way? Had feelings—feelings she once had thought of not only as respect but also as love—soured so much? She had felt a stranger; now she felt herself an enemy.

Ta-Tando was there, and he stood gaping. He tried to

make his face a mask of indifference, but he had never been good at hiding his feelings, this brother of hers.

"Ta-Tando." She touched his shoulder, and he only belatedly drew away from her hand. "Where are Pawago and Father?"

"They do not want to see you," he said shortly.

"What has happened, Ta-Tando? Do they speak so badly about me? Has Pawago's hatred infected everyone?"

"You left the tribe . . ." He hesitated. "It is said you are in league with the Algonquin."

"With the . . ." Crenna had to laugh, but it was a dry expression. Clever, clever Pawago. *Of course she speaks against war, she is in league with the Algonquin.* In Ta-Tando's eyes she read doubt. "You don't believe that, do you, Brother?"

"I am Pawago's lieutenant."

"That is no answer."

Ta-Tando shrugged. "How would I know what goes on beyond the camp?"

"How would Pawago?" she asked, and Ta-Tando could not reply. He appeared to be mulling it over. His eyes flitted from one place to the other, and now Crenna could see his entire body go tense. He grounded his teeth together, and when Crenna touched his arm, he nearly jumped.

"How have you been feeling, Ta-Tando?"

"What do you mean?" he demanded defensively.

"You know what I mean."

"My demons visit me," he admitted, looking shrunken and small suddenly. He took a breath, which seemed to inflate him. An anger, a strength, filled his eyes. Perhaps it was strength he had borrowed from Pawago. "Come along, I will show you."

They found Pawago and Yushta resting on a bed of pine needles, Pawago's head propped up on a log, his hands folded on his chest. His eyes sparked, became jewel-like as a rattlesnake's, and he pursed his lips contemptuously.

"Crenna . . ." It was Yushta who had spoken, and as he rose, first to his knees and then unsteadily to his feet, Crenna saw that age had finally crushed him. His hair was white, his gnarled hands were uncertain as he reached for her. "You are here! To bless us?"

"To beg you to stop before it is too late."

"I will not hear it." Yushta held up a hand and turned his back. "My son is dead."

"And so you would destroy a nation to avenge Manto?" she demanded.

"Yes. I will destroy the Algonquin nation with the help of my strong friends," Yushta answered, his voice cracked and slightly slurred.

"I was speaking of the Oneida nation," Crenna answered. "It will be destroyed."

"Why are you so certain that we will lose?" Pawago asked. "Why have you come to spy on us?"

She answered the first question. "There will be no winner in this war."

"Why do you support the Algonquin, Daughter?" Yushta asked almost with pain.

"I do not! Would not. I simply do not want the Oneida to fight."

"It is the same thing," Yushta said sadly. Pawago still rested against the log, his eyes unbearably self-satisfied.

"It is not, Father. Please, listen to me."

"We have already heard your arguments, Crenna. It is best if you go." He turned away from her again, a small, hunched figure bowed by age and by grief.

"Leave." Pawago rose. "You have nothing to say to us. You are a shame to your people, Crenna."

"Leave." Yushta would not face her again. Crenna glanced at Ta-Tando, who was staring into the distances. Once, briefly, he looked at her as if to say: You see how it is.

"Go, Crenna," Yushta said again, and Crenna knew there was no point in staying. These men would rush toward their death, dragging their women and children after them.

Yo had been right all along. It came back to her suddenly, strongly: "With the coming of the white man, the land shall flow with blood. It will be the end of our way, of our time." But they could not see it; they refused to recognize it. *How have we offended you, Manitou? Are we not your children?*

She turned away, and there were tears blurring her vision. Ta-Tando walked with her a way, saying nothing until they had passed through the great war camp and come to a slow-running ribbon of a stream. Crenna watched a maple leaf, curled with age, twist and float down the current.

"You should be frightened, Ta-Tando."

"I am a warrior."

"You should be frightened. You should feel it. All of our family has the gift of prescience. Mine is not so developed as Sachim's, but I can see the future; I know it. You must also, despite your denials, you must see what is to come, feel it prickle your skin, prod your soul, color your dreams."

"I feel nothing." Ta-Tando watched the leaf and nothing else. "Go home, Crenna. It is too late. It is over."

Then he turned and was gone. Crenna watched him sadly. He was an awkward, uncertain man, his soul tormented and driven. Yet he was her brother. She had cleaned him when he was a baby, made crude dolls for him when she was no more than a child herself. She had held him tightly in the night when he was frightened, when the thunder roared and he cried out in terror, believing Long Nose would come and take him to his terrible underground torture chambers.

Now he was gone. He was grown, and it was over. *Go home, Crenna. It is too late. It is over.*

There are times to speak, times to stand up and demand that things not be as they are, that human beings become what they can be, and not savage, lusting, bloody creatures seeking to destroy themselves.

But you cannot stand against the tide even as it destroys the earth; you cannot shout above the roar and constant thunder of the vast debilitating storms which roll across the land; there is no voice loud enough, no feeble body strong enough to roll back the tide, to demand that the war storms withdraw, and so you simply fall silent. Silent in the midst of destruction, as the twisting currents of time and the wind ruin all which might have been. You stand and if there is a horror in having to do so; there is also a peace. It is the point at which you can only throw up your hands and say: I have done what I could, the rest is the will of Manitou.

Crenna turned away from them. The weight was lifted from her shoulders, but not from her heart. The wind rustled in the trees, the early sky was already shading toward gray. From out of the north the sound of distant war drums came to her. She shivered, not from the cold, but from foreknowledge, and walked quickly down the long slopes, heading for home, for the only island of peace which existed in this forlorn and mad world she inhabited.

He watched her go and then turned toward the camp. There were small demons dancing in his head, small voices raised in mocking laughter, prodding his fears.

Ta-Tando saw his father slumped against the trunk of a tree, his old eyes open but lifeless. Pawago was self-satisfied, and despite his lean, hard body, gave off an aura of plump contentment.

This was the time of his glory. Now, when he rested on laurels yet to be won, when his reputation was secured by battles yet to be fought, by valor yet to be displayed.

The others sat solemn and dark, shadows against the earth. Their voices were sullen mutterings, splintered whispers like the voices of the small ones inside his skull.

Ta-Tando put his hands to his head, pressing hard against the bone, trying to suppress the wild chatter in his brain. The others were watching him, and so he took his hands away and stumbled off into the woods, away from their eyes.

He walked for a time and then broke into a run. They were still prodding him, shouting and cursing; demanding . . . What?

He stopped and leaned his head against the cool bark of a solitary cedar tree. The wind drifted leaves through the air. Far away a crow called twice.

What did they want? He had never known. They had simply always been there: raving, chanting, mocking, spurring, screeching.

He had tried to do what they commanded. He had burned and destroyed, yes, even killed to assuage their incessant, muddled demands.

It helped only briefly. Then they returned, stealing upon him in the night, or bursting upon him suddenly from out of the clear skies as he hunted or worked. At times it was enough to drive him to the earth, to send him into fits of uncontrollable fury when he slavered and bit his tongue, writhed and destroyed, tearing at his own body with his nails and teeth.

What did they want?

Back there, for a moment, it had become clear. A veil

drawn aside, a clear, echoic voice had spoken just once, lifting itself above the random cacophony to speak quite distinctly and say . . .

What? Ta-Tando banged his head against the tree, feeling the rough bark tear at his flesh, feeling the slow warm trickle of blood. Suddenly he stopped. Stopped and threw back his head and laughed.

It had all become quite clear. Ta-Tando was laughing, and he continued to laugh until the tears rolled from his eyes. He had to cling to the tree to keep himself upright. Hadn't he known all along? Known what the voices were saying, sensed it but not been aware enough to grasp the message and clutch it to his heart.

It came to him now, and he stepped away from the tree, his narrow chest rising and falling. He watched a bank of white stacked clouds approach from the northwest, watched the endless forest and the glassy silver of a river below.

I am destined for greatness. It was so simple. He was destined to be the great leader the Iroquois nation needed. He, not Pawago!

No wonder the spirits tormented him. His ears had been closed, his mind confused. Now it was all clear. Out of loyalty, he followed Pawago, and he supposed he would have to continue to do that for a time; but his destiny was clearly marked now. It was Ta-Tando who must watch as nations fell and then with the strength of his arms, the strength of his spirit—surely the others must feel its magnetism—it was he who must rebuild the world, forming a vast Indian nation with Ta-Tando as supreme ruler.

How could a man not recognize such a grand truth about himself? True, he had always vaguely felt he was favored among men, but just how had never been obvious. It was now. Now he would step forward, now claim his rights, now lead the Iroquois nation in a vast war of conquest. They had defeated and absorbed many tribes, but the old ones had turned their backs on their destiny, said in their councils, "This is enough."

If this war were to destroy the Algonquin, who then could stand in the way of the Iroquois? The British—that was laughable. They were hundreds to their one. Who else? There was no one. The Munsee were timid, the Leni-Lenape too few, the Susquehanna were women.

Once the Algonquin were defeated, Ta-Tando would step forward and explain it: "Brothers, we have our army and we have the world at our feet. I have been chosen; come follow me to the distant sea. We are invincible!"

Ta-Tando stood there, his pulse racing, his hands bunched into fists, his eyes aglow, his mind thrumming as he faced his destiny, as he stood at this twilight hour watching the Dawn of Empire.

He returned to the camp to find the army on its feet—his army. Te-al-Pantha was rushing somewhere hurriedly, bow in hand. "Where have you been!" he shouted. "We are ready. Pawago is looking for you."

Ta-Tando only smiled contemptuously. The fool didn't even recognize his leaders! Let Pawago wait. What did it matter? A man does not need to rush after his destiny. It will find him and carry him along like a great tide.

"Ta-Tando!" Pawago was gesturing with a frantic arm. Ta-Tando, still smiling, walked lazily toward his nominal leader as the Oneida warriors hastily packed and went to their assigned rendezvous points. "What's the matter with you?"

"What is it, Pawago?" Ta-Tando asked calmly.

"It's . . . What's the matter? Are you all right?" Pawago looked at him in the old superior way, and Ta-Tando had to smile. "A runner came from Creighton. We have our orders. Dawn will see the battle."

"All right. I am ready."

Pawago was still staring at him, still not understanding. "Take your party to the river." Pawago was sketching the location in the dirt. "Here is the bend, here the road. The bluffs rise—"

"All right." Ta-Tando interrupted Pawago before he could describe Ta-Tando's part in the battle. What did it matter? He was indifferent to the mechanics of Pawago's battle. They could not lose; Ta-Tando's destiny could not be altered.

"Is he all right?" Te-al-Pantha had returned again. With Pawago they watched Ta-Tando limp off, moving slowly, casually, toward his group of warriors. Pawago shook his head. His lips were compressed tightly.

"He wonders why he doesn't have your command," Pawago muttered. He cast thoughts of Ta-Tando aside. "Be at the ford at dawn. You will be the nearest to

Creighton as his forces emerge from the fort. If the Algonquin break through, you must hold them up until the cannon are in place." Te-al-Pantha nodded, and Pawago slapped his shoulder. "Fight well, Te-al-Pantha."

Then the subchief was off at a lope toward his force of two hundred which awaited him on the shady slope. As their leader reached them, Pawago saw them begin to filter through the trees toward the distant Hudson. Then he turned, snatched up his war bag, and strode to his own company of warriors. The sun was at their backs and the long shadows bled out from the bases of the pines. The wind was fresh and their hearts were light. Soon it would begin; soon it could be ended. Dawn would bring the death of the Algonquin nation and the triumph of the Oneida.

They ran on through the late hours, and then, with the coming of darkness, they slowed to a walk. The hundreds of warriors moved through the dark and solemn forest like the many parts of a great body. All silent, all with one thought, one aim.

The moon was rising when they reached the Hudson. Pawago, looking upriver and down from the high bluff, could see his forces moving into position.

"Pawago."

At Yushta's call he turned his eyes toward the forest. The white scout Creighton had been using as a go-between was squatting on his heels beside Yushta.

The man was unlike any Pawago had encountered. He was white, but wore his hair long and braided. He dressed in buckskins and carried a bow and arrows. He was from some distant place called Carolina, but seemed to have been a man of rank in England by the way Creighton addressed him. His name, or the name he used now, was simply Bill.

"What is it, Bill?"

"Just waiting to take the word to the general that you're in place," he said, rising. Pawago wondered where he had learned his Iroquois. From the Mohawk, it seemed by the accent, but when?

"We're ready. There's no change in the plan. We strike and fall back, leading the French and Algonquin into Creighton's cannon fire."

"No change." Bill rose, nodded, and was gone, running

as silently and swiftly as an Oneida warrior. Pawago watched the man for a moment, frowning. Then his thoughts were distracted by other matters and he returned to the bluff. With six men as runners, he ascertained the final positions of his forces and sent last-minute instructions.

The Algonquin with their French allies were still marching southward, their objective Creighton's fort, which the French meant to destroy at all costs.

They were already passing through Mohawk territory, and Wechakapi's warriors would slowly be cutting in behind them, preventing any retreat.

"Do you want to send runners out to locate the Algonquin?" Yushta asked. The old man was at his elbow, his eyes bright in the light of the coming moon; his voice was unsteady, but that was only the voice of age, and not of cowardice.

"No. I don't want to risk having a man intercepted now. We know where they are, know their objective. Now is the time for patience."

Yushta nodded and went away from Pawago, returning to the fireless, soundless camp. No one spoke, not even in whispers. The Algonquin too had ears.

Pawago stood on the bluffs, hands on hips, bare chest rising and falling. The moon, a silver crescent, topped the low, dark line of the pines and glossed the river. Now, looking north and south, he could see no movement, no shadow which did not belong. His men had gone to earth. The trap was ready to be sprung.

The moon was high in the sky; it was past midnight when the hand fell on Pawago's shoulder, and he sat immediately upright, throwing his blanket aside as he reached for his weapons.

"Where are they?" he demanded. Then his vision cleared and he saw that it was Ta-Tando, that the rest of the camp was quiet.

"They're not here yet; there's still time," Ta-Tando said, crouching over him.

"What are you talking about? You fool! What do you want, Ta-Tando?"

"They told me."

"Who told you? Told you what!"

"The spirits. They came to me and told me that this battle must not be fought in this way."

Pawago could only stare. Ta-Tando's face, silvered by the moon, was tranquil, his eyes distant. Another of his fits—and now!

"Go to sleep, Ta-Tando. It will be all right."

Clawlike hands gripped Pawago's shoulders. "They have told me. This battle must not be fought like this. Why are we at the point of attack; why are Creighton's forces behind us, shielded by cannon? The British cannot be trusted."

"We've been through all of this, Ta-Tando," Pawago said. His voice was a taut whisper. He had to restrain himself to keep from strangling the little madman. "I've explained it all to you already."

"What is it?" The voice was Moa-Telah's.

"Nothing. Go back to sleep." Pawago returned his attention to Ta-Tando. "You, Ta-Tando, you go to sleep as well. The battle plan has been drawn. I am sorry you do not agree with it, but it cannot be changed. Not now. Not because of spirit voices!"

"You do not believe in spirits?" Ta-Tando's eyes opened wider yet.

"Yes," Pawago said in exasperation, "only the rest of us do not hear so many voices as you."

"I know," Ta-Tando said gravely. "That is why I've come forward."

"Go to sleep! The plan is firm. Leave before I grow angry with you, Ta-Tando."

"You can't—"

"Leave now, or I swear I shall kill you."

Ta-Tando only nodded. He stood, watching the high moon for a moment as it drifted through the inky sky. No wonder these men did not recognize his true destiny. They did not even heed the spirits which whispered in the night. Did they not hear the river spirits murmuring, the revelations of Owl as he swooped low across the forest, the little chorus of the crickets? Suddenly he brightened. Perhaps this too was a part of destiny. Pawago would reveal his foolishness, suffer defeat, and then who would be supreme Oneida war leader—who else could there be but Ta-Tando?

Heartened by this warming thought, he walked back

through the forest, watching the shadows slip past. Twice he saw ghosts following him, encouraging him, and once the finger of Manitou beaming like a silver light through the black-pines. His blessing fell like a warm, encompassing waterfall. Molten silver spilling its revelation of destiny. Smiling, feeling warmth and confidence growing in his breast, Ta-Tando walked on.

Fools. Fools that they were, not to recognize the one true genius among them, the one destined emperor, the one great leader.

It did not matter; let them try their folly. Let them stumble and fall, let them suffer deception and death. Then, above it Ta-Tando would rise, and with Manitou's silver torch in hand, he would lead them to bright conquest.

He slept easily, deeply, warmed by his dreams, comforted by his expectations.

It was foggy, cold, when he was awakened from his slumber.

He looked up, saw Ya-tosphe, finger to his lips, and rolled silently from his bed. His heart was racing; his senses had come suddenly alert, extraordinarily so. Collecting his war bag and bow, he crept with Ya-tosphe to the edge of the river. There was nothing to be seen, but by lying still, listening, they could hear the cadenced marching of feet. The French!

He looked at Ya-tosphe and nodded, withdrawing deeper into the forest himself, looking around him as the warriors of his party flitted through the woods like silent specters and took up their positions. Ta-Tando looked across the river, noticing with satisfaction that the fog was heavy. He could discover none of Te-al-Pantha's men.

The fog curled through the pines, wraithlike, cold, and silent. Nothing moved. Moisture collected on the pines and dripped to the earth. Ta-Tando slowly notched an arrow and blew on his cold, stiff hands.

Now you did not have to be still to hear them; now the sounds of the French army were loud: the marching feet, the clang of metal against metal, the clopping of horses' feet, the screech of a wheel on a hub.

Fools. Ta-Tando smiled. All of the world seemed suddenly foolish and obvious. How could they believe they were secretly approaching Albany when they made a noise

262

like the Great Heads, like a forest of pines blown down before Manitou's wind?

All fools. Creighton, Pawago, the French. A superior understanding had come to Ta-Tando, and now he saw the folly of man, saw how easy it would be to outwit every force, each man on the broad continent.

He saw the first shadowy figure approaching through the white gloom of the fog, and his hand went up. He pressed himself against the sodden, pine-needle-littered earth and waited.

They came from out of the milky fog. Faceless, uniformed men, and Ta-Tando's fingers went to his bowstring, gripping the feathered nib of his arrow.

He laid his face against the earth, stilling his breath, his heartbeat, letting the French be drawn into the jaws of the trap. Now their feet sounded like thunder as they passed the Oneida position. Ta-Tando didn't dare look up. He lay silent and still against the dark earth, the wispy, concealing fog spread over him like a blanket.

He opened one eye and looked northward. Peering past the shadows of his lashes, through the whey of the fog, he saw them now. Algonquin. Painted, confident. Inwardly Ta-Tando laughed at their foolishness. They could not sense the coming calamity; their spirits did not speak to them of the rising star in the Oneida camp.

Their feet were hushed whispers against the earth. All the same, Ta-Tando could feel the ground vibrating as they passed. He saw one warrior with a flame-red face, his nose painted black. He heard a whisper pass between two enemy warriors and wondered what they had said. Did they speak of imminent death? He wanted to hear their horrified screams and look into their faces as death swept out of the forest and took them by their throats, as their blood ran into the river.

The last of them was past, and still Ta-Tando did not move. Ya-tosphe was looking at him expectantly. Ta-Tando lay still, as silent and unmoving as the dead. Minutes later a dozen more Algonquin passed.

Finally Ta-Tando nodded. The earth beneath him was silent, and he could no longer hear the thunder of the French boots.

It was time, and he lifted his hand again. They rose

silently, and moving toward the river, began to close the jaws of the trap.

Ta-Tando worked stealthily through the fog. There was no hurry, none at all. Pawago would strike from one flank, Te-al-Pantha from the other. Then they would retreat, after inflicting as much death as possible. The Algonquin and French were supposed to pursue the Oneida force toward the fort. If they did not, if for some reason they broke and ran, they would run into Ta-Tando's party.

If the Algonquin-French force followed their expectations and pursued the Oneida toward the fort, then Creighton's cannon would open up while Pawago and Te-al-Pantha reformed and joined Ta-Tando behind the enemy, effectively trapping them.

Ta-Tando trotted a way, seeing his men in the forest, appearing and disappearing at intervals behind the trees. The fog was low and heavy. At times all of them were lost in the river fog; at times it would suddenly part. Here and there, eerily, heads floated above the gray milk of the fog banks.

It was still. Everywhere, shadows moved, ghosts flitted through the dark cottony webs, the river spirits scrawled against the sky.

It came suddenly. A shout, a scream, a frantic order, a war whoop. It had begun, and Ta-Tando urged his body forward. Ya-tosphe's eyes met his, and they nodded to each other. *Slowly, now. Slowly.* They were not to expose themselves yet. Their presence must be guarded.

But it was difficult to hold back. Ahead, on the trail, the world had erupted into chaos. Arrows flew through the forest, thicker than raindrops in a winter storm. And the dead littered the earth, the dying dragged themselves away through the concealing fog. A Frenchman yelled and was silenced as an arrow pierced his throat.

It lasted only minutes. Minutes while the Oneida emptied their quivers, firing their arrows into the body of attacking Algonquin. Then, as the Algonquin loosed their own barrage of arrows, the Oneida retreated. Silently, swiftly withdrew into the forests, luring the Algonquin onward.

There was a loud shout, a foreign voice raised in command, and the bulk of the enemy force lunged forward. Ta-Tando could see them ahead of him, racing forward without method. Amazingly he could see their heads, decapitated by the fog, flowing toward the British fort, hear their war cries, their death songs, and yet they could not see him. The fog, the forces of nature, the fingers of Manitou—all had allied themselves with the Oneida cause, as the spirits had promised.

Ta-Tando slowed still more, lifting a hand. His lieutenants mimicked his gesture. Ta-Tando's force slowed; it was too soon for their presence to be known. Pawago was in full retreat—or so it seemed. And across the river, Te-al-Pantha still held his silent position.

Suddenly there was no fog, and Ta-Tando had the entire battlefield spread out before his eyes: Pawago leading his people in blind, panicked retreat; the British fort, stark and blocky against the green grass. A shout from the flank turned Ta-Tando's head toward the river. The Algonquin had split their force. Half of them were rushing across the river, their legs sending up silver spurs of water. Why?

There was the answer. Te-al-Pantha's position had been found out, and now the Oneida came forth from the woods on that side of the river, meeting the Algonquin force in midstream. The fighting was furious. Ta-Tando watched, his jaw working excitedly as an Oneida drove his war ax downward and severed the head of an Algonquin, as arrows pierced the heart of an enemy, as the Hudson ran red. A blunderbuss exploded from the bank of the river, and Ta-Tando shook with anger: Manto's murder came back vividly, and he had started forward, ready to strike back at the Frenchman who had fired the gun, before Ya-tosphe brought him back to himself by grabbing his arm and holding on savagely.

Ta-Tando halted and nodded, taking a deep, slow breath. It could wait. Retribution was written in the stars; it would come, but for now it must wait.

Ta-Tando, fascinated by the sounds and sights of the great battle, stood mesmerized for a moment more before Ya-tosphe's urging hand drew him back into the concealing fog, back to where the war was only a series of muffled grunts and disembodied screams, where reality was only the drifting, twisting fog and the dark, featureless faces of the warriors who squatted against the ground nearby, waiting for the final bloody phase of the action to begin.

The fog was cool against Ta-Tando's cheek, the message

of the spirits warm in his heart. It had begun. He wanted to leap into the air, to charge among the Algonquin, dealing death, to turn and proclaim his mission to his hunched, poised warriors, but he could not. Not just yet.

He only stood staring at the swirling mist, hearing the distant battle sounds, feeling destiny rush toward him like a wild mountain wind.

Pawago limped as he ran. A chance shot had sent an arrow into the calf of his leg. The wound was not serious, but he had been unable to get the arrowhead out. Wrenching the shaft of the arrow off, he had hobbled on, nearly tripping over Moa-Telah's body. The old Solitary Pine Tree had been touched by the finger of Death. He lay crumpled, still against the earth.

Pawago glanced over his shoulder, and as he watched, an Oneida warrior went down in a hail of arrows. The Algonquin were practically on their heels now. It had turned into a mad footrace, with the loser condemned to death.

Pawago knew now that Te-al-Pantha had been drawn out of position too early. He had seen the fighting at the river ford. Although that was not disastrous in itself, it weakened the flank heavily and reduced the element of surprise. If only that fool Ta-Tando had the sense not to show himself, it would still work.

Pawago labored up the wooded slope, his leg dragging, the pain increasing with each step. The Algonquin were close behind, far outdistancing the French, who had formed a rank and remained on the river path, doing very little actual fighting. They had turned loose their dogs and were now standing back, waiting to see what happened.

It took very little encouragement for the Algonquin to throw themselves at the Oneida. A lifetime of carefully nurtured hatred was more than enough impetus. Pawago stopped, fired three arrows downslope, and with satisfaction saw an Algonquin throw out his hands and crumple up.

The fort was just over the hill now; the plan was working, although everything was greatly accelerated, the actuality much quicker than the lines drawn on Creighton's paper plans.

They had only to crest the hill . . . Pawago was gasping with lack of breath and a surfeit of pain, but he knew he would make it. It was only the old warriors, those who had run their best races long ago, who would never see the end of the battle. These were outrun by the swift Algonquin and clubbed to the earth as they tried to make their escape—a flaw in the plan.

Pawago saw it as he seemed to see everything that foggy morning; his eyes were intently alert, aware of each shadow, of the painted, pursuing Algonquin rushing upslope through the timber, of his own men loping toward the crest . . . He saw it, but it gave him no more than a momentary twinge of sympathetic suffering.

It was Yushta. He had been taken down from behind. An Algonquin runner, no more than twenty years old, had easily caught Yushta as he tried to flee. A hand stretched out, and Yushta was dragged down by his hair, clubbed with the Algonquin's war ax as he fell, and then savagely beaten as he lay still against the pine needles.

Pawago ran on, ducking low to keep below the barrage of arrows which the Oneida who had already achieved the crest fired off to cover the retreat of those who were still on the slope.

Pawago himself was to the crest now. His leg was filled with fiery pain. He looked down the far side of the mountain, seeing the fort standing in the middle of the cleared field, stodgy and square as ever. By now Creighton would have manned the guns. Now the cannon would be primed and ready.

"Now, Pawago. We must go now!"

"One minute. Let them get closer! All right," he shouted, waving his arm. "Take them to the guns, lead the Algonquin to a deserved death."

The Oneida, some pausing to loose a last arrow, began to run downslope, the fort growing larger with each step they took. Pawago's heart was racing, racing with joy and exertion. *One more minute. One more.* They were on the very brink of victory. It required only one more step, and then another. Then the cannon would open up and the Algonquin force would lie strewn about the stump-littered field. *One more minute.*

He glanced up as he ran, and he could see the red-coated cannoneers at their guns, see sunlight on a bit of gold braid—Creighton's uniform, perhaps. He ran on, his leg nearly giving out on him as he leaped a stream-cut gully. He looked across his shoulder and then forward again. Now they were racing across the flats. *How much farther?* Weren't they in cannon range already? Why weren't the guns firing; why weren't the gates to the fort open?

Creighton was timing it too closely! It was time. Fire! He was near enough now to identify Creighton on the rampart. Through the sweat which stung his eyes and blurred his vision he could see the man, hands behind his back, watching the field coolly as another Oneida and another went down before the Algonquin arrows. Open the gates!

"Creighton!" he shouted. "Creighton!"

Lieutenant James Briggs turned his worried young face to his senior officer. "Sir?"

"What is it, Briggs?"

"Do you want me to call for the gates to be opened?"

"No."

Briggs simply stared. The general's face was granite, inexpressive. War whoops filled the air. The Oneida were dropping all across the field. They had no arrows left.

"Sir!" Briggs's voice was taut, thin. "Shall I have the cannon fire?"

"Where in hell are the French?" Creighton muttered to himself. He touched his chin thoughtfully, and mused, "They should be visible by now."

"Sir!" Briggs's voice was a harsh interruption.

"Be quiet, Lieutenant."

"But the Oneida . . ." Below, he could hear their voices; above the cries of battle he could hear fists pounding on the barred gate.

"Damn the Oneida!" Creighton snapped, his face going livid. "Let the savages fight it out among themselves. I'm holding the guns for the French assault."

Briggs had been watching as one warrior, set upon by three Algonquin, was hacked to death, his skull caved in by Algonquin war clubs.

"Sir—"

"Briggs, are you taking command? *Are* you, Lieutenant!"

"No, sir. Only—"

"They should have been here by now. Crafty devils, the French, holding back until they see what their Indian assault force can achieve." He actually smiled, perhaps in admiration of the French tactics. "Crafty devils."

Briggs had to turn away. Below, the Oneida were being slaughtered unmercifully. They seemed to have wasted all their arrows in their initial attack—of course they had not planned on needing more; they had trusted the British to keep their bargain.

Pawago turned away from the gate. His hands were bloody from pounding on it. He threw away his empty quiver and stood, war ax in hand, awaiting the onslaught of Algonquin warriors. There was no thought of running, no hope of making an escape.

He smiled thinly as he saw two bare-chested enemy braves rushing toward him. Ta-Tando had finally obeyed an order. He had held his position at the rear, and so Pawago's situation was an impossible one.

The Algonquin were nearly on top of him. He could see their painted faces, contorted with the exertion. There was nothing to do but to die bravely. They had called him many things, but they had never called him a coward. Now it was time to face a warrior's death.

Pawago threw back his head, and raising his war ax high, he charged forward to meet his adversary.

Ta-Tando stood counting the minutes. The fog lay like a ghost river along the Hudson. It hadn't thinned much since dawn.

"They should be there by now."

Ta-Tando slowly swiveled his head toward Ya-tosphe. He said nothing.

"What's happening? Look!" Ya-tosphe's hand was on Ta-Tando's shoulder, a gesture he did not like. He followed Ya-tosphe's pointing finger. The French, augmented by half a hundred Algonquin warriors, had wheeled toward the eastern flank. Now they were splashing across the river ford, the horses struggling against the current as they drew the wheeled cannon forward. "They've decided to assault Te-al-Pantha." Ya-tosphe's grip on his arm tightened. Ta-Tando shook it away. "What shall we do?"

"What we were told to do," Ta-Tando answered irritably.

"Something's gone wrong," Ya-tosphe said. "We should have heard the cannon long ago."

Suddenly they did hear cannon, but both men realized instantly that it was the French who were firing. From the opposite side of the Hudson, the French guns roared. Ta-Tando saw a small tree felled, saw the rising smoke, saw Te-al-Pantha's men rushing through the woods frantically like leaves before a storm.

"We could help them!"

"We are ordered to stand fast, to cut off retreat," Ta-Tando said. His voice was firm, but inside he was trembling with excitement. What Ya-tosphe said was true. They were in a position to flank the French, rain arrows on them while Te-al-Pantha made his retreat. But he had been told to stand fast, to conceal his force until the last possible moment.

"What if we reveal ourselves and then the Algonquin return from the fort? Then *we* are in a pincer. Then we are the trapped army."

"If we don't . . ." Ya-tosphe didn't finish his sentence. The cannon roared again, and the smoke from the cannon lifted to merge with the fog. They could hear agonized screams. Two Oneida lay dead on the riverbank; many more must have been dead in the woods. Te-al-Pantha had no choice. He had to break and run. His men could not assault the French through grapeshot.

As they watched, a tall Oneida who could have been Te-al-Pantha himself broke from the woods and tried for the safety of the river. A waiting Algonquin cut him down with a well-placed arrow.

"He should not have revealed himself," Ta-Tando said, as if to himself. *What was wrong?* Where was Pawago? Pawago would know what to do. He wanted to charge into the fray, but he feared Pawago's wrath more than the guns of the French, the arrows of the Algonquin.

They waited another hour while the battle raged and then faded to silence, while the fog-shrouded river rolled on; they waited in the shelter of the damp, dripping pines, and then Ta-Tando said, "We can wait no more. Something is wrong."

Then it was too late, but Ya-tosphe said nothing in response. Ta-Tando had followed his orders. It was not his fault he was no general.

They sifted southward, ghosts among the fog, the deep forest. Ta-Tando nearly tripped over the dead man. He could not identify him. His skull was battered, his face destroyed beyond recognition—but he was Oneida.

Ta-Tando froze, staring down at the dead man, before he shook himself and stumbled on. He had seen the dead before. But never so many, never so many of his own tribe. His friends and relatives. He found Yushta and knew him by his paint.

Ta-Tando threw back his head, and his mouth opened in silent anguish. He could not even cry out, for fear the enemy would hear him. He could sing no death songs for his father. He stood hunched over the body, and slowly he drew his knife as Ya-tosphe watched him. He lifted the blade to his face and slashed each cheek ritually. Blood streamed from Ta-Tando's face and mingled with the tears. The fog made the blood and tears both seem cold. He nodded to Ya-tosphe, and they walked on, silent, poised, their bows ready. Ta-Tando passed a dead Algonquin, and he stopped to spit on the corpse, reviling it.

Finally they crested the hill. Already it was dark, and growing colder. Fog lay across the cleared field below, forming a cottony skirt around the British fort.

Ta-Tando sank to his knees. A low, animal growl issued from his throat. Ya-tosphe could only stare, stare at his leader, who had begun to quiver and jerk, stare at the dead littering the field around the fort. He could not see them all at once. The fog, in its tantalizing, evil way, shifted and revealed here a part of the dead, there another, at times mercifully closing over the scene entirely.

Ta-Tando had gone to his knees and then toppled over. Now he lay on his side, his hands clenched so tightly that blood ran from his palms where his nails dug into his flesh. Spittle ran from his lips. His eyes were rolled back into his skull, and he shook like a dog in its death throes.

Ya-tosphe could no longer look upon the battlefield, and so he crouched beside Ta-Tando, resting a hand on his shoulder as he shook himself to pieces, as the fog rolled on, as the dead lay cold and stiff against the earth below them.

13

THE SNOW DRIFTED DOWN FROM out of the mottled skies, and Ta-Tando watched with unfocused eyes. The valleys below were roofed over with clouds. The long ranks of pines were snow-clad, hushed in their winter pallor. Ka-tash-hauht dominated the earth. His soft, cold weapons fell against his enemies—warmth, peace, comfort.

Ya-tosphe approached his leader, an extra blanket in his hand. Ta-Tando sat against the snow, unmoving. Snow had frosted his head, and it lay unmelting across his thighs and shoulders.

Ya-tosphe approached hesitantly. Ta-Tando, whose eyes had always been clouded, spiked with eerie light at moments of excitement, were now burning embers or black, lifeless obsidian, as his shifting moods dictated. Those terrible moods!

Paroxysms of rage were common. Then Ta-Tando ranted and stamped around through the deep snow, chanting words none of them could understand, pleading with unseen, tormenting spirits.

Now he was as silent as death, an effigy covered with glittering snow. He might have been sitting there through the ages, a stone memorial to a long-dead nation.

Ya-tosphe draped the blanket over Ta-Tando's shoulders and silently returned to the warriors at the fire, unsure whether Ta-Tando even knew he had been there.

Ta-Tando smiled. They thought him mad. They did not know what inner forces were working within. They did not know that the spirits, once vague and incomprehensible, now came with regularity, their message clear and strong.

The whites must die. Everything white must die, everything white must be wiped from the face of the land. Each tumor and wart the white man had built or carved into Manitou's earth must be reduced to ashes. *That was his purpose*, his final reason for existing.

For it had come with the white man, as Yo had

predicted. Death and turmoil and sickness and war. He had brought it with him from the dark side of the moon, or from beneath the sea—it made no difference where these children of the underworld had come from. All that mattered was that they be stamped into the ground, burned and buried, shattered and driven off until no trace of their poison remained.

The white man had taken Crenna away. The white man had taken Kala. The white man had killed Manto. The white man had taken their land. The white man had been the cause of Yushta's death. The white man had betrayed Pawago. What had he not been the cause of! He was death and destruction and disease—the dark side of man. Now he must be repaid, and the vision, once so vague, had become clear. *For this was I born.* For this had Manitou prepared him, toward this goal the spirits prodded him, had prodded him since he first set eyes on the pale, demon face of Van der Veghe.

The night he had gone to kill the Dutchman, he had not known what drove him to it. Now he knew, and now he felt remorse only in the knowledge that he had failed that night.

He would not fail again.

The snows fell, and thunder shook the skies. The snow slanted down, and the wind increased, buffeting his motionless body. Behind him the Oneida warriors watched him, wondering if his mind was gone, wondering what revelations had come to him, wondering what so transfixed him that he did not feel the icy fangs of the wind, the numbing cold. Ta-Tando threw back his head and laughed suddenly. And now they would wonder about *that*, another part of his brain told him.

Let them wonder. They would learn soon enough. They would learn as he stood before them and explained what had happened, revealed what must be done, undraped his true destiny. The winter would not last forever. Let Katash-hauht rumble and bluster, let him hold sway throughout the winter months. It meant nothing.

In the spring there would be a new sort of storm. A fierce, hot, vengeful wind which would roll across the land, dealing retribution.

She came out of the forest and stood silently, puzzled by the men who were gathered on the porch of the house. Crenna did not feel inclined to go forward, and so she waited in the shadows of the pines.

It was clear and cold. Patches of snow still lay in the shadows, but she had already seen signs of approaching spring in the forest. A black she-bear, sullen and gaunt, had waddled past her, two fuzzy cubs bounding along behind, pausing to wrestle when the mood struck them. Impatient flowers already lifted their heads beside the melting snow. There were ripening buds on the basswood trees and on the elms.

Crenna watched silently, only her eyes moving. There were six of them—men in long dark brown gowns, hoods hoisted protectively over their heads, shadowing their faces. Van der Veghe spoke to them a minute longer, raised his arm in what seemed to be a gesture of anger, and then stood, arms akimbo, on the porch as the six strange men turned southward, arms folded together beneath the vast sleeves of their robes.

Crenna emerged from the woods, seeing Sachim only now come out of the house, William and Cara beside her. Crenna hurried across the yard past the heaped cold ashes of the old outpost.

"Who was that?" she asked breathlessly. "What did they want?"

"Jesuits," Van der Veghe muttered, his eyes still on the river path, although the strangers had long since disappeared into the blue-green forest.

"Jesuits?" She shook her head. "What does that mean, Peter?"

"I'm sorry." He smiled. His thoughts had been far away. "They are priests—religious men. Shamans. And they are French."

"What did they want?" Crenna asked.

"The Oneida." Peter's mouth was turned up at the corners in a bitter smile. "They wanted to go among the Oneida and preach the Gospel—that is," he explained, "the message of the French God."

"What did you tell them?"

"I told them that the French God had already done enough for the Oneida. They didn't like it, I'm afraid." He paused. "I told them that the French had done enough, that the Oneida were no more."

Sachim spoke hesitantly. "I don't understand, Peter. How could these Frenchmen walk here with impunity? Aren't they afraid of the English, or is their trust in their God so strong?"

"Ah"—he nodded—"how could they walk here?" He smiled again, a distant, sublime expression. "It seems there is a truce in effect at present. The French and the British are at peace."

The irony was not lost on Crenna. She stood beside her husband, watching the river run. A peace! Now that they had laid waste to the Oneida nation, crippled the Iroquois League, devastated the Algonquin.

"They have run out of soldiers," Van der Veghe said. Then he turned and went into the house alone, leaving Crenna to watch the wind in the pines, the endless flow of the gray river, the coming of a spring which promised no warmth, no flourishing of nature, no joy.

A slow, soft rain twisted down from out of the skies. The Oneida crept forward across the deep, damp grass. Moving quickly, they dipped into a shallow gully and slowly lifted their eyes.

Still he worked; still he tore at the earth, burying the steel cutting edge of his plow in Manitou's heart. Here, a mile from the British fort, a party of farmers had built their homes. They tilled the land—the land which was not theirs and would never be.

Ta-Tando lifted a hand and pointed emphatically. Six men slipped off down the gully, running in a crouch. Six others moved off to the north, disappearing through the fine, swirling mist.

When he could see them no more, Ta-Tando's head lifted again until he could peer through the long grass and see the silent farmer walking stolidly behind an equally stolid, rain-darkened mule.

Ta-Tando turned and nodded to Ya-tosphe, then soundlessly they crept from their hiding place, waiting until the last minute, until the farmer's head came up, his face reflecting terror, before they broke into a run, their screams filling the air.

The farmer threw up a hand defensively, but Ta-

Tando's war ax broke his forearm and embedded itself in the white man's skull. A cry brought Ta-Tando's head around. A white woman herding two children before her was running toward the woods to the south, her skirts lifted high. They did not make it; Ta-Tando's men met them before they reached the trees. Their death cries were shrill, short, muffled by the rain.

"Burn the house," Ta-Tando said, and they did so. He himself walked to a small enclosure where a pig, two geese, and a cow watched him with growing trepidation. Ta-Tando slipped under an enclosure rail, and walking to the hog, he slit its throat as it squealed in futile protest. Next he dispatched the geese, finally the brown-eyed cow.

One of his men, a young warrior called Mheti, who had joined him only a week ago, started to pick up the geese, and Ta-Tando asked sharply, "What do you think you're doing?"

"The birds are good to eat, Ta-Tando, my chief."

"They are poison," Ta-Tando said. "They are white and unclean. Leave them!" Mheti dropped the heads of the dead geese and, shamefaced, wiped his hands on his leggings.

Ta-Tando walked nearer the house. Despite the rain, the flames burned brightly, licking at the eaves, charring the walls. It was good to watch it burn, good to feel the warmth on his face, good to know that another four whites lay dead.

He watched the flames writhe and twist, spelling out magical incantations; he watched the smoke rise into the sky, an offering to Manitou.

Then suddenly he turned and nodded to Ya-tosphe, and they departed, running toward the forest, leaving no more sign of their passing than did the rising smoke.

The man opposite Creighton was Captain Maxwell Harrison, Etonian, gentleman, and now Indian fighter. Behind Harrison, standing against the wall near the sideboard, was Lieutenant James Briggs, his brick-red face emotionless as he watched the two higher-ranking officers.

"No trace at all?" Creighton demanded.

"None but the ashes, the bodies," Harrison replied, his intonations decidedly upper-class. He sipped at the madeira Creighton had placed before him.

276

"The bastard," Creighton said, slamming his fist against his desk. "Twenty-four dead. The man's no respecter of women and children, either! Finally . . ." He rose and paced the floor, hands behind his back. "Finally we manage a truce with the Frogs, finally we can offer immigrants some measure of security, and then this . . . this"—he waved a hand, grasping for a virulent-enough term—"*rapacious madman* has to turn on us and begin murdering the whites."

"He was your ally, was he?" Harrison asked, lifting a bored eyebrow. Harrison's boots were still muddy. He hadn't shaved. He had been six weeks in the field searching for Ta-Tando. It was, in Harrison's words, like pursuing a phantom. He struck and then vanished like a pebble in a pond, leaving only the dark and deadly ripples to mark his passage.

"He *was* an ally—damn these savages! They're absolutely unpredictable."

Briggs had to turn his face away; he feared his eyes would reveal his thoughts. Maybe Creighton really didn't know why the Oneida had turned on him. Could he be that stupid, that myopic? Briggs decided he could.

"Well, we'll find him, sir," Harrison said, rising. "Thanks for the wine. It takes the chill off a bit." He put on his hat, and with a nod toward Briggs, he turned sharply on his heel and was gone.

Creighton sighed, finished his own wine, and glanced up to find Briggs staring at him. There was no malice in those eyes, no humor, no accusation, no expression of any kind. He simply stared, and he didn't even hear Creighton the first time he dismissed him.

"Boy's been over here too long," Creighton muttered as he watched Briggs's departing back. He made a mental note to see about transferring the man. Then, with another heavy sigh, he returned his attention to the report he was composing.

They came out of the willow thicket, seemingly untroubled by the rain. They walked in a file, the six of them, their hoods shielding them from the falling mist. The willow brush was silver with water; it trembled in the breeze. The glutted Hudson, muddy and gray, flowed southward beneath the wind-twisted clouds.

They came suddenly from out of the brush. Two dozen painted, shirtless savages. The Jesuits raised their hands and turned, trying to run, to hide, but there was no hope of either. The Indians swarmed over them, hacking them to pieces, and they fell to the earth and lay still, the rain washing the blood into the freshet-swollen Hudson.

Ta-Tando stood over them, a frozen, humorless grin on his narrow face. The muscles in his face seemed to have petrified. His mouth, drawn back, revealed almost all of his slightly crooked teeth. His eyes were wide—ivory spheres with pinpoint black dots painted onto them. Every tendon in his throat stood out distinctly. He leaned forward suddenly, and before Ya-tosphe could catch him, he had fallen on top of the body of one of the Jesuits.

Ta-Tando lay practically embracing the corpse, and as the others watched with fascinated horror, Ta-Tando lifted his ax time and again, burying it into the already dead flesh of the French priest.

When the flailing arm had stilled, Ya-tosphe helped Ta-Tando up, whispering, "You can kill them only once, Ta-Tando."

"Yes." Ta-Tando regretted that, but it was true. They walked on a mile through the rain, and then Ta-Tando let his men rest. They had come far that morning, perhaps twenty miles. There were only a few miles to go.

He sat against a tree, his arms wrapped loosely around his legs, thinking of that, letting the thought warm him. Only a few more miles to go.

For he knew now what he must do to exorcise his demons. He had killed many whites, many. He had destroyed all they owned and loved and had constructed, but it was not enough, and now Ta-Tando knew why.

The original sin had not been atoned for. The original error, the first mistake, the first stain, the first white man.

Van der Veghe. It was Van der Veghe who must die. He had come, and until then there had been an age of innocence, a stable and peaceful world where man knew his place, where duty was clear, where demons did not tear at your heart and throw you to the ground in their rages.

And then he had come, bringing the sickness. And still he lived. But he was the summoner of demons, the filth of the deep sea, the dark face of man, the dark moon-voyager, the criminal, the deceiver, Death! And so he must die. So he would.

They rested in the shelter of the pines, watching the river, listening to the rain and the silence of the forest. They rested, and then, when it was time, Ta-Tando rose and gestured to his men.

Silently then, with Ta-Tando's small spirits impelling them forward, they filed off through the deep vaulted forest, the scent of hot blood in their nostrils.

Van der Veghe's head came up and he turned toward the woods. But there was nothing to see. He shrugged and returned to his work. The rain was collecting in the horses' pen, and he was digging a trench to drain the water. The roan switched its tail and nickered. When Van der Veghe glanced at it, he saw that the animal's ears were pricked, its eyes intent on the woods beyond the burned outpost.

"What is it, boy?" he asked, placing a hand on the roan's damp, glossy neck. "See something?"

Perhaps the wildcat was back. It had killed the chickens Van der Veghe had purchased from the departing Dutch, and frightened the horses.

He continued to look toward the forest through the veil of fine, constant rain, but he saw nothing, and the horse seemed satisfied, and so he returned to his job.

He heard nothing until the body collided with his and he was knocked to the sodden earth, twisting wildly, trying to free himself. Only then did the war whoops reach his ears, only then did he see other men swarming over the corral, tearing down the corncrib, destroying the shed. But he saw all of that only secondarily as a blurred violent background to the stark immediate terror he felt as the warrior on top of him lifted his war ax and clubbed downward with it.

He had time in that fragment of a second, as the ax poised against the rainy sky swept downward, to recognize the features of Ta-Tando behind the paint. Then the ax bit deeply into flesh.

He had rolled enough to prevent it from splitting his skull, but the steel ax practically severed his arm at the shoulder, and Van der Veghe screamed with pain, seeing the crimson flow rush down his sleeve and mingle with the rainwater.

Ta-Tando was grinning, but it was no human expression. It was a demented, loathsome face, and Van der Veghe saw no light at all in those black, lusterless eyes.

"Ta-Tando . . ." he bellowed, his words broken by fear, by pain. The pain in his arm was excruciating. He was certain the arm had been cut cleanly away, and now he saw Ta-Tando's arm rise again, saw the ax poised.

"Ta-Tando!" The voice was Crenna's, and Ta-Tando hesitated. "Ta-Tando! Fool! What are you doing? Murderer!"

Van der Veghe heard the rushing feet, and then, as Ta-Tando's ax, still poised for the downstroke, wavered in his hand, he saw Crenna outlined against the sky, her dark hair washed down over her face, her eyes fiery, her mouth grim. She lunged and caught the handle of Ta-Tando's war ax, yanking violently on it until she and Ta-Tando fell in a heap against the muddy earth.

Van der Veghe heard her voice. It seemed to come from far, far away. Her words echoed as if she were at the end of a long dark tunnel. He clutched his shoulder, feeling the warm seep of blood, the flash of pain, watching the rain and the long feathered pennant of smoke rising against it. Somewhere a warrior cried shrilly. Van der Veghe lay against the earth, his teeth chattering, the rain washing against his face. He rolled his head, wanting to see her, wanting to hold her memory.

Ta-Tando fought back with all of his strength, but there was a lion's strength in the woman.

She shrieked at him and pounded her fist against his face. "Are you insane! Give me the ax. Now."

Ta-Tando suddenly stopped struggling; he looked up, saw Crenna clearly, saw her eyes, which met his with anger and despair. "Yes . . ." he muttered, feeling all of the strength leak out of him. He had started to say, "Yes, Mother," and had just held himself back. But she was not his mother; he had known none—only Crenna. There had always been Crenna to love him and keep him warm, to listen to his troubles. Ta-Tando fell back, his head sinking into the mud. The rain washed his war paint away. He watched Crenna, watched her throw the ax away, watched her eyes alter, become pitying.

She rose and went to her man, and still Ta-Tando

watched as she bent over him, kissing his waxen face, murmuring soft musical things to him.

The tears came from nowhere. They flowed from Ta-Tando's eyes and mingled with the rain. He did not move for a long while. He lay watching the rain, as motionless as if it were he who had been clubbed down.

Then slowly he rolled over, remaining for a minute on hands and knees in the mud before he rose shakily. She shielded Van der Veghe with her body, clung to him, loved him. Ta-Tando saw Sachim standing in the yard with two children beside her, one, the boy, as white as Van der Veghe. He looked away, and when Ya-tosphe, bow in hand, ran up to him, Ta-Tando said angrily, "Get out of here! Go away. Leave this place."

And he left. Smoke curled into the skies. The house would burn and would crumble. The rain, in time, would wash it all away. But their love would endure. Ta-Tando went into the dark forest and buried his face against his arms as he sagged to the earth, sobbing. He could still smell the smoke, still see Crenna bent over her man; and so, after a little while, he rose and walked on, the rain drawing a curtain behind him.

❊ 14 ❊

VAN DER VEGHE HELD THE horses while Crenna helped
William up onto the two-wheeled cart they had salvaged
from the Dutch settlement. The day was clear and bright,
the river smooth and placid.

"Well?"

Crenna looked up into Van der Veghe's face. She
shrugged; what was there to say? It all lay in ashes. Ta-
Tando had finished the dream. They would not have survived long under any circumstances, however. The Dutch
would never come again, the British were hostile. Indian
warriors still roamed the forest; the war alone endured.

Ta-Tando's ax had not severed Van der Veghe's arm,
but it had been so badly damaged that Crenna herself had
been forced to amputate it. Then for weeks Van der
Veghe had lain in a fever, fighting off the greedy,
clutching hands of death. Crenna had never left his side.
Sachim had seen to the children, who had to be forced out
into the fresh air. They sat enduring their father's trial
along with him, their small round faces pale and still as
Sachim moved about the camp gathering what she could
find for the soup pot.

Then one day his eyes had blinked open and they were
clear, unfevered. He had stretched out a weak hand and
clasped Crenna's wrist, and she had wept with joy.

It was another month before he had been up and about.
By then spring was well along, and they had taken slow
strolls through the forest and across the flower-splashed
meadows.

"It is a beautiful, beautiful land," Peter had said, gazing
far away as he held her hand, as the fresh spring breeze
gently flowed over the meadows, bending the long grass.
"But we cannot stay."

"I know it," she answered.

They had said nothing else. Separately their minds traveled old roads, remembering all that had gone before. All

of it gone now, destroyed by war, by men's ambitions and nature's fury. Yet they knew, as Ta-Tando had come to know, that their love could not be burned or battered down or blown away by harsh winds—and their love, after all, was all that did matter. The rest could be rebuilt; the rest could be, with time, forgotten.

Where they were bound, they did not know, but this was a vast country, and to the west and south there were lands where the war had not yet reached, where hatred did not yet dominate, where the rolling clouds of destruction had not yet penetrated.

There they would build again. They were taking all that really mattered with them.

"Ready, Sachim?" Crenna asked, and Sachim, perched on the cart, her arms around the children, nodded.

"Peter Van der Veghe?"

"Ready," he replied.

He started the horses forward, and the cart rolled out of the ruins of Dutch Albany, past the ashes of their effort, their dreams, and they left a little of themselves behind.

But it did not matter. Their life now lay ahead of them, beyond the forests, beyond the distant hills, and Crenna turned her eyes that way, walking beside her husband as the cart and its precious cargo rolled on toward the silent, deep green forest to the west.

ABOUT THE AUTHOR

PAUL JOSEPH LEDERER is a native Californian with an intense interest in the history of the American frontier. His family tree includes six great uncles who fought in the Civil War, three for the Confederacy and three for the Union, one of whom survived to become one of the original Texas Rangers.

He attended San Diego State University and served as a noncommissioned officer in Air Force Intelligence. While waiting for his writing to provide his livelihood, he worked in the San Diego Police Department Crime Lab, as a heavy equipment operator for the County of San Diego, and held such varied jobs as Good Humor man, exterminator, fruit peddler, librarian and delivery man.

Mr. Lederer is the publisher and full staff of his own Cormorant Press, which releases literary efforts outside the mainstream "when funds are available."

A student of Eastern religion and philosophy and American folk music, he lives in Southern California with his wife, Sandra, four children, and four cats (one for each child).